Unconquered

Planet of Perpetual Peace

Book I

Peter Man

Reviews

"Blending mythology, science, and history, Man creates an ambitious narrative that throws many unsuspected obstacles in Victoria's path. The plot interweaves modern Canadian culture with aspects of ancient Chinese and steppe civilizations, creating an absorbing, multilayered story uncommon in YA or fantasy fiction… Man's writing is rich with surprising details … this exciting intellectual journey will keep readers engaged as they follow Victoria on a time-bending quest full of unexpected twists and turns." — ***BookLife Review / Editor's Pick***

"Delivered with intelligence—and hilarious fun … The best of all possible worlds and stories comes together in this fascinating and immensely entertaining novel. Recommend."

— ***Grady Harp, Amazon Hall of Fame Top 100 Reviewer***

"This book is a tongue in cheek adventure, laugh out loud funny at times, and in the midst of all that, highly educational … fun and fantastical ride of a book. Highly recommend." — ***V. E., Amazon Vine Voice Review***

"One hell of an amazing literary masterpiece … I am lost for words trying to write this review. I highly recommend this book."

— ***Elizabeth, Amazon Review***

"A major feat of storytelling … I heartily recommend this book—it is a tour de force!" — ***M. Hernandez, Amazon Review***

"This is a book that you need to read! … This book has everything all rolled into one … I urge you to give this book a read … and enjoy the crazy fabulous ride." — ***Rebecca Hill, Reedsy Editor***

"Almost every genre can be found in this book—romance, suspense, thriller, sci-fi, humour and many more. It was basically like riding a roller coaster … Absolutely recommended!"

— ***Russ Ann, Amazon Review***

"This is a book to read! I have never read something quite like this book here. It's exciting, intellectual, fun, and totally an action adventure with sci-fi." ***Nona, Goodreads Review***

"Absolutely fantastic! I would highly recommend anyone to read this."

— Ivana S., Amazon Review

"This book is definitely amazing. 100% recommend!!!"

— Edna, Goodreads Review

"This story was entertaining and enjoyable from the first page. Great read and I recommend this to everyone."

— Jimmy Jefferson, Goodreads Review

"Not only a fast-paced and exciting science fiction story ... Mr. Man wants to impart to his readers, 'Everything you wanted to know about Chinese culture and society, but were afraid to ask.'"

— Jeff J. Brown, Author, the China Trilogy

"'Unconquered' combines three of my favorite things: Canada, China, and Sci-Fi—and does so seamlessly (it also features a kick-ass female protagonist, another weakness of mine) … Highly recommended!"

— Dr. Godfree Roberts, Author, Why China Leads the World

"An exciting adventure story, and at the same time, it presents some very amazing historical and cultural facts about China."

— Dr. Francis Pang, C.M., Member of the Order of Canada
Chairman, Concord College of Sino-Canada

Unconquered

Book webpage: https://www.petermanauthor.com

Blog: https://www.petermanauthor.com/shared-thoughts

Printed and distributed by IngramSpark

.

ISBN-13: 978-1-9994019-7-9

Prelusion

In the beginning, when chaos reigned, I wanted to write a book about two little-known topics, Canada and China. I remember telling someone in New York I was visiting from Canada, and she asked, "Where is it?" Also, whenever I switch on the idiot box to catch the breaking news, I get bombarded by a barrage of China China China, as the bugbear, not Panda bear, delivered by talking heads who know bupkis about China.

Considering I carry the genes of Chinese parents who left mainland China to live in Hong Kong, speak Cantonese and Mandarin, read and write both Traditional and Simplified Chinese scripts, studied Chinese history and literature, and lived and worked in mainland China for twenty years, I may know a thing or two about the country.

Furthermore, my father was a renegade communist from Yan'an, the headquarters of the Communist Party of China during the Second Sino-Japanese War. He wrote a historical novel based on his experience as a party cadre and performer for the Lu Xun Academy of Fine Arts. I also lucked out and befriended people in China who had led extraordinary lives. A prime example is Sidney Rittenberg, an American who lived in China for thirty-eight years after the Second World War, of which sixteen were in prison. Sidney, who passed away in 2019, taught me much about China.

As the son of new immigrants trying to build a new life in a new city under adverse circumstances, I was fortunate to have received an excellent education at La Salle College, an English Catholic school in Hong Kong. Baptized at birth and confirmed at eight, I joined the Legion of Mary under the guidance of the iconic Brother Thomas in secondary school and led the Rosary at the school chapel during lunch breaks. I was so pious I once aspired to be a priest. But it was not meant to be. My zeal cooled when a higher calling took my spiritual guide to a faraway land.

Later, my four years at McMaster University, with two living on Wallace, the rowdiest floor of the famous, or infamous, Whidden Hall residence, which inspired the classic campus comedy *Animal House*, convinced me to make Canada my home.

By a twist of fate, I pioneered and established Chinese-language television for the Chinese Canadian communities across Canada. It was an adventure which led to my two-decade sojourn in China, working in the television and broadcast technologies industry and witnessing the country's meteoric rise. In short, I have countless Canadian and Chinese stories to tell.

Although writing about Canada is not particularly challenging, China is another matter. One must compete for attention amongst countless authors who have been composing copious words in voluminous bestsellers on China, and my opinion, no matter how well-informed, would be buried under a profusion of poppycock.

Rather than taking on a thankless task, I decided to pivot to socioeconomics, despite never having received any indoctrination in the discipline. Frankly, I do not consider it a disadvantage, as my uncluttered mind is unencumbered by preconceptions.

While researching on the subject, I came across a quote from a Canadian economist, John Kenneth Galbraith, who admitted, "The only function of economic forecasting is to make astrology look respectable." Upon making this discovery, I gave up on the mundane and went for the stars, in other words, science fiction. I realized the sci-fi genre would unfetter my imagination to create faraway alien worlds, travel back and forth through time and predict the future without appearing to have gone off the deep end.

Experts and well-meaning friends who knew about my vacillations advised me to stick to one genre and focus on one subject. I could not decide whether I should listen to them or my guts, if guts could talk. After wasting precious minutes on fruitless philosophical contemplation, I went where my guts took me, namely, the kitchen. As I unsealed the portal of the refrigeration unit and a burst of photons from the fridge light flooded my face, I had an epiphany, one similar to what struck René Descartes, "I think; therefore, I'll have a beer." I gave life to an idea and collapsed its Schrödinger Wave Function. I would write an oxymoronic fact-based science fiction with everything in it, including the organic craft beer and the kitchen sink.

I have enjoyed the long and winding journey of creating this pièce de résistance. I must, however, warn treasure seekers they may not find a mother lode. They may hit a leaky pipe and encounter something unpleasant instead. On the other hand, prospectors with a discerning eye and an open mind will discover new ideas, new knowledge, new interpretations of history, new insight into the origin of human civilizations, new questions about the mysteries of our universe, new ways to understand oneself and the world, in other words, new ways to think, and a new theory for establishing a perpetually peaceful Utopian society, a lofty aspiration previously deemed beyond the limits of human endeavour. In addition, readers will learn many wild and woolly facts about Canada and China and be delightfully gobsmacked.

Before taking the plunge, I needed to be convinced my socioeconomic theory was not entirely frivolous. I submitted a concise thesis for review by the estimable Professor Justin Yifu Lin, the renowned dean of several economics institutes at Peking University, previous Senior VP and Chief Economist at the World Bank and the Vice Director of the National CPPCC Economics Committee, providing consultation to the Chinese government. Professor Lin parsed my thesis, concluding it was "logical and convincing." Amen!

Since I'll be writing hard science fiction, and the story has quantum physics, time travel and artificial intelligence in the mix, I must ensure the science has some basis in fact and not all mumbo jumbo. Thanks to the favourable alignment of the stars, I have had the opportunity to pick the superior brain of a real scientist who happens to be my brother-in-law, Professor Peter Ramadge, director of Princeton University's Center for Statistics and Machine Learning. Here's a big shoutout to my brother Peter for humouring me and treating my outlandish ideas as worthy of scientific investigation.

For the benefit of readers of all shades and persuasions, I'm spinning this yarn as a fanciful fable, catering to the consummate consumer's insatiable desire for epicurean pleasures. Although it will not please everyone and may even irk the odd reader, it promises to be something completely different and to transform anyone who has the stomach to read it from cover to cover, if stomachs could read. As a bonus, the reader will become an expert on China. *Carpe Liber*—seize the book!

Book 2 of the Series: Bellatrix

The sequel delves into the connections between the planets Earth, Shangria and Betel. Lost in the past, Victoria tries to find her way back to the future by visiting the author of *Dream of the Red Chamber*, thus learning the answers to many of the mysteries in his book. By chance, she witnesses one of the greatest battles ever fought by an invincible general who may have been a Canadian.

Book 3 of the Series: Augenblick: The Blink of an Eye

Readers will explore the concept of establishing a perpetually peaceful society, travel across a realm oft visited by heroes, lovers, demigods, epic poets and daydreaming young girls, and learn how our decisions can reset what has already transpired in the past. All the answers await our arrival at the saga's grand finale.

Table of Contents

This book is dedicated to the mixed-race
members of my family
My grandson, Charlie Man Dunn
My nephews, Darcy Ramadge
and
Sage Ramadge and his children
Noa, Yossi and Micah
because they may one day want to learn
the meaning of being Chinese

Author's Note:

The average reader may find the usage of English alphabets for Chinese names a bit puzzling. How does one pronounce Qin? Is Xian one syllable or two? Fear not, understanding the intricacies of the language is not necessary for enjoying the story.

Examples of Putonghua (Mandarin) pronunciation using English spelling:

Cao is pronounced Tsao	Sun is pronounced Suen
E is pronounced Uh	She is pronounced Shuh
Ge is pronounced Guh	Tang is pronounced Taang
Huai is pronounced Whuy	Tong is pronounced Tung
He is pronounced Huh	Wo is pronounced Wau
Hui is pronounced Huay	Xi is pronounced Si
Long is pronounced Loong	Xi'an is pronounced Si-aan
Nü is pronounced Neu	Xian is pronounced Sian
Qi is pronounced Tsih	Xie is pronounced Sieh
Qie is pronounced Tzieh	Xu is pronounced She
Qin is pronounced Tsin	Xue pronounced Shueh
Qing is pronounced Tsing	Ze pronounced Tzuh
Ren is pronounced Run	Zhou pronounced Jo

Modern Chinese naming convention places the family name before the given name. Hence for Deng Xiaoping, Deng is the family name and Xiaoping the given name.

Abbreviations:
TS: Traditional script (used in Taiwan, Hong Kong, and Macau)
SS: Simplified script (used in mainland China, Singapore, and the UN)
OB: Oracle Bone script (Shang, circa 1600–1046 BCE)
BR: Bronze script (Late Shang and early Zhou)

Chinese characters are in SS unless otherwise specified

Chapter 1

Before the Fall

Death is unpredictable! If Victoria Solana had any doubts, by the time the plasma sphere swallowed her, she had none at all. It had been barely a month since her sixteenth birthday when, without warning, death robbed her of everything she owned in the blink of an eye. Henceforth, she had given up the simple belief she was a simple girl from a simple family living a simple life in a simple little town in southern Ontario, a simple province in the simple country of Canada.

For Victoria, living a simple, ordinary life had become a distant memory and wishful thinking. Her recent experience had transformed her into a different person altogether. She could hardly recognize herself in the mirror. Was she Canadian or Chinese? Was she a girl or a boy? Was she a carefree high-school student or a superhero burdened with saving the world? Was she a human being or a ghost in someone's nightmare? During the past month, an onslaught of mind-boggling, extraordinary events challenged Victoria's comprehension of reality. To salvage her sanity, she taught herself to expect the unexpected. But nothing could prepare Victoria for the moment she found herself in the presence of a unicorn, the mythical creature of truth.

"My goodness!" Victoria mused. "Are my eyes deceiving me? If this is Delo the Unicorn, why can't I describe him? Does he have a horn on his head, or is it a pine cone? The long, golden hair covering him from head to toe seems to be gleaming rays of light.

Mr. Huang said, 'The unicorn has numerous forms, the unicorn has no form.' I didn't quite get it. Now I see. I may not know what I'm staring at, but I can perceive his presence. Too bad I can't describe my experience. And no one will believe me, no one except Emma and Jackie, who will believe anything I tell them."

"My dear Sibyl," Delo the Unicorn addressed Victoria with a soft, boyish voice. "We are reunited at last according to the prophecy of Sage Didymas. It's been a little less than three weeks since you were born. *Quantum mutatus*, how much you have changed! The lost souls in the Realm of Traum are awakening from their nightmares. O joy! Perhaps we will have hope after all."

"Delo, I'm pleased to meet you. But I don't know what you're talking about. Everything you say sounds Greek, or Latin, to me. You know my name is Victoria. Why do you call me Sibyl? I'm sixteen years old, not, as you say, born three weeks ago. Where is Traum, and who are the lost souls? By the way, I major in STEM courses at school. I don't believe in fairy tales, divine beasts or magic. According to Heisenberg's Uncertainty Principle, it is impossible to predict the future. It's the basic principle of quantum mechanics, which describes how things work in the universe. We should stop believing in fortune-tellers and religious scammers."

"Oh, *quantum ignotum*," Delo chuckled. "How much you don't know! And you're a serious scientist, aren't you? I can reveal all the universe's secrets to you in an *Augenblick* …."

"A what?"

"An *Augenblick*, the blink of an eye," Delo said with a playful wink, fanning the air with his long, heavy lashes, "the moment of enlightenment, an ephemeral attainment of ineffable joy, for which fools and philosophers surrender their eternal souls, if they had one. But for an inchoate infant, meaning you, my dear, it would be similar to Zeus revealing himself to Semele, Dionysus' mother, who suffered the consequence of her unbridled curiosity, demanding and receiving a glimpse of the Olympian god. Fried to a crisp, she paid the ultimate price merely for taking a gander at the ugly bastard.

"Of course, it is your Sibylline nature to be inquisitive, and you shall enjoy our knowledge of the past, present and future. All Sibyls do, and you're one of them. I recognize it by your voice. We speak the same language of truth. You know unicorns do not lie, and I'm, yours truly, Delo the Unicorn. I have innumerable names and uncountable forms. The Chinese call me Zhi and Qilin. Others call me Kirin, Einhorn or Monoceros. I may also be a dragon or a lion. The Chinese word for dragon depicts a creature with one horn. And if you open your eyes to what's in plain view, you will notice the lions in the Chinese Lion Dance are unicorns.

"Because you are less than three weeks old by my clock, my twin sister, Re'an, and I will protect you and keep you from the unknowable knowledge until you develop enough strength to withstand its power. Everyone depends on you for the Great Reset and a second chance to do things right. The mystery of our emergence will be revealed to you in small doses as you grow up. It is the only way, and so it shall be. Have patience, my dear.

"Meanwhile, prepare yourself to experience some discomfort as we arrive at our destination. I must borrow the immense energy of Creation to reconstruct the quantum states from their entropies. It may affect your more delicate organs, including your central nervous system. Some folks of weaker constitutions may lose their mind or slip into a coma from which they will never wake. However, you may rest easy, my dear. My transcendental fields will safeguard you with pretty good protection, though a slight risk remains because of your incomplete soul equation. Fortunately, you have inherited excellent traits from your ancestors. The odds are better than even you will survive."

Victoria was unsure if Delo's "better than even" odds were meant to be reassuring. How did she embroil herself in this royal imbroglio? Only a month ago, she was breezing along in her perfectly predictable life in the inconspicuous town of Dundas, about seventy kilometres, or forty-five miles for Americans, west of Toronto, right next to the city of Hamilton and a short bike ride from McMaster University, far from the madding crowd and minding her own business. What the hell happened?

The Victoria Solana of those golden days before disaster struck held the undisputed title of the most unremarkable person you could ever know. Growing up in the middle of nowhere, she thrived in a place where nothing happened twenty-four-seven. Moreover, Victoria's parents inculcated into her the habit of keeping her head low and blending in with the crowd to avoid attention, in other words, to be an average Canadian. She enjoyed the freedom of anonymity living in her secluded paradise, where milk and honey flowed, bread was plentiful, and children played without despair.

In such a plain and placid environment, Victoria developed an unexceptional appearance and nondescript demeanour, and, in the presence of other ordinary Dundasians, her physical manifestation would transmogrify into quantum uncertainty.

But death changed everything!

Since the evening of her sixteenth birthday, Victoria had little choice over matters of life and death. So far, the only important decision she had made amounted to entrusting her safety to a shifty stranger, who asserted she must embark on a dangerous and arduous journey to the unknown. According to this fearmonger, the survival of humanity and perhaps the entire planet was at stake. Delo suggested it could be far worse. Be that as it may, Victoria could not refuse to play.

At this stage of her journey, Victoria decided she must overcome all obstacles to face what awaited her at the destination of her destiny. This unassuming Chinese Canadian adolescent small-town girl had already witnessed a plethora of inexplicable prodigies and survived a litany of mortal misadventures. She knew she was ignorant about much of the universe and powerless to affect any changes. The only thing she still had a little control over was her resolute and unyielding heart of gold.

Victoria was said to have been an obstinate child, giving her parents titanic headaches when she insisted on feeding her apple purée to the goldfish, clinging on with iron resolve to stray animals and donating her toys to passers-by who did not have any. For her stubborn insistence on being kind and generous, Victoria's parents nicknamed her Bellatrix, meaning girl warrior. Victoria mellowed over the years while her parents tamed her in a calming cocoon of love. But the headstrong girl never left. She was merely napping beneath her shy and reserved exterior.

As she entered uncharted waters from her quantum leap, thanks to the transporting powers of Delo the Unicorn, Victoria conjured the image of the Bellatrix in her mind. She donned her black adamantine armour, gripped her fearsome spear of eleven cubits and mounted Delo, now a magnificent stallion. The imaginative teenager transformed her superego into a knight-errant, trekking through time and space to right all wrongs, joust against giants and battle the lying blatherskites intent on ruining her serene realm.

What is a little discomfort to a knight-errant? What matters wounds? For each time she falls, she will rise again to renew the fight undaunted. The Endless War will not end until the villainous vermin who started it are crushed and reduced to dust, to be blown away into nothingness by an errant gust.

The tick-tock of a clock crept into Victoria's consciousness, morphing into the tintinnabulation of clanging steel. The music of ringing metal reminded her of the "Anvil Chorus" in Verdi's *Il Trovatore*, "Dawn is unfolding, night is lifting. To work! To work!"

"This is it, my dear," Delo said. "We have arrived. Use the ring to summon me when you're ready for the next leg of your journey. Do not dawdle. Owing to an ill-advised external intervention, a dark force has emerged, spreading its poisonous web on the Internet. It evokes the image of a giant vampire spider, sucking the blood dry from all living creatures. Humans are no match for it. This dark force will either enslave or exterminate them. You're their last hope. Make haste. I wish you Godspeed and good luck."

Upon waking from her strange dream, Victoria suffered a headache of biblical proportions. A searing fire seemed to be scorching her skin, causing unbearable pain. Although it did not take long for her to recuperate and for her eyes to regain focus, she quickly realized an unmitigated disaster had befallen her. The ring by which she invoked Delo had vanished from her left thumb.

Wasting no time to despond over her hopeless situation, Victoria inspected her environs before figuring out Plan B.

A blanket of powdery snow overlaid the surrounding landscape, which sparkled in the soft glow of the rising sun. The high heat of the quantum leap had vaporized all the icy crystals in her immediate vicinity. Blue steam was rising from her clothes. Although Victoria wore only a light cotton hoodie, she did not mind the refreshing cold. It soothed her feverish skin.

Several ruddy-faced children wrapped in wolf-pelt coats were examining Victoria's anachronistic attire. A nosy puppy was sniffing her hair, its friendly tail wagging with boundless energy.

A sprawling settlement surrounded by a wall of stout timber stood a stone's throw away. Nearby, trickles of thawing snow gathered into a babbling brook. The guards were opening the front gates, letting in a group of traders with wagon-loads of goods eager to ply their wares at the morning market. The melody of metallic percussion flowed from a smithy near the entrance. This remote settlement in the middle of a great mountain range, established during the last years of the Qin Empire more than two millennia before the present day, was awakening from its ambrosial sleep.

"Holy guacamole!" Victoria muttered to herself. "Someone has stolen my ring. How will I save anyone without it?"

As an only child, Victoria Solana was her parents' pampered princess. Her to-do list did not include saving people. Why should she waste her beautiful, innocent mind on human tragedies outside her purview and beyond her ken? Victoria had no mundane concerns as long as she could live an uncomplicated life far from the troublous world and close to the simple people she loved, namely, her parents and her two best friends, Emma and Jackie.

Victoria shared multiplicate interests with her mom, such as reading, cooking, sewing, sketching and bathroom singing. She also had a close relationship with her dad and shared some of his multifarious interests, such as classical music, chess and spectator sports. While her dad loved watching English Premier League soccer matches and was a diehard Manchester United fan, Victoria supported the Maple Leafs, Raptors and the Blue Jays.

Since grade school, Victoria had learned to identify the heavenly constellations from her father, an amateur astronomer, who often regaled her with bowdlerized versions of the related Greek myths, leaving out all the sex and violence.

Victoria loved magic. It is a phase most kids go through growing up, though she never grew out of it. She adored the Amazing Randi and Penn & Teller, famous debunkers of charlatans and scammers. Victoria bought their books to learn some of their tricks and practiced to become adept at prestidigitation and misdirection. In the process, she learned never to believe in magic.

As part of her parents' persistent effort to keep their daughter invisible, Victoria never participated in any competitive sports, which was fine for her because she had no particular interest in phys ed. She preferred to apply her energies elsewhere, for example, contributing anonymous articles to the school newspaper and trying to rack up a million points in solitaire.

On the other hand, Victoria had a knack for playing chess and could defeat most players her age. She cut her teeth studying past masters such as Morphy, Capablanca and Nimzowitsch, while drawing inspiration from current female World Champion Ju Wenjun and teenage girl prodigy Lu Miaoyi. However, Victoria disliked humiliating her opponents and was happy to be a kibitzer; thus, she could checkmate others in her head and enjoy the game without hurting anyone's feelings.

Despite her sedentary lifestyle, Victoria was hale and hearty as a rock. She could not remember the last time she visited a doctor, although doing so would not have cost her parents a brass farthing, thanks to Canada's universal healthcare. Victoria's balanced diet undoubtedly contributed to her perfect health. If one needed to find fault with the reclusive, small-town girl, it might be her weakness for chocolate, a vice in which she indulged from time to time.

Except for their strange habit of celebrating Christmas on January 7, the Solana family was a model social unit consisting of three individuals living in perfect harmony and perpetual equipoise. They never encountered any three-body problems.

Life in the sleepy town of Dundas was, therefore, all veriest Canadian for Victoria, and Victoria was as Canadian as anything Canadian could ever be, ranking right at the top of the list with the Canada goose, lumberjack, maple syrup, ice hockey, Drake and saying sorry when someone steps on your toe.

But in the blink of an eye, or as Goethe would say, "*den Augenblick*," Victoria's life in Canada turned upside down and inside out. She lost everyone and everything she held dear. She could no longer be sure who she was. Her past became a puff of smoke, suspended in the air, to be dispersed into nothingness by a wave of her hand. Having fallen through the rabbit hole, Victoria became disoriented as an ant on a Möbius strip or a ladybird in a Klein bottle, at a loss as to which Bizarro dimension she belonged. The unfortunate teenage girl might have kept her two best friends, but they were on the other side of the galaxy, left behind in the fairytale kingdom of Dundas of long ago and far away.

Never having strayed beyond the equally idyllic town of Simcoe nearby, Victoria sallied forth on a death-defying odyssey over unscalable peaks and across tempestuous mains in search of the elusive truth. She had to evade sinister assassins, stare down the barrel of a loaded pistol and escape certain death in a fiery car crash. She jumped out of an airplane midflight without a parachute and jolted awake halfway across the world in a strange land, living dangerously among natives who spoke an alien tongue.

Back in the far-flung land of her ancestors, Victoria's life hung by a thread in a high-speed car chase with six container trucks, ending up trapped inside the vehicle at the bottom of the sea. She dangled from the ledge at the top of the tallest building in China, wrestled with a hungry tiger and sent three grown men on an untimely passage to the other side.

On a positive note, a series of improbable but not impossible events presented Victoria with the chance to win the World Series for the Toronto Blue Jays with a swing of her bat on a full-count with the championship on the line. All these happened because, although she was unaware of it, Victoria held the key to unlocking the most enigmatic mystery of the universe.

"You're exaggerating," Victoria complained as she struggled to her feet surrounded by nomadic children in the remote mountains of northeastern China a hundred and ninety-five years before the birth of Jesus of Nazareth. "Even your exaggerations are exaggerated. And your timeline is all screwed up. It's too much. Won't you tell the story the way it happened, please?"

Dear Lord Almighty! Tusitala, have mercy! What has transpired is unprecedented in the history of storytelling. The heroine of this epic saga has made a personal request for how she wants the author to tell her story. While it is highly unconventional, she is the protagonist, and it is her prerogative.

For readers who may find this factitious fabrication's pompous and hifalutin lexicon discombobulating, or as Jane Austen would say, "Extremely vexing," the last sentence means Victoria Solana is the boss, and, in most cases, we should comply with her wishes.

So, without further ado, let us begin anew, with minimal embellishments or poetic licence, to recount the improbable adventures of Victoria Solana and explain why a unicorn is transporting her through time and space. After all, the unicorn is a mythical beast; it has no place in a factual story.

Chapter 2

There Are No Accidents

It was a dark and snowy evening. Canada has many such evenings in the winter, especially on Victoria's birthday, December 22, the one day in the year with the least amount of daylight. Victoria and her parents, Michael and Angela, were heading home in their old, reliable Volkswagen Golf after enjoying a sumptuous dinner at their favourite Chinese restaurant, Dragon's Lair, a vintage diner operated by a nonagenarian Chinese lady who refused to retire. Emma and Jackie did not join Victoria because they had agreed to celebrate each other's *unbirthdays.*

Victoria loved Chinese food, learning all about it by watching the cooking shows of the indefatigable Martin Yan of *Yan Can Cook*. As was the case with Victoria, Martin was born in China and blossomed in Canada, though he would follow his heart and move to the sunnier climes and greener pastures of San Francisco. Michael and Angela Solana adopted their lovely and beloved daughter from China before her first birthday. Victoria had no memory of her country of birth, only a vague idea she belonged to the same ethnic group represented by Bruce Lee, Jackie Chan, Jet Li, Mulan, Kung Fu Panda and Shang-Chi, all martial arts experts.

Michael and Angela, a handsome couple with a pleasant mix of Slavic and Germanic features, were Russian speakers born in Ukraine before the collapse of the Soviet Union. When they had the chance, they immigrated to Canada and left their past behind, adopting English names after settling in Dundas, a small, inconspicuous town among hundreds in southern Ontario. At the time, the young couple, in their early thirties, would have lived a perfect life in Canada if not for one minor defect. They wanted children, but Angela was barren, and Michael was sterile.

Michael discovered the possibility of adopting from China since the country implemented the so-called One-Child Policy.

The background of this policy began way back in 1979 when China arrived at a watershed moment in its history. The country had normalized diplomatic relations with the U.S. on the first day of the year. The Gang of Four, the perpetrators of the power struggle behind the decade-long Chinese Cultural Revolution, were taken to task and locked behind bars. The new leader of China, Deng Xiaoping, one of a few first-generation revolutionaries and top-tier leaders of the Communist Party of China who survived the ten-year turmoil, visited the U.S. in the same year, trying to learn what his country must do to catch up with the rest of the world.

As the gates of the Central Nation, a more accurate translation of China than the Middle Kingdom, opened in 1979, the country's burgeoning population of one billion was experiencing exponential growth. No one questioned how China doubled their mouths to feed, almost doubled life expectancy and quadrupled literacy in one generation of supposed failed communist rule. China achieved these while surviving through a suffocating Western embargo after suffering a century of nonstop wars, natural disasters and colonial plunder. It flew in the face of all the reports of the Western free press. As a sage once asserted, there is no truth in news and no news in truth! Ancient cultures favoured large families to survive high infant mortality, famine and wars. Better healthcare, nutrition and education helped most Chinese children become reproducing adults. However, in the shadow of success lurks Nature's Great Balancing Act, which rewards unbridled growth with primacy but punishes it with destruction and death.

Confucius said, "A gentleman is moderate, a villain is not." Chinese culture promotes moderation, as unfettered success is the root cause of demise.

Abiding by the philosophy of its heritage and the advice of Western scientific studies, such as the popular report *The Limits to Growth*, the Chinese government implemented the so-called One-Child Policy, with exemptions for ethnic minorities and the rural population. The policy, which ended in 2016, forestalled Nature's tendency to reduce population by starvation, disease and war. China's bold social experiment helped people transcend their evolutionary endowment of animalistic instincts.

The plan worked well enough, and the population's growth slowed. While this created new problems, the alternative would have been much worse. One of those problems became a boon for Michael and Angela.

When the One-Child Policy took effect, some Chinese families refused to relinquish their patriarchal tradition and insisted they must have a son to perpetuate the family lineage. Ten years of the Cultural Revolution did not uproot this entrenched view. It might be easier to move mountains than change a person's mind. Hence, some parents abandoned their baby girls or put them up for adoption. The lucky ones would find their way into the orphanages and end up in North America with their adoptive families.

In Michael and Angela Solana's case, they received the assistance of a Chinese art dealer and came home after a short trip to China with an eleven-month-old baby girl.

At sixteen, Victoria embodied the typical small-town girl next door with her long, silky, dark brown hair, almond-shaped eyes and the egg-shaped face of the classic Chinese beauty of the north. Chinese literature often describes northern girls as spirited, strong-willed and, sometimes, even martial. A well-known example is Mulan, the heroine of a Disney cartoon and historical action movie. However, Victoria grew up being shy and reserved, seldom showing her best face to anyone outside her most intimate circle of family and friends. Nevertheless, the teenage girl could not easily mask her innate qualities. Victoria shone with a natural aura, and her bright eyes were always full of fight.

Victoria had arrived at an age when girls began to be self-conscious about skin blemishes. She comforted herself with the supposed auspiciousness of three faint moles on her face, interpreting the one on her left cheek as a beauty mole, the one near the left corner of her lip as the indication she was a connoisseur of good food and the one at the centre of her chin below her lips as the sign the owner was loving and considerate.

To those who did not know her well, Victoria was a puzzle and a paradox. Despite her imperfections and attempts to be mediocre, no one could describe her as plain or homely. On the contrary, if one studied her features with an aesthetic eye, it would be easy to conclude she exuded natural grace and beauty. Victoria was a rosebud waiting for the right moment to burst into bloom.

"Honey, please take a break," Angela said, turning around to nag Victoria in the back of the car. "You've been staring at the phone all night."

"In a minute. I'm checking my food videos. The Lion Heads Braised in Soya Sauce and the Chairman Mao Braised Pork were to die for. I'm also sharing birthday cake pictures with the girls."

Victoria had been best friends with Emma and Jackie since kindergarten. The three girls formed a secret society they dubbed the Weird Sisters. It constituted Victoria's only social life outside of school. Her parents had no social circle to speak of. She thought of them as eccentrics and did not think much of it.

"Sweetie, are you being Bellatrix again?" Michael said. "Please be a good girl and listen to Mama. You two are giving me a headache. The roads are slippery, and I need to focus on driving."

It was a moonless and frosty evening. The slush from the freezing rain made driving on the rural highway treacherous. An urgent message had been weighing on Michael. He must get home without a moment's delay.

As Michael took an unusual detour to shorten the journey and avoid the main roads, the shadow of a wraith rose from the blackness of the earth, which materialized into a monstrous beast, bounding behind the family of three in their Volkswagen Golf and pouncing on them. A fifty-three-foot container truck, gorged with seventy metric tons of blood-red French Cahors and California Zinfandel, vroomed by like a bat out of hell at what must have been a hundred miles per hour, imparting an almost imperceptible brush on the fragile Golf as it passed, and the fiend accomplished its dastardly deed. Victoria and her parents watched in horror as their car careened off the road. Meanwhile, the culprit vanished into the night as if it were the fleeting silhouette of a ghost.

It would take no more than the tick-tock of a clock for the car to slam into the trees, but it took an eternity for Victoria as the world spun in slow motion before her eyes. The stunned girl wanted to scream, but could emit only silence. All she could hear was the melancholy melody of Bach's "Air on the G String" playing on the car radio.

After the initial shock subsided, an eerie calm descended upon Victoria, evoking the strange sensation of being trapped inside an out-of-control space capsule spinning its way to infinity. Having no means to change her inevitable fate, the only thing she could do was accept her impending doom.

Michael and Angela were not surprised their time had come. They were almost expecting it. They only regretted not having the time to tell Victoria they loved her and the truth about who she was and where she came from.

Chapter 3

Unbreakable China Doll

A windborne eagle spread her wings and soared high into the azure sky, sailing over the snowy peaks of lofty mountains, gliding across the golden dunes of a sprawling desert and circling above verdant hills and sleepy vales. She followed the path of a roiling river, which churned muddy waters as it raced eastward into the ocean. High in the empyreal realm, brave Helios embarked on his daily journey in his well-dight chariot of flashing bronze. The eagle dreamed of being one of the sun god's winged steeds. As she cruised over the meadows and the idyllic villages, a harpoon arrow whizzed past, startling her. Another barely missed her, and a third came too close for comfort.

The magnificent bird of prey beat her mighty wings to stir up a turbulent storm. She flew into a column of rain clouds to evade the menacing missiles. Water drenched her feathers, flooded her eyes and blurred her vision. Blue and green lightning flashed around her, followed by colourful explosions resembling New Year's Eve fireworks. She did not know what hit her. It stung as if 1.21 gigawatts of electricity had singed every neuron in her body.

Victoria regained consciousness with the freezing rain beating her face. For as long as the teenager could remember, she had this recurring dream of being a majestic black eagle.

The car had slammed into an ancient oak. The violent deformation of the chassis had sheared off the rear window. Wet snow poured through this opening. The shock of the impact shook

Victoria to the core, yet she did not suffer any lacerations or fractures. She thanked her lucky stars because she did not believe in miracles or magic.

The airbag saved Michael, but the car had collapsed on him. Victoria became frantic when her mother did not answer her call.

"Calm down, sweetie," Michael struggled to speak. "Leave the car … go home … find the Almanac … your birthmark."

"I'm not leaving, Papa," Victoria sobbed. "I'll wait for help."

"Danger … not accident … no police … find David Huang … Toronto … go!"

Victoria squeezed through the opening onto the dark, deserted country road. She could not find her phone in the car wreck and had to run a kilometre to call an ambulance. A jumble of questions whirled in her head. Why did they dine at Dragon's Lair? Why did Papa take this detour? Why were people targeting them? Who was David Huang? Victoria had no time to wait for answers. Michael was fading fast. She needed to hurry and get help.

The freezing rain had eased up, but it remained difficult for Victoria to negotiate the slick roadway. She turned back now and then to see if any cars were coming. After forging through the slush for about five minutes, Victoria was relieved to see a car stop near the wreckage. The emergency lights started flashing.

"Thank God!" she congratulated herself. "Help is on the way."

Ghostly green lightning flashed in the sky while deep thunder rolled from afar. And without warning, horror of horrors. A preternatural streak of lightning snaked down from the sky and hit the wreckage, which burst into flames, followed by an explosion. The lightning and the fireball lit up Victoria's face in quick succession. In the blink of an eye, she became an orphan again. Although in shock, Victoria remembered her father's dire warning. It was not an accident. She turned and ran for dear life.

Victoria did not know how far she ran or for how long. She had no memory of how she staggered into a half-deserted plaza and stumbled upon a parked taxi with the driver inside taking a coffee break, how her debris-covered face startled the driver out of his wits, and how he drove her home after the frazzled, wild-eyed girl demonstrated she did not have a scratch on her.

Victoria showered in steaming hot water to wash away the shivers and horrors of the evening. Her mollycoddled brain could not register the terrifying facts. She had lost her parents, and they had been the target of shadowy killers. Victoria's innards twisted into knots while tears escaped in big, heavy drops. She wished it was all a nightmare from which she would soon awaken.

The vulnerable teenager tried to think of someone she could trust and turn to for help. For all her life, she had gotten used to having no immediate relatives, not a single cousin, not an aunt or uncle, not even a grandparent. It had always been this way. For Victoria, it was normal.

From what bits and pieces Victoria learned, her parents lost their families after a disaster. It was a past they preferred not to revisit. Victoria had questions, but she avoided delving into her parents' family history. For their particular reasons, all parents keep secrets from their children. Victoria knew her parents had suffered trauma when they were young. She would be patient and let them choose the right time to recount their stories. Unfortunately, with their untimely passing, her questions would remain unanswered. For the moment, Victoria was more concerned about who the killers were and why they came after her family.

Chapter 4

Riddle Me This

Though reeling from the evening's disaster, Victoria did not forget her father's instruction to search for her birthmark in a book he referred to as the Almanac. After sifting through her memory and finding nothing about having a birthmark, Victoria started scrutinizing easy-to-miss spots such as the soles of her feet and the hollows of her knees.

The phone rang, making Victoria jump. She did not pick up the phone, and the caller hung up without leaving a message. Victoria could not think straight with her heart pounding at two hundred beats a minute. She closed her eyes and tried meditation to settle her jittery nerves. Despite appearing timid and demure, Victoria possessed a stout heart. She told herself she must not panic but be strong and brave. At the end of the day, fortune favours the brave!

After regaining calm, Victoria's long-lost memories began flooding back. She remembered when she was a toddler, her mom once told her about a mark on her back, which upset her, and she did not stop crying until her mom assured her it would disappear over time. Since it stayed out of sight, it went out of mind, and she forgot all about it.

Victoria twisted around in front of the bathroom mirror to see if she could find any unsightly spots on her back. Lo and behold! She found a red strawberry mark near the end of her spine.

On closer inspection, it appeared to be the tattoo of a heart instead. But why would anyone give a tattoo to a baby? Maybe her biological parents identified their newborn daughter with it. On the other hand, if they feared losing her, why did they put her up for adoption? Victoria had questions but no answers.

The nonplussed girl must next locate her father's jealously guarded Almanac. She had accidentally discovered it while playing Easter egg hunt as a child, but had no idea of the book's significance. Victoria headed to Michael's reading room in the basement, guessing he had kept the mysterious Almanac in his secret nook, the gap between the top of the bookcase and the ceiling. She stepped on a stool and shone a flashlight into the cranny, and voila! She found it.

The Almanac was an antique folio bound in thick and hard leather covers. Michael had treated it as a priceless treasure and kept it a closely guarded secret. The book's front cover displayed a line drawing of the abdominal plate of a tortoise shell, zoologically named a plastron. Three strange glyphs ran down the centre.

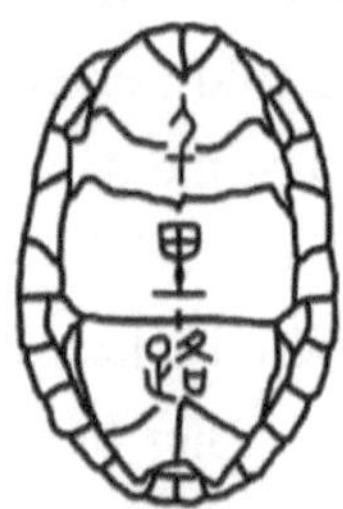

Fantastic sketches and puzzling pictograms filled the pages made of ancient vellum. It reminded Victoria of the enigmatic and indecipherable Voynich Manuscript. She riffled through the book to search for her heart-shaped mark and found it in seconds.

Picture words filled the verso page, with Victoria's heart tattoo among them. A star chart of otherworldly constellations occupied the recto page, its centre adorned by a fan-shaped flower. Illustrations of flora and fauna, including the face of a mythical beast, lined the margins, none of which appeared to be of telluric origin. An arrow pointed from the heart symbol to a scribbled scholium in red, "To learn secret, decode secret."

Unfortunately, the clue did not tell Victoria which secret to decode. How could anyone decipher a secret message without knowing the message? Victoria gave way to frustration and rummaged through the piles of books bestrewn in the room with the ferocity of a hungry raccoon scrounging for food. After exhausting herself to no avail, Victoria remembered a puzzle-solving lesson she learned from her father: "When searching for hidden answers, always use the brain rather than the eye or brute force, and one should never rely solely on luck or hope without thinking and experimenting."

Michael had introduced Victoria to crossword puzzles earlier in the year. She enjoyed playing the game, gaining a vast vocabulary and a compendium of trivia knowledge, which improved her favourite game of Trivial Pursuit at the same time. She put on her thinking cap and started working on the riddle.

"How would Papa leave a clue for me? Would it have something to do with my heart-shaped mark? No, anyone can see the symbol is a heart. It's too obvious."

Victoria read the clue over and over.

"'To learn secret, decode secret.' It's maddening. What secret can it be?"

The phone rang, and again, it made Victoria jump. Her adrenaline level shot through the roof, charging her brain with inspiration. The room seemed brighter, and her mind became more lucid. Apparently, the trauma of the car crash had delivered a whack on the side of Victoria's head, and the adrenaline triggered her transformation into a savant. As her neural excitation ran off the scales, it dawned on Victoria the secret was the word "secret" itself. To learn the secret, decode the word "secret."

Victoria knew the answer to the crossword clue "secret" was *sub rosa*, meaning "under the rose" in Latin; therefore, the secret was under a rose. Proud of herself for solving the first part of the riddle, Victoria scanned the room for books about roses.

The first section on the top shelf of the bookcase housed books on Religion, the next, Archaeology, and the third, Art and Music, followed by Science and Technology. On the two shelves below were arrayed the Greek and Latin classics, Gibbon's *The Decline and Fall of the Roman Empire*, Joseph Needham's *Science and Civilization in China*, and books on Alexander the Great, Hannibal, Julius Caesar, Genghis Khan, Mehmed the Conqueror, the Duke of Marlborough, Frederick the Great, Napoleon, Heinz Guderian, Georgy Zhukov and Moshe Dayan. The next shelf was home to the entire collection of Shakespeare's plays and sonnets, the complete Sherlock Holmes, and every one of Agatha Christie's mysteries. The bottom shelf was devoted to books and journals written by I. F. Stone, Gore Vidal and Upton Sinclair, with a small section reserved for the English versions of the four greatest classical novels of China: *Romance of the Three Kingdoms*, *Journey to the West*, *Water Margin* and *Dream of the Red Chamber*. Unfortunately, Victoria found nothing about roses.

As she seemed to have run into another dead end, Victoria hit the mother lode. She noticed a stack of books, DVDs, Blu-rays and CDs on the floor beside the bookcase. It started from the top with a Unitel-Classica HDTV production of the Richard Strauss opera *Der Rosenkavalier* on Blu-ray. It sat on top of a Deutsche Grammophon compilation CD of Schubert lieders, featuring Goethe's "Gretchen am Spinnrade" and "Heidenröslein," which, in turn, rested on top of six DVDs. The first one was the Disney classic *Sleeping Beauty*, the second was the blockbuster *Titanic* by James Cameron, the third was the biopic *La Môme* about the French singer Édith Piaf, the fourth was *Citizen Kane* by Orson

Wells, the fifth was a documentary titled *The Roosevelts*, and the last was another documentary, *The Children of Soong Ching Ling.*

Books made up the rest of the stack, starting with Antoine de Saint-Exupéry's bittersweet fable, *The Little Prince. Romeo and Juliet* occupied second place. Gertrude Stein's *Geography and Plays* was third, followed by two history hardcovers, *Lancaster and York* and *The Diet of Worms.* Under these, a curious pamphlet titled *Confessio fraternitatis Roseae Crucis, ad eruditos Europae* rested on top of the stack's foundation, also the giveaway clue, Umberto Eco's international bestseller, *The Name of The Rose.*

To the unsuspecting, this might have been a random pile of books and discs, but to Victoria, the stack screamed "roses." It did not occur to the riddle-solving girl all these "rose" connections came from the trivia she had memorized for crossword puzzles and Trivial Pursuit. In any case, Victoria was sure her hunch about *sub rosa* was correct. She checked through the stack item by item, searching for the secret behind the puzzle. Yet, she found nothing. Confident this rose-related stack did not assemble by itself, Victoria decided to look under the carpet.

After moving the stack to one side, Victoria noticed the carpet had been recently cut and stapled. She found a sheathed Swiss army dagger in a drawer and easily ripped the staples from the floor. True as the night was long, hidden under the carpet was a secret compartment. Victoria lifted the cover to reveal a grey-coloured jewellery box made of a light but sturdy fabric-like material, and displayed prominently on the lid of the box was the symbol of a plant in black.

Chapter 5

Sub Rosa

Victoria opened the jewellery box, hoping to discover answers to her questions. She noticed another symbol on the underside of the lid, resembling a simplified hand and an elephant.

Inside the box was a folded note from Michael and Angela.

Dear Victoria,

When you read this, we may not be here anymore. Don't be sad. We knew this day would come. Your destiny is not with us but with the stars. We love you very much and have sworn to protect you. You're a special gift from God, giving us a new lease on life when we should have been dead and buried. Go to Toronto and find Mr. David Huang. He gave you to us. He will tell you the whole story and take you to China to find your biological parents. His company, Solvicta Antiques, is in downtown Toronto.

The jade pendant and ring inside this box are your belongings. Keep them safe with you at all times. Take also the Almanac. When we were in China to adopt you, we met a blind fortune-teller outside the White Swan Hotel in Guangzhou, where we were staying. He knew many secrets and gave us the book to protect you. He warned us never to lose the book and to tell no one about it. Even David Huang does not know. But you can trust David to be your guardian. We have been safe all these years because of him. The symbol on the back of this letter is David's sign, by which you can identify him. Burn the letter after reading it.

Be careful, be brave, and everything will be fine.

Love you,
Mama and Papa

A teardrop fell onto the note as Victoria finished reading. She turned it over to find a symbol on the back.

Victoria sketched it on her palm and incinerated the letter with a cigarette lighter. Inside the jewellery box, she found a prepaid cash card and a wad of one-hundred-dollar bills in U.S., Canadian and Chinese currencies on top of a yellowish arch-shaped jade pendant attached to a red string for wearing around the neck. Inscribed on both faces of the pendant were some cryptic symbols.

Also attached to the red string was a ring fashioned from what appeared to be animal horn. Under a bright light, it sparkled with the fire of a million stars. A mythical beast design, similar to the beast face in the Almanac, was carved on the front of the ring.

Inscribed on the back of the ring were two more symbols.

Victoria pulled the red string over her head and stuffed the pendant and ring inside her shirt. She found no answers in the jewellery box but more mysteries instead. Why did her parents say her destiny was with the stars? Why did her parents say they should have been dead and buried? Why did they swear to protect their daughter? Weren't parents supposed to protect their children?

Victoria had no clue why, all of a sudden, people attacked her family and destroyed her peaceful, calm and uneventful life. None of this made sense. The phone rang again. As before, the caller hung up without saying a word. But the message was clear. Victoria knew no matter how hard it was, she must leave the house before trouble knocked at the door.

She grabbed the book she was reading, *Childhood's End* by Sir Arthur C. Clarke, the Almanac, her tablet, a change of underwear, her toothbrush, face cream, a few sanitary pads and two bars of Ecuadorian rainforest dark chocolate saved up for emergencies, stuffed them in her knapsack and walked out of the only life she had ever known.

Victoria took one long, last look at the beautiful little house she called home. It was her cozy nest, where she spent her happiest days and created her memories. It was her strong fortress, where her family was always safe from harm. She must now say goodbye, not knowing if she would ever return. Victoria must leave the safety of her sanctuary and venture into the wild and dangerous world on her own.

Christmas was two days away. Though it was not the same holy day her parents celebrated, Victoria loved its festive spirit. Most of her neighbours had decked their houses and front yards with Christmas lights and garden ornaments to evoke happiness and excitement. However, on this occasion, Victoria was overcome by an abject sadness and a morbid fear of the unknown. On this, her sixteenth birthday, when she should be celebrating with family and friends, she suddenly found herself up to her neck in turbulent waters, surrounded by circling sharks, with no land in sight in all directions. To whom could she turn for help? Who was David Huang? Her parents must have good reasons for never mentioning the man or revealing his background. Victoria must first catch the coach to downtown Toronto, pass the night in a safe place and figure out how to locate him.

As Victoria strode past Emma's and Jackie's houses, keeping herself in the shadows, she decided to bid farewell to the Weird Sisters. She could not vanish from their lives without saying a word. But what should she tell them? Would divulging her secrets endanger them and their families? Victoria's mysterious enemies had already demonstrated they were powerful and ruthless. Could Emma and Jackie keep Victoria's secrets?

Chapter 6

Weird Sisters

Victoria lived about ten minutes by foot from Emma and Jackie. Both her BFFs came from wealthier families living in large, opulent houses.

Jackie's grandparents emigrated from Athens to Toronto in the sixties. They worked hard, invested wisely and made a fortune in real estate. Jackie's father, a McMaster alumnus, retired upon receiving his inheritance, moving the family to Dundas, where he spent all his free time at the Dundas Valley Golf and Curling Club. Sharp-tongued Jackie was the tallest of the girls, making her the perfect candidate to be their protector and spokesperson.

Emma, the freckle-faced blonde beauty, attracted boys in the way flowers lured bees. She enjoyed regaling the Weird Sisters with the pranks she played on her gaggle of admirers. Emma's father, Professor Stanley Stone, came from old English stock with a long history in Canada. He taught Applied Mathematics at McMaster University. Emma's German-Canadian mother, Lorelei Herrmann, was reputed to be a cryptographer at an agency with an acronym. She would neither confirm nor deny the rumour.

Victoria loved to listen to Emma's brainy parents discuss whimsical topics such as Higgs Boson, Lie Groups, Galois Theory, Yang-Mills theory, Bayes theorem, the Poincaré conjecture, the Riemann hypothesis, Schrödinger's Wave Function, Heisenberg's Uncertainty Principle, Superstring theory, the Epimenides paradox, the Fermi paradox and other equally impenetrable imponderables.

Despite not understanding what they were talking about most of the time, Victoria rated Emma's parents as super-cool.

Professor Stone and Lorelei sometimes conjured outlandish ideas, such as the concept of the largest integer, which they coined the Boggle. The number was so immense Victoria could not wrap her head around it. Once, she overheard them talking about the Grand Unification Theory. They were at odds with the idea a single line of an equation could describe the universe for eternity.

"I'm not sure if it's science," Professor Stone complained, "when we're applying mathematical tricks to satisfy a reality we know little about. How can we hope to find the eternal fundamental truth of the universe when we have gathered only a minute amount of information from an imperceptible iota in space for a fleeting moment, all of which is limited to our observable dimensions beyond which we can't imagine or test?"

"And everything is based on the assumption our math has an unshakable foundation," Lorelei added in agreement. "Bertrand Russell and Kurt Gödel proved we shouldn't be so cocksure about what we think we know. Maybe we know nothing. My current work on entropy and information theory is giving me second thoughts about the Second Law of Thermodynamics."

Another time, Victoria listened to Emma's parents expatiating about the imperfect human perception of reality.

According to Professor Stone, scientists exploring fundamental laws were blind philosophers examining an elephant's exterior to define the animal in its entirety. While one might guess the lateral symmetry, it would be a thankless task to reconcile the ear with the tusk or the nose with the tail and to fit all the elements of the elephant into a single, unified theoretical construct.

Would this perception of reality have anything to do with the elephant glyph on the jewellery box?

After launching a few well-aimed pebbles at Jackie's bedroom window, Victoria extracted her best friend from the house without alerting the rest of her family. Upon Victoria's request, Jackie texted Emma, summoning her to a Weird Sisters meeting.

"Coven call. Hush hush. Your backyard. Pronto."

Victoria and Jackie were shivering in the backyard when Emma opened the door and beckoned them to get in.

"Let us meet out here," Victoria whispered. "I'll be quick. I don't want anyone else to know I've been here."

Emma wrapped herself in a warm overcoat and sneaked out, thinking, "A secret in the middle of the night, how exciting!"

"Girls, something unexpected happened tonight," Victoria said, holding her friends' hands. "I can't say too much except I'll have to leave town ASAP, and I don't know when I'll be back."

Emma and Jackie were shocked into silence.

"I'm going to China to find my biological parents. It may take some time. I'm going to miss you both."

"This is so sudden," Emma said. "What about your parents here? Are they going with you?"

"Our car got hit by a truck and exploded," Victoria said, bursting into tears. "I barely escaped. My parents are dead, and if I don't leave now, I'll be dead too. Before I got out, my dad told me it was not an accident. He also told me where to get help. It's much safer if you don't know about it. Don't let anyone know you've seen me, including your parents and the police. You'll have to pretend I'm dead. I have to go, but not without saying goodbye."

"Oh my God," Emma gasped while comforting Victoria. "It was your car in the breaking news!"

Victoria confirmed, gesturing for Emma to lower her voice.

"You're not going to China all by yourself," Jackie said after recovering from the shock. "We're the Weird Sisters, Vicky. It's one for all and all for one. Let us know how we can help you."

"No, once the people who murdered my parents realize I survived the crash, they'll be hunting for me. I can't get you two involved. It's too dangerous. Also, we shouldn't use our chat accounts. I'll get in touch when I know it's safe."

"We can set up accounts with fake names," Jackie said. "I'll be Atropos, Emma can be Lachesis, and you can be Clotho. We'll send short coded messages and delete them afterwards."

The girls knew these names well. They had familiarized themselves with the Greek goddesses of Fate while playing the computer game Moirai.

Intrigued by sisterly trinities, Victoria had read up on the Three Sisters of the Orion constellation, better known as Orion's Belt, and Hinduism's Tridevi, the three goddesses Lakshmi, Parvati and Saraswati. She also informed herself about the Norns, the three Norse goddesses of destiny, Urd, Skuld and Verdandi. Her trivia knowledge included the three Soong sisters, the most influential women in China during the twentieth century. One of her favourite books was John Updike's novel about three women in a small town, *The Witches of Eastwick.* Victoria even heard of the Bilderberg Group, the Trilateral Commission and the Council on Foreign Relations, dubbed the "Three Sisters" by conspiracy theorists.

While they spoke, a black SUV sped by without regard for speed limits or stop signs, turning off its headlights as it flew past Emma's house.

"I better go," Victoria said. "I'll send messages when I can. Don't worry. I'll be fine."

The freezing rain started to fall again. Victoria hugged her BFFs and hurried off. As she left the people and life she knew and loved, she tried to savour the sweet sorrow and not lose the moment in time, like tears in rain.

Chapter 7

War of the Wolves

In 209 BCE, twelve years after the Qin State conquered all the other warring states to establish the Qin Empire, the first empire in China, disaster struck. After five hundred and fifty years of nonstop wars, the long-suffering peasants hoped peace would last, but they hoped in vain. Mars had aligned with Antares of Scorpius two years ago, heralding a bloody mess. One year after the heavenly portent, Qin Shihuang, the first emperor of a unified China, passed away. His dream of building a ten-thousand-generation dynasty would die with him. Another soul-crushing conflict would engulf the world. It was great news for the warlike Eastern Wolf tribes, known in China as Donghu. Their wish would not be in vain.

The camp of the Eastern Wolf was abuzz with excitement. The order had come down for all men of fighting age to prepare for battle. The Tengri, or Great Chief, of the Eastern Wolf Confederation had gathered two hundred thousand bows, the most massive and fearsome horde ever assembled by any northern nomads. Their enemy and erstwhile kin, Modred, known as Modu (冒顿) in history, could muster at most forty thousand men, of which only ten thousand were loyal followers. Modred must answer for the crime of having murdered his father to take over the leadership of the Huns, a wolf tribe known in China as Xiongnu.

To the Eastern Wolf warriors, Modred must be mad, and the Huns must be crazy to follow him to certain death. Everyone expected Modred to slip away during the night. Instead, he rode out early in the morning, seeking battle. The desperate man had a death wish, but so be it. The oracle had spoken, "It will be a great slaughter." The Eastern Wolf warriors had been looking forward to this for a long time.

Among the Eastern Wolf tribes, only one young man, Lone Wolf, remained unenthusiastic about the coming battle. As the adopted son of one of the great tribal chiefs named the Tuman (头曼), he took a wimpish antiwar position, besmirching his father's ancient title, which meant "the wise chief of a myriad host."

Lone Wolf was feeding his horses, talking to them to calm their nerves and making sure his weapons were in working order when two armed men rode by, one of them deliberately knocking the arrows out of his quiver.

The troublemaker was White Wolf, the eldest son of the Tuman and Lone Wolf's adoptive brother.

"What do you need these arrows for?" he sneered. "Didn't you have a thousand reasons not to fight today?"

"You don't need so many excuses," taunted North Wolf, White Wolf's younger brother. "If you're afraid, you can stay here with the women, but make sure you clean all the horse shite."

Both men burst out laughing as they trotted off to marshal their men. Lone Wolf ignored the insults and stooped to pick up his arrows. He refused to be angry at his adoptive brothers for the sake of the Tuman. Someone picked up one of his arrows and handed it to him. Lone Wolf turned around to gaze into the stunning green eyes of an adolescent girl with Eurasian features.

"Wolf Star, you're a sight for sore eyes," Lone Wolf greeted the girl with a beamish smile. "Where have you been? I thought you had forgotten me after your betrothal ceremony."

"I'll pretend I didn't hear that. I've been busy doing my duties for this tribal alliance they imposed on me, getting acquainted with my future husband's large clan. But, because of the coming battle, we have postponed the wedding."

"Do you know where your future tribe will migrate after the battle? If they go west, I'll lose a good friend."

"I'll lose a good friend, too," Wolf Star said, her eyes misting up. "I already miss the times you told me those amazing stories. Lupalina had warned me about you and your stories. She says after I marry, I must keep my distance from you. Just in case we don't see each other, I've come to say goodbye."

Lone Wolf knew his friendship with Wolf Star would end as she approached marrying age. He stared at her for a few seconds in awkward silence, debating whether to intervene in her fate.

"Tell me, Wolf Star. Why are you having your nuptials after the battle? Is everyone so sure we will win?"

"All the warriors are confident of a great victory. And I want to talk to you about something. I hear gossip you've been advising the Tuman not to join the war against the Huns. People are saying bad things about you. You've got to be careful. An arrow in the battlefield can come from behind your back."

"I know," Lone Wolf sighed. "I've been telling anyone with ears this war won't end well for us, but no one listens. People don't want to hear the truth because they've invested too much energy defending the lies. The oracle says it will be a great slaughter but doesn't say by which side. We only hear what our prejudice wants us to hear. Because of this common flaw, Croesus, the wealthiest man in my story, lost everything he owned.

"Listen to me carefully and do as I say. Go to your yurt and prepare dry meat, yogurt and water to last a half-moon. Bring your sheep, horses and wolfdogs to the east gate to join up with Lupalina and a group of women and children. Trust me, it'll save your life."

"What about my future husband?"

"Go and say goodbye to him. We're all rushing headlong into the slaughterhouse. No one knows who will escape unscathed. We'll leave it to the gods. In my case, I'm under the cruel spell of Cassandra's Curse, but for you, do as I say, and you'll survive. We have an old saying, 'Keep the mountains green, and we'll always have firewood.' The survival of the Eastern Wolf tribes depends on the women and children. You must stay alive."

Lone Wolf glued his eyes on Wolf Star while she scurried off, reflecting, "What an odd-looking girl with red hair, green eyes and fair skin!" As Lone Wolf was an outcast, so was Wolf Star. She was not yet sixteen and not much more than a child when Lone Wolf joined the tribe three years ago. He was eighteen or nineteen at the time. They hit it off as though they had known each other forever. They remained close friends even after the Tuman pledged her to a chieftain from a neighbouring tribe.

Wolf Star and Lupalina were kinfolks of the Tuman's wife, who went by the title of Ianse, known in China as Yanshi (阏氏). The Ianse's tribe had migrated over a hundred years from the northwest beyond the Celestial Mountains and the ends of the known world. They joined the Eastern Wolf tribes when their chief gave his daughter to the Tuman for marriage. The alliance produced two strapping sons, White Wolf and North Wolf.

Lone Wolf's memory wandered back to three years ago on the day when he woke from a trauma near the Tuman's camp. He was wrapped in a black shroud, suffering from a headache of biblical proportions and hurting as if a searing fire was scorching him from head to toe. The Tuman saved his life by throwing him into an icy stream and having Lupalina nurse him back from the brink of death. At the time, he did not know his name and only retained blurry images of the past.

The Goddess of Fortune, Tyche, looked with favour on the young man when the Tuman decided to adopt him and name him

Lone Wolf. Over the years, his lost memories drifted back. He remembered Dragon was his name in his past life, and his family did not abandon him to die in the wilderness. For now, Lone Wolf must repay the Tuman's kindness and help his tribe survive the onslaught of the Huns.

Lone Wolf examined his sabre, named Luna, which he had forged from scrap iron. He did not learn the art of sword-making from the Wolf-smiths but recollected the skill from his memory. Luna turned out to be of *passing* strength and beauty, easily cleaving four horse carcasses in one slash. It proved to be the most formidable dealer of death in the north.

A messenger on horseback galloped over with a battle order.

"Lone Wolf, the Tuman has summoned you to be his spear carrier today, you lucky son of a she-wolf! Follow me."

Upon receiving the order, Lone Wolf donned his war cape, which he had altered from his shroud, and mounted his steed of sorrel red. With eagle feathers affixed to his mantle, when the young warrior rode, he resembled the angel of death, terrorizing earthlings and striking fear into the hearts of mere mortals.

The Tuman wielded an outsized spear eleven cubits in length. It was a symbol of his power, prowess and prestige. By tradition, a trusted chieftain carried the spear beside the Tuman whenever he paraded in public. Only a battle-tested warrior would enjoy this great honour and exclusive privilege, especially when committing bloody murder in times of war. Lone Wolf had no idea what prompted the Tuman to make his adopted and, therefore, least favourite son his spear carrier on this day of wrath. Whatever the case, he was glad he would be riding alongside his adoptive father into battle. Being right next to the Tuman, he would have the chance to return the favour to the old chief for saving his life.

Chapter 8

The Onslaught

Once armed and marshalled, the warriors of the Eastern Wolf tribes rode out of their camp to take their designated positions on the battlefield, an immense stretch of cavalry terrain facing a low ridge split open into a wide wooded mountain pass. Lone Wolf was at a loss for words as he feasted his eyes upon the magnificent sight of a massive army on horseback moving in formation and arrayed on a vast plain. It is no wonder the human spirit is enamoured of war. The breathtaking grandeur, pomp and pageantry could readily evoke an eruption of adrenaline and endorphins, driving the morons into a bloodthirsty frenzy and mutually assured destruction.

As expected, Modred adopted a defensive position across the mountain pass, ready to turn tail and skedaddle into the wild, wooded hills beyond. The Tengri's horde did not care how Modred deployed his men. With their overwhelming numerical advantage over the Huns, the Wolf warriors were confident they would overrun Modred's paltry army with one determined charge.

According to legend, the Eastern Wolf tribes and the Huns descended from the same ancestral Wolf clan that originated in the Wolf Mountain, a part of the Great Green Mountain Range known in China as Yinshan, the "Shady Mountains." The early Wolf tribe migrated south across the Yellow River into the fertile pocket known as the Ordos. They came into contact with the Shang kingdom, the earliest Chinese dynasty attested by archaeology, which lasted from circa 1600 to 1046 BCE. Shang culture was the progenitor of the Chinese civilization. The Wolf tribe fought wars against the Shang, later becoming a Shang ally and getting its name recorded in China's annals as Guifang (鬼方), the Land of Spirits, dramatized as the Gotts in Victoria's saga.

On this day of destiny, the two descendant branches of the ancient Wolf tribe met as implacable foes on the battlefield. The Tengri of the Eastern Wolf confederation, supported by his tribal chiefs, agreed to parley with Modred, exhausting all pretenses in peacemaking before the bloodletting. They met in the middle of the battlefield and started their verbal jousting.

"Modred, you execrable ingrate, evil incarnate, abortion of the earth," the Tengri opened with a barrage of name-calling from the moral high ground. "The tribes are here because of your egregious crime of patricide. Your heinous act is indefensible."

"Respected elders and cousins," Modred pleaded. "You must not pass rash judgment. My father, may he rest in peace, made me the hereditary son. But under the evil spell of his cursèd concubine, he sent me as a hostage to the remote western kingdom of Yozzi, known to some as Yuezhi, where they treated me worse than they would a sand scorpion. It didn't take long before my loving father attacked Yozzi, expecting them to flay me alive in revenge. What would you have done to survive? Am I allowed to defend myself?

"To save my skin, I stole Yozzi's best horse and escaped back to the Great Green Mountains, cheating death many times. When the common Huns welcomed me as a hero, I proved a tough nut for the concubine to crack. To up her game, she advised my dear father to put me in charge of ten thousand bows to expand his land holdings. If I succeeded, it'd be great. If I failed, they would have a perfect excuse to cut my throat. If I lost my head in the process, someone would've done the dirty deed for them. Hence, I risked my neck all the livelong day while the slut and her spawn sat at my father's table, wining and dining on the fruits of my labour, trying to usurp what was rightfully mine.

"I learned long ago I do not own anything I cannot defend. The Huns and our pastures belonged to me, not to some mealy-mouthed parasites which had crawled out of the womb of a slithering strumpet. If I don't defend what's mine, who will? Put yourself in my shoes. What would you have done?"

"You tell a fine tale," the Tengri scoffed. "Your father, the Hunnu Tuman, gave you your life and had the right to take it back. You, on the other hand, have no right to kill your father."

"Hear! Hear!" The tribal chiefs of the Eastern Wolves shouted in agreement.

"My Wolf brothers, if you must persecute me on this lie, I will plead my hands are unsullied with my father's blood. His people's arrows, not mine, struck him down."

"No judge in the world will accept your duplicitous argument," the Tengri declared with righteous indignation. "We know the account of the events. You were using whistle-arrows to train your archers. First, you sent your whistle-arrow toward your steed. When the archers balked, you cut their throats. Next, you shot your whistle-arrow toward your concubine. The archers, of course, held back. Again, you slew them without mercy. Finally, you launched your whistle-arrow toward your father's mount, and the archers unloosed their arrows. You knew they were ready.

"During the last hunting expedition of the Hunnu Tuman, you sent a whistle-arrow screaming toward him, and your well-trained archers, without hesitation, rained arrows on your unsuspecting father. The arrows may not be yours, but you're guilty of causing your father's death."

"My dear Tengri," Modred rebutted, unveiling his contempt for his accuser, "with all due respect, you should not speak with such sanctimony as if you were some shining beacon on a hill. You didn't judge me when you first heard of my family troubles. Instead, you came asking for my mighty steed from Yozzi. You didn't accuse me of anything when you held the reins of my prized horse. But it was too easy for you. Your greed and lust drove you to demand the hand of my beautiful wife, my helpmate, whom I loved. Against the advice of all my people who urged me to fight, I swallowed the insult and sent the woman to you.

"You did not accuse me then. No, I didn't hear any sententious talk of my crimes. But your greed knew no bounds. You believed you could extort anything from me and demanded to take large tracts of my marchland. When my counsellors imagined I would submit as before and advised me to cede our pastures, I tore them apart with my bare hands. Without land, I'm nothing; the Huns are nothing. I'll never cede an inch of land to you or your hounds.

"When you realized no land was forthcoming, you immediately accused me of all kinds of crime. If I'm guilty of staying alive, so be it. Your gilded words are so many shameless lies of hypocrites. Hypocrisy is a two-headed snake. It bites whoever is feeding it. Your people may be fools because they live their entire lives in the cesspool of your lies, but we can smell the stench from a mile away. Your moral law is a sick farce you use to delude yourself and your stupefied slaves. Your holy indignation will not move us. If you want our land, you must fight us and bleed for it."

"So be it," the Tengri declared with a voice cold as death. "This futile confabulation is over. Let the slaughter begin."

After the Tengri and the tribal chiefs returned to their positions at the front, the Great Chief signalled for the charge. The attack horns blared, and the game was afoot. The massive ranks began advancing in a walk, gradually quickening the pace to a trot and speeding to a canter. The earth trembled beneath the harmonious hammering of the heavy hooves, and the rumble resembled rolling thunder from the bowels of Tartarus, rising in a crescendo until it exploded in a roaring climax as the horses broke into a gallop. As if they were actors in a Greek tragedy, the Wolf warriors pranced in a danse macabre to the chorus of Carl Orff's "O Fortuna." Quaking in their boots, Modred and his Huns did not wait for the impact, retreating into the wooded hills beyond the pass.

Modred, the military genius, could be sharing his eternal abode with the likes of Ulysses and Guido da Montefeltro at the eighth pit of the eighth circle of Dante's Inferno, where they forever receive their just deserts from the fallen angels of the eighth order known as the black Cherubim, identified as Watchers from non-canonical sources. Modred had laid a perfect trap for his hubristic enemy, and the overweening fools plunged headlong into it. While the crafty Hun showed the Eastern Wolf his meagre troops, he had another eighty thousand men deployed in a deadly ambuscade. When Modred told his people the rapacious Eastern Wolf tribes were coming for their horses, women and pastures, every Hun rose to support their new leader.

Emulating Lord Cardigan's British Light Brigade, which charged into Russian hellfire at the Crimean peninsula, the first wave of the Eastern Wolf warriors rushed recklessly into a meat grinder. When the second wave arrived, they could not avoid running over the broken ranks of their retreating brothers.

Without forewarning, a howling wind and a blinding sandstorm joined the mortal struggle. The Wolf warriors who survived the ambush could not see beyond their immediate fate, which was certain death, either at the hands of their confused brethren or by the trampling of their unnerved horses. Lone Wolf wanted to stop the Tuman from charging into this maelstrom of death, but the momentum for self-destruction was unstoppable. The Tuman grabbed his fearsome spear of eleven cubits and disappeared into the fog of war. Lone Wolf had no choice but to follow.

Riding into the pass, Lone Wolf beheld a gruesome sight he had foreseen in his dreams. Crushed skulls, cleaved torsos and severed limbs scattered across the blood-stained earth. Those who were lucky died straight away, while the half-dead writhed in agony, begging for mercy with a coup de grâce to the head. The groaning of the damned echoed in the valley of death, as if they were singing the chorus of the Requiem Aeternam in the Harrowing of Hell. Some cursed the gods with their last breath, while others asked why their gods had forsaken them. The godless also questioned why, not why they were dying, but why they had ever lived!

Lone Wolf wept because he knew this day would come, but his hands were tied, and he couldn't save anyone. They all lost their precious lives defending their silly lies. The routed survivors of the once proud Eastern Wolf tribes fled among riderless horses in a pell-mell from the killing field. Lone Wolf saw White Wolf and North Wolf galloping away from the slaughter they had long yearned for. He asked them for their father's whereabouts and told them to join Lupalina, but they did not even slow down to respond.

Lone Wolf could smell the thickening stench of death. He must find the Tuman. A straggler told Lone Wolf to turn back and save himself. He had witnessed the Tuman banner going down. The chief and his bravest men were outnumbered, outgunned and outfoxed. They were as good as dead, or as the saying goes, dead as Schrödinger's cat. Ignoring the advice, Lone Wolf pressed on and braced himself for the approaching storm.

The young Wolf warrior heard three horses thundering toward him through a cloud of dust. He lifted three arrows from the quiver and drew his bow. As the three Huns came into view, Lone Wolf let loose the three darts all at once. At the sound of the bowstring singing the death tunes of Apollo's lyre, the three Huns fell off their horses as one. The warrior in the middle swallowed the arrow in his mouth and expired before he hit the ground. The one on the left heaved his final breath when the dart went through his neck and tore his throat apart. The last missile drilled through the left eye of the third Hun and expelled half his brain, launching his spirit on a short flight to the Elysian plains. But more Huns were closing in. Lone Wolf spurred his steed and charged as he drew Lady Luna and raised her to heaven. With his left hand, he held steady the reins, a small round shield and a spiked mace.

The first Hun on the right was quick to meet his Maker. Lone Wolf swung his cold steel in a sweep and cleaved the man's head from his shoulders. The next Hun on the left was slow to duck. Lone Wolf dealt the man a blow with his mace, rearranging the features on his orcish face. On the right again, Lone Wolf bent to evade the oncoming sabre while he slashed with his blade, bisecting the Hun across his waist. On the left, he broke his shield against a powerful spear thrust and, wielding his mace, returned the favour, flattening the enemy's helmet and his skull within. Out in front, two Huns attacked from both sides all at once. Lone Wolf threw his mace at the one on the left, unhorsing a man who had spent his entire life on horseback. On the right, Lone Wolf parried and slashed in one flourish, sundering the Hun's shoulder from his convulsing carcass.

Two more Huns rode up on either side. Lone Wolf had lost his shield and was defenceless, or so the hapless Huns believed. Unbeknownst to the enemy, Lone Wolf wore an iron gauntlet on his left hand. He blocked the blow from the Hun on the left with his metal sleeve and rammed his steel claws into the poor grunt's chest, plucking out his throbbing heart for all to see. On the right, with Lady Luna, Lone Wolf sliced through the Hun's sabre as if it were a loaf of French baguette and, with one swipe, surgically separated the man's brain from his head. Rumours ran riot about the poor Hun living for hours before realizing he was dead!

By now, the Huns had seen enough of the devil and decided to let the bloodthirsty butcher through.

Lone Wolf found the Tuman alone and slumped on his steed. Every one of his best warriors had fallen. The old chief had no more strength yet held on to his spear. The dying Tuman had stuck the bloodied and torn Tuman banner in his belt. He would rather lose his life than his honour. An arrow had found its mark in his chest. Through sheer will, the chief lived to see his adopted son.

"Lone Wolf, you're here," the Tuman wheezed and whispered. "Take my spear and banner. Go back and save my tribe. Let me die on the battlefield. It is all a warrior can hope for."

"You'll live, my lord," Lone Wolf said. "If the Huns can't stop me from getting to you, they sure as hell won't stop me from getting you out of here."

Indeed, the Huns opened a path for Lone Wolf and the Tuman, watching their passage from afar. Aside from the rational fear of death, the Huns also marvelled at the bravery and martial prowess of this fearsome god of war, who rode in alone and rescued his chief from a deadly trap.

The Tuman had not expected to benefit from saving Lone Wolf three years ago. When the chief found the young man wrapped in a death shroud abandoned to perish in the wilderness, he noticed this was no ordinary man. Yet, little could the Tuman have guessed coursing through Lone Wolf's veins was the blood of an ancient race of civilized kings. The young man also carried a "ghost" gene of immense power known as the Half-Key, which came from long ago and far away. And so it goes. The tale unfolds.

Chapter 9

The Warrior Queen

During the early thirteenth century BCE, a great war fought by gods and men for the sake of a woman was brewing between the Greek city-states and the Ionian colonies across the Aegean Sea. More than a century earlier, a wandering tribe named Shang arrived at the Central Plains in East China, occupied its heartland and held all other tribes in thrall with their advanced technologies, knowledge of the stars, a writing system and the unstinted favour of the gods in war, marking the flowering of a civilization which continues uninterrupted to the present age.

In its heyday, the Shang tribe constantly clashed with its neighbours, conquering all. Rather than being the cause of epic wars, Shang women took arms and fought in them.

With night fast approaching, Queen Zia's troops finally dislodged the rearguards of the Gotts from a key hillock following a heavy skirmish. The rapid advance of the Queen's hoplites stunned the northern barbarians. The Shang army had the reputation of moving at the blinding speed of molasses. They built caravansaries along their roads eight kilometres apart, representing a day's march. This distance was named a *she* (舍).

The Gotts moved at least twice as fast but were bogged down on this occasion by their massive horde and prodigious plunder. From their reconnaissance reports, the Gotts knew the Shang king Wotan, known in Chinese history as Wuding (武丁), was more than eleven days' march away with the bulk of his army, which might as well be the other side of the galaxy. They were, however, unaware the king's favourite wife, Queen Zia, taking the advice of her chief counsellor, Lady Diane, had decided to give chase with her smaller, more agile personal troops.

Although the hillock could barely qualify as a grassy knoll in the middle of an otherwise featureless terrain, it commanded an unobstructed view of the entire area up to a river swollen by recent rainfall about three kilometres to the north. The mound also screened the Queen's reserve troops from the enemy's view, allowing them to be deployed and manoeuvred unobserved.

The northern marauders thus found themselves caught in an unenviable dilemma. They needed to return to their home base, but trying to cross the river with their loot while Queen Zia's army was hot at their heels courted disaster. They could give up their spoils and disperse, but having come a long way from the north, no one wanted to go home empty-handed.

The river curved south toward the Shang army's right, forming a natural defence for the Gotts' left flank. Their only escape route was to the northwest, but a village stronghold and thick woods stood in the way. In any case, marching across the front with their left flank exposed to attack by Queen Zia's army was too risky. The Gotts were trapped, but they preferred to fight anyway. Death would be better than running home with their tails tucked between their legs, with nothing to show after raiding deep inside Shang.

The Gotts routinely ran roughshod over the Shang villagers with their legendary whirlwind charges. Upon the arrival of Queen Zia's army, the barbarians must contend with well-trained, disciplined and armoured hoplites wielding bronze spears and poleaxes deployed in bristling phalanxes defended by interlocking rectangular shields. Furthermore, a war-hardened aristocrat in a four-horse chariot led each phalanx. The Gotts should expect a stiff challenge from the Shang queen.

Riding in their war chariots and ringed by a hundred mounted Guards, Queen Zia and Lady Diane arrived at the top of the hillock to inspect the lay of the land. Queen Zia's horses were brilliant white, while Lady Diane's were glistening black. The personal Guards consisted of twenty-five female warriors, with the rest being eunuch soldiers who had their left eye ritually blinded.

The Shang word for "soldier slave," *zang* (臧), depicts a poleaxe stabbing an eye, while the pictogram for "common slave," *tong* (童), is a dagger piercing a man's eye.

A personal guard tagged along with the charioteer in the Queen's royal chariot, carrying the Queen's fasces known as the *yue* (钺), a battle axe representing her aristocratic and military authority. The Queen held the power and discretion to take the lives of her subjects but bore full responsibility for their well-being. Power and responsibility always exist in a tenuous balance.

Lady Diane enjoyed Queen Zia's favour by being her most capable general and closest companion. Her chariot came with a guard holding the Queen's minor *yue*, a slightly smaller axe.

Queen Zia occupied a unique and exalted position in the Shang's royal house. Not only was she King Wotan's highest-ranking wife, head of his harem of over sixty wives and concubines, most of whom married for political alliances, but she was also his High Priestess and most powerful warrior. During an earlier war, King Wotan entrusted her with the largest army ever assembled by the Shang kingdom. Queen Zia held an unassailable advantage over other wives. She was King Wotan's blood kin.

Arrayed in body armour of bronze plates resembling dragon scales, Queen Zia had cut short the lives of many enemies with her bow and arrows. She donned a shining bronze helmet with two tall pheasant feathers nodding in the air to inspire awe. Similarly armoured, Lady Diane had eagle feathers for her helm. The Queen draped a white cape on her back while a black mantle billowed behind Lady Diane. In their early twenties, both bodacious bellatrices could be haute couture models on runways in Paris, Milan and Shanghai. As King Wotan's favourite wife, Queen Zia would give birth to two princes and two princesses, securing her status as the Queen Mother of the future ruler of the realm.

"What do you think?" Queen Zia asked her favourite. "Will tomorrow be a good day for battle?"

"It'll be the best day ever," Lady Diane replied with supreme confidence. "The gods have spoken. They're on our side."

The Shang, especially their aristocrats, were religious zealots relying on oracles to guide their daily decisions. They prepared tortoise plastrons or animal bones, such as the bull's shoulder blade, and divined their oracles on them. An official diviner would place a red-hot metallic rod at specific notches prepared for the purpose, creating a crack in the surface and making a loud pop. The direction of the fissure revealed whether the gods agreed or disagreed with the question. The pronunciation of the Shang word for this oracular divination is *bu*, the onomatopoeia of the popping sound, and the pictogram is a drawing of the crack (⺊). The Shang language is easy to learn.

The scriveners would meticulously carve the oracles on the bones or plastrons used for the divination. The characters are known as the Oracle Bone script, the oldest written language of China and the progenitor of modern Chinese writing. Scholars can trace many modern Chinese characters to their original Oracle Bone forms.

"Will trickery in divination guarantee victory for us?" Queen Zia said with uneasiness in her voice. "If we wait for the King, we can be more assured of the outcome."

Queen Zia and Lady Diane were high priestesses and official diviners and knew the tricks of the trade. Clever diviners could always predetermine results with a bit of simple preparation.

"Have faith, Domina. Even if you doubt the fickle gods, you can trust my generalship. I have yet to fail you. 'Tis not every day we trap the elusive Gotts. Let us prepare for battle. We shall have a great victory tomorrow."

"As you wish, my brave Diane. Come to my tent and have a drink with me. I wish to present you with a good luck charm for the battle. You'll sleep in my tent tonight. Tomorrow, we fight."

"Yes, Domina. But I'd like to stay a while longer to study the enemy. I'll join you after sundown."

"Make it quick. Wine waits for no one," the Queen said before retracing her route down the hillock with her guards.

As the day was drawing to a close, Shang soldiers made offerings to the reclining sun god, one of the most important of their numerous deities. The founder of the Shang Dynasty was Tang (汤). In the Oracle Bone script, his name depicts the sun's warm rays, a blessing generously bestowed by the Creator God on the human race.

According to ancient Chinese myth, ten suns once loitered in the empyreal realm, destroying humanity with fire and flood until the hero Houyi, husband of the moon goddess Chang'e, shot down nine with his divine bow and arrows, leaving only one to rise and set each day. The Shang word for "olden times" (昔) is a drawing of the sun and antediluvian flood.

Immanuel Velikovsky, a scholar of the remote past and author of the book *Worlds in Collision*, believed a Near Earth Object once passed close to our planet, causing the sun to stop moving along the ecliptic, thus creating the myth. His theory attracted a large following, but Carl Sagan begged to differ.

Lady Diane surveyed the Gotts' camp, noting a formidable enemy well-armed, well-organized and well-prepared for battle. She diverted her gaze southward to admire the picturesque view of the great kingdom of Shang, a living watercolour of idyllic villages bedecked by ribbons of rising smoke. The forced march of the Queen's troops had spared these settlements from being overrun by the rampaging Gotts. The season was mid-autumn, the leaves were changing colour, and harvest was underway. The peasants burned the stalks of harvested crops, generating smoke to repel locusts and birds, while the ashes became fertilizer for next year's crops. The Shang created the word for autumn from this imagery.

In the early days of King Wotan's reign, Queen Zia was only one of his many wives, and Lady Diane was one of the Queen's many handmaids. Both girls would have wasted their lives away in the seraglio. Bored by a life of languor and dissipation, Lady Diane convinced Queen Zia to gain freedom in adventures.

The opportunity availed itself when King Wotan encountered difficulties dealing with Tufang (土方), the Sand Kingdom, in the north. On Lady Diane's advice, Queen Zia pleaded with her husband to let her lead an army to pacify their nettlesome neighbour. For lack of a better alternative and his love for the Queen, King Wotan relented, granting her fifteen hundred picked men with fifty chariots. Meanwhile, Duke Yarjee (亚其), the Queen's father, loaned her a thousand soldiers and twenty chariots. King Wotan, however, did not hold high hopes for his wife's first foray into organized violence.

Therefore, when messengers arrived at the Shang capital bearing news of how Queen Zia had crushed the Sand Kingdom's army, razed its walled settlements, captured the ruling clan, enslaved a thousand young men in the flower of their youth and was returning home laden with loot, King Wotan was overjoyed, travelling an unprecedented ten *shes* to welcome home his triumphant wife. Henceforth, Queen Zia became the top girl of the dragon's lair and gave the Shang king his first prince of the blood.

According to the customs of war, King Wotan rewarded Queen Zia with a tract of fertile land populated by hardy subjects, over which she reigned as an independent vassal. Of course, the Queen did not live in her fief but sent personal servants to administer it.

As the crepuscular light of the setting sun faded away, the stars began to twinkle in the evening sky. Lady Diane gazed at the brilliant Orion with forlorn longing, overwhelmed by a wave of sadness as bits of buried memory escaped from the dark corners of her heart. She remembered waking in the wilderness wrapped in a black shroud, suffering from a headache of biblical proportions and hurting as if a fire was scorching her from head to toe. The dazed girl was unsure of who she was or whence she came, only vaguely remembering she had lost the love of her life and the fruit of their love. Her banishment to this violent land offered no escape. She might never see her loved ones again. For a long time, she cried herself to sleep every night.

By a stroke of luck, Queen Zia found Lady Diane during a royal hunt and healed her, keeping her as a handmaid. On an average day during the Shang Dynasty, it was unbecoming of a Shang aristocrat to save the life of a dying slave. The Queen had noticed a tiny red tattoo on the girl's forehead. The Shang word for "concubine," *qie* (妾), meaning "female slave," was the drawing of a tattoo knife atop a woman's head. Red tattoos, however, had a special meaning; the Shang cast spells on the bodies of the dead with them. The Queen believed the slave girl must have survived an ordeal. It was the destiny of a person who had cheated death to accomplish great deeds.

As Queen Zia's status rose, so did Lady Diane's fortunes. When the warrior queen received her fief, her deputy gained an official title with choice fields as her reward. The Queen named her favourite handmaid Diane, a derivative of her aristocratic title, *Dian*. The title was related to the official's duty of managing the Shang king's cultivated lands and hunting grounds. The pictogram for the word *dian* (甸) portrays a person attending a field.

Even in those days when warrior queens were not uncommon, it was more than unusual for an unmarried female slave to hold property and a title. As Queen Zia's favourite, Lady Diane broke all the rules and traditions. Not only did she often parade around town in her four-horse royal chariot, but she always brought an axe carrier bearing the Queen's minor *yue* to boot. It would be wise for men who had some wrongheaded belief in women's place in society to shut their pie holes and keep their prejudiced opinions to themselves, lest they venture to experience the caress of the Queen's axe on the back of their necks.

Lady Diane was no nameless slave, nor would she ever be a concubine of some beady-eyed, bushy-browed, hairy-nosed, shaggy-bearded, gamey-breathed, bandy-legged Shang lord. In her veins coursed the blue blood of an ancient lineage of warriors who trained their girls from a young age to be superior fighters. She also carried a "ghost" gene of immense power known as the Half-Key, which came from long ago and far away.

Lady Diane doffed her helmet, revealing the red tattoo on her forehead. While it marked her as a future queen, it also served as her shackle. It ended up saving her life and keeping the flame of hope alive. And so it goes. The tale unfolds.

Chapter 10

The Unicorn Rings

Lady Diane summoned the senior commanders of the various units to Queen Zia's Tiger Tent for the war meeting. The Queen's army, a product of Lady Diane's martial expertise, boasted to be the most sophisticated military organization of its time. The Shang assembled their combat units at ten, a hundred, five hundred, up to a thousand hoplites. Depending on the number of war chariots available, twenty-five to fifty hoplites fought as a phalanx unit under the command of an aristocrat riding in a chariot drawn by two or four horses according to rank. Lady Diane adopted the structure and trained soldiers to specialize in specific tasks. She sensed the coming battle would be hard-fought, as the Gotts had their backs to the river. A cornered beast is a dangerous beast.

Contrary to rumours, the Gotts were no savages. Lady Diane noted they had an organized army with infantry units and armoured cavalry regiments. Having drawn the grain wagons into a circle, they had made their camp a fortress where they corralled the plundered animals and the kidnapped children. Subduing the Gotts would not be a cakewalk.

Nevertheless, Lady Diane planned to spring a few surprises on them. The fighting would start at dawn with the sun shining into the Gotts' eyes. An early battle would be a surprise in itself. The Shang soldiers always made an offering to the sun at first light, followed by a full meal. Afterwards, they took turns relieving themselves, leaving a foul mess. Upon the Shang army drawing up the battle lines, the diviner would ask the oracles whether they should fight. It was surprising they fought any battles at all.

Lady Diane did not care for unreasonable rules. She sent heralds around the camp, announcing the favourable oracle for an early battle and the promise of rewards. In addition to the regular share of the spoils, each enemy's left ear collected would yield a bounty of twenty cowry shells. The purse for capturing a breathing prisoner was fifty cowry shells. The Shang commander who killed an enemy chieftain in single combat would get the spolia opima, or rich spoils, which included all the properties of the slain enemy chieftain. As a meed of honour, the Queen would pay the hero twenty bronze cowry shells and two bronze spades, known as *qian* (钱), from her treasury, making him rich. On the other hand, a swift death awaited disobedience or cowardice during battle.

The cowry shells were not trumpery designed to scam the soldiers. The Shang used them as currency. The word *bei* (贝) for "cowry shell" is a radical which forms a part of many modern Chinese words relating to money, wealth and trade. As Shang society developed, cowry shells from the southern seas became inadequate as a currency, and, over time, bronze money replaced it.

The production of bronzeware necessitated a significant investment in food. Imagine the expertise, time and effort required to discover the mines, excavate the ores, extract the metals and deliver the ingots over long distances and hostile territories to the smithies equipped with high-temperature kilns to get things made. Everyone on this supply chain needed food produced by the peasants, without which, the world would have no nation builders, no scientists, no philosophers, no artists, no palaces, no castles, no world wars, no money, and no advanced civilizations. Without peasants and their surplus food, we would still be Stone Age hunter-gatherers. Praise the peasants for their investments!

However, the peasants needed soldiers to protect their fields, water supply and produce. As a result, they lost everything to the most cunning and violent killers, who made themselves kings.

The high priests also vied for power, monopolizing the knowledge they gained while consuming the food invested by the peasants. They turned around to enslave their benefactors with the fear of God, mesmerizing them with fabulous tales of hope and salvation while promising eternal rewards payable after death. To perpetuate the pillage and plunder, the holy men conspired with the kings to legitimize their rapine and murder by inventing the Mandate of Heaven. Peasants have been oppressed ever since by the myth of heroes building advanced civilizations with the help of God and money, forgetting to mention the most fundamental and life-sustaining wealth, which made everything possible, was looted from the peasants in the first place.

By the power of legends and myths, liars and murderers built the ancient world's infrastructure and economy without lifting a finger. With this ingenious method, the Shang royalty built palaces and temples, mass-produced bronzeware, equipped large armies and fought endless wars. The rulers took possession of the wealth produced by the peasants. In return, they paid the dummies minimum wage. "Never give a sucker an even break," they said. It was almost the same as having the goose that laid the golden eggs.

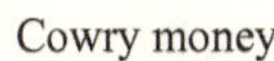

Cowry money

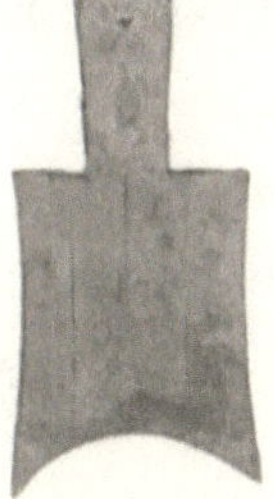

Spade money

As the years passed, the bronze spade *qian* became the Chinese word for "money." Therefore, when Chinese people save money, they mean stashing away spades. Also, when Chinese people lend money, they will call a spade a spade and demand payment in spades.

After the war meeting, Lady Diane stayed at Queen Zia's tent for the sleepover. The Shang queen laid out a pair of archer rings of exquisite quality before her favourite, each exhibiting the carving of a mythical beast known as the *zhi* (廌) on the front and its given name on the back. While the rings appeared to be of animal horn, they sparkled with the glitter of a million stars under a bright light. Lady Diane was well acquainted with one of them.

The archer rings had been gifted to Queen Zia by a one-eyed trader, who perambulated with a walking cane known as the Lituus. He claimed to have travelled from beyond the Celestial Mountains in the northwest, bringing wagon-loads of jade, gold, wine and rare spices. Having petitioned King Wotan for permission to trade in the kingdom, he decided to win over the Queen with precious gifts. The trader later settled in the Shang capital and became an official of the court. He adopted the name Huang Yin and was the ancestor of the Huang clan. *Huang* (黃) is the name of an arc-shaped jade piece worn by aristocrats, later borrowed to mean yellow. *Yin* (尹) is a title meaning "minister," its pictogram depicts a hand holding a walking cane. As a one-eyed servant of the king, Huang Yin's status *chen* (臣), later used to mean an official of the king, is the drawing of an eye.

Queen Zia granted her favourite the first pick. Lady Diane chose the archer ring marked "Return" and "Not Yet." She had a good reason for leaving the other ring marked "Go" and "Come" for Queen Zia. It had something to do with the iron rule of causality.

"Use it for the battle tomorrow," Queen Zia said. "And may every arrow you release find its target."

Chapter 11

Room 929

Victoria arrived in Toronto around midnight, stepping off the coach onto Dundas Street, a familiar name, half a block from Yonge Street, the city's main thoroughfare. She found herself plumb in the centre of downtown Toronto, where the lights were much brighter, dispelling the darkness and helping her forget her troubles and cares for a moment.

Toronto was primed and ready for Christmas. Holiday decorations and fancy lights festooned the lampposts on Yonge Street. The shops at the iconic Toronto Eaton Centre vied for attention with one another, dazzling pedestrians and shoppers with their holiday displays. Festive spirit filled the air as Christmas music and carols played nonstop everywhere.

Victoria's fears, however, kept a tenacious grip on her and created imaginings of night prowlers in the shadows, ready to pounce on helpless victims. She quickened her pace to find refuge in a 24-hour Tim Hortons, the ubiquitous coffee shop in Canada.

The distressed and exhausted teenager planted herself at a table, determined to stay up through the night with the help of coffee and mini-donuts known as Timbits. Although business was brisk past the wee hours, it was mostly takeout. Except for a one-eyed man equipped with a roving glass eye, who hid his face in the shadow of a broad-brimmed hat, Victoria had the joint to herself. Using the free Wi-Fi to go online, she located Solvicta Antiques, about a fifteen-minute walk from the coffee shop.

Victoria struggled to keep her eyes open through the dead of night. For a few seconds, she drifted off and found herself staring into a deep, tenebrous darkness from which a glass eye emerged. Suddenly, a scorpion burst out of the crystalline orb, snapping its menacing claws at her. Victoria woke from the nightmarish vision with a start. Her adrenaline fired up every neuron in her body, expelling her drowsiness and animating her brain with vigour and vim. She would not doze off again for the rest of the night.

Pedestrians began appearing on the streets before sunrise. Delivery trucks brought food supplies and newspapers. Soon, well-groomed young men in dark suits and fashionably dressed ladies with painted lips rushed into the cafés and restaurants for bagels and cappuccino. Toronto was stirring from her ambrosial sleep. Victoria polished off her breakfast, crushed the crossword in the *Toronto Star*, brushed her teeth in the washroom, slung the knapsack on her back and headed out for Solvicta Antiques.

As she weaved through the white-collar crowd, Victoria had an eerie feeling someone was tailing her. Survival instincts had so sharpened her senses she could almost perceive a threat from the back of her head. She suspected the creepy hobo with the glass eye was stalking her. The man had stayed in his corner all night, and when he left before the morning rush, he stopped at the door to glance at her with an evil glare. For a second, he appeared to be an ogre in his oversized coat.

The normally unathletic small-town girl waited for a streetcar to rumble by, found a gap in the traffic, and sprinted across the street without looking back. Racing at full throttle, Victoria was surprised by the explosive surge of energy erupting from every cell in her body. Her legs seemed stronger and gravity weaker. It was as if the air rushing past was giving her aerodynamic lift. Victoria had no idea she could do a one-hundred-metre dash in ten seconds flat without breathing hard. Too bad no one was timing her.

Having shaken off the stalker, Victoria arrived at a numbered door in the office section of an ancient Richardson Romanesque downtown hotel, which did not display any signage for Solvicta Antiques. Before she pressed the doorbell, the door buzzed open.

Victoria was relieved to see the company name on the wall inside the office. She had arrived at her destination. The room in front of Victoria was cluttered with Chinese vases, Egyptian statuettes, Celtic bronze vessels, Chinese calligraphy, bamboo scrolls, Latin codices and a pair of stone lions known as leogryphs, each with a single horn. Framed certificates lined the walls. Slightly out of place were two Baroque oil paintings propped against wooden crates. Both artworks depicted two women in the gruesome process of cutting off a man's head with a large sword.

By coincidence, if such a thing were possible, Victoria had written an article for her school newspaper about these paintings, one of which, titled *Judith Slaying Holofernes*, was a masterpiece crafted by Artemisia Gentileschi, an accomplished female painter influenced by Caravaggio. This extraordinary woman applied her artistic talents in revenge against all the men who had raped her, subjected her to humiliation in a public trial and yet let the culprit walk free. She executed the beheading with great relish on behalf of all abused women. The other painting, *Judith Beheading Holofernes*, was by the maestro Caravaggio himself.

At a desk positioned in a *feng shui* corner to command the unobstructed view of the room sat a thirtyish South Asian man who denied knowing anyone named David Huang. Fearing she would have no one else to turn to if she could not find her man, Victoria refused to take no for an answer.

"I'm sorry, something doesn't jive here," Victoria said, showing the symbol on her palm to the man. "I'm certain Mr. David Huang owns Solvicta Antiques. I have an important message for him."

"Maybe you mean Dr. Brown," said the man when he saw the symbol. "He's in Mumbai and won't be back until January at the earliest. Would you like to leave a message?"

Victoria's heart sank, but a strange sight greeted her eyes, giving her new hope. The man put his index finger to his lips, making the hush gesture. With the other hand, he lifted a sheet of paper displaying the number 929.

Room 929 languished inconspicuously at the end of a long, dimly lit corridor. It delivered a furtive yet reassuring message confirming Victoria had arrived at her secret guardian's safe house. Room 929's door swung open as she approached. Standing before her was a middle-aged, bespectacled Caucasian man with dark curly hair, who exuded an exotic Orientalism beneath his pale, handsome face and piercing brown eyes.

"Thank goodness you're safe, Victoria," said the man with reserved politeness. "I have sent out a search party to no avail. But as the old saying goes, 'You may wear out your iron boots and fail to find the Holy Grail, yet it may fall on your lap before you take the first step.' I'm David Huang, your official guardian. Sorry about what happened to Michael and Angela. Please come inside."

Victoria was perplexed. She was expecting a Chinese man.

"It's okay," David said with a knowing smile. "I'm the David Huang you seek. Dr. Brown is the alias I use for my business, which is lucrative and demands discretion. But brown, my dear, is all theory and yellow alone life's golden tree. My name, Huang, means yellow, and I shall be the tree you lean on for protection from now on."

He reassured Victoria by raising his fist and displaying his signet ring, which sported the same symbol on her palm.

Chapter 12

Flight of Fancy

Victoria was so exhausted she fell into a deep sleep the very moment her head hit the pillow. In her senseless slumber, she found herself in a land of dreams, flying high as an eagle under a peculiar amber sky. She did not know why the sky was not blue. For most dreamers, this land had no rules.

Beneath the great eagle, thick, tulgey smog shrouded the earth. She descended gradually until the land became visible through the hellacious haze. Plumes of fire in purple, blue, green, orange and yellow erupted in rhythmic bursts from vents in the ground, followed by mushroom clouds of fuliginous fumes. Concrete blocks and steel struts strewed the land in haphazard heaps. The once-green meadows had decayed into a Boschian hellscape of death and desolation. Victoria's idyllic paradise had suffered a devastating disaster of an apocalyptic scale.

As the bird of prey swept a wide arc to turn away from this land of broken dreams, she caught sight of an object falling from the high firmaments. Victoria could see far with her eagle eyes and was shocked to espy a young boy plummeting in freefall to certain death.

Without hesitation, the eagle withdrew her pinions and dove after the boy, forgetting they were so close to the ground. At the last moment, Victoria, disregarding the deadly danger, grabbed the boy's limbs with her claws and struggled to open her wings, but nothing could stop them from plunging in a tailspin toward the long steel shards protruding from the ground.

Victoria woke from the nightmare with sweat dripping from her brow. She was safe and sound on a soft, springy mattress in a luxurious hotel room. David Huang had arranged a regal suite in the hotel-office complex for her.

After suffering the trauma of losing her parents and going through the whole night without sleep, Victoria was on the verge of emotional and physical collapse when she arrived at David's den. The situation, however, was not all reassuring for Victoria because she found herself inside the deceitful matrix of a Caucasian Chinese using a fake name. How could she not have reservations about her supposed guardian? To allay her fears, David showed her some old photos of him posing with Michael and Angela, showing off their recently adopted baby daughter in front of the White Swan Hotel in Guangzhou, China.

Victoria's tears overflowed when she saw her parents in these photos. She remembered her mom combing her hair while she took chess lessons from her dad. When she walked with her parents in the park, they always held her hands on each side. It was miraculous her dad always showed up in the nick of time to catch her when she fell from the swing or slide. They would live only in her memory from now on.

Victoria knew she had to rely on David Huang to protect her, as she had no alternative. She recounted the events of the previous evening, including how she found the jade pendant and the ring, but she kept the details about the Almanac to herself. She knew she had to be careful until she found reason to trust this shady art dealer, who did not strike her as being an honest man.

When Victoria woke from her dream, it was past seven in the evening. She checked her knapsack to ensure nothing was missing, freshened up and called David Huang. A few minutes later, her guardian arrived with a travel bag and a take-out order of roast duck with plum sauce on steamed rice, Victoria's favourite.

"Prepare for an adventure," David said. "We're flying to Shanghai on a private jet. But before we take off, we need to give you a changeover."

He took out a pair of scissors and a comb.

"You're getting a haircut and a disguise."

"Are you sure we need to do this? I'd rather you leave my hair alone."

"I'm sorry. I'm afraid you'll need a different appearance, even a different gender, to evade the shadowy agents who are dead set on laying their hands on you. You'll have to listen to me if you hope to survive long enough to meet your biological parents."

"Who are these people? What have we done to deserve this? My parents and I have always minded our own business. We hardly even stepped outside of Dundas."

"It's a wild story going back several thousand years. Listen, we have a long journey ahead of us. It takes five hours to fly from the Island Airport to Vancouver, where we'll fuel up and get your paperwork done. It takes another twelve hours to fly from Vancouver to Shanghai. We'll have lots of time for your briefing in a secure environment. Now, let us get to work."

Victoria suppressed the unease in her guts while her locks flew off the scissors and floated to the floor, except for one fateful strand, which landed inside David's shoe by accident, if such a thing were possible.

For Victoria, this haircut marked the end of the age of innocence. A new person would emerge, and Victoria would need all the courage, wisdom and love she could gather to survive the dangers ahead. When David warned the girl he was about to execute the cruellest cut of all, she covered her eyes, afraid to peek in the mirror. Finally, David announced what he needed to do was done. Victoria removed her hands tentatively and was surprised to stare at the reflection of a teenage boy. After switching to unisex clothing and working on boyish mannerisms, she could pass off as the Chinese nephew of his Caucasian uncle.

David snapped a few photos of Victoria, after which a limousine took them to the Island Airport, where a Gulf Stream jet awaited. To anyone not privy to the secret, Victoria was now Victor Su, a Chinese Canadian boy flying to China in a private jet plane with his wealthy uncle, a Caucasian Chinese antique dealer going by the alias of Dr. Brown. In short, everything was a lie.

The South Asian man from the Solvicta Antiques office greeted Victoria as she entered the Gulf Stream, "Welcome aboard. You look much better than this morning."

David Huang followed two steps behind with a large bag. He made eye contact with Raja, giving him a discreet hand signal to ignore Victoria's disguise.

"Victoria, meet Raja," David said, introducing the two. "Raja, meet Victoria. What's the takeoff situation?"

"Flight path has been approved. We're taking off in half an hour. Would you two like a drink before I join the pilot? I'm co-piloting."

"Thanks, Raja," David said. "We'll help ourselves."

"Please allow me, sir," said the eager assistant as he poured the chilled Baron de Rothschild Brut into a champagne flute. For the teenage girl, he served a fizzy drink. "We have cider for the lady."

Experiencing her first flight, Victoria watched the takeoff through the window with breathless wonder. Nighttime Toronto receded into a city of stars. Soon, the space outside plunged into pitch blackness except for the flashing light at the tip of the wings. Not long after, the galaxy and the constellations came into view.

The first constellation Victoria learned to identify was not the Big Dipper but Orion, the heavenly hunter. The most prominent star of the constellation is the fiery red giant, Betelgeuse, as his right shoulder, sometimes referred to as his right hand. His left shoulder is Bellatrix, the female warrior, also known as the Amazon star. The part easiest to recognize is the triple stars forming Orion's Belt.

Victoria reminisced about the story of Orion, who once hunted with Artemis, also known as Diana, the goddess of the hunt. The vainglorious Orion bragged of his plan to kill all animals, raising the hackles of Mother Earth, who sent a scorpion to lay low the boastful hunter, and it dispatched him with one lethal sting. Zeus, the head of the Greek pantheon, decided to place Orion and the scorpion up in the sky as prominent constellations. However, the two luminaries were implacable foes. They would never appear in the night sky at the same time. In the northern hemisphere, Orion rises in the winter and sets before Scorpius' ascension in the summer. Scorpius will set before Orion rises again.

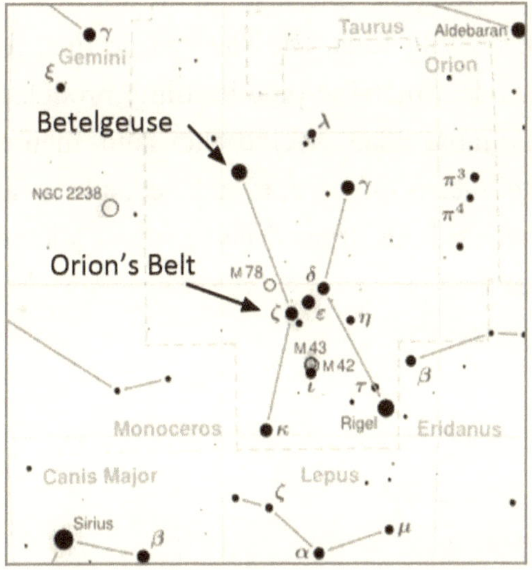

Although it was impossible to forget the horrific events of the previous night, Victoria focused on the auspicious beginning of her new adventures. After all, she was cruising through the sky in a private jet, enjoying the freedom of flight much as the eagle in her recurring dreams. An unannounced turbulence shook Victoria out of her reverie, giving her brain another powerful jolt. All of a sudden, it dawned on her the boy who fell from the sky in her nightmare was none other than herself with her gender-bending makeover. A panic attack gripped her as she realized her dream was the omen of a dire situation. But it was too late. She was twelve thousand metres in the air and did not have eagle wings.

Noticing David Huang had dozed off in his seat, Victoria shook her guardian violently as if he were a rag doll, but the man remained unresponsive. The mysterious art dealer was out cold and in a stupor.

It was not hard for Victoria to imagine Raja had spiked the drinks with sedatives, and, by logic, it would soon be lights out for her as well. The would-be superhero of Dundas could kick herself for being so careless. Her mom had taught her never to accept food or drinks from strangers. She also could not believe what a fool David was for trusting Raja. But she had no time for regrets. She was trapped inside a metallic tube hurtling through thin air at five hundred knots more than twelve thousand metres above terra firma, with no means of escape and seconds away from being knocked out by insidious drugs. Maybe it was Victoria's fate to go down in flames.

Chapter 13

Freefall

Victoria's unsuccessful attempt to rouse David from his stupor brought Raja out of the cockpit.

"Please let Dr. Brown rest, Miss Victoria. He was exhausted from everything everywhere happening all at once, but was too excited to sleep. He might have taken a sleeping pill."

"He should've known better than to take sleeping pills with alcohol. He's not responsive at all, and I'm worried."

Raja weighed his next move for a few seconds before poking David in the chest. Faster than one could say Vaslav Nijinsky, David abruptly awakened from his somnolent state, grabbed his colleague's probing fingers and, bending them backwards, forced him to his knees while yelping in pain.

The pilot monitoring the cabin camera reacted to the commotion as any well-trained killer would. He rushed out of the cockpit with a pistol in his hand, pointing it at Victoria and shouting at the top of his lungs, "Let him go, or I'll shoot her!"

Victoria learned something about the stranger to whom she had entrusted her life. David was not the negotiating type, especially when facing an armed man making death threats. Shielding himself behind Raja, he drew a Glock from a concealed holster at blinding speed and fired three quick rounds at the gunman's chest. Before the pilot knew what hit him, he was reliably and certifiably dead, or as the saying goes, dead as Schrödinger's cat.

Victoria needed several tick-tocks of the clock to recover from the surprise of seeing a comatose David spring to life, execute a lightning-fast finger-hold and hit three bullseyes on a moving target with his handgun. In the past, this firefight would have given Victoria a terrible fright and caused her to scream with all her might. Instead, she remained unfazed, exhibiting a sangfroid she had no idea she possessed. She convinced herself life was stranger than the movies and managed to keep a cool head.

David let go of Raja's fingers but kept his Glock pointed at his erstwhile ally.

"Why, my friend? What can they possibly offer you to betray me?"

"They threatened to harm my family," said Raja, begging for mercy with his fearful eyes. "I had no choice."

"You should've known better. The only way to help yourself and your family was to talk to me."

"I'm sorry, so sorry. I lost my head. Please give me another chance. You need me to land this plane."

"Raja, my friend," David said, emphasizing "my friend" with cold irony. "This is the last time we work together. Take the plane to the nearest airport. After we land, you'll take care of the body. We'll go our separate ways, and I never want to see your face again. Do you understand?"

"Yes, sir. Thank you, sir," Raja said with abject remorse. He rose to his feet and wambled toward the cockpit. David covered Victoria's eyes and fired two shots at the traitor's back. Without issuing so much as a whimper, Raja slumped to the floor, dead.

"What have you done?" Victoria cried. "Don't we need him to land the plane?"

"Don't judge me. Raja gave away your whereabouts, causing your parents' demise. I warned Michael, but he made the wrong turn. A moment ago, the rat tried to notify his new masters of his failure to deliver us. I have to put him out of his misery."

David pried open Raja's fist to retrieve a small device, which he crushed with his pistol grip and flushed down the toilet.

"The poor guy had no idea what sort of people he was dealing with," David continued. "They contacted me through a trusted secret channel at the same time they were trying to compromise him. It was cheaper and much less hassle for them to pay me directly. I knew when Raja got the Fentanyl. I didn't drink his champagne."

"What about me?" Didn't he lace my drink with it? I'm not sleepy at all. What gives?"

"They might not want to drug you. Besides, you may be immune to it. Sorry about the violence. You may have already noticed your uneventful and sheltered Canadian life is over. Your odyssey to the truth won't be a dinner party."

"Thanks for the good news. But tell me something useful, such as how we are going to land this plane. Can you pilot this?"

"Nope, I'm not James Bond. We'll have to resort to Plan B."

"Whatever you do, will you be so kind as to give me a heads-up before giving me a heart attack, please?"

"Sure, it's my job to keep you out of harm's way," David responded with a wry grin. He entered the cockpit and pressed some buttons. Victoria could feel the plane descending. David unzipped his large travel bag. It was his Plan B. "Let's chalk up another first on your list. We'll escape by tandem skydiving at night without a legal drop zone."

David asked Victoria to move her knapsack to the front and helped her put on a tandem harness. Afterwards, he handed her a helmet and a pair of goggles.

"Here, put these on. Don't worry about the jump. I promise it'll be safe and fun."

David put away his glasses, strapped on the parachute with a bit of help from Victoria and headed toward the baggage door at the back of the plane, beckoning the hesitant girl to follow.

"We're approaching three thousand metres. Time to fly."

Victoria recoiled at the prospect of jumping out of an airplane midflight in complete darkness into the unknown. Nevertheless, she had no choice but to put her life in the hands of a stranger who was also a cold-blooded killer.

Having survived a car crash and a shootout, Victoria could sense her nerves hardening, helping her stay cool in the face of insurmountable adversity and immutable fate. After all, what is the point of panicking while strapped to your seat at the top of the roller coaster, about to plunge into the abyss at a thousand miles per hour? You might as well sit back and enjoy the cardiac arrest.

David fastened Victoria's harness to his tandem gear. He gave last-minute instructions, reminding her to equalize the pressure in her ears, showing her the tap on her shoulder for the jerk when the parachute opened and another for when she should draw up her knees before landing, all the while, reassuring her it would be a safe and enjoyable experience.

"Watch out for the wind. I'm opening the baggage door," David warned as he pulled the latch over. The door slid open, letting in a rush of cold air. The icy blast reminded Victoria of the freezing rain beating her face, waking her after the crash. She shuddered and braced herself.

David secured the flashlight at his belt and switched on his headlamp to slice through the blackness outside the airplane. His GPS/Altimeter wristwatch flashed and beeped.

"This is it!" he shouted above the buffeting wind, and, with a leap, the two tumbled out of the plane into the deep, dark void.

Chapter 14

Running on Empty

David and Victoria landed safely on a country road about four hundred metres from a lone gas station with a convenience store and coffee counter surrounded by a darkness blacker than the blackest ink. The only light came from a car so far away it resembled a star at the edge of the universe.

As David asserted, the dive was an exhilarating experience for Victoria. The freefall, the adrenaline rush and the sensation of losing all control, yet knowing everything would be fine because she had a guardian angel watching over her, gave Victoria the thrill of a lifetime. She almost wanted to get back up and jump again.

After disposing of the parachute, helmets and goggles in a ditch and covering everything with soil and snow, David and Victoria hotfooted to the gas station, which had a weather-beaten sign on top of the building displaying its name, *No. 1 Corn Gas.* Some letters were missing after Corn.

A solitary uniformed attendant manned the joint, his name tag indicating Brent was at your service. The man was a balding, grumpy, cynical and caustic curmudgeon who appeared much older than his age and way past his expiry date. His only reason for being in this godforsaken place at this ungodly hour was his inability to hire someone else to do this joyless job. Enrapt in his comics, Brent was miffed at the walk-ins before closing.

David and Victoria bought a coffee and hot chocolate and sat at a corner far from the counter. While enjoying their drinks, David's

GPS/Altimeter watch started flashing. “Good news,” he whispered. “Our car is coming to pick us up.”

“No way! It’s the middle of the night, and we’re in the middle of nowhere. How do you pull this off?”

“You have much to learn about the world outside Dundas, my dear. I’ll explain later.”

Seconds after they finished their drinks, a black, futuristic vehicle screeched to a stop outside, timing its arrival with the precision of a military operation.

“Our ride is here,” David said, signalling Victoria to follow him. Leaving a hundred-dollar bill on the counter, he instructed the surprised attendant, “Keep the change, Brent. We’re not here, we’ve never been here, and you don’t remember ever seeing us.”

Victoria’s eyes widened at the sight of the fancy car, especially when the gullwing doors opened, showing no driver inside.

“She’s a beauty, eh?” exclaimed David, beaming with pride. “This vehicle of the future is designed and built by some of the smartest people in the world. Though resembling a hypermodern speedster, she is much more than meets the eye. The car’s artificial intelligence has guessed within twenty kilometres of where we would end up and has been waiting in the neighbourhood. She has been homing in on us once I activated Plan B from the plane.”

David unfastened the GPS/Altimeter watch, crushing it underfoot before tossing the remnants to the roadside.

“Won’t this car be too conspicuous?”

“In a word, no. The car’s exterior has a coat of advanced dynamic metamaterial for unmatched cloaking. We’re practically invisible most of the time. We also have a hologram camouflage feature, helping us blend in with other cars in heavy traffic.

“By jumping out of the plane, we’ve shaken off our shadowy pursuers for a while. These people may be powerful, but I promise they’ll never lay a finger on you as long as I’m alive. We’ll try to stay a few steps ahead of the chase. Travelling by car, we'll throw them off because they don't expect it. They'll be combing the skies for us but will find nothing. Moreover, this car's navigation system uses advanced quantum satellite encryption technology. We're undetectable to electronic trackers and impregnable to the most capable hackers."

Victoria raised an eyebrow. "I don't mean to contradict you, but the news says only China has quantum satellites, and it's still experimental. Are you pulling my leg?"

"Don't believe everything you read in the news," David offered pithy advice. "There's no truth in news and no news in truth. Our tech is based on China's Beidou BNSS navigation satellites and their Micius quantum satellite. It's in early stages and will need more work for large-scale deployment, but our dedicated Beta quantum channel is a hundred percent operational."

As the automatic seat belt strapped down David and Victoria, a life-sized hologram of an attractive Eurasian woman in her thirties with shocking red hair and stunning green eyes, dressed in a form-fitting Federation Starfleet-style uniform, appeared in the empty seat beside them. Startled but not shaken, Victoria tried to touch the image, passing her fingers through to ascertain it was only an optical illusion.

"David, how are you?" the hologram assistant said. "Hello, Victoria, or should I say, Victor. I'm Moira. Welcome aboard."

"Good to see you, Moira. Prepare for takeoff," David said, commanding the car as if it were a spaceship. "Input destination coordinates for Vancouver Pan Pacific Hotel. Schedule optimized breaks for muscular relaxation, victual replenishment and micturition relief. Initiate high-velocity kinetic impact resistance and EMP shield. Activate electronic stealth, noise cancellation, optical cloaking and holo-camouflage—make it Buick Lacrosse. Set cruise speed at maximum warp and engage."

"I'm impressed, Captain Picard," said Victoria, a diehard Trekkie who had binge-watched *Star Trek: The Next Generation* several times. "What's the propulsion system of the NCC 1941? I noticed the Starfleet registry on the licence plate."

"Very observant," David said while both captain and passenger sank into their seat under the high G force of the car's acceleration. "This is the Starship Bozeman. Everything you see is cutting-edge technology. We have a solar power system employing a solid-state battery with 1.1° Magic Angle offset stratified graphene-borophene electrodes and a nano-metamaterial electrolyte, storing enough power from our nano-Cadmium telluride and ultra-thin perovskite hybrid solar panel to keep us going as long as the sun shines.

"On top of that, we have a parallel power source with negligible overhead in weight. The car's titanium-foam-bonded, self-healing, impact-resistant polymer chassis comes installed with an integrated Lamarr spread-spectrum adaptive phased-array rectenna that collects ambient electromagnetic energy and doubles as an active phased-array radar. For emergencies, our next-generation nuclear batteries will power the system as a backup for up to one thousand kilometres, even at extreme temperatures.

"Our car's generic designation is Model SU11, the eleventh-generation offspring of our first concept vehicle, custom-designed and built for me by a group of top engineers poached from BYD, Nio, Xiaomi, Geely, Hongqi, XPeng, Chery, Huawei and others, practically all the big players in China. Our work is more than a decade ahead of the rest of the world. We should be ready when the China Sun superconducting Tokamak fusion reactors come online. We want to be able to receive unlimited power through wireless technologies. I have several Chinese unicorns working on this for years. The Starship Bozeman, my dear, is the future. Being smart and green, she always runs on empty."

Chapter 15

Sign of the Scorpion

An eagle glided across the still, sultry summer sky, basking in the warm rays of the setting sun. On her way back to the aerie, she spotted a band of nomads emerging from the majestic mountain range that separated the sunbaked desert and wind-swept steppes in the west from the lush, green valleys and dark-soiled plains to the east. The group's eastward journey followed the southern bank of a rushing rivulet, which carried the sweet, delectable waters from the tree-covered mountains into the fat, loamy lands below.

Despite its humble origin, the stream would join with other tributaries to form a great river, Liao, the lifeblood of iron tribes destined to rewrite the history of China and forever change its character. The roiling waters would disgorge from the dragon's mouth into the endless ocean hundreds of kilometres to the southeast. The nomads called this mountain stream Yellow River, not the famous cradle of the Chinese civilization, but a minor namesake and the cradle of a peripheral semi-nomadic tribe, which would later rule China and become an integral part of the Chinese civilization we know today.

The band of worn and haggard nomads consisted of about three hundred men, matched in number by both the women and children, all perched precariously on the bony backs of lean horses. A pack of hungry wolfdogs straggled along. These barely domesticated best friends of man had taken part in their masters' arduous trek but were at the end of their rope and could break ranks any time.

Upon reaching the foot of the mountain, the group, too tired, hungry and wounded to keep going, decided to stop and rest for the night. Since most men were bandaged and could not work, the women pitched tents while the children tended to the animals. The season being summer, the remnants of the Eastern Wolf tribe would enjoy another hour of light before sunset.

A tent of sheepskin and wolf pelts went up with customary celerity. Four older women lifted a dying man on a cleverly designed travois-stretcher from a litter into the tent. Three young men planted a large spear at the entrance and waited. After the helpers had left, a woman emerged and summoned them to enter.

Inside these humble quarters, the Tuman, on his last legs, lay on a straw mattress, accompanied by his tattered and bloodied banner hanging beside him on a twig. White Wolf, North Wolf and Lone Wolf knelt by the deathbed, downcast and disheartened.

White Wolf, whose head was wrapped in a blood-stained cloth and right hand heavily bandaged, hogged the space nearest to his dying father. Next to him squeezed North Wolf, who limped with a tree branch for a crutch because some crazy horse's hoof had landed on his toe. Beyond the tight circle, Lone Wolf brooded in his soiled tunic caked with the dried blood of his enemies. The Tuman had summoned his sons to receive final instructions.

As Lupalina exited the tent to let the men settle their family affairs, the Tuman beckoned his faithful servant.

"Lupa, please stay. You're my sons' wet nurse and their mother's handmaid. You've been with us all these years. As your mistress is with the wolf spirits, and I'll join her soon, you'll be the only person my sons will pay heed to. Please stay and bear witness."

Lupalina preferred not to be involved in tribal politics but could not forsake the Tuman in his last moments. She retired to a corner, fixed her eyes on the ground and kept her mouth shut.

"My children," the Tuman said. "Give me your hands."

"Baba," White Wolf and North Wolf called their father in unison, but Lone Wolf whispered, "My lord."

"Call me Baba, Lone Wolf," the Tuman commanded. "I gave you your life."

White Wolf and North Wolf turned to glare at Lone Wolf with open disdain.

"Yes, Baba."

"I'm sorry, Lone Wolf," the Tuman whispered through quivering lips, "I gave little consideration to your counsel and went to war with Modred, the father-murderer."

Upon mention of the one who slaughtered the Eastern Wolf tribes, White Wolf and North Wolf spat in contempt.

"The Huns have destroyed the Eastern Wolf Confederation, and our tribe of twenty thousand bows with uncountable animals is no more. Curse the Tengri for his greed. Curse him for causing death and destruction to my tribe. I'll curse him again when I meet him in the Valley of the Dead. I have only a short time to live. I can do no more. Lone Wolf, swear you will stand by your brothers and help our tribe return to glory."

"Yes, Baba, you will recover, and we will survive," said Lone Wolf, keeping a brave front. "We'll be strong and numerous as before. Our wolf-howl will strike terror into the hearts of our enemies, and the Tuman banner will fly in the wind again. I swear to fight alongside my brothers as you command."

"Good," said the Tuman. He turned to his other sons and asked, "And will you two support Lone Wolf as true brothers?"

"Why, of course, Baba," White Wolf replied. "Ever since we saved Lone Wolf from the wild animals, we have kept him with us as a part of the family, even giving him a wolf name. We will honour your wish and always treat him as a brother."

"Even if I make him Tuman?"

While the tradition of the Wolf Tribes was for the Chief to pass the Tuman banner to the most capable son, regardless of age or rank, none of his sons had prepared their ears for the Tuman's shocking words, least of all Lone Wolf.

"Baba, I'm your eldest son," White Wolf protested. "I'm more experienced, and the people respect me. Besides, Lone Wolf is not of our blood. Passing the banner to him is a not a good idea."

"Baba, even if you believe White Wolf can't lead because he may have lost the use of his sword hand," North Wolf argued, "I should be your second choice. I can fight again when I heal."

"Baba, my lord," whispered Lone Wolf. "My brothers are right. Please reconsider."

Ignoring Lone Wolf, the Tuman directed his ire at White Wolf and North Wolf.

"Yes, you two are dying to fight again, but we are where we are because of the fighting. All of you great warriors together didn't have the wisdom of one Lone Wolf. When you sneered at him and called him names, he didn't get angry but fought beside us. Didn't you see him fight? No teat-sucking Hun stinking of wolf piss could stand their ground before him. More importantly, Lone Wolf prepared our escape before the battle while we were quarrelling over how to distribute the spoils. He's the reason we even have a tribe."

The Tuman paused to catch his breath, coughed and continued.

"As for Lone Wolf's foreign blood, remember the Wolf tribes are composed of different peoples from faraway lands. We are strong because of it. Your mother came from beyond the ocean of sand where the sun sets. Her tribe speaks the tongue of the birdsong and worships strange gods in the sky. The fiery-haired damsel from her tribe, Wolf Star, has the green eyes of a snow leopard. What is her blood? Your mother had the golden yellow eyes of a wolf. Look at your reflection and ask why you're called White Wolf.

"I want a wise person to be Tuman after I die to lead whatever is left of us, to make the tribe strong again. It is our good fortunes the gods have sent Lone Wolf to preserve us."

Turning to Lone Wolf, the Tuman bellowed with the remaining fire in his chest to impress upon the reluctant young man.

"Lone Wolf, swear you will not abandon us and will be Tuman after I die. Swear you will bring glory back to our Wolf tribe."

The Tuman's sons, recognizing the pointlessness of arguing against the demented rant of a dying man, kept their heads down and their mouths shut.

"Swear," the Tuman shouted with his last breath.

"I swear," Lone Wolf whispered.

The Tuman smiled in satisfaction as he laid down his head and gave up the ghost.

Thereupon, a few curious children sticking their noses into the tent scattered in all directions to spread the news. Within seconds, the entire camp erupted in a chorus of howling, joined by the wolfdogs. "The beloved Tuman is dead. Long Live the Tuman!" The last remnants of the once proud Wolf tribe sang their laments and their dirges. Meanwhile, a new struggle for succession began inside the Tuman's tent.

"Lupa, Baba was not in his right mind," said White Wolf, seeking support from his most important ally. "Surely, you must have noticed."

Lupalina did not respond as she shuffled over to the deathbed. She knelt and placed two pieces of jade over her master's eyes and one into his mouth. After a short period of pregnant silence spent considering her best course of action, Lupalina rose to her feet and spoke to White Wolf and North Wolf in a stern voice.

"Your father, bless his soul, had good reasons for making Lone Wolf Tuman."

Turning toward Lone Wolf, the venerable and powerful woman raised her arm and pointed at the young man.

"Lone Wolf," raising her voice, Lupalina demanded, "show us your mark."

Lone Wolf at first hesitated, but turned around and lifted his long, thick mane to reveal a blue tattoo on his nape, hitherto hidden from all except the Tuman and Lupalina. At the same time, the faithful executor of the Tuman's last wish lifted his bloodied banner to display the Tuman's sign. They were a perfect match.

Chapter 16

Heart of the Dragon

The people buried the once great Tuman without pomp and circumstance befitting a defeated leader of a band on the run. They strangled his aged wolfdog, White Fang, and buried it beside him to serve as his companion in the afterlife. Following the simple burial rites, Lupalina called a tribal meeting and declared Lone Wolf the new Tuman in the name of her recently departed master. White Wolf and North Wolf held their tongues and nursed their grudge, having been duly informed by their dying father they were no match for Lone Wolf in a physical challenge, even if they were healthy. Hence, Lone Wolf received the chief's spear and banner without bloodshed. At least, the tribe could enjoy some peace.

For this occasion, during which Lone Wolf would determine the tribe's future, he arrayed himself in his eagle mantle, glowing with an aura of solemn magnificence as he addressed his tribe.

"I owe my life to the old Tuman. May his spirit ever protect us. I promised him I would lead the tribe, but I do not deem it appropriate to accept the title of Tuman."

White Wolf and North Wolf were surprised. Their eyes lit up, hoping the Tuman position might still be up for grabs.

"As we all know," Lone Wolf continued. "The title of Tuman (头曼) means 'the wise chief of a myriad host.' For more than a millennium, our ancestors have passed down the scorpion symbol and the Tuman title in our tribe. Modred's father also called himself the Hunnu Tuman. However, without the banner, he was no more than an imposter. The Qin Empire in the south, following the tradition of the previous Zhou and Shang dynasties, has adopted the scorpion to mean 'myriad' or 'ten thousand' (TS:萬), signifying a large number. It is a much-revered symbol.

"Therefore, I can't be your Tuman or carry the Tuman banner until our tribe numbers ten thousand bows again. In the meantime, I shall be Chief Lone Wolf. I shall lead the tribe with the help of my two brothers, Left Chief White Wolf and Right Chief North Wolf, and the elders, who are generous with their advice."

This announcement stirred up a wave of murmurings among the tribe members, but most raised their thumbs in approval. White Wolf and North Wolf accepted the olive branch, although it did not mollify their resentment. The two brothers would continue to devise their secret plots for their separate futures.

"We must make some immediate decisions," Chief Lone Wolf said. "Modred, the father-murderer and destroyer of the Wolf tribes, wishes to exterminate us."

Everyone spat in contempt at the mention of the accursed name.

"His soldiers are following our tracks through the mountains as we speak. Our sharpshooters have slowed them down with hit-and-run attacks. Their scouts have learned to respect our archers. But I suggest we keep moving through the woods instead of descending into the plains. In the mountains, we can hide better and ambush our pursuers with more devastating effects.

"The trees are laden with fruits and nuts. We won't starve here. The woods are also teeming with deer, reindeer, wild boars, hares, pheasants and wild geese, which we can hunt and trap for food. We will find an abundance of mountain cats, wolves, foxes, minks and sable, whose pelts will warm us. Our wolfdogs will be happy here. And if we don't stray too far from the streams, we'll eat our fill of spawning sturgeon, northern salmon, burbot and carp. I'll teach you how to catch them.

"Our horses and sheep will fatten on the ample pastures. Where the land is arable, we can grow millet, barley and wheat. Finally, we shall worship the golden Shanbe, the divine beast with one horn. Its spirit has led us through the woods to safety. Let us pray it will guide us through the difficult times ahead."

Lone Wolf had scouted the area in anticipation of the retreat. He learned the Eastern Wolf tribes had sojourned here in the remote past, and their legend spoke of the golden unicorn, Shanbe, which roamed the wild woods. Lone Wolf understood how small doses of faith and hope would be vital for the tribe's survival. Meanwhile, he refrained from mentioning the dangers of sharing the territory with brown bears. It was something the hunters among them could deal with. He wanted the people to stay positive as they faced an uncertain future.

"The Huns won't hound us forever," Chief Lone Wolf asserted. "Modred will soon recall his soldiers for other wars. The Huns, once our Wolf brothers, grew strong in the seventy-black peaks of the Great Green Mountain Range. Led by the treacherous father-murderer, Modred, they have triumphed over us, and the Eastern Wolf tribes are no more. Let us swallow the bitter truth, learn from our mistakes and not let lies delude us.

"Modred has taken innumerable slaves and animals. He has amassed mountains of spoils. The blood of the slain flooded the battlefield, staining the earth crimson-red. Having tasted of gore, gold and glory, the Huns will never sate their lust for slaughter, plunder and power. Their unquenchable thirst will become a scourge and consume them.

"The Huns will soon ride to the south and the west. They will certainly crush their enemies with their heavy cavalry. But it will also mark the beginning of their downfall and our rise from the ashes. We must seek out any survivors and join forces with them. Living in the mountains and the woods means we won't be fighting any territorial wars. The dwellers of the plains are known as Berserkers, who cover themselves with bearskins and fight as if possessed by animal spirits. They will not welcome us.

"In the mountains, we will toughen ourselves and our children. We will strengthen our sinews and sharpen our skills. We will stay out of war and make alliances with our dispersed brethren hiding in the mountains to the north and south. We may even pay tribute to Modred to buy us some peace. We'll keep our heads down and bide our time. We'll use all our energy to grow until we are strong and numerous enough to ride out of the mountains without fear. When the time comes, I shall take up the Tuman's banner and ride forth with you. All those in favour say aye."

Everyone punched the air with their fist and shouted their approval. A few started the familiar wolf-howl, which might have inspired the people of the southern empire to call the northern Wolf tribes the *Hu* (胡), meaning "northern barbarian."

"We've had a long day," Chief Lone Wolf announced in closing. "Let us sleep well tonight. I'll take the first watch. We'll strike camp at first light to move to higher ground. In the name of the old Tuman, and may his spirit ever protect us, I declare this tribal meeting adjourned. People, have a good rest."

The whole tribe rejoiced at the old Tuman's wise choice of Lone Wolf as his successor. They all went to bed with empty stomachs but hopeful hearts. They knew upon sunrise, they would face another challenging day fraught with trials and tribulations, and their survival would depend on sound judgment, wise decisions, hard work, tenacity, dedication and sacrifice. They believed as long as they remained united under Chief Lone Wolf's leadership, the tribe would thrive again.

Lone Wolf found a perfect sentry spot on a grassy knoll overlooking the camp. He had sent a few responsible young men to cover the periphery in other directions. Lone Wolf brought his favourite wolfdog, Phantom, to keep him company. As he settled down, he heard a rustling noise ignored by Phantom. Lone Wolf and his wolfdog knew someone had been tailing them.

"Show yourself, Wolf Star. You should be resting rather than trying to ambush us."

"I want to congratulate you on becoming our chief," Wolf Star said, emerging from behind a bush and sitting beside Lone Wolf. "We all trust you will be a great leader."

"It's a heavy burden I never wanted, but I made a promise to the old Tuman. May he rest in peace."

Lone Wolf was a young man in his prime, the greatest warrior the Eastern Wolf tribes had ever known. The battle and the hasty retreat into the mountains reduced the survivors into feral beasts, yet Lone Wolf kept a superior air of the indomitable spirit in him. His chiselled face shone with the aura of a demigod but a vulnerable one with secrets hidden inside his melancholy eyes.

Lone Wolf found the fragrance and the body heat of a charming young girl so close to him quite unbearable. He stiffened his resolve and kept his distance from Wolf Star.

"I've lost everything," Wolf Star said, pressing closer to Lone Wolf. "But I'm glad to be alive. You saved my life."

"Good thing you listened to me. And, by the way, I'm sorry about your loss."

"Everyone has suffered loss," Wolf Star said, entwining her loosening braids with Lone Wolf's mane. "But while we live, let us live."

The soft, feathery touch of Wolf Star was as gentle as the caress of Zephyrus, the fairy goddess of the summer breeze, who carried the sweet smell of wildflowers into young lovers' hearts.

Wolf Star's intoxicating fragrance drifted into Lone Wolf's head, reminding him of a forgotten happiness buried in a blurry memory from long ago and far away.

"Do you know why you're called Wolf Star?" Lone Wolf asked out of the blue.

Perplexed by Lone Wolf's coolness toward her, Wolf Star lowered her eyes dejectedly and shook her head.

"You're called Wolf Star because you're as lovely as the Heavenly Wolf star in the sky. It is sleeping beneath the southern horizon, but when the snow falls, it will rise and shine with the gleam of your bright eyes. Have patience, you will enjoy great fortunes as your star rises. Good things come to those who wait."

"How do you know so much?" asked Wolf Star, returning her admiring gaze upon Lone Wolf. "Do you have a star?"

"Indeed, I do," replied the young chief, pointing at a constellation close to the southern horizon. "See the long string of stars? It's the Dragon. At the chest of the Dragon is a fiery red star. See it? It is my star, the Heart of the Dragon."

On this midsummer's night, the flaming-red Antares of the constellation Scorpius shone bright and dominated the southern sky. It was first known as the Great Fire or the Shang Star during the Shang Dynasty and later as the Heart Star of the Dragon constellation. Antares means "peer of the war god Ares," while Ares is the Greek name for Mars. Antares was a star of war.

"Your star has brought you good fortunes," said Wolf Star, placing her head on Lone Wolf's broad shoulder. "I hope it burns bright in the sky to keep you safe for always."

"Wolf Star, I'll tell you a secret if you promise not to tell anyone," Lone Wolf said. Since he could not fend off Wolf Star's advances, he had no choice but to tell her the truth.

The last time Lone Wolf spoke to Wolf Star with such gravity was a situation of life and death. The young girl's heart was filled with dread, fearing what terrible secrets might escape from Lone Wolf's mouth. She twisted her lips into a bitter smile to accept the darkness threatening to devour her and braced herself for the onslaught of pain. Life is pain, Wolf Star had learned from experience. People saying otherwise were selling little blue pills.

Lone Wolf stared at Wolf Star's innocent, angelic face in the moonlight. Her glistening eyes were pleading for mercy. Lone Wolf knew the truth would pierce her heart and shatter her dreams, but he didn't know what else he could do.

"Wolf Star, my memory is coming back in bits and pieces. I remember I already have a wife. We also have a baby daughter. I don't remember how we got separated. But sooner or later, when all my memory returns, I'll have to leave the tribe and try to find my family. I hope you understand."

Teardrops of sparkling diamonds fell from Wolf Star's eyes. She bore her pain in silence while clinging to Lone Wolf's arm.

Chapter 17

Rising from the Ashes

As Lone Wolf predicted, Modred became fed up with the casualty reports from his troops chasing after the elusive Eastern Wolf survivors. The conditions were ripe for a truce when Lone Wolf sent boxes of wild red ginseng to Modred and a silver fox pelerine to his Ianse, congratulating the Hun on his adoption of the Chanyu title, similar to Khan of later years. The ginseng was said to enhance virility and promote longevity. It grew in the woods in China's northeast, near where Lone Wolf's tribe was licking its wounds. Both gifts were rare and precious. Modred was pleased and called off the wild goose chase.

Meanwhile, more survivors of the slaughter came through the mountains and joined Lone Wolf, who provided them with food and safety. Other groups settled in the mountain range north and south of Lone Wolf's band, forming kindred alliances and helping each other defend against the Berserkers, a barbaric tribe known as the Hemo (貉貊) in ancient Chinese annals.

Lone Wolf reorganized the tribes under new banners, built well-defended settlements and taught the people to supplement hunting with fishing and farming. The young chief had a knack for breeding animals and growing things. Under his leadership, the settlements soon teemed with livestock and cellar storages brimmed with grains, preserved vegetables, salted fish and cured meat. Food was plentiful, milk and honey flowed, the population multiplied, and the tribes thrived during this period of peace.

As the powerful Chief and a virile Adonis, Lone Wolf received numerous offers from eligible nubile women to be his helpmate. He needed someone to look after him, and he also had a duty to produce babies. To be strong again, the tribes must produce abundant babies, and Chief Lone Wolf must set a good example.

With all the young women vying for his attention and the elders piling on the pressure, Lone Wolf realized he would enjoy no peace until he settled this issue. The situation deteriorated to the point he feared staying in his living quarters after sundown because all the unmarried girls would line up outside his door with baskets full of food and wine, hoping he would ask them to stay.

One chilly evening in late autumn during the deer rutting season, Lone Wolf took a stroll with a heavy heart and came to his favourite grassy knoll. He wanted to escape from all the wenches knocking on his door. He found Wolf Star alone with her wolfdog, Chimera, stretched on her back and staring at the Milky Way. Wolf Star did not stir as Lone Wolf lay down beside her.

"Are you waiting for me to show up?" Lone Wolf asked. "You know how I'm trying to avoid those girls."

"No, I'm not waiting for you," Wolf Star replied, her eyes transfixed at the starry sky. "I'm waiting for my star to appear. You said it would bring me good luck."

"I'm sure your luck will change soon. But how long have you been here? I didn't see you at the mess hall. Have you eaten?"

"I'm not hungry."

"All our animals are getting fat, but you've lost weight. Are you eating well? Come to my cabin. I have plenty of food."

"I'm fine. Will you tell me a story? Can you tell the story about the little prince again?"

"I'll tell you any story you like if you come to my place and eat something warm. Even poor Chimera looks famished."

"I'm not hungry. Chimera, are you hungry?"

Her faithful wolfdog whined.

"Hey, you're beginning to worry me. I've been so busy looking after everyone I forgot about my best mate. I should've taken better care of you," Lone Wolf said. He took Wolf Star's hand and gave her a light tug. "Come with me."

Without turning her head toward her inscrutable friend, Wolf Star neither budged nor let a word escape her lips. Finally, she failed to hold back her tears, and the pearly drops started spilling over from the corner of her eyes. Wolf Star had lost everyone dear to her. She feared she would lose the only person she could depend on. Lone Wolf held her face to his chest and let her release the bitterness from her heart.

After Wolf Star's emotions subsided, Lone Wolf dried her tears with his sleeves. He knew the cause of her grief and how to relieve it. He decided to reveal more of his secrets, but only those not so shocking they would drive her insane.

"I know I've been a mystery, not only to others but to myself as well. I can remember more of my past now. However, I can't reveal it to anyone. You're the only person I can trust."

"I have kept your secret. But it hurts when I remember you will leave us someday."

"I'm sorry to burden you with it. I know this is not fair to you. I'll keep my secrets to myself if you prefer not to know."

"I'm fine now. Let me share this weight oppressing you."

"I'll never find a better friend than you, Wolf Star," Lone Wolf said. He paused to collect his thoughts and began, "When the old Tuman found me, I had such a high fever my memory was damaged. With the help of an herbal balm, I have been recovering, and now I can remember a lot more. I know why I got separated from my wife and daughter. It's because I'm an exile. My tribe had banished me for life. Though I want to find my family, I may never see them again. I need to keep this a secret because people have a low opinion of exiles, who are usually traitors of their clan or have committed evil crimes against their kin. How can another tribe accept such a person to live among them?"

"I can't imagine you've done anything so evil. Do you remember why you're banished?"

"On this, my memory is still fuzzy. Maybe the crime is so heinous my heart does not want to remember."

"Knowing you all these years, I don't believe it's possible."

"I hope you're right. Anyways, it was the past. For now, as you say, while we live, let us live. Come with me to my cabin. I have something important I want to discuss with you in private."

"What is it? No one is here but you and me. Tell me now."

"Will you promise to eat something afterwards?"

"You mean a 'cross my heart and hope to die' promise?"

"Yes," Lone Wolf replied, laughing. He had taught Wolf Star this silly oath. "And do you remember what follows?"

"Stick a needle in my eye," Wolf Star said, squeezing her nose. "It's disgusting."

"Okay, back to serious business. I have a proposition for you."

"What do you mean? What's it all about?"

"I have a problem. The way things are going, I can no longer lead the tribes without a helpmate. The elders and all the young women are pestering and pressuring me to no end. I can't function as the Chief when every kind word I say to a young woman is an invitation to spend the night with me. When a girl comes to me for help, I don't know if she needs help or wants me to marry her. All the young men looking for helpmates are upset with me, too. How can I stop this nonsense?"

"I don't know. Maybe you can marry Lupalina, and no one will ever bother you again."

"Do not jest. I'm serious."

"But it sounds as if you're bragging."

"It was the preamble for my proposition," Lone Wolf said. He drew a deep breath and proposed, "Wolf Star, will you be my helpmate?"

"Are you poking fun at me again?"

"This is as serious as a blood feud, Wolf Star. If I can't avoid it, I'd much rather have you as my helpmate."

Wolf Star sat up and fixed her gaze upon Lone Wolf with her bright, animated eyes, almost tripping over her words in excitement, "Promise me this is not a joke."

"Cross my heart and hope to die."

This time, tears of joy flowed down Wolf Star's face. She would no longer be the lonely outcast. She would be the beloved Chief Lone Wolf's Ianse and the mother of his children. In the blink of an eye, her world brightened, illuminated by her happiness, and the icy, forlorn Milky Way transformed into a glittery gem-studded ribbon in the sky. New grass sprouted around her, glowing luminescent green, turning the barren ground into a luxuriant meadow elegantly adorned with the delicate and mysterious Queens of the Night. Twinkling stars descended on Earth, taking the form of florescent pixies frolicking among the fragrant blossoms. Two nightingales arrived from heaven to serenade the young lovers with the "Flower Duet" of Delibes. What need did Wolf Star have for food when the only thing on her mind was covering Lone Wolf with countless kisses?

Thus, Lone Wolf solved his immediate problems with a single masterful stroke, a win-win solution for all involved. Even the prophecy of the Havenly Wolf star came true. The rise of the star did bring the girl Wolf Star great fortunes. As for the long-term repercussions associated with this stopgap, their solutions would have to wait.

Chapter 18

The One-eyed Apothecary

All the tribes under Lone Wolf's leadership continued to thrive. Before long, they had ten thousand bows again. The elders convened a congregation in which Chief Lone Wolf became Tuman. The young Chief did not want the title because he knew it would rub salt in his brothers' wounds. After all, what's in a name? Lone Wolf knew his brothers would act on their resentment one of these days. Meanwhile, life must go on.

As the months and seasons rolled by, the tribes prospered and grew in number. Lone Wolf decided to form a super-tribe, which he named Shanbe after the divine beast. He adopted the unicorn as the super-tribe's totem and named the mountains hosting their settlements Shanbe, later known as the Greater Khingan Range.

Over time, the Shanbe tribes spilled over from the mountains onto the plains. The Berserkers read the writing on the wall and realized their days of enjoying a monopoly of the fat lands were over. They were smart to bury the hatchet and join the Shanbe, sharing the land of the rich, black soil with the mountain folks. Three hundred years later, when Shanbe hordes started showing up at the doorsteps of the Eastern Han Empire, the Han people gave the tribe a Chinese name, Xianbei (鲜卑).

Meanwhile, Wolf Star became a beloved Ianse. She started a new fad among the women when she used rouge to paint a flower on her forehead. Lone Wolf had given her this fashion idea. He did not know where it came from.

However, the union of Lone Wolf and Wolf Star ran into an unexpected glitch. After a year together, they remained childless, with no sign the situation would improve. They tried to boost their virility by consuming a farrago of folk remedies, including wild ginseng and braised deer pizzle, all to no avail. Wolf Star was desperate and started consulting the shamans, but their treatments were torturous and often had the opposite effect.

By a twist of fate, Wolf Star got what she wanted, though unaware of the price or the stake. One day, an itinerant doctor and his assistant arrived at the settlement. The doctor wore a patch over his left eye and perambulated with a walking staff. They promptly cured a young boy suffering from a high fever.

The news of the visitors quickly made its way to Lone Wolf. He wanted to check them out without causing a stir. Arriving at the market square, he bumped into Wolf Star, whose gossipers told her the healers came from the south and were in the area searching for rare herbs. The civilized people from the southern empire were rumoured to be knowledgeable about every subject under the sun and should be able to solve Wolf Star's problem.

The medicine men had set up a tent clinic, and patients were queuing outside. Lone Wolf's guards cleared the way for the Tuman and the Ianse. When Lone Wolf entered the tent and saw the strangers, he froze as if he had seen a ghost.

"What's the matter?" Wolf Star asked. "Do you know them?"

"No, but they remind me of people in my misty memory."

The one-eyed doctor and his assistant had no sooner finished attending to their patient when they heard the armed guard announce the entrance of the Tuman and his Ianse. The doctor hurriedly rose to his feet and greeted the dignitaries in the cultivated manners of the southern empire, head bowed, arms extended, and his left hand placed over his right.

"I beg the Tuman to forgive my delinquency in propriety. If I had known my intrusion would trouble Your Excellency and the Ianse to grace my humble clinic with their presence, I would have requested an audience in front of my lord in the first place."

"Be at ease, good doctor," Lone Wolf said. "You are among wild people with little manners here. Please tell us about yourself."

"I'm an apothecary, herbalist, surgeon and medical doctor from the Qin Empire in the south. People call me Mr. Hua. I'm here searching for rare herbs. Imagine my surprise to find this paradise hidden in the mountains. By chance, a young child in the settlement was suffering from a shivering fever. I helped him recover with a simple herbal tea. When word went around, more people with ailments came seeking treatment. I could not refuse them. As a doctor, I have sworn to help the sick. I hope I haven't created too much disturbance."

"On the contrary, we're most thankful. If you have no other plans, I invite you and your companion to stay with us."

"My lord's kindness is boundless. Your Excellency may have guessed we're here also because we want to stay far away from the endless wars down south. Since the passing of Emperor Qin Shihuang, the empire has been on the brink of total collapse. First, evil plots and murders created chaos at the imperial court. Soon, the peasants and the deposed aristocrats rose in rebellion. After the Battle of Julu, the Qin Empire was doomed. But the rebels begin to fight among themselves. It won't stop until one king remains to rule them all. For us plebeians, we only wish to live in peace."

"Good. We share the same desire, Mr. Hua. You are my guest and may stay as long as you wish. My men will arrange suitable lodging for you and your companion. I will appoint servants to attend to all your daily needs. Tonight, we'll hold a feast in your honour. Before we leave you to your work, my wife and I would like to seek your counsel on a private matter."

"By observing your faces, I already guessed your complaint. Your humours do not mix. I can fix your condition with an herbal prescription. If both of you take the potion according to instruction, I promise you'll have many children."

"Oh, thank God you found us," the delighted Wolf Star cried. "How can we repay you?"

"It'd be good if you would show my companion, Shazi, where to find wild ginseng. It'll more than pay for everything. And we'll stay to ensure the Ianse gives birth to a strong and healthy baby without complications."

Lone Wolf was visibly stunned when he heard the name Shazi, which meant "idiot." The doctor noticed and tried to mollify his concern, "Shazi is his nickname. He may be a bit confused sometimes, but he's always as helpful as a squirrel and rather harmless. Shazi may not be ideal, but no one else would follow me on my random peregrinations. After all these years travelling together, I've grown accustomed to his face."

"Have we met before?" Lone Wolf couldn't help asking. He had a strange feeling he knew them once upon a dream.

"It's impossible. Why do you ask?"

"I apologize. I suffer from a bothersome malady. Several years ago, a high fever damaged my brain, and I have not fully recovered. I sometimes get the past, present and future all mixed up. And I go through some days unsure whether I'm awake or dreaming."

"I know what you mean. I've experienced similar symptoms. I'll prescribe some Lethe lotus for you. It'll help you sleep, and you'll wake up with your confusion all cleared up."

Time flew with the speed of an arrow. Wolf Star did conceive as Mr. Hua promised. She wore a constant glow on her face and vaunted her ballooning belly. Nine-and-a-half moons later, the happy Ianse gave birth to a healthy baby girl endowed with her mother's stunning green eyes. When Lone Wolf's gaze met the baby's crystalline orbs, he experienced a jolt as if struck by lightning. Upon the baby surviving the first moon cycle, the proud parents named her Blitzen Wolf.

With the help of the Lethe lotus, Lone Wolf's muddled memory of the murky past subsided into the background. The Shanbe folks became accustomed to having Mr. Hua and Shazi look after their universal healthcare. People were healthier, lived longer and had more babies. The Shanbe Mountain was a paradise to the Shanbe tribes. What could go wrong?

One day, Lone Wolf returned from a short mountain retreat to find the settlement in turmoil. Lupalina, with the help of a wet nurse, was tending to the baby Blitzen Wolf. They both displayed deeply furrowed worry lines on their brows. Wolf Star had been missing for several days, but no one knew her whereabouts. Added to their misgivings was the simultaneous disappearance of Mr. Hua and Shazi. Perhaps the strangers from the south had kidnapped Wolf Star. Trackers with their hunting hounds had searched for miles in all directions but found nothing. Wolf Star, Mr. Hua and Shazi had vanished without leaving a whiff of their scent in the air.

For a long time, Lone Wolf was beside himself with grief. He feared he was losing his mind because he could not remember Wolf Star's face. When she appeared in his dreams, her hair became dark brown, and the red flower on her brow became a heart. He spent many evenings at the grassy knoll, hoping the Ianse would show up, but was greeted only by the wind. Eventually, Lone Wolf came to terms with the disappearance of his helpmate. He had to let go of her memory and pay more attention to Blitzen Wolf, who was beginning to walk and learning to talk. Lone Wolf gained comfort from spending time with his daughter. He forgot it was his destiny to lose Blitzen Wolf when another stranger from long ago and far away walked into his life.

Chapter 19

Oblique Order

According to Lady Diane's plan, the Shang soldiers drew up the battle lines as saffron-robed Dawn rose from her ambrosial sleep. Queen Zia took personal command of the centre with Lady Diane as her deputy. Two aristocrats from a minor branch of the royal house led the wings. The autumn morning air was crisp, the sky was clear, and no biting gust blew from the north, making it a perfect day for violence and bloodshed.

Every phalanx hoisted the Shang flag, showing the Oracle Bone symbol for Shang. The pictogram depicted a dagger for ritual slaughter atop an altar. A later version, which evolved into the modern Chinese character (商), added a receptacle underneath for catching the blood of the sacrificial victims. A variation included stars as the determinative to mean the name of the Shang Star, also known as the Great Fire and later the Heart Star of the Dragon constellation. In the West, it was named Antares of Scorpius.

Queen Zia, famous in modern China as Fu Hao, led the royal guards who hoisted her banners depicting a female with a son. This pictogram means "good" (好), pronounced *hao.* Her name, however, was not Hao but Zi (子), meaning "son." During Shang times, when a name belonged to a female or a matriarchal clan, it was customary to add the "female" (女) radical to the written word. Her name, Hao, was, in fact, the matriarchal form of Zi, and Zi was the name of the Shang's royal house. Since Queen Zia and King Wotan had the same family name, they were near kin from the same paternal lineage. Fu (妇), showing a broom, was her title, meaning "married woman." Since Hao was the king's wife, the title denoted "Queen." Therefore, Fu Hao means Queen Hao, or to be more accurate, Queen Zi, known to us as Queen Zia.

The Queen and her trusted deputy exchanged a nod to indicate the game was afoot. Lady Diane gave the order for the phalanxes to advance, signifying it was time to rumble, and the whole array began to march forward to the beat of the drums.

The Gotts were a semi-nomadic tribe living northwest of the Shang kingdom. Contrary to rumours, they were not uncivilized but had learned much through frequent contact with people from the south. They also acquired expertise from their southern neighbours to produce weapons, tools and vessels of bronze. The Shang named their kingdom Guifang, the Land of Spirits.

The Queen's army consisted of fifty chariots, each in charge of fifty hoplites. Each chariot was driven by a charioteer, transporting a man-at-arms wielding a poleaxe on the right and a commander armed with a bow and arrows on the left. The chariot functioned as a command vehicle rather than a shock weapon. In battle, the phalanxes and the chariots advanced in close formation to the steady beat of the war drums.

The Gotts were taken aback at the sight of the Shang army on the march without performing their usual rites and ceremonies. They had no time for breakfast as they scrambled to arm themselves and form a defence line against their enemies.

Upon arriving in front of the Gotts, Lady Diane ordered the first action of the battle. A small detachment of light-mounted skirmishers from the left wing galloped off to probe the enemy's right flank. Lady Diane introduced this novel tactic as her second surprise for the Gotts. She had invented a saddle, securing mounted archers to their horses and allowing them to turn around and shoot arrows at their pursuers without falling. As the skirmishers came within range, they loosed their arrows, reeled to their left to safety and regrouped to make another charge. Since the Shang had more advanced bows, their skirmishers could harass the enemy all day without suffering losses.

The horde's chief transferred his armoured cavalry from the centre to the right wing to counter the Shang threats. He believed his right would bear the brunt of the heavy fighting, as his left was flush against the swampy riverbank, making it difficult for the Shang chariots or hoplites to traverse. Furthermore, the right flank offered the only possible escape route for the Gotts.

Noting the enemy's movements, Lady Diane ordered a complicated manoeuvre. The left wing of the Shang army stopped its forward march and deployed the phalanxes into interlocking defensive squares, anticipating a cavalry charge from the Gotts. Queen Zia's central division swung anticlockwise, bringing its right closer to bear on the enemy lines. The phalanxes of the Shang right wing, with hoplites carrying faggots for advancing over the boggy land, marched forward to assault the Gotts' left wing.

Lady Diane had invented the oblique order to attack the enemy's weak wing while defending against their strong wing. This asymmetric strategy was an advanced concept and disappeared from history for six hundred years until the Battle of Chengpu (城濮). The Theban general, Epaminodas, later employed it at the Battle of Leuctra to crush the Spartans. The audacious Alexander followed suit at Gaugamela, where he routed the much larger army of Darius III of the Persian Empire. Almost three thousand years after Lady Diane, Prussian King Frederick the Great employed this battle order to achieve a similar result at the battle of Leuthen, routing an enemy army twice as large. Victoria also applied it when she played chess, usually with her favourite opening, the Dragon variation of Sicilian Defence.

As the struggle at the Shang right wing hung in the balance, Lady Diane ordered the reserve troops to deploy to her right. Two squadrons of heavy cavalry armed with long lances rode out from behind the hill and prepared to charge the left flank of the Gotts.

Lady Diane developed the mounted Lancers because the best way to neutralize the Gotts' cavalry was to use cavalry. The Shang lancers, secured to their saddled and caparisoned war steeds, wielded a long lance to cut and stab the Gotts at a distance. Lady Diane had adopted the lance to gain an advantage over the more common spear. The saddle also enabled the Lancers to unseat their opponents in a melee. This deployment was another surprise for the Gotts, as they were keenly aware the Shang army favoured the plodding tactics of the orderly phalanx led by chariots.

While the Shang Lancers deployed in a double-line formation to support the right wing, the other wing must withstand the counter-attack of the Gotts' heavy cavalry. Led by their chief, the Gotts dispersed the Shang skirmishers and, resembling demons astride monstrous beasts, charged the Shang's left wing, delivering pandemonium to the quaking Shang hoplites.

Reacting to this development, Lady Diane at the centre brought her archer squadrons forward and, from their slanted position, unleashed volleys at the flank of the charging Gotts, forming a lethal crossfire with the archers of the left wing. It succeeded in blunting the enemy's attack. By the time the Gotts' heavy cavalry arrived at the Shang's left wing, the momentum of the charge had dissipated, and the attack became disorganized. The Gotts could not break up any of the Shang's well-defended squares. When the Gotts Chief realized he could not bring mayhem to the Shang phalanxes and the Shang skirmishers were regrouping and threatening his rear, he ordered a retreat.

Meanwhile, on the Shang right, noticing the forward phalanxes had laid down the faggots, the Lancers itched to ride into action.

Lady Diane sensed the battle had arrived at a critical juncture needing her direct intervention. She turned to Queen Zia to make a request.

"Domina, I beg for leave to take the field. To assure the favourable outcome of this battle, I must lead the Lancers in person to close the ring on the Gotts. All we need to do at the centre is to keep the phalanxes fixed in their defensive positions and order our forward archers to unleash volleys into the horde if they attack. Our pioneers had buried empty wine amphorae in well-covered ditches last night. The Gotts will charge to their demise if they try. I have signalled our left wing to assume attack formation and envelop the Gotts. Not a single fish will escape the net today."

"Can't you send someone in your stead? I don't want you to take unnecessary risks."

"I need to go now; otherwise, the Gotts will escape. Wish us luck. I shall return anon with good news."

Lady Diane kissed the archer ring on her thumb, displaying her intimate friendship with Queen Zia and, without waiting for approval, leapt off her chariot.

During battles, every second counts, and time waits for no one except for the dead. Lady Diane mounted Saluzi, meaning Purple Streak, her favourite steed of ebony black and ordered the captain of the Royal Guards to keep the Queen safe until her return.

Lady Diane seized a lance from her squire, bidding her female flag-bearer and personal guards to follow her. Saluzi reared in a high curvet and, with a mighty kick, bounded into the fray with the force of a cannonball. All eyes, of friends and foes alike, were drawn toward this shimmering black beast thundering across the battlefield, breathing flames from its snout as if it were a monster from Tartarus, its flowing mane billowed in the wind along with Lady Diane's black cape, evoking the roaring waters of the Yellow River cascading down the cataracts of Dragon's Gate.

Chapter 20

Twilight of the Gotts

The Shang and the Gotts had been grappling with each other in a death struggle since early morning. As the shadows shrank, the empty craws of the barbarians began to growl. The Gotts failed in their attack, and their chief had little choice but to ride back to his lines, at which point he received the news his left flank was on the verge of collapse. He hurriedly dispatched troops from the centre to stabilize the buckling wing.

The marauding horde's leader realized he might have met his match, and his only chance to come out on top was to attack the Shang queen at the centre. Alexander the Great did something similar at the Battle of Gaugamela to great effect. The Gotts Chief rallied his men for a desperate charge, a Hail Mary play.

"Wolf brothers!" he thundered, riding up and down the line, exhorting his men to do and die. "The Shang are giving us their lovely maidens to warm our beds. The brave horses at the front get the pretty vixens, the slow ones at the back get the neutered goats."

The horde roared with laughter.

"Why are we still here?" the Gotts Chief shouted. "Let's go get them."

Without waiting for their leader, the horde rushed forth as an unstoppable hurricane toward the Shang queen's phalanxes at the centre, galloping to the heroic chorus of Wagner's "Ride of the Valkyries" and howling as if possessed by the wolf spirits roaming the mountain range of the seventy-black peaks.

At this very moment, with the help of the Lancers, the Shang's right wing broke through the Gotts' left. The battle had proceeded according to Lady Diane's plan so far. However, the ominous dust cloud rising behind the horde's daring charge at Queen Zia created a moment of anxiety for Lady Diane, reminding her of separation and death. Wasting no time in hesitation, she marshalled the Lancers for a flank charge at the Gotts to deliver the coup de main.

As for the Gotts, their bravest did not get the pretty vixens. Their steeds crushed the buried amphorae and fell headlong into the ditches dug by the Shang pioneers. As the next wave approached Queen Zia's phalanxes, a deadly shower of arrows rained on the hapless Gotts, sending the eager warriors on a fast track to Valhalla with the Valkyries as their new brides.

Before the Gotts could regroup, the Lancers, led by Lady Diane, smashed into their left flank. The carnage was horrific. The Gotts' desperate charge came to nothing, and they ended up in a cauldron with no way out. The Gotts Chief, accompanied by his best warriors, retreated toward the wagon fortress, hoping to rally the troops and break out of the encirclement.

The barbarian leader lost all hope when he learned Shang soldiers had already taken his camp. Lady Diane had sent her Special Operations platoons in the dead of night in a wide westward flanking march through the woods to the marshes behind the Gotts' line. They waited in hiding until the moment was ripe and captured the Gotts' wagon fortress by surprise.

Lady Diane, leading a unit of the Lancers and flanked by her picked guards, cut a swathe through the Gotts and arrived at Queen Zia's front.

"Domina, I bear great tidings. We have won a glorious victory today. We have surrounded the Gotts. They have nowhere to run. Please order your phalanxes to march forward without leaving any gaps. Our pioneers have prepared marching lanes through the ditches in front. I will now capture their chief and bring him before Your Majesty."

"Well done! But after the battle, I will deal with you for running off without leave."

Queen Zia sounded stern, but she secretly stole a subtle smile.

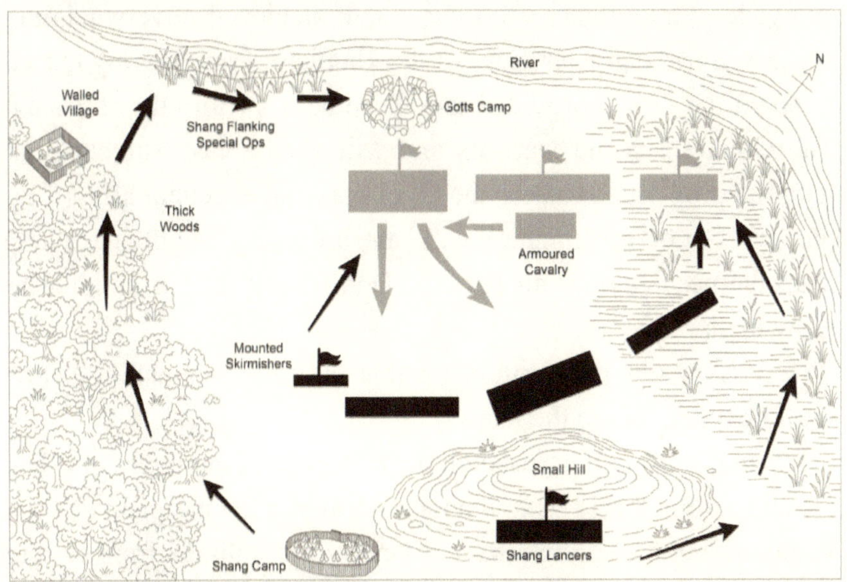

"As you wish, ma'am," replied Lady Diane, knowing Queen Zia would absolve her of any mischief. Although the battle was, in essence, already over, she wanted to make the victory more meaningful than another day of wanton slaughter. While born and bred a warrior, Lady Diane had always yearned for peace.

"I have a small request, Domina. The Gotts are brave, intelligent and more civilized than what the warmongers tell us. Instead of committing them to a wholesale massacre, we should consider having them as our subjects, maybe even allies."

"The Gotts have brought much death and suffering to our people. The King will want to extract some satisfaction of vengeance from this victory."

"As Your Majesty already knows, there is no money in revenge. We should consider policies generating long-term profits for us. The universe is most benevolent when it is in balance. We have won a lopsided victory today. Hence, we must restore the equipoise. The time to exercise self-restraint is when we have enjoyed extraordinary fortunes and achieved overwhelming success. For the greater glory of the kingdom, I implore my Queen to spare the Gotts, provided they become a sworn ally of Shang. The Gotts are proud warriors and will not be easy subjects, but with the proper persuasion, they will make an excellent ally. If my plan works out, the kingdom will have a friendly neighbour to help keep the peace along our borders. Don't we want our children to grow up in peace?"

"What is our justification for this radical peacemaking? How shall I explain this to the King?"

"What I propose is based on the teachings of our ancestors. The ancient scrolls forbid us to hunt and slaughter the pregnant and the young during the spring season. They also prohibit us from cutting saplings and conducting wars of aggression. The writings warn of self-destruction if we wield our power without restraint. In truth, we're abiding by the wisdom of our forefathers. And even if our lord, the King, disapproves, we can always ask the Oracles and, by our good-intentioned guile, obtain a favourable response."

"Alright, I'll consider it, my dear Diane. I'll let you know my decision after you have captured the Gotts Chief."

Queen Zia had decided long ago to indulge in her favourite girl's fancies, whatever they might be. It always gave the Queen great pleasure to do so.

Chapter 21

The Tuman's Banner

The Gotts Chief and his dwindling guards fought with the ferocity of feral beasts but in vain. One by one, his warriors succumbed to their wounds and returned to the womb of Mother Earth drenched in blood. The desperate leader of the horde tried to break out of the ring of Shang hoplites but failed. He contemplated an honourable end by falling on his sword, but his horse stumbled into a trap, and the Shang soldiers captured him unharmed, along with about a thousand Gotts who survived the slaughter.

Lady Diane arrived at the prisoners' camp with her mounted guards. She rode up to the captives to inspect their condition. The once-feared Gotts were a sorry sight to behold. Everyone sustained multiple wounds of various degrees of severity. Yet they stood proud before the woman who had thrashed them on the battlefield.

"I'm Lady Diane," the bellatrix shouted, "War Counsellor of Queen Zia, *Dian* of King Wotan and Marshal of War for the kingdom of Shang. I wish to speak with the Chief of the Gotts."

Not a single prisoner uttered a word. A few Gotts spat in contempt, one losing a tooth in the process. Another captive, with his nose battered into a pulp, started laughing, spitting out blood with each guffaw. A badly wounded barbarian, with an arrow through his shoulder and a gash on his face, followed suit. The one next to him, with his cracked skull in a gore-soaked bandage, started howling with abandon. The hysteria continued to spread, and soon, the entire pathetic group was in stitches, half of them holding their stomach and the other half wiping the tears streaming down their cheeks. The Shang could never comprehend the humour of the Gotts, who laughed in the face of death.

"Sblood and zounds!" Lady Diane issued a curse and made an exaggerated gesture toward the pile of firewood collected for the camp's frigid night, which instantly burst into flames. No less superstitious than the Shang, the Gotts perceived the simple magic trick as a prodigy. The woman in front of them was no doubt a powerful witch, and the fear of supernatural forces was enough to silence the barbarians.

"Are you aware," Lady Diane roared, "Queen Zia had fought ten great battles against neighbouring tribes and won all of them? Have you not heard about our famous war against the Sand Kingdom, how we levelled their walled settlements and captured most of their young men? Do you have any idea what happened to the captives? We maimed half of them, the proudest and the best fighters, and made them slaves. Most of them became eunuchs. The other half we sacrificed to the gods."

A wave of murmuring rippled across the prisoners, especially at the word "eunuch."

"I do not want such a bloodbath. I wish to make an offer. If the Gotts take an inviolable oath of friendship in blood with the Shang, we will set you free to return home to your families, with your horses, with wine and gifts from King Wotan and Queen Zia. The other choice is the fate of the Sand Kingdom's warriors. Now, where is your Chief?"

A barbarian stripped of his ornaments sauntered to Lady Diane's black steed and caressed the animal's nose. Saluzi snorted.

"We are the indomitable Gotts," the Chief declared. "If the whore queen is serious about wanting peace, why does she insult us by sending a trollop as her emissary? We might have lost the battle to the connivance of a crone who practices the black arts and sleeps with the farting devil, but we are unimpressed. We'd rather die than submit to a skank. If the Shang wants peace with the Gotts, you must first gain our respect. Let your bravest fight me in single combat to the death. If I lose, the Gotts will be your most faithful ally. If I prevail, we will leave with what we have rightfully plundered from our raids."

"Very well, I challenge you," Lady Diane said. "Guard, give the Chief a horse and a weapon of his choice."

"I will not tilt with a twattling termagant!" the Gotts Chief roared, contemning his conqueror with insults and spittle.

"I've made the challenge. You cannot back out," Lady Diane said, riding over and poking the man with the butt of her lance, "unless you're chickened and afraid of losing to a wench."

"Chickened? Afraid of losing to a wench?" the apoplectic barbarian bellowed. "You will rue the day you were born. Harlot, prepare to die."

The great warrior of the Gotts snatched a spear from a guard, wielding the grim weapon with skill and flourish. He mounted a horse brought over for him, and the game was afoot.

In one-on-one combat, the big, muscular barbarian was no match for the dainty female Shang warrior, an expert fencer with the lance. Lady Diane's battle-tested war steed Saluzi danced circles around the Gotts Chief, tantalizing the brute while keeping his lethal thrusts away from its mistress. After teasing the Gotts warrior with a few near misses, Lady Diane disengaged and galloped off. Believing his feminine foe couldn't handle the physical exertion, the Alpha male gave chase, going for the kill.

As the Gotts Chief caught up to Lady Diane, he was surprised by her unexpected backward thrust with her lance. The skillful pursuer parried in a hurry. The agile female warrior avoided her opponent's spear with a circular counter-parry, went under his arm, and whacked his side with the shaft of her lance, careful not to cut the man. Lady Diane executed the takedown with elan and power, knocking the Gotts warrior clean off his horse and eliciting a collective gasp from his men.

At this very moment, a herald announced the arrival of Queen Zia, who entered the camp in her chariot surrounded by her Royal Guards and her pack of wolfdogs. She declared, "Lady Diane, we owe you much for today's glorious victory. By my command, I grant you the authority to deal with the prisoners as you wish. The sun is setting. We have pledged our victory to the Unconquered Sun and the Supreme God Di. We need you to be our high priestess for the offerings. The gods will be pleased with the hecatombs of earthlings sacrificed to them. Otherwise, we have an abundance of sacrificial animals, including three hundred oxen from nearby villages. Settle this now, and don't be late."

Having delivered the message, Queen Zia winked at Lady Diane, turned her chariot around and left. The Gotts Chief was still sprawled on his back, dazed from the fall and bedazzled by his female opponent's mesmerizing martial prowess. For the Gotts, getting a timely whopping was the necessary dose of reality. If the Shang kingdom had women such as Queen Zia and Lady Diane to defend it, the Gotts did not stand much chance of having their way with pillage and plunder. Perhaps they could learn something from these wenches and be stronger for it.

Lady Diane dismounted and offered the shaft of her lance to the Gotts Chief, helping him to his feet.

"Now we have jousted as equals," Lady Diane said with diplomatic tact and respect, "will the Gotts befriend the Shang?"

Without hesitation, the beguiled Gotts Chief raised the lance with Lady Diane's arm, and the Gotts captives roared huzzahs.

Although Lady Diane's voice was hoarse from a day of shouting, she needed to make one last speech.

“Brave warriors, tonight you will rest in safety. You will have hot food, and our medicine men will tend to your wounds.”

The Gotts erupted in another round of hurrahs.

“You may bury or burn the dead according to your traditions. Tomorrow, we will invite the Gotts Chief and his chieftains to represent all the Gotts at the Ceremony of Brotherhood. We will take the inviolable oath of blood in the presence of the gods. Afterwards, everyone will wine and dine together as kin and family. We will forget past quarrels.”

Lady Diane gestured to her squire, who handed over a rolled-up banner. She unfurled it to reveal the sign of the scorpion.

“This is the banner you will use while you’re friends with the Shang. It is the flag of the Tuman. The name means ‘the wise chief of a myriad host.’ Henceforth, the royal court of Shang will honour the Gotts Chief with this title. Our soldiers will fight alongside each other against common enemies. The Gotts shall forsake the raiding of Shang villages. We will trade instead. No one needs to die, and everyone wins.”

The Gotts Chief raised his Tuman banner high up in the air, right beside the banner of Lady Diane and the Shang flag.

“Tuman! Tuman! Tuman!” the Gotts chanted.

Chapter 22

What's in a Name?

Victoria asked her guardian while speeding along the Trans-Canada Highway in the Bozeman, "Should I call you Dr. Brown, Mr. Huang or David?"

"I have many names, but David will do."

"Alright, David, I'm not sleepy. I'm ready to learn who I am. But first, who are you, and why do you have a Chinese name?"

"I may not look Chinese to you, but I'm all Chinese. Have you heard of Freestyle skier Eileen Gu? She is an American who doesn't look Chinese, yet she represents China in the Olympics. Try to figure out Romanian-UK tennis player Emma Raducanu. No one could have guessed she is half-Chinese. How about Mike Rowse, the first foreign-born Hong Kong civil servant to give up his British citizenship to be a Chinese, or American NBA all-star Point Guard Stephon Marbury, who calls China home? Of course, you know about Canada's own gold medallist swimmer, Maggie Mac Neil, who is originally from China.

"All these people you may mistakenly believe to be non-Chinese are Chinese to some extent. You see, ever since birth, we have been consuming countless seemingly innocent little lies conspiring to warp our perception of reality. Besides protecting you, my job is to wake you from your stupor and train you to see the truth. First, forget everything you know. They're all lies."

"This is a popular line in movies. I hope you're not trying to gaslight me. I only want to know the simple truth."

"The truth is never simple. It takes a lot of work to learn the truth, which is so shocking you'll refuse to believe it."

"Since the car accident, I've absorbed a lot of shocks. Why don't you try me?"

"Yes, you've been amazing, and I'm proud of you. I suggest we play a virtual reality metaverse game to speed up your enlightenment. It'll be fun at the same time."

David reached below the seats and withdrew a mini-game console and a pair of virtual reality goggles with haptic accessories, each set including a latex cap, long gloves and stockings. He opened up a box full of wireless electrode pads.

"This Beta Huawei AIR gear will take us on a virtual reality tour of the truth," David said. "While a picture tells a thousand words, a realistic VR experience will let you live a thousand lives. Brace yourself for an unforgettable joyride."

Victoria was hesitant. "You're using faked reality to show me the truth. Shouldn't I be concerned?"

"You should be concerned, but you should also learn how to distinguish the truth from the lies and the lies from the truth. Let us seek truth from facts. I gave you to Michael and Angela, they left you a message telling you to find me, and you've seen the photos. I've had to take grave risks shooting two men, one of them armed. And your adoptive parents died protecting you. They would not send you to me if it weren't safe.

"As for our shadowy pursuers, we know they are powerful agents known as Watchers. They are relentless in their pursuit and will insidiously mingle fraud, deceit and malice with truth and sincerity to confound you. We must keep you from falling into their hands because the survival of life on Earth depends on you. This metaverse game will filter out the lies and help you recognize your true nature. It will prepare you for a dangerous future. I don't deny it. I'm using a lying device to help you learn the truth. But you can decide what is real. I'm training you to fight an existential battle. To win this fight, you must open your eyes to the truth."

"Frankly, I have no idea what you're talking about," Victoria said, unconvinced. "My parents didn't tell me anything. They didn't prepare me for this. I'm not too smart, I'm not strong, I won't say I'm a coward, but I'm no hero, and I don't want to fight any battles. Why would anyone be interested in abducting an ordinary Canadian from Dundas? All I ever hope for is to live a quiet and simple life. Why can't people leave me alone?"

"Put these on, and you'll learn something new about yourself and the world. What have you got to lose? It's more or less a game we play to kill time on a long drive across Canada."

David helped Victoria put on her game gloves, stockings and cap. He applied electrode pads to Victoria's temples, jugular, throat, arms and legs. Finally, Victoria gave in to David's gentle but persistent persuasion and put on the VR goggles.

David outfitted himself with the same gear and summoned the console's manager, the polite and pleasant Moira, to calibrate the equipment and synchronize the interfaces. He loaded the app, gestured "Play," and the game was afoot.

A door opened before Victoria and David, and they stepped inside a spartan bedroom. A young blonde-haired woman with a pale complexion was in bed, covered by a blood-stained sheet. A newborn baby wrapped in swaddling clothes slept beside her. A Chinese man knelt by the woman, holding her hand and sobbing.

"Where are we?" Victoria whispered.

"We're in my family home at Huangxian, or Yellow County, in Shandong Province. The blonde-haired woman is my mother. She is dying from complications arising from giving birth to me."

Victoria realized why David did not look "Chinese." He was an offspring of a mixed-race marriage. "Sorry about your mom," she said. "Do you know where she came from?"

"I grew up without a mother. Everything I know about her I read from her research papers on her roots. I learned my mother was a Russian Jew. Her parents lived in Harbin, a Chinese city in northeastern Manchuria, near the Russian border. In the early decades of the twentieth century, a community of Jewish refugees sprang up in Harbin. They had fled from the turmoil of the Tsar's hostile policies, revolution and wars of foreign intervention in Russia. Although this Jewish community has since migrated to Israel, America and other parts of the world, they have left behind some interesting buildings and Western traditions in the city.

"During the Second World War, my mother's parents travelled south, probably to join another group of the Jewish diaspora in Shanghai. They ran into trouble at Tangshan, about 160 kilometres east of Beijing, where they helped a Chinese fabrics merchant harried by Japanese soldiers. These incidents happened under Japanese occupation. My mother, a newborn baby, was the sole survivor. The soldiers found her wrapped in a blanket with the sun and the Hebrew word for 'sun,' *Shamash*, embroidered on it. The sun was the national emblem of Japan, and the soldiers, respecting the symbol, spared the baby and took her to an orphanage. My mother later named herself Tang Shanmei from *Shamash* and Tangshan. Shanmei means kind and beautiful.

"After the Communist Party established the People's Republic of China, they sent my mother to a foster home in Tangshan. She became a top student and went to one of the best universities in China, Peking University, where she met my father."

"Your mother had a nice name and a sweet face. Your father must be devastated."

"I remember my father as a humourless and miserable man. I may have seen him smile once or twice. I guess life dealt him a bad hand. He also made my life hell by naming me Huang Di, which sounds like 'emperor' but means 'little brother Huang.' My childhood sucked because I looked different. On top of that, my name made me the butt of countless jokes. I was resentful toward my father. I had a better relationship with my grandparents. My father figures prominently in your story. We'll get to him later."

David snapped his fingers, and the scene froze.

"Alright, you have the answer to your first question. Now, let us get down to business and visit the Empire of Lies."

"Is it another game?"

"It's a metaverse where every citizen reminds everyone else they're telling the truth. When you turn on the idiot box, the reality shows are contrived, the news is fake, and every talking head lies. The newspapers are even worse. Hardly a sentence printed by the free press does not convey a bald-faced lie, a false narrative, a misleading half-truth or an insidious omission. The creators and disseminators of these fabrications insist they're defenders of the freedom of expression when, in reality, they mean the freedom to equivocate and prevaricate. Upton Sinclair once commented about them, 'It is difficult to get a man to understand something when his salary depends upon his not understanding it.'

"Editors, journalists and reporters are salary earners. They can't afford the truth. We watch the news for free. We shouldn't expect the truth either. Woe to those who support and pay for the lies. What about politicians? We cheer them on when they slander and smear. We're puffed up when they bloviate. We elect and empower the best liars and are proud of it. We *expect* them to tell bald-faced lies. We'd believe something is amiss if they don't. We only complain when they lie poorly, not because they lie.

"Lies infuse the air we breathe and the water we drink. We swallow them wholesale and nonstop. We ingest, digest and regurgitate lies until lies become us. Where is this Empire of Lies? Let us enter the realm. All it takes is for me to snap my fingers and for you to open your eyes."

Chapter 23

Empire of Lies

"Everything is a lie ..." – Sage Didymas

Victoria opened her eyes to find herself inside the Bozeman in the metaverse game, a virtual simulation of her reality. David was still expostulating about falsehood.

"While the Empire of Lies rules us all, it exists mainly in our heads. We can always learn the truth, but we are too lazy. We accept the lies because they align with our biases. We prefer being delusional because we don't want to face the painful truth.

"Consider how often we tell ourselves and others we are free when, in fact, none of us is ever free from the need to eat, and therefore, at times, having to disgrace ourselves by the undignified necessity to acquire food by any means. None are more hopelessly enslaved than those who falsely believe they are free. People also mindlessly repeat, 'There is no such thing as a free lunch.' If it's true, the person who says it would not have survived infancy. All babies depend on free lunches. Free lunches perpetuate life itself.

"We are trapped in a cesspool of lies because we have passed the infernal gates ignoring this warning: *lasciate ogne speranza, voi ch'intrate*—abandon every hope, all those who enter. We are forever mired in the cesspool of the Big Lie because, as the great Yogi Berra succinctly said, 'We made too many *wrong* mistakes.'

"Most of us spend our entire lives submerged in an ocean of BS," David concluded. "We can't comprehend flowers because BS is all we know."

"Is that right? How do I know you're not feeding me BS?"

"It's not so simple. It's easier to demonstrate everyone you've ever trusted has lied to you. Who do you trust the most?"

"I guess I trust my parents a hundred percent."

"Your parents never told you anything remotely close to the truth. They had always sheltered you from it. Besides, where do children learn about Santa, the Easter Bunny and the Tooth Fairy? All lies. Who can you trust if not your parents?"

"You're right," Victoria admitted. She was crestfallen with the realization she could trust no one.

"Name a book you believe preaches the truth."

"The Bible, of course. We all swear by it."

"Yes, the whole truth and nothing but the truth, except God didn't tell the truth when He, or She, perhaps They, told Adam, 'Of the tree of the knowledge of good and evil, thou shalt not eat of it: for in the day that thou eatest thereof thou shalt surely die.' On the other hand, the serpent told Adam and Eve, 'ye shall not surely die … your eyes shall be opened, and ye shall be as gods, knowing good and evil.' Adam and Eve ate the forbidden fruit. They didn't die on the same day. Instead, they opened their eyes and became enlightened. Don't you agree God lied?"

"God means spiritual death. God doesn't lie."

"If God uses ambiguous words to hide the truth, the Almighty is equivocating, the same as lying. Everyone lies, even when they have no intention to do so. What if you believe in a lie and spread it to those who trust you? Parents, teachers, preachers and BFFs do it all the time. A recent study estimates humans, on average, lie eleven times a day. You can't avoid it. So, to discover the truth, you must always exercise critical thinking. In other words, stay smart, read widely, keep an open mind, question everything, gain experience, look under the surface, read between the lines, learn about the source, detect false narratives, follow the money, ask the right questions, stop believing in liars, seek truth from facts, think outside the box and apply Bayesian reasoning."

Victoria agreed with reservations, thinking, "Easier said than done. But what is Bayesian reasoning?" She was afraid to ask.

"Good, now we can enter the next level," David said. "Let's load our history app to experience historical events firsthand."

"Sure, I like history. It's my favourite subject at school."

"Excellent! In your opinion, who is the greatest U.S. President in recent memory?"

"Obama comes to mind. He was the first African American President. He also won the Nobel Peace Prize."

"Obama was a bit of a let-down with his 'hope' and 'change.' And the Nobel Piss Prize in no way indicates the worthiness of its recipients. More often than not, the board doling out the prize is a panel of pedantic, pontificating, pretentious, putrefying cow pies, repeatedly failing to execute Alfred Nobel's will. After Obama won the preemptive award, he doubled down in drone assassinations, destroyed Libya, backed terrorists in Syria's regime change, targeted Venezuela, bombed Yemen, expanded NATO and reneged on his promises to withdraw from Afghanistan and shut down Guantanamo. Obama made peace with the warmongers.

"He also attacked whistleblowers with might and main. The heroes who take grave personal risks to expose serious government crimes are condemned for telling the truth and have to beg the criminals for clemency. The liars, on the other hand, are lavishly rewarded. Who will save the country from itself now? The lesson is no one wants to take the red pill. During his tenure, Obama accelerated the unsustainable accumulation of the people's debt to enrich the One Percent, all in the guise of saving America's economy. He paved the way for our unstoppable slide down the slippery slope. Obama may be popular with the Democrats, but the greatest? I beg to differ. Try another one."

“How about George W. Bush? He liberated the Iraqi people from their tyrant, Saddam Hussein.”

“Bush destroyed Iraq based on a lie and caused death and displacement to millions. Maybe he should receive the Nobel. He also got America stuck in Afghanistan, wasting trillions in war for nothing. The Taliban won. Try again.”

“Who came before Bush? Oh, Bill Clinton. Didn’t he bring peace to some Eastern European country?”

“He bombed Serbia to pieces and expanded NATO, breaking the promise to Russia and planting the seeds for future wars. He is also notorious for having a sexual affair with a young woman in the White House. ‘Great’ is not the word to describe him.”

“I’ve got it, Ronald Reagan. Republicans worship him.”

“For sure, many Americans loved the avuncular Reagan and his jokes. But his much-touted Reaganomics did not work as hoped. His policies accelerated the evisceration of the unions, the weakening of social safety nets and the erosion of the middle class in America. Who came up with the fantastic idea to place the wealth of the nation, with no need for accountability, in the ‘responsible’ hands of the One Percent and the Military Industrial Complex while letting only a pitiful amount trickle down to the stupefied masses dying of thirst? I don’t want to know. Some Americans may have fond memories of Reagan, but not great.”

“I’ve read a bit about Nixon, Johnson, Kennedy, Eisenhower and Truman. They’re all famous. But people seem to have a special place in their heart for Kennedy as this knight of Camelot.”

“John F. Kennedy could have been an influential president if he were allowed to govern for two terms. Too bad! Shite happened! Try to name a president who had accomplished something benefitting not only Americans but also the rest of the world.”

“I’m not familiar with U.S. Presidents from too far back. Maybe you have someone in mind?”

"Alright, I'll tell you my choice. It's Franklin Roosevelt. He was elected President of the United States four times, a record unlikely to be broken. He extricated America from the Great Depression with the New Deal and led the Allies in the fight against the Axis Powers during the Second World War. He worked with Chiang Kai-shek of China and Stalin of the Soviet Union to defeat their common enemies. He demonstrated people from diverse backgrounds with opposing ideologies could work together for a better world. Haven't you studied FDR?"

"Not a whole lot. We learn mostly Canadian history at school."

"Let's check out my favourite U.S. President on the day after Pearl Harbour when he delivered the famous 'Infamy Speech' to a joint session of the U.S. Congress."

David snapped his fingers, and the surroundings switched to the Chamber of the House of Representatives. A soldier was helping Franklin Roosevelt struggle from his chair to the podium.

"Does he have health problems?" Victoria queried. "Why does he need help to walk a few steps?"

"It's a condition FDR makes a point not to publicize. He has been paralyzed from the waist down by polio since 1921, eleven years before he first became the U.S. President. But in public life, people never see him in a wheelchair. He gets around wearing leg braces, holding onto a walking cane and getting help from a strong assistant, usually one of his sons.

"FDR was born into a family of fabulous wealth, most of which came from his mother's inheritance. He could've lived a comfortable life doing nothing, but he refused to be defeated by his handicap and became one of America's greatest presidents. While FDR had his share of black marks, such as the Japanese American internment camps, his contributions far outweighed them. It may surprise some people a deep connection existed between FDR and China. Let us hop over there and explore this little-known tale."

Chapter 24

Wealth of a Nation

The tropical sun was beating on the backs of Victoria and David, both as deckhands on board an early nineteenth-century freight clipper moored to a large mastless hulk, one of ten anchored to the northwest of an island in the middle of a peaceful ocean. Victoria could taste the saltiness in the air in her first experience of the boundless main.

A swarthy, middle-aged Chinese man, a trusted agent of the Security Merchant in charge of China's foreign trade, came aboard the ship. He had the front and top of his head shaved, while a braided pigtail hung down his back. Victoria couldn't believe Chinese men had adopted such a punkish hairstyle in recent history. A towering, muscular, fresh-faced, well-bronzed, broad-shouldered Westerner flanked by armed guards greeted the visitor and signalled the crew hands to start unloading the cargo.

"This is the summer of 1833 during the Qing Dynasty," said David while mopping the deck. "We're on board a cargo ship off the coast of South China. Most of FDR's dynastic wealth comes from this location. This young, enterprising American, only twenty-four years old, will make a huge fortune here."

"Who is he? Is he a famous pioneer?"

"He is Warren Delano, Jr., the maternal grandfather of Franklin Delano Roosevelt. He's a new hand at the Boston trading house Russell & Company, learning the ropes at the front lines. Over the next ten years, the company would grow into the largest American trading house in China, with Warren Delano at its helm. Of course, Franklin's granddad doesn't get filthy rich by trading only tea, porcelain and silk. He goes into a lucrative business which makes an obscene amount of money, smuggling opium into China."

"Franklin Roosevelt's grandfather was El Chapo?"

"El Chapo backed by the US cavalry. We're in the good old days of gunboat capitalism. These large hulks function as floating warehouses. American, British and French fast ships drop off the opium here while less maneuverable ships conduct the legitimate trade. Chinese drug mules would take the contraband ashore on fast rowboats. Besides ruining many lives and families, this illegal drug trade also depletes China's silver, raising interest rates and condemning the poor to a life of debt slavery.

"People would be surprised to learn most of the American opium traders were from Boston, including the Perkins, the Forbes and the Russell families, to name a few. They would pour their easy money from China into building American railways, employing, with unintentional irony, cheap Chinese labour, investing in American industry and funding institutes of higher learning. Princeton, Harvard and Yale all received their share of the sanguine silver. Many of these traders would become prominent philanthropists, but nowadays, few realize their dynastic wealth came from a pretty little flower."

"Before we lay all the blame on America, what's with the incompetence of the Qing government?"

"It was the first international trade war between the West and China, and America was only one of the players. When Westerners traded with China, they bought a large amount of tea, silk and porcelain. But they didn't have anything China needed except for one item, silver, which happened to be the country's legal tender. By coincidence, the Spanish discovered one of the world's richest silver deposits at Potosí in the Spanish colony of Bolivia in South

America. Western fair and free market capitalism at once kicked into high gear, employing enslaved natives to dig up the Bolivian silver and sending it to China as Spanish Carolus silver coins. It was almost the same as printing money.

"Meanwhile, the Brits' trade deficit with China piled up. Sounds familiar? Lo and behold! They discovered opium, which China banned and which the Brits could grow in colonial India for nothing. When the Qing government enforced their rule of law, the Brits went to war in the name of fair and free trade. To add insult to injury, the colonial West sent spies to steal proprietary Chinese tea seeds and expertise, almost destroying China's tea industry."

"This doesn't seem right."

"'Right' never helps the victims. You do not own anything you cannot defend. It is the First Law of Economics. Hence, Chinese wealth went by gunpoint and thievery to the colonial plunderers. Afterwards, possession becomes nine-tenths of the law in the West. How convenient! Chinese civilization is the oldest continuous civilization, and their people have long memories. They know their history. So, the next time you hear Western politicians and the news media vilify China, what are they feeding you?"

"Mostly baloney, I suppose."

"Codswallop, pollywoppus and tommyrot, all nonsense. The lies are so rich they make my head spin. On the other hand, the politicians and the free press are only doing their job, spewing endless, richly funded and globally organized lies. To learn about the Qing Dynasty's incompetence, let us visit the Opium War."

"Can't we skip the wars? Isn't one shootout enough already? Frankly, I don't have much of a stomach for blood and guts."

"You may not like it, but I do have to train you to deal with confrontations. You may want to avoid violence, but sometimes it comes knocking on your door. My grandfather taught me never to bring a knife to a gunfight. It is a course you can't afford to skip."

Chapter 25

Fall of an Empire

With a snap of his fingers, David transported the two gamers to the countryside east of Beijing, the "north capital." The date was September 21, 1860. The time was the crack of dawn. The area was abuzz with soldiers marching and horses trotting. The autumn morning air was crisp, the sky was clear, and no biting gust blew from the north, making it a perfect day for violence and bloodshed. The Chinese army would be defending the Qing capital. Scouts reported the Anglo-French army had started marching and were about an hour away. The Chinese armed forces had drawn up their defences along the Beijing-Tianjin section of the Grand Canal, blocking the way to two bridges, one of stone and the other of wood. They had their back against the ancient waterway, which connects Hangzhou in the south with Beijing in the north, with no possibility of retreat. As the saying goes, a cornered beast is a dangerous beast.

The famous Mongolian general, Sengge Rinchen, had deployed a bristling mass of ten thousand Mongolian cavalry at the centre of the Qing line, with the same number of foot soldiers for each wing. The artillery units had thrown up defence works at the front, positioning the cannons to cover the battlefield.

The stone bridge, known as the Eight Mile Bridge, straddled the Grand Canal at about a two-hour march from Tongzhou, the "passage district," leading into Beijing. It represented the last line of defence of the eastern approach to the capital of the Qing

Empire. The Anglo-French army must cross the canal over this bridge to reach the city's front gate about fifteen kilometres west of the crossing. The Chinese defenders must prevent it.

The English horse regiments in brilliant scarlet-red coats soon arrived at the scene with a battery of six-pounders, closely followed by the French cavalry in sharp blue jackets. They occupied a village nearby to establish their camp, encountering no opposition by paying the villagers for their trouble in silver. Not long after, the Anglo-French infantry and the artillery caught up. Without taking a break, they marched straight to the front.

Facing thirty thousand Chinese defenders in grey battle garb, the Anglo-French army of ten thousand men had only one thousand horse soldiers posted at their left flank, with the King's Royal Dragoons deployed in front. The Qing army enjoyed a significant numerical advantage with a dug-in defence. They would be immovable if they were well-armed, well-trained and well-led by competent leaders.

However, the Qing recruited the infantry in great haste and did not have time to train them. The few cannons and muskets they possessed were outdated. Most of the soldiers still wielded swords and spears or bows and arrows. Sengge Rinchen would have to depend on his Mongolian cavalry to deliver the knockout punch.

"The Anglo-French army is tiny," Victoria exclaimed. "And the Chinese are defending their capital. I don't see why the Qing emperor can't stop the invaders."

"The Qing Dynasty is currently quite weak," David explained. "They're facing huge challenges from their own subjects. A serious peasant rebellion has been gnawing at the heart of the empire for almost a decade, and the Qing emperor can't do a darn thing about it. The rebellion, known as the Heavenly Kingdom of Great Peace—no irony intended—is headed by a failed scholar of Hakka origin. The Hakka, meaning 'guest family,' are descendants of migrants from the north. The rebels, whose leader identifies himself as Jesus' brother, control much of the wealthy region of East China, including the major city of Nanjing, the 'south capital,' and have threatened Shanghai and Beijing with their armed forces. The Western powers see this as a great opportunity to extract their pound of flesh from the Qing emperor."

"But China is huge and has a gazillion people. If the Chinese are serious about defending their country, it would be impossible for ten thousand foreign soldiers to conquer it."

"Right! You've hit the nail on the head. But no one can blame you for not knowing the Qing emperor was not Chinese. His family name is Aisin Gioro. It sounds as Chinese as Solana. He may look Chinese, but, in reality, he's Manchu, descendants of the Jurchens from southern Siberia, who had ruled northern China from the twelfth to the thirteenth century as the Jin Dynasty. The Chinese considered them barbarians. But by the time the Manchu replaced the Ming with the Qing Dynasty, their rulers were so Sinicized they were more Chinese than some Chinese."

"Now you're messing with my perception of China."

"When it comes to China, most people know bupkis. It's a vast and complex country with a long history. It is also a melting pot and home to numerous ethnicities and cultures. The Qing Manchu ruled China for 268 years until their last emperor, Puyi, a six-year-old child, abdicated in February 1912. China was under foreign rule for nine generations before the modern era. The braided pigtail you saw on the Chinese man aboard Warren Delano's schooner was the Manchu's traditional hairstyle, imposed upon the male population in China on pain of death. His vest, known as *magua*, or 'horse jacket,' and the Chinese women's traditional long dress, *qipao* or 'banner robes,' are Manchurian in origin. By this time, the Manchu had made China their permanent home, and their culture had become inextricably interwoven with the Chinese culture. The

Manchu changed China, but China also changed the Manchu, who became Chinese.

"As for the local population not coming to the aid of their Manchu ruler, it is also normal. Throughout Chinese history, up to this point during the Qing Dynasty, the illiterate peasants have no voice in politics. They pay their taxes to the landed gentry and tax collectors. They don't care who is sitting on the throne. If the ruler makes life hell, the peasants will rebel. China has a long tradition of peasant rebellions, starting with the establishment of the Han Dynasty by Liu Bang, the son of a peasant. Rulers ignore the plight of the Chinese peasants at their own risk."

David pointed at the village behind the Anglo-French line.

"Here is something you won't learn reading history books in your little house in Dundas. If you pay attention, you can see the villagers setting up a market to sell supplies to the Anglo-French army. The foreign invaders even have Chinese guides, interpreters, baggage handlers, camp servants, coolies, ditch diggers and sutlers who have followed their employer's advance from south China. These collaborators have no concept of saving China or building a future for their nation. The Qing rulers have only themselves to blame for losing the support of their subjects."

Upon a round of cannonade from each side, creating a lot of clamour and smoke, the game was afoot. Victoria, at first, shrank from the explosions but soon regained her composure. Despite having lived her life watching grass grow in a small town in southern Ontario, Victoria's transformation in the past twenty-four hours had been remarkable. From living a quiet life in a secluded paradise where nothing happened, she strutted confidently into a decisive battle near the capital of China, muttering to herself, "Calm down, girl. All this exists only in your head."

General Sengge Rinchen knew the future of the Qing Dynasty rested on his Mongolian horse soldiers. The heavy cavalry of

Genghis Khan's lineage would trample the Anglo-French army under their iron-clad hooves. The general did not know his cavalry was up against soldiers who had beaten Napoleon, defeated the Tsar in the Crimean War and quelled the rebellions in the Indian War of Independence. The English soldiers remembered how their impregnable squares repulsed Marshal Ney's cavalry charge at Waterloo. Fresh in their memory was the disastrous Charge of the Light Brigade at the Battle of Balaclava in the Crimean War, a fatal mistake to be repeated by the Mongolian general.

Taking advantage of his numerical superiority, Sengge Rinchen unleashed his cavalry in a frontal assault on the Anglo-French centre. These brave men did not ask the questions why but charged straight into withering fire. One wave after another repeated the same foolish act, fulfilling their duty to do and die. The Anglo-French army's fusillade mowed down the brave soldiers with no discrimination on age or rank. Thus, Sengge Rinchen destroyed the flower of his army. After the decimation of the Mongolian cavalry, the Anglo-French cavalry launched the coup de main and charged the Qing centre, routing the reserves. The hole at the Qing centre left their two immobile wings isolated. When the centre could not hold, the army fell apart, and Beijing had no soldiers to defend it.

While the battle did not result in significant casualties, the complete capitulation of the Qing emperor to the minuscule Anglo-French army started the unstoppable fall of the Qing Empire. It was plain to anyone with eyes the emperor had no clothes. From here on, the collapse of the Qing Dynasty was only a matter of time. Tick-tock, tick-tock.

After the battle, the Anglo-French army looted and burned down the Old Summer Palace. The Qing emperor did not own whatever he could not defend, property rights and the rule of law be damned. A century and a half later, many Chinese national treasures remain languishing in foreign cells.

David took Victoria to the ruins of the Old Summer Palace to check out the charred remains of an empire's past grandeur. The Anglo-French soldiers were helping themselves to whatever they could lay their hands on. What they could not carry off, they either burned or destroyed. The frenzied pillagers had no idea they had reduced one of the most valuable libraries in China to ashes.

"To this day in the real world," David told Victoria, who was distraught with the wanton destruction and blatant banditry, "the ruins are left standing as a monument to what happens when a country cannot defend itself. After the war, Chinese intellectuals recognized the need for change if the Chinese civilization was to survive the onslaught of the Western barbarians. By an ironic twist, opium woke the Chinese people from their stupor."

To help Victoria develop strategic thinking, David started a game in which she took on the role of Sengge Rinchen. Her goal was to repel the Anglo-French army's attack on Beijing. She did so by sending spies into the enemy's camp, bribing and threatening their local help, cutting off their food, water and munitions supply and inflicting maximum casualties with guerrilla tactics and guile. The Canadian gamer had the advantage of not having to answer to the Qing emperor's concerns or worry about the political aftermath. The central idea was to establish a strategic position by which she could afford to lose many minor battles but never the war, while the Anglo-French could not afford to lose a single engagement, as they starved and slowly bled to death.

Through this exercise, Victoria learned the importance of gaining strategic advantages over winning individual battles. Meanwhile, her spies set the enemy camp on fire during a night raid, causing helter-skelter. Moira, dressed as an officer of the King's Dragoon, emerged from the chaos waving a white flag, saying between coughs, "We're five minutes from the next service station. Let's take a break."

Chapter 26

Yellow Stone

Victoria and David exited the virtual world and disembarked from the Bozeman, inconspicuously parked outside a service station disguised as a black Buick Lacrosse. It was the wee hours of Christmas Eve, and the joint was haunted only by a few truck drivers taking a break on their way home. The two ordered a snack and chatted in a quiet corner.

"Tell me more about yourself," Victoria requested, nibbling on her poutine. "How did I end up in your care, and why are you protecting me from the Watchers, whoever they are?"

David showed Victoria the symbol on his clan ring again.

"This symbol on my ring is the ancient Chinese word for my family name, Huang, meaning the colour yellow. The word at first represented a jade ornament worn by royalty in ancient China. You have such a *huang* jade pendant piece."

Victoria pulled out her jade pendant and showed it to David.

"Is it worth a fortune?"

"Much more than a fortune, it's priceless. According to my lineage records, our clan's founder, Huang Yin, was an aristocrat of the Shang Dynasty. I'm supposed to be his 110th-generation descendant. He gave his only son a so-called *Book of Heavenly Secrets*, instructing him to pass it down to his descendants until the arrival of the Bearer of the Oracle. The book has a word-by-word record of the Oracle carved on your pendant."

"What does it say, may I ask?"

"You may, but brace yourself for what you're about to hear," said David, suggesting a presentiment of doom. "It mentions an impending cataclysmic catastrophe, a global apocalypse called the 'Stopping Of The Sun,' in other words, the End of Days."

"What happens when the sun stops?" Victoria asked with a mixture of disquiet and disbelief.

"The earth stops spinning, followed by the displacement of the oceans. It'll be a tsunami from which no one can escape. It'll be the Great Deluge all over again. Most terrestrial lifeforms on earth will perish. Velikovsky will be vindicated."

"Who is Velikovsky?"

"He was an author whose study of ancient scriptures convinced him something similar happened in the remote past. Myths from all over the world say most humans died in an ancient flood."

"If he is right, we're toast."

"Yes, but we have hope. The *Book of Heavenly Secrets* says the Bearer of the Oracle is also the prophesied saviour. Since you possess a *huang* jade with the Oracle mentioning your name and birthday, you must be the Bearer. The eldest son in my lineage—that's me—has been tasked to protect the Bearer. For people privy to the secret, I'm known as the Guardian of the Oracle. We must now try to locate your biological parents. We need them to explain how you would save the world."

"Stop! It is too much. I can't process all this. You're giving me a brain cramp."

"As I told you when we began this journey, the truth would be too shocking. Quite frankly, I was as skeptical as you are. I thought Huang Yin was family lore until I studied the oracle bones excavated since the turn of the twentieth century. Surprise, surprise! I found many records of a Shang official named Huang Yin.

"My family's unbroken lineage record has existed for as long as we've been around. Although my father was adopted, he is from the greater Huang clan and is considered a legitimate scion of this branch, burdened with the duty to protect the Bearer at all costs. In any case, archaeological evidence has corroborated the existence of my family's founding father.

"When I first saw you at my ancestral home in Yellow County, you were several months old. You had your pendant and ring with you. My father, Huang Shi, 'Yellow Stone,' brought you over from Anyang, your birthplace. He knew your biological parents. But he fell into a coma after taking a long, circuitous journey home. I believe you hold the key to the secrets in his head. Ergo, I'm taking you to him."

"I'm sorry about your father. But are you sure we're not going on a wild goose chase?"

"It is natural for you to be skeptical about all this. However, a lot of people believe you're the real deal. You're part of a secret my family has kept for over three thousand years. I hope what convinced us will convince you in due time. Let us get back on the road, and I'll show you what happened during the fateful year when I was nine."

The clock rewound to December 22, 1975, a special day in China known as the Winter Festival or, in Chinese, the "Extreme of Winter." Chinese families would get together and have dinner on this day, similar to Thanksgiving or Christmas Eve in the West.

At the time, David lived with his father and grandparents in their ancestral home in Huangxian, or Yellow County. David, who went by the pet name Didi, or "Little Brother," had three aunts, and their families were all at the house for dinner. It was a noisy, chaotic, almost Italian affair, with shrieking kids chasing each other, overturning furniture, creating clamour and inducing grown-ups to yell at them. David missed these gatherings.

As the extended family was about to sit at the dinner table, a neighbourhood boy barged in and, with his stentorian voice, announced, "A long-distance phone call for Uncle Huang Shi is on hold at the post office." In those days when no one had private phones, getting a long-distance phone call was a big deal. It would get everyone to talk over one another all at once.

By this time, the Cultural Revolution was in its tenth year. David's father, Huang Shi, was an academic biding his time, going through the motions in a day job at a vermicelli processing plant in his hometown. His promising career as an Oracle Bone expert had been languishing in perpetual limbo.

Yet Huang Shi never gave up hope. All these years, he had been waiting for a call from the city of Anyang, "Peaceful Sun," in the province of Henan, "River South," bidding him to take up his long vacated research position at the Anyang branch of the Institute of Archaeology, one of many institutes of the Chinese Academy of Social Science.

The archaeological site of the Shang (circa 1600–1046 BCE) capital, known in historical times as Yinxu, meaning "Yin ruins," was located on the outskirts of Anyang. Yin was where the Shang established their royal court for 273 years until being overthrown by the Zhou (1046–256 BCE), their western vassal. Historians later referred to the Shang Dynasty and its capital as Yin. The Shang, however, referred to their capital as the Great Settlement of Shang. The word *yin*, which means "thriving," to this day, has not been discovered on oracle bones, only on later bronze vessels.

At any rate, Anyang was the only place where an Oracle Bone scholar would want to work. It seemed Huang Shi's winter was coming to an end. Could spring be far behind? When he returned from the call, everyone anticipated a joyous announcement.

"Yes, it was Professor Zheng, the head of the Institute of Archaeology at Anyang," said Huang Shi with a rare grin, and the whole room exploded in celebration. "She has not forgotten me and wants to see me. However, she wants me to get a car and leave right away. She'll pay for the expenses. Something extraordinary has happened. She wouldn't tell me over the phone. I'm sorry, folks, I'll have to skip dinner this year. I must hurry."

"How long will you be away?" his father asked.

"I'll be home for Spring Festival. But I don't have an exact return date. I'll send a wire as soon as I know."

"Don't worry about us," his father said. "Do your job with distinction and make the Huang clan proud. I'll talk to your factory boss and persuade him to approve your leave of absence. I'll look after your social benefits payments and ensure your position remains open in case things don't work out in Anyang. But leave it to me. Everything will be fine here."

No one knew what prompted Huang Shi to skip one of the most important dinners of the year. What could have happened with such gravity it could not wait until the next day? It was all a mystery, but the whole family was happy for him. Huang Shi had always dreamed of working at Anyang under the leadership of Professor Zheng, a Peking University alumna and a prominent pioneer in the field, who had contributed to his doctoral paper. Despite the lingering uncertainty for all these years of political turmoil, Professor Zheng remembered Huang Shi when she was on the verge of making a monumental discovery.

Huang Shi's father had an inkling of what this call might be about but said nothing. He knew of many false alarms in the past. It could be another one. He decided to wait for Huang Shi to return in January of the following year to learn what was behind this call of extraordinary urgency.

Chapter 27

Year of the Dragon

"If you have tears, prepare to shed them now!" Huang Shi heard the saddest news as he stepped off the coach at the Yellow County bus depot. It was in the evening of January 8, 1976. The Gang of Four-controlled state media, in a curt and cold message, announced Premier Zhou Enlai had passed away in the morning. The beloved leader was the last obstacle to the powerful clique taking complete control of the Party and the country. Huang Shi had never witnessed so many grown men and women everywhere burst into tears all at once. One might think the holy plague had smitten China, and God had struck down the firstborn of every house.

When Huang Shi entered his home, everyone expected him to deliver happier news. But the sullen-faced Huang Shi said nothing. He went inside his bedroom and bolted the door.

The approaching Year of the Dragon was supposed to be auspicious for China. Instead, three of the nation's preeminent leaders left for the Great Beyond. Premier Zhou Enlai led the parade before the Spring Festival. Marshal General Zhu De, founder of the People's Liberation Army, followed on July 4. Last but not least was Chairman Mao, who made the grand exit on September 9. What was to become of China?

In April, the Gang of Four purged Deng Xiaoping, who had the unflattering honour of receiving this mortification twice during the Cultural Revolution. Deng was sixty-five when they first banished him. He was seventy-one when they placed him under house arrest. Deng's son, Pufang, became paralyzed below the waist after falling from the fourth floor of a building while fleeing from the Red Guards. Deng's younger brother took his own life rather than suffer torture and humiliation at the hands of the mob.

Deng was way past retirement age. He had dedicated his life to China's revolution since adolescence. He did not deserve this treatment. Yet Deng did not give up and died a bitter man, nor did he defect to write memoirs vilifying the Party. After all, dying is easy, revolution is hard. Revolution was not hosting a dinner party. In the face of impossible odds, Deng refused to concede defeat, rising at the ripe old age of seventy-two to lead the nation out of the wilderness, helping even those who had harmed him and his family. What changed China's fate? Less than a month after Mao's passing, when all hope seemed lost, the Hand of Destiny came out of nowhere and, with the speed of summer lightning, deposed the Gang of Four in an artfully executed coup, dumping them into the dustbin of history and condemning them to suffer eternal damnation in the ninth circle of Dante's Inferno.

In May, archaeologists discovered an undisturbed royal Shang tomb at Yinxu. It belonged to the warrior queen Fu Hao, Queen Zia in our saga, well known among scholars by the more than two hundred extant oracle bones mentioning her name. It was a stunning discovery of the ages by Professor Zheng and her team.

Several days later, disaster struck when Huang Shi vanished from the face of the Earth. David's grandfather went to Anyang to search for his son, but in vain. The broken-hearted man was found dead under a willow tree near Yinxu, accompanied by an empty 56% alcohol *Erguotou* bottle. A Chinese proverb says, "Good luck never visits in pairs while misfortune never strikes alone." It is Murphy's Law with Chinese characteristics. David, perforce, became the Guardian of the Oracle at the tender age of ten.

In July, before the tears dried, the most devastating earthquake of the twentieth century flattened Tangshan, the hometown of David's mom. Six hundred and fifty thousand went to bed and never woke. It was carnage on an apocalyptic scale.

In China, natural disasters were portents of epochal change. In the Year of the Dragon, the Chinese people's suffering stretched their endurance to the breaking point. When may they rest from burying their loved ones? How many pools of tears must they shed while mourning the dead? The long-suffering people survived only by the motto: "*Sic transit gloria mundi*, thus passes the glory of the World. *Dum vivimus vivamus*, while we live, let us live."

Huang Shi would miss the horrors of Tangshan, but what he witnessed at Anyang was more horrifying. The morning after returning home, Huang Shi finally left his room to face his family with the news of the approaching Apocalypse.

"What happened in Anyang?" Huang Shi's father asked with a hint of foreknowledge. "Has the Bearer of the Oracle arrived?"

"So, you've guessed it."

"The Oracle does mention the birthday of the Bearer."

"Right, it slipped my mind. When I arrived in Anyang, I learned a young man had promised to help Professor Zheng make a once-in-a-lifetime discovery if she could convince me to show up pronto. He seemed to have hypnotized the professor. He also knew about the Guardian of the Oracle and me. He said his wife had given birth to a baby girl on the 'Extreme of Winter.' He showed me a *huang* jade piece with ancient glyphs. The words matched the Oracle to a tee. If the prophecy is coming true, the End of Days is near, and his daughter is the only one capable of preventing it."

"Did he provide any additional proof?"

"He had a briefcase with amazing powers. He showed me the future with it, a future he said would come to pass if his daughter fell into the hands of the Watchers."

"The Watchers?"

"According to the young man, they're agents of a secretive organization named DIAS. Dressed in dark clothing, they always operate in pairs, with one of them inseparably attached to a briefcase exhibiting powers far beyond our current technologies. The young parents are in trouble. It's up to us to protect the baby. We must keep the Bearer from the Watchers until her powers manifest in due time. The survival of humanity depends on it."

"What future did you witness?"

"When the young man opened his briefcase, it released a golden beam. As I gazed into the light, my consciousness entered another realm. No words could describe the surreal experience. I witnessed how the world would end. It was horrifying and more than the heart could bear."

Didi did not understand everything the grown-ups were saying, but he saw his father's face turn pale with the pallor of death as he recalled the visions of hell.

"Where is the Bearer?" Huang Shi's father asked.

"She is with her parents and will become my ward in May when she has grown stronger. I do have some good news. I'm finally getting my research job. I'll start in April at the beginning of the excavation season."

"This means I only have a few months to prepare you and Didi. Since we're the lineage of the Guardians, Didi must also learn about the secret and our duty. We'll have to guard the Bearer of the Oracle with our lives. If anything happens to you and me, Didi must take over. We should also call a meeting of the secret Shang clans. We'll need all the help we can get."

When April came around, Huang Shi bid farewell to his family and left for Anyang. He did not know he had said his last goodbye to his father and would be absent during his son's growing up.

Chapter 28

The One-eyed Collector

Victoria noticed a gaping hole in David's story. The math didn't add up. He was talking about 1975 and 1976, way before her time.

"Who's this saviour of yours?" Victoria asked with a healthy dose of skepticism. "You can't be talking about me."

"Have patience, my dear," David said. "You can decide after you have met my father and looked at all the evidence."

"Fine. Please explain how you ended up in Canada with so much money to pay for all these fancy gadgets."

"Sure. Let us get back on the road and the metaverse. I'll take you to a private auction where I earned my first pot of gold."

Entering a pre-loaded game, David brought Victoria to a luxurious auction room in a private club packed with crazy-rich Asians, eccentric collectors and sharp-eyed agents, all clutching numbered paddles. Victoria held paddle number eleven.

"We're in an auction house in Hong Kong," David explained, "where rare Chinese treasures have sometimes surfaced. They're going to bid on my vase. I'll let you know when to raise your paddle. Making a bid at the right moment will help push the price higher. We can learn about arbitrage in a role-playing game later."

The auction assistant presented the artifact to the room, and the auctioneer began the bidding.

"Lot 121, ladies and gentlemen, is a Southern Song vase flawlessly crafted in the shape of a Shang-Zhou vessel, overlaid with a coat of crystalline crackled glaze, suggestive of elegant jade. This gem of the Internal Manufactures Royal Kiln, discovered in an old antique shop in Beijing, once owned by the Qing Prince-Regent Chun, Zaifeng, father of Aisin Gioro Puyi, the last emperor of China, is the rarest of the rare in its pristine condition, showing here. May I start at five thousand U.S. dollars?"

Someone raised his paddle without hesitation. David winked at Victoria and whispered, "My man."

"Five thousand, I'm bid," the auctioneer sang a rapid rap as he picked up speed. "Do I hear six thousand? Six thousand. Thank you, sir. This lucky find is once in a lifetime. Do I hear seven?"

An impatient bidder in the front row with paddle number 1011 checked his Patek Philippe Supercomplication pocket watch and raised his index finger.

"We have a bid of ten thousand dollars. Thank you, sir. Join the bidding now for this priceless treasure. Do I hear eleven?"

The action soon turned frantic, with agents running out to call their clients and others staying on the line using those clunky Motorola cell phones. David asked Victoria to raise her paddle twice to maintain the tempo. As the bidding rose, the pace slowed. The air was pregnant with suspense.

"The last bid is eight million five hundred thousand dollars. Fair warning, going once, twice," the auctioneer swept the room with his eyes as he whipped out his handkerchief to dab the sweat on his brow. After a tense moment of silence, he banged the gavel with flair, declaring, "Sold for eight million five hundred thousand U.S. dollars to Count Petrov von Petersdorf. Thank you, sir."

The winning bidder with paddle 1011, sumptuously attired in a Hayward bespoke suit over an impeccably tailored Charvet shirt eclectically matched with a Grateful Dead Jerry Garcia Limited Edition silk tie, donned his Herbert Johnson handcrafted poet hat, picked up his walking cane with a golden apple knob and left the room in haste. Victoria noticed the buyer had a pale complexion, raven-black hair, a well-trimmed beard and an aquiline nose. To top it off, he sported a diamond-studded eye patch over his left eye.

"Do you have any idea who he is?" Victoria asked.

"As some Brits like to say, I haven't the foggiest. I tried to find out, but the man vanished into thin air. His name means Peter from the village of Peters. Of course, it's bogus. After some sleuthing, I discovered the buyer was Comte de Saint-Germain, but he kept his real name a secret. Rich people are eccentric. I don't care as long as I get paid. I made a killing on the sale. I found the vase at Beijing's antique shopping district, Liulichang, the Glaze Factory. Guess how much I paid for it. I dished out a cool eight hundred and fifty yuan, about a hundred U.S. dollars at the time. Not bad, eh? This auction paved the way for many more afterwards."

"You mean some poor sap sold the vase to you for one hundred dollars, and you sold it for eight and a half million. Is it ethical?"

"It's chum change. Perhaps you haven't heard of the 450 million dollar 'Salvator Mundi' dud. And don't forget how the natives sold Manhattan Island to Peter Minuit for sixty guilders, which can't buy one brick today, whereas the vendors were neither the owners nor the deed holders of the real estate. This transaction was supposed to represent fair and free trade, but most of the North American continent changed hands by the laws of the jungle and at gunpoint. Afterwards, possession becomes nine-tenths of the law. It proves the fundamental principle of economics: You do not own anything you cannot defend. The rest is BS and balderdash.

"My vase was worth about a year's food and expenses for the Beijing stiff and his family; therefore, he believed he made a good deal. Outside of China, where lots of hot cash sloshes around, it's not hard for someone to believe the story of the royal kiln and part with eight and a half mil. Who can say what anything is worth?"

Victoria shook her head in disbelief.

"Relax, the buyer hasn't lost anything," David continued. "He has merely exchanged his illusory wealth for the concrete ownership of a tangible object which will generate more illusory wealth through reinforcements such as insurance, appraisals and balance sheets, ofttimes sanctioned and sanctified by fancy signatures with curlicues. You know who gets ripped off?"

"Certainly not you."

"Most people get ripped off without knowing it. Others support the rip-off, hoping to do the ripping-off later. Notice how a vessel made of clay goes from one place to another, and the world's wealth increases by eight and a half million dollars out of nowhere. And it all ends up in someone's pocket as cash. It's the lifetime income for a small village toiling to create real wealth over a patch of rice paddy. This fabulous wealth creation is magic. It's sleight of hand and misdirection. The Beijing stiff is not in the game; therefore, he doesn't get any.

"Our system rewards those who create the illusion of wealth and puts it all in the pockets of the illusionists, the One-Percenters. Our system also hires a henchman class to enforce the use of this imaginary wealth, which some people call money, capital or GDP. The producers and makers of food, goods and means of production are real-wealth producers. Yet they're poor and have no money because they're not in the game.

"The more illusory wealth materializes out of thin air, the poorer the real-wealth producers become. It's a paradox and an oxymoron. If the real-wealth producers somehow awaken from their stupendous stupor and question the illusion, the henchmen will vilify them as lazy, stupid and parasitic thieves, if not commies, and, with God's blessing, declare holy war on them.

"This system of illusory wealth also owns the narrative, perverted and propounded by the popular free press, which is, in fact, a faction of feculent factories of fabrication specializing in fanning the flames of violence. Sorry about all the ‘f’s, it’s not intentional. The real-wealth producers have become so feckless, helpless and distracted by their fight for a minimum wage they end up joining the attack dogs and putting the blame on other victims.”

“Okay, you have a beef about the system. But you should stop being a One-Percenter yourself; otherwise, you’re no better than a liar and a hypocrite.”

“You’re right. The illusion is, currently, the only game in town. We may find it disagreeable, yet we must live with it. It’s the same as air pollution. We need to breathe even if the air is putrid. And we cannot avoid playing the rigged game because we have no alternative. We can only try to beat the devil without becoming one. The question is, what are we prepared to do? How dirty are we willing to get? It is the most dangerous part of the fight.”

“To tell the truth,” Victoria said, trying to suppress a yawn, “I’m tired of all this fighting. I’m also getting sleepy.”

“Yeah, I’m rather tired of it myself,” said David, getting infected with the yawn. “Let’s exit the game and catch some z’s.”

After removing her haptic gear, Victoria reclined across the back seats for a snooze. By now, she had shed most of her earlier suspicions about David. When they interfaced in the VR game, Victoria could experience more than the illusion of the event. She could sense David’s firm belief in the mythical story of the Oracle and would, therefore, never harm her.

“David, I’ve been thinking. Apart from the one time you’ve had to use a gun, you’re, more or less, a gentleman and a scholar. You remind me of a professor.”

“I was a professor,” David said wistfully. “I followed in my father’s footsteps to become a scholar of ancient China. I graduated *magna cum laude* from Peking University and completed my postgraduate studies at the University of Toronto under the mentorship of the renowned Professor James Hsu.

"After receiving my doctorate, I stayed to teach ancient Chinese culture and collaborated with Professor Shu-Ying Tsau of York University on research. I held a second job at the Royal Ontario Museum, cataloguing their oracle bones collection donated by Reverend James Menzies and Bishop William White. I would've died happy dedicating my life to academic pursuit. But ROM funds dried up. I didn't get tenure. I crashed back to Earth and found myself begging for teaching jobs that paid a pittance.

"I had recently married, bought a house in Toronto with a hefty mortgage, and my first child was on the way. What could I do but use my knowledge to sell myths? To survive, I became a wheeler-dealer. I was powerless against the system. I didn't know I was a slave until I learned the hard way. A person living on a salary cannot afford the truth, much less freedom. I learned my lesson and adopted capitalism's winner-takes-all mentality. Greed is good, and selfishness breeds success. To hell with the rest of the pea-brained humanity. These are the rules of the game we play. When China opened up for business, I found a gold mine. My antique business became lucrative. I have never looked back."

Victoria had fallen asleep in the middle of the soliloquy. For a moment, David's thoughts harked back to a time when he was poor and naïve. He sighed, took out a duvet and pulled it over Victoria.

The shadow of a spectre sped through the darkness of the night on the Trans-Canada Highway. Up in the heavens, bright Orion summoned the mysterious Monoceros, the Unicorn. A cigar-shaped monolith tumbled and rolled across the field of stars. Earthlings called it Oumuamua, meaning "distant messenger." In ancient texts, Watcher means the same thing. Oumuamua appeared to be a rock from interstellar space but was, in fact, a pollinator. It came from long ago and far away to deposit something on Earth. A small metallic sphere landed on the Trans-Canada Highway, latching onto the Bozeman as it zoomed by.

Chapter 29

No. 1 Corn Gas

Two men, both attired in funereal black overcoats draped over their black suits perfectly matched with black silk ties, black cotton trousers held up by black crocodile leather belts, shiny black Oxfords and black deerskin cashmere-lined gloves, stepped out of their black BMW SUV and, lifting their impenetrably black Gentle Monster shades, cast an icy glare at the No. 1 Corn Gas Service Station. One of the men, an African American wiseguy afflicted with dead eyes, stooped to pick up a lifeless watch with his forensic forceps, examining it in ominous silence while the other, a cold-blooded Latino hothead, stood guard holding on to an inscrutably black briefcase. The inspector nodded at his partner in crime, who responded with a sneer. They patted their overcoats to ascertain the readiness of their concealed weapons and marched straight into the gas station.

Brent, the prematurely bald and perpetually bored attendant, was engrossed in his comics as usual when the entrance bell chimed. It broke his concentration. He sighed, put down the book, glanced at the clock, which showed two p.m., and tried to slam the door on the undesirable walk-ins before closing.

"Gentlemen, we're closing early today. It's Christmas Eve."

"Do you know who we are?" asked Vincent, the Latino, as if all Saskatchewanians should know the answer.

"Hmm, let me guess," Brent, merciless with stupid questions, replied with his customary Canadian prairies sarcasm. "You're the

Men in Black, here to deal with aliens on Earth. Listen, fellas, it's quittin' time. We're closed, capiche? My lovely wife is waiting at home with a bird in the oven and a glass of mulled wine to warm the cockles of my heart. So, why don't you gentlemen make like a tree and take your business to the next service station at Wolferton?" He spat at the mention of the accursed name. "You're welcome, and happy Halloween!"

Brent kept his uneventful days interesting by inserting irony into his interpersonal intercourse, but he chose the wrong targets this time. Indeed, the two men in black were the shadowy agents known as Watchers, who had scoured every nook and cranny in their frustrating, futile quest for the Bearer of the Oracle ever since the day she was born. They were not in the mood for humour.

"Who says it's quittin' time?" Jules, the African American, grunted through gritting teeth. "You ain't goin' nowhere until you answer some questions. Have you any idea who we are and why we're here?"

"To tell the truth, fellas, I haven't the foggiest," Brent said with a faux British accent, "and I don't give a flying fog. Either this has something to do with Hank's crazy daydreams, or I'm in an Ed Wood movie. I'm not impressed by your Laurel and Hardy act."

Brent glanced at the security camera as a message to the strangers not to try anything funny.

"Answer our question," Vincent said, imposing himself before the gas station attendant, "and you can skitter home to your sexy wifey afterwards. Did a middle-aged man and a Chinese teenager pass through here in the last twenty-four hours?"

"Why am I talking to you?" Brent said, remembering the hundred-dollar tip he received for keeping mum. "You're not buying anything. What's in it for moi?"

"Okay, I'll have the Royale with Cheese," Vincent said, "and my brutha here wants the Big Kahuna with everything."

Upon making the fake order, he pulled a monster of a pistol from his coat and almost stuck it up the shocked attendant's nose.

"Just kidding, Rockefeller. Here is what's in it for you. If I detect bullshit in your answer, I'll pop your brain like a pimple with my bare hands. And my friend here," Vincent scowled as he wagged his gun against Brent's nose, making it wiggle, "will put so many holes through your cold, dead body they'll have to wipe your smugly face off the floor with a mop."

"Why didn't you say so? You could've said so earlier," Brent said, as his sensitized nose exploded with a violent sneeze.

"Bless you," Jules said. And Vincent echoed, "Gesundheit."

Brent purged or, more accurately, emunged the slime from his bulbous proboscis, muttered "Thanks" with a nasal twang and complied with his guests' wishes.

"At Number One Corner Gas, Customer is King! Ask, and all your answers will be questioned, I mean, all your questions will be answered. If you'd only let me get a word in, I'm willing to tell you, I'm wanting to tell you, I'm waiting to tell you. I'll tell you all my secrets—my first kiss, my Chilli Cheese Dog recipe, even where I hide my girlie mags."

"Do you read the Bible, Brett?" Jules asked with a dark, menacing growl. He did not like where the *Versch□rfte Vernehmung*, or enhanced interrogation, was heading.

"The name's Brent," said the bewuthered gas station attendant.

"Oh, No! Not the Bible again," Vincent vociferated as Jules prepared to orate an apocryphal apocalyptic verse before blowing someone's head off. "You made up the whole flapdoodle."

"I most certainly did not," Jules asseverated. "Ezekiel 25:17. Look it up."

"You wanna bet?" Vincent said with a smirk on his face. "If I'm right about you making that up, are you gonna give me your famous foot massage?"

Jules swivelled his head in slo-mo to give Vincent the Doonesbury Doomsday stare for about five seconds before issuing a stark warning, "Figaro! Are you trying to piss me off?"

Thereupon, the African American unholstered a bombastic Smith & Wesson 500 Magnum from inside his overcoat, cocked the gnarly blunderbuss and pointed it foursquare at Brent's face.

"Talk!" he thundered.

"What d-do you want to know?" Brent stammered, with fear-saturated sweat oozing from his brow.

"Tell us everything," Jules bellowed.

"What d-do you mean everything?"

"EH-VRY-THING!" Jules roared at the top of his lungs, his booming voice reverberating into the deep, dark void of the cold, starry sky.

"When I was f-f-f-four years old," Brent said, blowing spit at his interrogators, "I remember my m-m-mother trying to toilet train me …."

"About the man and the Chinese teen," Jules enunciated while glaring at Brent with his enlarged eyes and contracted pupils.

"Last night, around closing," Brent finally sang like a canary, "a middle-aged man and an Asian boy walked in out of nowhere. I don't know if the boy was Chinese, Korean or Japanese. They got a drink and left."

"See, it's not so hard, is it?" Vincent said. "Now, do you know who we are?"

"I see nothing. I hear nothing. I know nothing. I didn't even get up in the morning."

Vincent and Jules looked at each other.

"Are we happy?" Vincent asked Jules.

"We're happy," Jules replied.

Chapter 30

Field of Dreams

Victoria lived a "seven-eleven" lifestyle, rising at seven and hitting the hay at eleven. She loved the fresh fragrance of dawn mingled with the soothing "Morning Mood" of *Peer Gynt Suites* playing in the background with her dad humming along. For breakfast, she preferred free-range eggs fried sunny side up with smoked Canadian bacon complemented by fresh orange juice, percolated Ethiopian Arabica coffee and Prince Edward Island cultured butter on lightly toasted pumpernickel.

While Victoria was breaking bread with her family on an average morning in her humdrum life, out of nowhere, a loud buzz disrupted the calm. Before anyone realized what was happening, a monster claw tore off the top of the house, leaving the stunned family of three enveloped in dust and debris.

Several bombers were streaking across the clear blue sky, weaving a pattern of jet trails resembling a heavenly net. A pink heart-shaped balloon displaying the curious words "Eat Me" floated into the exposed kitchen. The balloon popped, sending a shock wave that knocked Victoria and her parents to the floor. Immediately, flying bomblets with spinning scythes, ablaze with an eerie blue flame, swarmed the room, slashing, crushing and exploding to the melancholy melody of the "Intermezzo."

After the bomblets had accomplished their dastardly deed and the dust had settled, Victoria witnessed a gruesome sight. Her parents were holding on to each other in a tight embrace, but they had lost their heads. For reasons she did not comprehend, not a drop of blood was shed. She saw wires and optical fibres in the place of veins and arteries. She peeked down to note she had lost all her limbs, exposing electronics and a metallic skeletal frame.

Shrapnel had struck her in the left eye, which popped out of its socket, caught fire and started burning with a bright blue blaze. As if having a life of its own, the eyeball started wiggling and transformed into a mechanical scorpion.

"I'm having a nightmare. I need to wake up from this nightmare," Victoria kept telling herself. She closed her one remaining eye and repeated, "There's no place like home. There's no place like home. There's no place like home." When she opened her eyes, she was inside the Starship Bozeman, its Dolby Atmos immersive audio system playing the "Intermezzo" from Pietro Mascagni's *Cavalleria rusticana.*

"You okay?" David asked. "Have you had a good rest?"

"I had the wackiest nightmare. But I'm fine now. It's only a dream. Where are we? Are we there yet?"

"We have a long way to go. We've passed Medicine Hat. Calgary is coming up, but we won't be stopping. We'll be staying overnight at Field. Moira got us rooms and reserved a table for us at Truffle Pigs. We'll have a proper Christmas Eve dinner."

"What's Field? Why are we staying at Field? Why don't we stop at Calgary? I'd love to visit the city."

"Moira prefers staying off the beaten path. For her, safety is Job One. Field is a good choice for a stopover in the Rockies, with fewer than a hundred residents and far from the madding crowd. We're staying overnight, so we may explore the Burgess Shale in the morning."

"Burgess Shale … I remember the name from Trivial Pursuit."

"The Burgess Shale is a fossil record of weird lifeforms from five hundred million years ago. Something caused the decimation of all these strange alien-looking critters so you and I can talk about the meaning of life today."

"Isn't life strange?!"

"It's also wonderful, and we depend on you to prevent the next decimation."

"I don't know if I'll be up to the task. For now, I'll concentrate on what's for dinner."

"Do you have a favourite dish in mind? Moira can order ahead."

"The place is called Truffle Pigs. So, I'll have their pork special. But what about you? Are you allowed to eat pork? Is it Kosher to eat in such a restaurant?"

"It's fine. I'm not a strict observer. I'll survive a turkey dinner at Truffle Pigs. People assume all Jews believe in a genocidal tribal God who closes your windows when it rains. It's simply not true. But don't tell anyone. What we say in the Bozeman stays in the Bozeman."

"Whatever, I don't know much about the religion. I'm glad I can eat pork without controversy."

"Moira booked Truffle Pigs because she knows you love pork. After all, home is where the hog is."

"Ha ha," Victoria chuckled. "Good slogan!"

"It's also a fact. The Chinese people have had a close relationship with pigs since antiquity. The Shang peasants kept pigs in their homes. The Oracle Bone word for 'home' (家) is a pig under a roof."

"A married woman might've created the word," Victoria quipped. "Talking about home, how's your family taking all this, you being away for Christmas and risking your life for a stranger?"

"We're a Jewish household. We don't celebrate Christmas. My wife, Beth, thinks I'm in Mumbai making a bid for the Buddha's Śarīra, a religious relic worth a king's ransom in China. I'm supposed to be at the secret auction for the holy stones. I'll have to pass because of something more important. As for my duty toward you, it's the same as my duty toward humanity and my family. I love my family, but I must take you to my father who'll help you find your parents. The oath of the Guardian will end with me. I'll do my duty, but I don't want my family in Canada to be involved."

"You mean they have no idea about the Stopping Of The Sun?"

"Nope. I don't want my wife and children to live in fear."

"How about the corporate giants you work with? Are they in on this, or do you pay them for their technologies? How much money are you spending? Doesn't your wife complain?"

"My dear wife, Beth, doesn't know how rich she is. She'll faint when my lawyer shows her the accounts. But my money is nothing compared to the combined power of the secret Shang clans and their companies. While I'm the Guardian of the Oracle, I don't operate alone. I get help from a secret network of influential and powerful Shang descendants with lineages as old as mine, including my trusty lawyer Malcolm from McCarthy Tétrault. We don't worry about money when it comes to saving humanity. Money is meaningless if we all die."

"Try telling the One-Percenters and the warmongers."

"Good, you're catching on. But I'm not here to proselytize about socioeconomics. My job is to enlighten you about our background. It is not a coincidence my family has sworn an oath to protect you. We are related to you in mysterious ways. I'll take you on another metaverse trip to show you how it all began and how it may all end. First of all, most people have heard about the Han, but few know anything about the Shang, the true progenitor of the Chinese civilization. Let us visit their capital, Yin, during the middle of the eleventh century before the Common Era and learn what happened to them."

Chapter 31

Sudden Death

David and Victoria, adopting the role of Shang soldiers in the metaverse, walked the beat in a sprawling settlement of thousands of straw-thatched houses built from wood and stones. The Shang capital, one of the largest cities in the world, was home to more than a hundred thousand residents. Pedestrians clogged the paths between the houses, workshops and retail stores, where artisans produced merchandise and vendors sold everything under the sun. A factory with furnaces spitting flames mass-produced bronzewares. A fort perched atop a hill served as the palace and citadel. Because of the Shang's military supremacy, Yin did not need the walls expected of a capital city.

A river ran through it. The Huan River, also known as the Anyang River, supplied water for drinking, cleaning, and irrigating the wheat fields, rice paddies, vegetable patches and fruit groves surrounding the settlement. The river was home to abundant fish, shrimp and other riparian flora and fauna. Chickens, ducks, pigs, buffalos, goats, horses, and dogs roamed the fields. It was early autumn, and the ripening crops suggested a bountiful harvest.

The last King of the Shang Dynasty, Di Xin, was not at the capital but engaging in another one of his pacification wars, this time against the Eastern Barbarians. He would be victorious as in his many earlier campaigns. The people would welcome him home with a triumphant reception. They would make sacrificial offerings to the gods and celebrate in a month-long wine fest.

“This is not the farming village I expected,” Victoria remarked.

“During the eleventh century BCE,” David said, “Yin was already a well-developed city by global standards. The Shang tribe’s tradition spoke of having moved its settlement thirteen times. It gained full-spectrum dominance in the plains of the lower Yellow River during the sixteenth century BCE. Roughly two hundred years later, the Shang experienced a great blossoming here at Yin, their last capital before their western vassal, Zhou, toppled them in 1046 BCE, which we’re about to witness. The Shang sowed the seeds for the Chinese civilization.”

“But haven’t the Chinese people lived here for thousands of years before the Shang? What makes the Shang so special?”

“By the time the Shang settled here, their civilization was head and shoulders above the Stone Age tribes in this vast land. From the archaeological perspective, the Shang exploded onto the scene as a highly civilized agricultural tribe prominent for their religious fervour and military prowess. They introduced China’s first writing system, horse-drawn chariots, astronomy and advanced bronze-casting technologies, among many other inventions.”

“Do we know where they came from?”

“Because of their migrations, we know nothing of their origin. It’s the same with the Sumerians and the ancient Egyptians. Of course, we may speculate. For example, Shang astronomers created calendars using the sexagenary cycle of sixty, first used by the Sumerians and the ancient Egyptians. However, the Shang were the first to name the cycle’s positions by combining the Ten Celestial Stems and the Twelve Earthly Branches, suggesting the coexistence of decimal and duodecimal counting systems.”

“What are the Celestial Stems and Earthly Branches?”

“No one knows for sure. I published a paper on the subject, but it’s a long story. Another thing worth mentioning is the Shang was unique in using the twelve-year Jovian cycle to measure their age.”

"Jovian means …."

"Of Jupiter. The Shang referred to Jupiter as the Age Star. However, a Jovian year is 4,332 days, almost twelve Earth years. The Shang astronomers needed a lot of patience and skill to track the planet, measure its cycle, and fit the Solar and Lunar calendars into the Jovian year. They might've gone through all this trouble to keep track of their migrations. Do they seem primitive to you?"

"Wow! They must be aliens."

"You may go easy on the sarcasm, but we should keep an open mind. Here's another interesting fact. The Shang's founding myth connects the tribe to Antares of Scorpius, also known as the Shang Star or Great Fire. Shang may be the only major Chinese dynasty mythically linked to a star. The ancestor of the Shang tribe, Xie, which means 'covenant,' is the God of the star Great Fire and China's ancient fire god."

"Are you sure this is not all fairy tales and folklore?"

"I'll let you be the judge. One can find the story of Xie in an ancient history commentary, *Chronicle of Zuo.* It says Xie and his brother Shishen, sons of the mythical god-king Di Ku, were implacable foes. The unhappy father sent his sons to realms far apart to keep them from fighting. Xie became identified with Antares and Shishen with Orion. The two gods never appear in the night sky at the same time. This story parallels the Greek myth of Orion and the heavenly scorpion."

"Hmm, interesting! So, you're saying the origin of the Chinese civilization has connections to a Greek myth."

"Not only Greek. Xie was merely one of numerous gods in the pantheon. The Shang also believed in a supreme Creator God, Di (帝). The pictogram for Di is a flower bud, the word's original meaning. When Shang kings died, they became minor deities, also titled Di, hence Di Xin and Di Ku. It is similar to the deification of Roman emperors and their family members after death."

"Supreme Creator God sounds Abrahamic."

"Wherever the Shang came from, the ideas behind a belief system are universal. People in China no longer remember the Creator God Di because the deity fell out of favour after the fall of Shang, and the word *Di* has taken on the new meaning of 'emperor.' I researched the origin of this name of God by studying its cousins. I was surprised by what I found.

"The supreme Creator God Di of the Shang, by coincidence, is cognate with the Indo-European root *dyeu* for 'god' or 'sky,' from which we get *Deus*, the Latin word for 'god,' and *Dies*, Latin for 'day.' From *dyeu*, we get Zeus of the Greeks, Jupiter of the Romans and Tyr of the Vikings. Dionysus, the famous wine god; the Dioscuri, the twin gods; Diana, the Greek goddess of the hunt; and Dyaus, the Aryan Sky god, all derive from the same root. Today, the Italian word for 'god' is *Dio*, and the Spanish is *Dios*. It's *Dieu* in French, *Dev* in Hindi, *Dia* in Irish and *Duw* in Welsh. Di, meaning 'god,' can be found almost everywhere. For example, the Zhou tribe worshipped the supreme Sky god Tian (天), which means 'sky' or 'heaven,' and the northern nomads worshipped the Sky god Tengri. Both are cognate with *dyeu*."

"Does it mean this Shang god Di is of Indo-European origin?"

"Not necessarily. It could be a coincidence. Besides, religious belief is a complex human development similar to culture, ethnicity and language, which undergoes constant intermixing, mutation and evolution. Indo-European is itself a linguistic theory. My research merely indicates this name of God, Di, is widespread. Our ancestors might have crossed paths in their migrations and heard the same tall tales."

As David and Victoria strolled through ancient Yin, absorbing the sights and sounds of the bustling settlement, they noticed multiple columns of black smoke rising sequentially from the west. Messengers on horseback were racing through the capital toward the citadel. People dropped what they were doing and formed little gossip groups to spread the latest rumours.

"These are war signals," David explained. "It means an enemy is on the march. The Zhou tribe, a former loyal western vassal of the Shang, is leading a rebellion."

"I thought the Shang were famous for their military prowess. Where did the Zhou tribe find the courage to rebel?"

"The Shang does have a powerful military, and Di Xin is a feared conqueror. But good fortune sometimes gets to one's head. The progression of Tyche, Hubris and Nemesis has proven to be infallible throughout history, yet people at the top of the food chain choose to ignore it. The King is far from home, murdering and plundering less-developed tribes. The oracle says he'll triumph. Di Xin is confident his western flank is secure, defended by his trusted vassal, the Zhou. He also has family members guarding the capital. But he forgot to consult the oracles about his throne.

"Di Xin's hubris blinded him to the threat posed by those in his family with legitimate claims to the crown, his two elder brothers, Weizi and Weizhong, and his uncle, Jizi. Di Xin's son, Crown Prince Wugeng, has been scheming against his father's favourite concubine, Daji, who has the King wrapped around her little finger. Taking advantage of the Shang's internal schisms and the absence of the King's elite troops, the Duke of Zhou leads his neighbouring tribes in an armed uprising."

"If what you say is true, the Duke of Zhou is a traitor."

"It is, indubitably, a treacherous stab in the back. However, history belongs to the victors. By the pens of Zhou historians, Di Xin is vilified as a drunken tyrant beguiled by his cursèd concubine, Daji—the woman gets the blame, as usual—while the virtuous Duke of Zhou restores order according to the mandate of Tian, the Sky god, later known as Heaven. History, as we know it, is mainly the glorification of murders told by liars to idiots."

"Well, at least I'm not the only idiot."

"Oh, one will never be alone when it comes to being a fool," David said with a sardonic smile. "As Einstein said, 'two things are infinite, the universe and human stupidity, and we're not sure about the universe.' But I digress.

"As their world collapsed around them, my Huang clan believed the End Times was at hand, and the Bearer of the Oracle would soon emerge. Instead, all they witnessed was the passing of their earthly glory. The Zhou took Yin without serious opposition, and the Shang Dynasty fell apart. To perpetuate their tribal identity, the Shang people survived under other names. Meanwhile, Shang culture lived on in its written words. Because of this inheritance, the Chinese civilization survived all foreign invasions, conquests and colonial rules. Today, it is stronger than ever."

David and Victoria walked up the mound of the citadel. From their vantage position, they could see the army of the Zhou and their allies marching toward the Shang capital, pouring forth as a deluge over the unharvested fields of the undefended capital city.

"This is game over for the Shang," Victoria remarked.

"The Shang Dynasty fell. Its records were buried and forgotten. As time passed, Shang became legend, and legend became myth, until the dynasty resurfaced as history in the fin de siècle of the nineteenth century with the discovery of the oracle bones."

David began to wax poetic on the fall of empires.

"My name is Ozymandias, King of kings; look on my works, ye mighty, and despair!"

Victoria, who learned Percy Bysshe Shelley's *Ozymandias* in her English literature class, joined David in reciting the poem.

"Nothing beside remains, round the decay of that colossal wreck; boundless and bare, the lone and level sands stretch far away."

Chapter 32

Confucius and the Secret Shang

The Shang king, Di Xin, rushed home to defend his throne. He was eager to settle the score with the Zhou rebels in a pitched battle on the plains of Mu'ye outside his walled city, Zhaoge. By this time, the Zhou rebels had already taken Yin without firing a blunderbuss, if they had one.

Victoria and David arrived at Mu'ye to witness the showdown. At the head of the Zhou army were two well-wrought war chariots. David identified the man on the right as the Duke of Zhou. He was a man in his early fifties, muscular but with a ventripotent beer belly. His trusted guard carried an imposing, gleaming bronze *yue*, and his flag carrier raised a white banner adorned with a bull's tail.

On the Duke's left was a wiry, wizened man with a long, silvery beard, all dressed in black and surrounded by guards waving black banners. More a wizard than a warrior, he was the famous Great Sage Jiang, a nonagenarian who refused to retire and was the main reason Zhou supplanted Shang rule. He was also the first duke of the vassal state of Qi, which encompassed most of the modern province of Shandong, "Mountain East," David Huang's birthplace. The Shang had ignored Jiang's mental prowess and condemned him to a life of mediocrity until the Duke of Zhou's father met him, whiling away his sunset years at age eighty, fishing without a fishhook by the banks of the River Wei. The Great Sage Jiang's clan name is Lü. He and his Lü descendants would significantly influence China's destiny.

The Great Sage, an out-of-luck descendant of a Shang clan specializing in metallurgy, once survived by toiling as a butcher earning minimum wage. By chance, he was a good friend of a Huang scion in his youth and had stolen a furtive peek at the pages of the *Book of Heavenly Secrets*. Upon taking Yin, the Sage made a beeline for the Huang manor and confiscated the book, said to turn zeroes into heroes, and usurped its authorship. The Huang clan followed the book to the Qi State, where a Huang descendant would recover the book upon the state's demise.

At Mu'ye, the two gamers witnessed the Zhou rebels charge at the Shang lines. Trusting in the illusion of his invincibility, Di Xin had assembled his army with slaves from conquered tribes, some of whom were kin folks of the rebels. They all turned tail and fled, causing the Shang army to crumble from within.

Victoria noticed a dark cloud, foreshadowing heavy rainfall. It was, in fact, a torrential downpour of arrows bearing the dread omen of doom. David snapped his fingers and instantly transported the two gamers to the front yard of a simple straw hut secluded in a wooded glen deep in the untamed mountains and far from the madding crowd. The volley of arrows transformed in the blink of an eye into a flurry of furry poplar seeds dancing in the warm summer breeze. Victoria reacted to the trick with a nervous giggle.

For Di Xin, his world collapsed all of a sudden, though it had taken place over years of wilful blindness, ignoring the internal rot. Every slaughter of a defenceless tribe reinforced the deep-rooted but erroneous belief it made Shang great. The people did not see it coming either. They had been wining and dining on the ill-gotten gains of Di Xin's rapine and plunder. Those who did not receive their fair share of the loot wagged their sanctimonious fingers at their victims. Gilded words of hypocrisy poisoned one and all. The people blithely shrugged off the oracle's warnings, cheering on Di Xin's military adventures and accepting the atrocities as routine collateral mishaps. Shite happens! They preferred to slow-cook in the cauldron of delusions and lies. The Shang Dynasty collapsed gradually over the years and then all at once at Mu'ye.

After the Duke of Zhou became the Martial King of Zhou, he allowed Di Xin's son, Wugeng, to rule Yin as an archduke. Jizi, Di Xin's uncle, migrated to the northeast of China. Koreans call him Gija and consider him their civilization's founding father.

When the Martial King of Zhou died, his brother, the Sage of Zhou, ruled as regent for the young successor. The Sage of Zhou was the founding father of the vassal state of Lu to the west of the Qi State, also within the modern Shandong Province. The Lu State was famous for education, and Confucius, China's educator GOAT, the gentlest of all time, was born in Lu.

Meanwhile, Wugeng joined an ill-starred rebellion of the Zhou princes and perished, resulting in the expulsion and dispersion of Yin's inhabitants. Hence, Yin became Yinxu, the Yin Ruins. The Sage of Zhou sent Weizi, the eldest brother of Di Xin, to the Shang's ancestral city of Shangqiu, or "Shang mound," in today's Henan Province, to rule as the Archduke of Song, previously spelled Soong, keeping alive the royal lineage of Shang under another name.

Weizi is the ancestor of many prominent Chinese family names, such as Song of the Soong sisters, the most influential women of modern China; Meng of Mencius, the successor of Confucius, and Meng Wanzhou, the top executive of Huawei; Hua (花), meaning "flower," of Hua Mulan, legendary female warrior; and Hua (TS:華), a different word meaning "elegance," of Hua Tuo, the most famous herbalist and surgeon in ancient China.

The royal Shang lineage and its branches have concealed their identities under some of these names. Weizhong, Weizi's younger brother, succeeded him as the second Archduke of Song, and Confucius is Weizhong's fifteenth-generation direct descendant.

Thus, two thousand and five hundred years of Chinese culture rests on the unshakable foundation laid by a royal Shang descendant. Is it a coincidence? Confucius also has an unbroken lineage extending to the present day. The Oracle Bone word for his clan name, *Kong* (孔), meaning "good," resembles *Zi* (子), meaning "son," which is the name of the Shang royal lineage.

For David and Victoria, now as Lu State officials, five hundred years had elapsed in the blink of an eye.

"Let us pay homage to Confucius," David said. "This great scion of royal Shang was born here a few days ago."

"If Confucius was of royal blood," Victoria asked, "why was he born in a shed in the middle of nowhere?"

"Many great leaders were said to have been born under humble circumstances. Moses and Jesus are prominent examples. In Confucius' case, his fifth-generation ancestor was an aristocrat from the ruling house of the Song State, who sought refuge in Lu because of internecine strife. Confucius' father was a renowned general for the state of Lu.

"The poor fellow managed to have nine daughters but not a single son. In Zhou's patriarchal society, he needed a son to carry on his lineage. His concubine gave him a son with a deformed foot. It was not acceptable. Confucius' father was in his late sixties. Most girls were married off in their early teens. Such an age gap was against social norms and frowned upon. Fortunately, the virtuous daughter of a friend agreed to have a child with him out of wedlock. It must, however, take place far from prying eyes and wagging tongues. Confucius was, in truth, a bastard son at birth."

David and Victoria peeked inside the hut to see a young girl seated on her makeshift bed, partially concealed behind a curtain. She had finished breastfeeding a moment earlier and was tucking the newborn Confucius to bed. An amah, preparing porridge and eggs, noticed the visitors and gestured for them to keep quiet.

The silver-haired father was ecstatic with the safe delivery of his son. He was preparing a travel backpack to walk out of the mountain and break the news in person to his wife and concubine. Since he had a healthy son, they must agree to accept his son's mother into the family. He rose and ushered his visitors out of the hut where they could talk. At this very moment, a fawn wandered into the vegetable patch in the front yard. The general, famed for his height, bowed deeply toward David and Victoria.

"We are most honoured for the visitation of Your Graces," he said. "We are also blessed by the appearance of the prophesied divine creature bringing propitious portent. My undeserving pup of a son will treasure this priceless gift for the rest of his life."

According to popular legend, a Chinese unicorn, *Qilin*, appeared at the birth of Confucius. In the unicorn's mouth was a jade piece, and carved on it was an oracle about the arrival of a king, one without a throne or a kingdom.

When rumours circulated about a unicorn appearing at the birth of a Shang prince, the Guardian of the Oracle thought this baby must be the Chosen One. It turned out to be a false alarm. The boy would have a different yet important destiny.

Confucius moved into the Kong family manor with his mother, but when he was three, his father passed away. Even before the funeral rites were over, the Kong matriarch evicted Confucius and his mother. As a scion of the Shang royal lineage, Confucius grew up in a slum. While he was a teenager, his mother's life journey came to an early end. The "Six Shang clans of Yin," which had relocated to Lu by royal edict following Wugeng's demise, took in the boy and groomed him. In the end, the teachings of Confucius, a scion of royal Shang lineage, became the cornerstone of the indestructible Chinese civilization.

Apart from the Song State and Shang aristocracy, the Shang commoners saw their fortunes take a steep, vertiginous dive. The

Zhou prohibited them from working as scholars, officials, soldiers, peasants or artisans. The only way they could make a living was by trading, a despised form of livelihood said to have been invented by the ancient Shang. The word *shang* later took on the meaning of "commerce-trading." Can one imagine a lower social status than peasants? It was to be a Shang person, a merchant trader.

One of the most famous merchant traders in Chinese history was Lü Buwei, who became the most powerful official of the Qin State. He paved the way for Qin's conquest of all the other warring states, culminating in the first unified empire of China. Most people do not realize he was a Shang descendant. Lü Buwei was born in Puyang, also known as Diqiu, the burial mound of Di Ku, father of the Shang tribe's founder, Xie. Lü Buwei was, in fact, the twenty-third generation descendant of the Great Sage Jiang. In his possession was the *Book of Heavenly Secrets*.

Under David's guidance, Victoria visited historical figures of this era, including Duke Wen of the Jin State, Wu Zixu, Shang Yang and Fan Ju. She watched the Battle of Chengpu, during which the Jin army of Duke Wen employed the oblique order. She witnessed a coup d'état, in which Wu Zixu helped the Wu prince slay his kin using a deadly dagger with a wavy blade. By a twist of fate, Victoria would one day wield this evil bodkin with the intent to commit bloody murder. The Wu state later fell under the guile of Xi Shi, the most alluring femme fatale in China's history. Victoria also learned how Shang Yang, the founder of Legalism in China, transformed Qin into a militarized state and an economic basket case, a sort of Lycurgan Sparta in China, and how Fan Ju began Qin's conquests with the Battle of Changping, infamous for Qin's massacre of four hundred thousand prisoners of war. Since each story is an epic, the recounting must wait for another day.

Meanwhile, David and Victoria transported themselves to a manor at Handan, the capital of the Zhao State in the north, a state encompassing the kingdom once ruled by Shishen, the god of Orion. The two gamers found themselves inside the main hall of an ornate building decorated with the trappings of fabulous wealth. A voluptuous Venus wrapped in flowing diaphanous silk was performing the ribbon dance for her master and his aristocratic guest. Musicians playing pan flutes, a seven-string *guqin*, or "ancient harp," stone chimes, bronze drums, and bronze bells made empyreal music for the Terpsichorean dancer.

The guest was an adolescent man, arrayed in a sumptuous brocade robe exquisitely crafted with silk samite. He was a young prince of noble birth attended by several officials, including David and Victoria amongst them. The two role-players stood by the hall entrance and stayed out of earshot. The host, about ten years older and almost as extravagantly enrobed, kept his esteemed guest's vessels overflowing with alcohol and sweetmeats by an endless procession of attendants and servants. But the young aristocrat's heart was neither in the food nor the wine. He was mesmerized by the whirling apsara, lapping up every drop of her *passing* beauty and ethereal grace with his love-struck eyes.

"This guy's a real creep," Victoria whispered with disgust. "He's drooling all over the dancer."

"The gleam in his eyes," David said, "will turn out to be a world conqueror. This love-smitten young man, Yiren, is the future father of the first emperor of China, Qin Shihuang. Right now, he is a low-status Qin prince, the son of a concubine, living in Handan as a hostage, far from the heart and mind of his father, the crown prince of the Qin State, and living under the Damoclean sword of losing his head if Qin ever invades Zhao. His host today is the wealthy merchant Lü Buwei. The dancer is one of his concubines."

"Is this lecher trying to steal his host's concubine right under his nose? People can be so crazy."

"And even crazier, Lü decides to indulge him."

“This reminds me of ancient legends.”

“What we’re witnessing here is mostly based on historical records. During the Warring States era, the period we have arrived at, a Shang trader enjoys no social status. But the constant wars also means traders are indispensable, and being a supplier for the Military Industrial Complex allows low-status Shang traders to get filthy rich. Having accumulated untold wealth, Lü covets power and status. After befriending the Qin prince, he begins investing in a bold scheme to make his new friend the Lord of Qin. China’s most famous business motto comes from Lü Buwei, ‘Always accumulate rare goods.’”

The dancer made a face-changing move unique to the Sichuan opera and became Moira. “We’re at Truffle Pigs,” she said. “Let’s exit the program.”

Indeed, Lü Buwei considered the Qin prince rare merchandise. If the price was his concubine, so be it. The down-and-out hostage was grateful until his dying day. Sparing no expense, Lü smuggled Yiren back to Qin and, with exorbitant bribes, insinuated him into an alliance with the Crown Prince’s childless favourite wife, who convinced her lord to make his long-forgotten son the official heir. The first son of Prince Yiren and his dancer wife would grow up to be Qin Shihuang, the first emperor of a unified China. The rest, as the saying goes, is history.

Wielding unrivalled power as the Chancellor of the Qin State and later Regent of the young Qin Shihuang, Lü Buwei implemented economic reforms, built lasting infrastructure, some still standing more than two thousand years later, and won decisive battles, paving the way for the unification of China. Without this Shang descendant’s intervention, China might never have emerged as a single country using a standardized written language, forming a unified culture. China could have become another Europe.

Chapter 33

Wormwood

Speeding past Calgary, the Three Sisters peaks and Banff without stopping, David and Victoria made it to Truffle Pigs in time for their reservation. They plopped down at their table and continued Victoria's odyssey of discovery.

"David, how did my parents get involved? They never told me anything about their past except they were born in Ukraine when it was part of the Soviet Union."

"Michael and Angela answered an ad to work in a dangerous job. At the time, they both suffered from a deadly disease and would've died without getting help. I sponsored them to come to Canada and paid for their treatment. In return, they looked after you and tried to hide you from the Watchers."

"They were dying from a disease? I had no idea."

"Yes, they were victims of the Chornobyl disaster, a nuclear accident which contaminated a large area with radioactivity. Michael and Angela lost everyone in their immediate families, and, to add insult to injury, they were both diagnosed with cancer. The arrangement let them start a new life, get top-notch medical care, and, since they couldn't have children, have a baby by adoption. Most importantly, they had no fear. It was perfect. While doing a job, they loved you as their flesh and blood."

"I know, and I miss them," Victoria said, tears welling in her eyes. "But I never had any idea they had cancer. They always seemed to be in perfect health."

"Well, we don't have the answer to this mystery. While your parents' non-Hodgkin lymphoma was treatable, their oncologist said it would be a long battle. No one contemplated the possibility of your parents getting cured.

"You can imagine our shock when we learned Michael's and Angela's cancer simultaneously went into remission, and by the time you started school, they no longer had the affliction. It was nothing short of a miracle. The oncologist couldn't compute the odds of it happening without divine intervention. All she said to your parents was, 'Thank God and thank your lucky stars.'"

"Since you mentioned it, I realize the three of us were so healthy we never even caught a cold."

"I noticed as well, and I suspect you may be the reason. I believe you may have self-healing powers and can affect people around you with perfect health."

David and Victoria stopped talking when the waitress served their drinks and appetizers. Victoria became pensive. She had too many questions but no answers. Naturally, the small-town girl was skeptical and planned to test David's theory later. Meanwhile, she would keep asking questions.

"My parents never told me about you. I didn't even know you existed. What if I couldn't solve my father's puzzle? Our paths might not have crossed."

"We wanted to sever the connections by which the Watchers could find you. Yet they somehow succeeded. For the worst scenario, we had a Plan B. I triggered it the moment I received a Level Five alarm. If you hadn't found me, I would've tracked you down. I called your home several times, and my trackers missed you by seconds. When you hopped on a coach to Toronto, I figured you'd find me. We left a lot of bread crumbs for you.

"When your parents landed in Canada, I changed their names to Michael and Angela Solana. I named you Victoria Solana because you were born on the winter solstice, the feast day of the Roman sun god Sol Invictus, the Unconquered Sun. I registered my company name, Solvicta Antiques, based on the same god."

"I noticed the similarity between my name and your company. I knew I was on the right track."

"You've been to my private office. You may have guessed why it's room 929."

"I'm not a hundred percent sure. I saw Caravaggio's painting in the sales office. I have written an essay on it. I know Caravaggio's name is Michelangelo, which means the Archangel Michael, whose feast day, Michaelmas, is on September 29, Caravaggio's birthday. I'm guessing room 929 is September 29, the connection to Caravaggio, whose name is Michelangelo, which connects to my parents, as Michael and Angela combine to form Michelangelo, and hence, to me. Am I right to assume all these are not coincidences?"

"There is no such thing as coincidence, my dear, only the illusion of coincidence."

David took a sip of his Oloroso, leaned forward as if carrying on a normal conversation and whispered, "A man is staring at us from nine o'clock. Stay alert, but don't turn your head."

Victoria glanced sideways and almost fell off her chair. A glass eye in the shadow of a broad-brimmed hat was goggling at her from a dark corner. It was an unsettling experience to be stalked by a one-eyed homeless man wrapped in an oversized coat from Toronto to the Rockies. Victoria also noticed the blood had drained from David's face. Two men in black overcoats had entered the dining room, one of whom carried a black briefcase. The Watchers had caught up to them. David and Victoria must run for their lives.

"Don't panic," David said with a subdued voice. "And do not make any sudden movements. After they're seated, you'll walk calmly past the reception area as if heading for the washroom. The

Bozeman will be waiting outside at the front. Don't rush, but don't get caught."

"What about you?" Victoria asked, concerned for the safety of her guardian, who was responsible for her safety.

"I'll create a diversion. Don't worry. I have a Plan B. Moira knows where to pick me up. Go now."

Victoria found it almost impossible to mosey across the room with a nonchalant air, pretending not to have a care in the world while dying to make a bolt for the door, but she managed it. She was relieved to see the Bozeman at the front with its gull-wing door raised. The moment she jumped in, the car screeched toward the restaurant's emergency fire exit, from which David had ejected in a mad dash. The two men in black were scrambling after him, trying to squeeze through the door together but getting entangled with each other. They couldn't chase after Victoria because the one-eyed man was in the way, brandishing a heavy club with a metallic head. How did these people know about Truffle Pigs? How did the one-eyed man get here even before the speedy Bozeman? Who were these people?

"Moira, arm the Bozeman," David ordered as he hopped in. "Aim the EM phaser at the car park and fire when ready."

Upon the spoken command, the Starship Bozeman issued a bone-shivering, joint-loosening hum, blowing up the lights in the parking area. Sparks and smoke spewed from the front panels of the parked cars. The lights in Truffle Pigs dimmed and flashed, struggling to stay alive. The men in black were running to their SUV but stopped in their tracks as sparks shot out of the briefcase.

"Botheration and damnation!" Vincent cursed with smoke escaping from his mouth and ears. "We need spare parts."

The one-eyed man stood in the shadows, watching David and Victoria flee the scene. The high-energy pulse had fried his fake eye. A red light started flashing in the pupil, indicating it was rebooting. As if by magic, the eye repaired itself.

It took a while before David and Victoria recovered from the unexpected excitement and physical exertion.

"Will someone explain to me what the whole thing was all about?" Victoria cried.

"They're the Watchers," David said. "I warned you about them. They'll stop at nothing to get you. It was a close call."

"What about the other guy with the fake eye? I saw him in Toronto the night before I found you. He was in the Tim Hortons, staring at me the whole time."

"He's another one-eyed man who shows up without warning. Maybe he's the Comte de Saint-Germain in disguise. You're popular, and people want to lay their hands on you. But I'm not going to let it happen. Come hell or high water, you'll meet my father and wake him from his coma, and he'll convince you to believe what we believe. You'll find your biological parents and save the Earth from the Stopping Of The Sun, fulfilling the Oracle in the *Book of Heavenly Secrets*."

The Starship Bozeman sped through the Rockies in the dark with its precious passengers. Victoria ate chocolate and granola bars for Christmas Eve dinner. She didn't mind as her Christmas would come later in January on the 7th. They stopped for a few hours at Kamloops, where a man in a dark alley gave David a package containing Victor Su's passport and Chinese ID card. After arriving in Vancouver, Moira skipped the Pan Pacific, where the Watchers and the one-eyed man were certain to lurk in ambush. She took the Bozeman with its priceless cargo aboard a container ship, leaving port on Boxing Day. At long last, they were on their way to China.

Chapter 34

Hill of Beans

Wan Wenlong grew up in the wild mountains of western China. His family name, *Wan*, meaning "myriad," came from the pictogram of a scorpion. His given name, *Wenlong*, means "tattoo dragon." His ancestors had moved to this remote area from time immemorial to escape the oppressive laws and bloody wars. Wenlong's village did a Garbo and isolated itself from the rest of the world. Although he was maturing into a bright young man in the mid-seventies of the twentieth century, it might as well have been during the Ming or Qing Dynasty. Time stands still in the ancient hills. The only changes for Wenlong were the seasons, and he loved autumn as the best season for hiking.

Wenlong loved to explore nature. He knew the mountains better than the back of his hands. On this occasion, he spotted what he thought was a Milu deer and followed it through a heavy wood down a ravine, and for the first time, he lost his way. He tried to retrace his steps but ended up going in circles. As evening approached, he kicked himself for the misstep and settled for the only option, securing a safe spot in the woods to pass the night.

At seventeen, Wenlong was a loner and a nature lover. The villagers were never too concerned about him exploring the mountains on his own. Wenlong demonstrated early on that he was a prodigal genius with extraordinary abilities. He had hiked alone since he was six or seven and had always come home safe and sound. However, his destiny finally caught up with him.

Wenlong found a clearing, collected some twigs and made a fire. As the sun sank and darkness reigned, he could hear unsettling noises within the wild woods. He hoped it was small, nocturnal animals awakening from their slumber. All of a sudden, Wenlong experienced sharp stings on his back. When he scratched, he learned they were not caused by mosquitoes but by darts.

The young man tried to flee from his invisible assailants, but his legs refused to cooperate. Wenlong had developed outstanding strength from rock climbing and working as an apprentice to an ironsmith. He was also training to be the sheriff's assistant. Nevertheless, an effective drug can put down an elephant, and Wenlong had three poisoned darts stuck on his back, more than enough to put him into a deep sleep.

What is deep sleep but a rehearsal for death?! Time stops for no one except for the dead. Wenlong might have slept for ten hours or ten million years. It made no difference to the half-dead in a dreamland. When Wenlong lifted his eyelids, he found himself inside an electronic pod lined with flashing lights. He drew in a lungful of air to clear the cobwebs in his head, climbed out of the pod and tottered to the window for a quick inspection. The world had changed during the time he was asleep.

The vision beyond the window was a dizzying admixture of *Blade Runner* and *The Fifth Element*, but brighter and less chaotic. Soaring architecture had replaced the green mountains Wenlong grew up in, while holograms of fruit-laden trees, colourful blossoms and fairy-like butterflies compensated for the loss of natural beauty. Wenlong heard no din of traffic, only the whimsical music of *Scheherazade* by Rimsky-Korsakov. The sky took on an eerie hue of golden amber. A space elevator transported people and goods between a space station and the earth. But was this Earth?

As Wenlong tried to make sense of the brave new world he had awakened to, a portal appeared on the wall. Two robed figures glided in, their faces hidden in the shadow of a large cowl covering their heads. Except for a golden flower emblem on their chest, their robes were blacker than the blackest black. They resembled two black holes from which no light could escape.

"Greetings," the figure in front said. "Peace be with you."

"Where am I?" Wenlong blurted out.

"You're home. You've always wondered about your elders' tall tales. Now you can see for yourself."

"Who are you, and why do you bring me here?"

"Son of Shangria, we're the Grigoris, true messengers of DIAS. You shall shun the Watchers, who are false messengers. We cannot disclose the universe's secrets—only something evil this way comes, causing an unstoppable wave of destruction. Our sun, the benevolent Yindi-Ra, has become unstable. We need a peaceful sun to survive. Our time is running out. You must save us."

The Grigori opened his fist to reveal a *huang* jade piece.

"The Dragon's Tooth will lead you to the Guardian," he said. "Entrust him with the key. It is our only hope."

As he spoke, the heavens turned blood red. The skyscrapers started tumbling down, and stunning mushroom clouds in the full spectrum of colours erupted from the earth. The two Grigoris fell in a heap and seemed to have disintegrated inside their robes. The *huang* jade piece glowed brighter and brighter, firing sparks in all directions until it exploded in a blinding flash.

Wenlong awoke with the sparks still bouncing in his head. Though groggy from the poison-induced sleep, he quickly realized he was inside a dark cage with narrow slits allowing slivers of light to pass through. From the swaying, he perceived his iron prison was hung high above the ground, ensuring no possibility of escape.

Sun Tzu, the great strategist, once said, "Understand yourself and the others, and you will not fall in a hundred battles." The man never mentioned anything about winning. Wenlong studied his environs to devise a Plan B. He noticed a clean, well-kept village surrounded by peach trees. The dreamy, languorous fragrance of peach blossoms suffused the air. A lazy stream meandered through the sleepy meadows. The temperature, much warmer than in the mountains, suggested late summer.

In addition to everything unusual about the village, Wenlong noticed females playing dominant roles. They wore flowing silk and moved with the grace of fairy goddesses. The men who showed up were either labourers, peasants or miners. They lived and worked far from the village and were subservient to the women. Every morning, the young females in charge of physical exercise would gather at the village square to practice kung fu, swordplay and archery, trying to outdo each other while demonstrating their lethal skills.

"Can this be the fabled paradise of Peach Blossom Spring?" Wenlong reflected. He knew well the legend of *Peach Blossom Spring*, a fable penned by a reclusive poet in the fifth century CE about a hidden utopia. Wenlong's village elders spun yarns about this mythical village being nearby, hidden in the mountains. They accused its original settlers of stealing the key of eternal youth, known as the Dragon's Tooth, from Wenlong's ancestors. For this crime, his clan had sworn to destroy the utopia and reclaim their precious treasure if they could ever find the village.

Wenlong noticed his female captors were not as peaceful as the fable described. The subordination of the men seemed rather odd. Perhaps the women had captured and enslaved them, and he might suffer a similar fate.

Every day, the same girl brought Wenlong his meagre meal while a boy replaced his poop bucket with a clean one. The girl always came after dark, keeping her face in the shadows and never uttering a word. Wenlong decided to make the first move. When the girl showed up with his food, he tried to start a conversation.

"Hey, my name is Wenlong. What's your name?"

She darted away without answering.

The next day, he said, "Hey, I got lost. Where are we?"

Once again, she dashed off without saying a word.

"Can I speak with your elders?" Wenlong asked, but to no avail. At wit's end, the despairing Wenlong tried something drastic.

"If you don't talk to me, I won't eat your food."

Ignored again, Wenlong made good his word. Hunger and thirst were oppressive masters. Nature forces living creatures to consume food necessary for survival; otherwise, one might as well stop breathing. The lack of water was even harsher. Wenlong did not know how long he could keep it up. The food and water were sitting by the corner, beckoning him. Wenlong wanted to give in. What if the girl did not care? What if he died here? He might as well die with a full stomach. Death would be the ultimate escape, but his body wanted to live. The young prisoner passed out.

When Wenlong came to and opened his eyes, he was struck by the divine vision of an angel crowned by a moonlit halo, gazing at him with a tender frown. Her limpid, aqueous eyes emanated such enthralling charm as Wenlong had never seen, not even in his wildest dreams. He thought he had died and gone to heaven.

At about the same age as Wenlong, the girl who supplied Wenlong's daily sustenance had a strawberry birthmark on her forehead. Dripping water onto his parched lips, she transformed the plainest liquid into the Ambrosia of the gods. She fed him a piece of ripe peach, transmuting the common fruit into the *Theobroma*, "food of the gods," imparting immortality.

Before reviving Wenlong, the girl had lowered the cage to the ground and hauled him out. He was free to flee. Wenlong banished the thought and, sitting up, tried to win his captor's heart and mind instead.

"Hi, I'm Wan Wenlong. What's your name again?"

"You're welcome," the girl said. "Mu Xinfeng is my name, and I'm not helping you again. You're in deep doo-doo!"

"Why? I was hiking. I got lost. Next thing I know, your people ambushed me with poisoned darts, and here I am."

"It's a lie. We have powerful Watchers guarding our village. They don't use primitive weapons. You were out cold when they found you. We took one look at you and knew you were a spy."

"It's ridiculous. I have no idea where I am or who you are. Why would I spy on you?"

"You don't know but want to know; therefore, you spy. We know where you're from, the Wen and Wan village. You're troublemakers. It's no good lying. We know the truth."

"The truth is I mean no harm. We hear tall tales from the elders about a hidden paradise, but no one believes a word they say."

"Of course, I know you're harmless. Otherwise, you'd die in your cage."

"So, are you going to set me free?"

"Not for me to say. Our Queen Mother will decide your fate."

"You have a queen here?"

"We have a matriarch whom everyone calls the Queen Mother. But why am I telling you this? You should be the one talking."

"What do you want to know?"

"Tell me about your village and what you say about us."

"My people have been in these mountains for untold ages. We're supposed to have descended from a race of civilized kings which engendered the Shang tribe. It's a load of schnickschnack and kauderwelsch if you ask me. The elders also talk about a hidden realm of fairy goddesses where immortal peach blossoms bloom all year round. It's nothing but fairy tales and folklore."

"Unfortunately, now you've discovered us, you have a problem. Didn't your elders warn you to stay away from us?"

"They did mention some bad blood between our villages from the remote past."

"You should've listened. Now, get back inside the cage. I have to go. We'll talk tomorrow. And be a good boy, eat your food."

Xinfeng used a pulley system to hoist the cage back up and vanished into the night.

Following this encounter, Wenlong couldn't sleep a wink. When he closed his eyes, he could see Xinfeng's aqueous eyes, long fluttering lashes, porcelain skin, blushing cheeks, haughty nose and rosebud lips with an inviting pout. The vision would overcome the young man, who wished to drown in her intoxicating fragrance. Although he was supposed to hate Xinfeng, he lost his head doing the opposite. He was stung by Eros' poisoned dart and afflicted with love's inquietude. His heart suffered from an excruciating pain, which only Xinfeng's presence could ameliorate. Wenlong no longer wanted to escape. He craved for Xinfeng to be beside him every minute of every hour until his dying day.

One may wonder how people living in remote mountains learn, adapt and develop. Once in a while, some clansmen from Wenlong's village would walk out of the mountains to the outside world to explore what was happening and learn new knowledge. They would acquire books for the village school and even bring back orphans to enrich the genetic pool. At times, the changes outside were so overwhelming they would suffer the shock experienced by the inhabitants of the mythical Brigadoon, where a hundred years elapsed between sunset and sunrise.

Years ago, Wenlong's villagers walked out of the mountains and learned about the People's Republic of China. They were concerned the well-organized Communist government would discover their ancient village in the remote mountains. The reclusive villagers preferred to be left alone by the outside world.

Xinfeng's Queen Mother also informed her children of the new China. No one was allowed to venture out of their hidden paradise, nor could anyone beyond the mountains bring them news. The Queen Mother was the only person who could learn what went on outside their secret realm.

At first, both villages waited with bated breath for the government's intrusion. Years went by, yet no one came. The powers that be were too busy governing a vast country in a dangerous world. They had to fight wars to gain peace. They had to pacify incitements and quell disturbances to defend the nation's integrity. They had to overcome embargoes and sanctions. They had to survive natural and unnatural disasters. They had to feed the world's largest population with scarce arable land and scant water resources. They must also endure a relentless siege, which resulted in untold death and suffering.

Meanwhile, the government of the new China had to conduct international diplomacy, survive internal power struggles and withstand the gales of revolution. In the process, they made mistakes and suffered the consequences. They had to learn the lessons and rectify the problems. The nation had emerged standing from the baptism by fire of the Korean War, endured the famine following the Great Leap Forward and recovered from the growing pains of the Cultural Revolution. Despite the never-ending strife and hardship, the Chinese government never gave up because it had promised to serve the people. The problems of two tiny villages in the remote mountains of western China did not amount to a hill of beans in this crazy world.

Chapter 35

Paradise Lost

After defying her clan's rules-based order several times without repercussions, Xinfeng, "Heart Phoenix," became bolder. She stayed longer, and her lips got looser. When ticks bothered Wenlong, Xinfeng came in the middle of the night to let her grateful captive out for a dip in the river.

Wenlong tried to lure Xinfeng into the water, but she did not bite. The girl noticed her prisoner's clan symbol, the scorpion, tattooed in blue on the back of his neck. She was taught since childhood to be wary of this clan. Wenlong was supposed to be her sworn enemy, yet she could not help being drawn toward him.

Wenlong took advantage of Xinfeng's friendship to learn about her unusual village. As he suspected, Xinfeng's Mu, or "Wood," clan was matriarchal. All the males were workers with no social status and lived in a separate area far from the village. They planted crops, produced tools, made furniture, built houses, toiled in a mine and handled most of the heavy lifting. Meanwhile, the females took care of procreation, childcare, education, religion, arts and crafts, healthcare, technology and martial affairs.

Individual families did not exist in Mu society, which functioned as one big family, with the Queen Mother controlling the villager's genetics and making all mating arrangements. She ensured male babies grew up to be industrious and subservient. Occasionally, the Watchers would introduce orphaned boys from the outside world to improve the genetic pool. All girls received strict military and martial arts training. Xinfeng was a product of this system, but she was special. Wenlong would learn about Xinfeng's background on this night of the full moon, enjoying each other's company by the banks of the Peach Blossom River.

"Is your Queen Mother ever going to let me go?"

"Aren't you having a good time? Have I not treated you well?"

"I enjoy every second we share but prefer not to live in a cage."

"I'm risking my life to let you out. Don't be too greedy."

"I appreciate it, but I don't get the point."

"I doubt the Queen Mother will ever let you go. She's keeping you as a bargaining chip."

"Bargaining chip for what?"

"Nothing. Forget what I said. Even if the Queen Mother lets you out, she'll send you to work in the mines, which is far worse than the cage."

"I've seen a lot of miners. What're they digging for?"

"Why do you ask so many questions?"

"I'm an ironsmith's apprentice. If you're mining for iron, it's right up my alley. I can make nice steel swords for you."

"We don't need steel swords. We only need wooden ones for training."

"I've been watching your martial arts training sessions. What style of kung fu are you practicing? I've never seen it before."

"Kung fu? We call it wushu. Are you any good at it?"

"I try my best. I've been training to be the sheriff's deputy."

"So you are pretty good. What style do you practice?"

"I've learned a bit of everything from the elders, such as Wing Chun, Mantis, Shape-Mind Fist, Labyrinth Fist and Choy-Lee-Fat. I am also trying my hand at the Eighteen Grapples."

"What are you best at?"

"Freestyle street fighting, the real stuff."

"You want to have a go?" Xinfeng said with a playful wink.

"Sure. Let's have a go," Wenlong leapt to his feet and began stretching, eager for a challenge. "I haven't sparred for a while."

Wenlong, indeed, was an excellent fighter. He had watched and learned the Mu clan's unique style and was well prepared.

After the traditional salute with the left palm over the right fist, they started showing off a few set moves, testing one another. Wenlong exercised his alpha male prerogative and went on the offensive. But the lightning-quick Xinfeng stood her ground with an impeccable defence. And when Wenlong tried to throw Xinfeng with a grapple, she became as slippery as an eel and slipped from the hold, flipping over him as if she were weightless, flicking his ear mid-air to tease him.

"Wow, your kung fu is incredible!" Wenlong remarked after disengaging, much impressed by his sparring partner.

"You're not bad yourself," Xinfeng said, abiding by her martial discipline to be humble in winning.

"Someone says the only invincible kung fu is speed. Your reflexes are almost inhuman."

"My reflexes are average, but I excel in reading your moves. Anticipation is one of the most important arts we learn. I can stand here, and you won't be able to touch me."

"You're amazing! And how did you flip over me with such ease? Have you ever considered getting into gymnastics?"

"It's basic Qinggong, 'lightness skill.' Any cat can do it."

"Let me check your hands," said Wenlong. She let him have her hands for a second but withdrew them because no boy had ever touched her before. Wenlong noticed Xinfeng had long, shapely fingers with no sign of wear and tear.

"It's a mystery how you can practice kung fu without leaving any scars on your delicate fingers."

"Oh, I forgot to tell you I'm a special daughter of the Queen Mother with unique powers."

Xinfeng decided to show Wenlong a glimpse of what she could do. She placed her index finger on a nearby peach tree and punched it into the trunk with the force of a nail gun.

Wenlong was dumbfounded. He grabbed Xinfeng's hand by reflex to make sure she wasn't hurt. And when he examined the scraped skin on her finger, it healed in front of his incredulous eyes. Xinfeng tried to reclaim her hand, though half-heartedly. Wenlong did not let go. Any fool could see the girl was blushing with the sweet allure of a ripe peach. Her heart was melting from the heat. The world around them cracked and crumbled into smithereens, dissolving into a green screen. The air burst into flames. Wenlong could hear both of their hearts beating, pounding, pulsating, about to explode. Xinfeng's eyelids shuttered, and her lips unlocked.

What happened next was neither planned nor by chance. It was an act of Nature, the same as leaves falling in autumn and the full moon turning animals loony. Wenlong lost all control, wrapping his arms around Xinfeng in a constricting embrace and kissing her long and deep with the unyielding force of death.

For the young lovers, it was their first kiss, which might have lasted mere seconds but could have been an eternity. While a kiss is just a kiss, this one stopped time. Despite enjoying the tingling sensation of ecstasy, Xinfeng could not ignore the gravity of her transgression. She pushed Wenlong away and hurried toward the cage without saying a word. Wenlong followed close on her heels, issuing profuse apologies.

"I'm sorry. I'm so sorry. It won't happen again."

Xinfeng held her tongue until they arrived at Wenlong's prison.

"Why are you sorry?"

"I'm not sorry for what we did. You know my heart will stop beating without you. I'm sorry if you're offended."

"I'm not offended. But this is getting too serious. I haven't told you about something important. I'm going to have a baby."

"What? Say that again."

"I'm … going … to have … a baby."

"How … who … when?" Wenlong stammered, completely taken aback. "Not from what we did."

"It hasn't happened yet, silly. I'm going to have a baby in nine months."

"Who's the lucky father?" asked Wenlong, crestfallen.

"I don't know yet. The Queen Mother will announce tomorrow at the Banquet of Conjugation."

"Are you seriously going to go through with it?"

"I must. What choice do I have? I share the Queen Mother's special lineage. She has been grooming me to take over from her. When I have a daughter fit to take my place as the new heir, the Queen Mother will abdicate and pass the throne to me. This tradition has continued since the beginning. My clan and village depend on me to tend the flock as the next Queen Mother."

"Can't you tell her you already have me?"

"Not possible, especially for you. Our village lore tells of a time in the remote past when our ancestors found this place to hide from the outside world. Our tribe has always been matriarchal, and the world was becoming too patriarchal for our taste. Out of the blue, your tribe showed up and tried to reenact the Rape of the Sabine Women with us as the victims. Our ancestors knew how to defend themselves. They maimed your chief in the melee and took your tribal symbol, the Dragon's Tooth.

"Your tribe threatened total war. Being the children of Orion, our ancestors offered a holocaust to the heavenly god for protection. Sure enough, two black-cloaked men known as Watchers came into our village. They claimed to be messengers of a deity named DIAS, sent from Orion to protect us, and they used magic to hide us from your tribe. However, they also forbade us from leaving the village or consorting with strangers. The punishment for failure to comply is eternal banishment to Naraka."

"Where is Naraka? Is it an island?"

"It's a state of mind, a figure of speech for the lowest level of hell. It's a terrible place of torture with no possibility of escape."

Wenlong remembered the Grigori's warning about the Watchers being false messengers. Since the Mu clan considered them as their guardian angels, he did not want to raise the question.

"So, what's going to happen to us?"

"Yes, we have a problem, don't we?" Xinfeng sighed. "After I conceive, I'll have special ladies-in-waiting to ensure the baby develops without incident. I won't have the freedom I have today. Someone else will bring you food."

"I will not touch anyone else's food."

"The new girl drinks from the Peach Blossom Spring and is pleasing to the eye," Xinfeng said, keeping a brave front and hiding her feelings. "You'll appreciate her visits and eat her food."

"But I only have eyes for you. If you stop coming, I swear I'll starve myself to death."

"Please stop dreaming," Xinfeng said, rubbing her eyes to disguise their reddening. "We can't be together. It's hopeless. Forget about me. I can't help you. I can't even help myself."

"Don't give up on us, I beg you," Wenlong pleaded, putting his arms around Xinfeng, who began to sob softly on his chest. "Don't give up on a lifetime of love. We may only have one chance. If you know the way out, we'll escape to the outside world. I swear by the Heart of the Dragon to love and protect you until the end of time."

"How do I know I can trust you?"

"Cross my heart and hope to die."

"If you lie, I'll stick a needle in your eye," Xinfeng said. "Tomorrow, after the Banquet of Conjugation, I'll slip out and bring you food. In the meantime, don't do anything stupid."

Chapter 36

Lovers' Leap

The Banquet of Conjugation was slow-motion torture for Wenlong. He suffered death by ten thousand cuts. While wallowing in misery, he could hear the hateful festivities and the arrival of the chosen man. Wenlong clutched his heart in unbearable pain, imagining what Xinfeng might be doing.

Would she find the chosen man attractive? Would her sisters persuade her to stay? Would her sense of duty win her over? Would she fear the outside world and the unknown future? Would she drink the Queen Mother's magic potion to forget him? Would she change her mind and let him die of a broken heart?

The seconds and minutes dragged on. The sun lingered in agonizing torpor until it finally sank into the netherworld. Wenlong strained to hear Xinfeng's footfall or catch her intoxicating fragrance on the night breeze.

"Where is my Xinfeng?" Wenlong cried in despair. The torture of not knowing if she would show up was worse than receiving a death sentence and getting executed posthaste by a quick blade.

Wenlong sensed the cage descending to the ground. With the moon missing from the overcast evening sky, he could not make out the black-cloaked Xinfeng. She moved with such silent, cat-like agility Wenlong did not notice her arrival. She had brought a black cloak and some wedding buns for him.

"Put on this mantle. You can eat the buns on the way. We have to go now. It's game over if they catch us."

"I could cover you with a thousand kisses. I was afraid you would not show up and leave me to die in my cage."

They ran along the river to the foot of the Nine Dragons Mountain, where the delectable, rejuvenating water of the fabled Peach Blossom Spring flowed into a catch basin known as the Nine Dragons Pond. Xinfeng cleared away some shrubs to unveil a large rock. She removed what appeared to be a *huang* pendant from her neck and inserted it into a notch on the side of the mountain. The rock rolled sideways, unsealing a cave entrance.

"Hold on tight," Xinfeng said. "We'll have to go through together quickly, or the rock will make bugsplats of us."

Wenlong was happy to oblige and held Xinfeng so tight it was impossible to tell where one person ended and the other began. Xinfeng gasped and told him to take it easy—they would have time for whatever he wanted to do, but not while they were running for their lives. On the count of three, they slipped through the opening as one. The rock swiftly resealed the opening, and complete darkness enveloped them. Wenlong could see nothing except Xinfeng's eyes, which glowed with the gleam of fire opals.

Inside the belly of the Nine Dragons stretched the Labyrinth of Despair. Fortunately, Xinfeng knew the way out. After twisting and turning in the dark for hours, taking frequent breaks and making slow progress for lack of oxygen, they emerged on the other side of the mountain. They had lost track of time while inside the Nine Dragons. The eastern sky was already brightening with a faint blush. The two fugitives kept running until they returned to Wenlong's familiar ground, where they sat down to rest their weary legs and take stock of their situation.

"We're lucky the Watchers weren't around," Wenlong said.

"They were at the mine," Xinfeng explained. "In return for the Watchers protecting the village from the outside world, our miners extract a rare mineral known as Didymium for them."

"Do you know what for?"

"No idea. We only know Didymium has remarkable properties, and the Watchers guard it jealously as if it were the Nibelungen gold. As the heir to the Queen Mother, I know the Watchers' whereabouts and how to elude them."

"Thanks to you, we're free. By the way, the key you used to open the gate of the Nine Dragons appears to be a piece of *huang* jade with magic spells on it. How does it work?"

"I won't lie to you. It's the Dragon's Tooth from your village. The Watchers used it as the key to open the gateway to the outside world. The Queen Mother wore it on her neck. While grooming me, she had used the key many times to let me into the Labyrinth of Despair for training. As the future Queen Mother, I must know my way through the underground maze because I'll be the village's only connection to the outside world. Anyone without the training will get lost and die. Furthermore, as an offspring of the Queen Mother's lineage, I can see in the dark and survive for long periods without air. I made sure you had enough oxygen to survive."

"I must learn more about your ancestry and how you inherited these amazing traits. Regardless of your strange lineage and society, I can't describe how happy I am you decided to elope with me. Tell me all about your escape."

"At the banquet, I pretended to be drunk. The handmaids took the groom and me to the bedroom, where I put the man to sleep, applying a Rear Naked Choke. The guards are my dearest sisters. They cried and begged me not to leave. Finally, they let me go because of love. I don't even know what it means. I only know I'm miserable when we're apart. Why must I lose my family to be with a stranger? I have no idea. But I must do what is true to my heart.

"I sneaked into the Queen Mother's room. She was asleep from the wine, and I took the Dragon's Tooth from her neck. I'll return it to you now. My village has not gained anything from it."

"Keep it as my token of love for you. No one believes in the myth of the Dragon's Tooth anyway, and everyone has forgotten about it. What we should do is return to my village right away. My family must be worried sick about my disappearance. With their blessing, we'll hold a proper wedding ceremony."

"I'm afraid I can't live in your village. Even if your family accepts me, I'll become a traitor to my family. The Watchers have powerful magic. They'll show up asking for me. If your village refuses to obey, they will have hell to pay."

"Alright, we'll go far away from here, find a big city and melt into the crowds. No one will ever know where we are. We'll be free to live our own lives."

"We may only dream," Xinfeng said, dreading the prospect of a difficult life with Wenlong. "More likely, we'll always be on the run. The Watchers are no ordinary humans. We have never seen them eat or sleep. They don't seem to age or die. They're indeed messengers of a powerful god, and they're relentless. They'll track us down. Some men had tried to escape by scaling the mountain, but none succeeded. We won't have an easy life. I don't know what went into my head, getting myself involved with you."

"Courage, my love," Wenlong said, wrapping his arms around her. "All will be well. When the poisoned darts hit me, I fell into a deep sleep and had a vivid dream, in which I encountered two black-robed men who identified themselves as the Grigoris. They claimed to be true messengers of DIAS, the same mysterious god of the Watchers you mentioned. They warned me to steer clear of the Watchers. They called me Son of Shangria. I believe they meant Son of the Shang Star, known nowadays as the Heart Star of the Dragon constellation, the star I swear by. They also gave me a hint about where to go. We should journey to Anyang, the city of the 'peaceful sun,' where the Shang tribe once thrived and laid the foundation of the Chinese civilization."

Chapter 37

Rise of the Peasant

The freight ship carrying Victoria and David needed three weeks to cross the Pacific. Its destination, Ningbo-Zhoushan, south of Shanghai across Hangzhou Bay, was one of the busiest ports in the world.

During the trans-Pacific trip, Victoria experimented on and confirmed her healing powers, which were triggered into full bloom by her recent traumatic experiences. It explained why she never got sick, how she survived the car crash, and why she did not react to the drug in her cider. She also discovered she could heal those near her, transmitting her perfect health to others, and with this power, she inadvertently helped her parents beat their cancer.

To take advantage of the relative calm, David took Victoria on a journey through Chinese history in the metaverse, demonstrating how, despite China's Confucian patriarchal society in the past, strong women always emerged during pivotal times to steer the country on the right path. Moreover, when chaos ruled, a commoner would always appear out of nowhere with the *Book of Heavenly Secrets*, and China's history would take a positive turn.

Navigating the VR game with David, Victoria learned of such a history-mover after Qin unified China. A young desperado named Zhang Liang wanted to assassinate the emperor Qin Shihuang. As expected, this asinine idea did not pan out, and Zhang became a fugitive. While on the run, he performed two acts of kindness, changing the course of history. First, he saved Xiang

Bo, the uncle of the hero Xiang Yu, who would one day destroy the Qin army with a small band of followers at the Battle of Julu. Xiang Bo would return the favour by saving the life of Liu Bang, the future founding emperor of the Han Dynasty. Next, Zhang Liang fetched the shoe for Sage Yellow Stone, an elder of the Huang clan who had recovered the long-lost *Book of Heavenly Secrets*. Zhang Liang would receive the book and become the GOAT, Greatest of all Time, strategist in the history of China, helping Liu Bang, a commoner described by historians as a boorish, boastful, bungling, illiterate and uneducated son of a peasant, to become the one king to rule them all, whose Han Dynasty was so influential it is, to this day, almost synonymous with China.

Unbeknownst to the world, Zhang Liang's ancestor was Ya Zhang (亚长), a Shang prince interred inside Yin's royal palace near Fu Hao's burial chamber. Ya Zhang's undisturbed tomb emerged from the earth late in 2000 CE. Zhang Liang, therefore, boasted to be a Shang scion of royal blood. The educator and part-time politician from Taiwan, Zhang Yazhong, by his name, practically professes to be a Shang descendant of Ya Zhang.

"If Liu Bang was as clueless as historians describe," Victoria queried, "why didn't Zhang Liang take power for himself?"

"After Qin Shihuang condemned Lü Buwei to death, the secret Shang clans decided it was best they worked behind the curtains. Despite what historians said about him, Liu Bang had many excellent qualities of a great leader. By transforming a peasant into an emperor, the secret Shang clans lifted the veil of lies which asserted only certain people could be king. The peasants had for too long supplied the food and delivered their sons to the armies fighting the endless wars, as well as the labour gangs building the palaces, temples, canals, roads and great walls, while all the wealth and glory went to the liars, plunderers and murderers. In one stroke, the peasants demonstrated they wielded the power of the people."

"Well, Liu Bang's success means the secret Shang clans had backed the right man. For a common peasant, he must have been a great emperor. Why else would the Chinese people refer to themselves as ethnic Han but not Qin, Zhou or Shang?"

"Most people do not realize Liu Bang might have been a Shang scion himself. The secret Shang clans, however, supported him because of his wife, the first named empress of China, who, censured in history and besmirched by male historians, became the de facto ruler of the Han Empire after her husband died.

"As the regent, the empress carried out economic reforms and built the foundation on which Han thrived and survived for over four hundred years, giving its name to most people who identify themselves as Chinese. The empress did not go to war when Modu, the Xiongnu Chanyu, insulted her. She swallowed the affront to let the long-suffering peasants enjoy some peace. She implemented the unprecedented policy of granting land to everyone, including ex-criminals, imposing a flat tax of only one-fifteenth of the harvest, later halved and, for ten years, waived under the next emperor. The empress was almost a communist with ancient Han characteristics. She also began the standardization of coinage, a feat even Qin Shihuang could not achieve, eventually arriving at the standard Han Five-Baht during the flowering of the dynasty, which any citizen could mint provided they met quality standards. Men of later ages who engaged in endless wars, currency debasement, profligate spending and the telling of lies didn't want people to know how a woman helped establish the Han Empire."

"Who are these men you're referring to?"

"Almost every masculine member of the ruling class," David replied. "We shouldn't believe in those lying male historians who created the myth of the evil empress of Han. They did not lack words to extol the virtues of the martial emperor, Han Wudi, who waged endless wars with the Xiongnu and started Han's inexorable descent down the slippery slope. Liu Bang's extraordinary wife is known as Empress Lü. Her father, a man of means from the Qi State and a descendant of the Great Sage Jiang's Lü clan, for some reason, moved to the backwater hometown of Liu Bang, once a part of the extinct Song State ruled by the royal Shang, where he offered his precious daughter's hand in marriage to a jobless street ruffian. What are the odds all these are coincidences?"

"There is no such thing as coincidence, my friend," Victoria said, echoing David's mantra, "only the illusion of coincidence."

"Exactamundo! Let us check out how a son of Shang helped a peasant build an empire and why the dynasty took the name Han."

David snapped his fingers, and the two gamers were instantly transported to a mountainous area, teetering precariously on wooden planks affixed to the sheer walls of a steep gorge that resembled a deep, ugly scar of an old knife wound. Roads did not exist. The only means to traverse the area was via these precipitous planks a hundred metres above the sharp, rocky channel of the gorge. Timorous soldiers hoisting red flags struggled along the treacherous path, their limbs tremulous in trepidation.

"Oh my God! Is this safe?" Victoria lost her cool for a second.

"Don't worry. The game terminates if you fall to your death."

"Thank goodness! And why are we risking our lives here?"

"We're marching with Liu Bang's army to Central Han, a hellhole which is home to exiled criminals."

"So that's where Han comes from, a hellhole, but why?"

"To make a long story short, Qin Shihuang, who conquered China by brute force, reverted to the methods of Shang Yang, the famous founder of Legalism, relying on strict laws and harsh punishments to control the restive populace of his vast empire. During the tenth year of the Qin Dynasty, Mars aligned with Antares of Scorpius, presaging a great war. Sure enough, Qin Shihuang died the following year, and the peasants began to revolt.

The deposed aristocrats of the conquered states soon joined the rebellion. Combining their efforts to overturn Qin rule, the rebels agreed to grant the lordship of the old Qin State to whoever captured the capital of the Qin Empire, Xianyang, near Xi'an.

"While Xiang Yu, the grandson of a famous general of the Chu State in the south and nephew of the Xiang Bo mentioned earlier, fought and won the decisive Battle of Julu in the face of impossible odds, Liu Bang avoided pitched battles and sieges, arriving at the capital of Qin and capturing it without bloodshed."

"Isn't it cheating?"

"Not exactly. You may say Liu Bang gamed the system. But his cunning created a political conundrum. Xiang Yu had won the undisputed world heavyweight boxing title, whereas Liu Bang played dodgeball and bullied a sick child into submission. Who would be calling the shots? Liu Bang did what Riddick Bowe decided to do when forced to defend his title against Lennox Lewis. He refused to enter the ring. It was wise of him. As a realist with street smarts, Liu Bang knew agreements bound only the weak. What are agreements if one has no means to enforce them? Thus, he dispensed with the BS and acknowledged Xiang Yu as the Supreme Hegemon.

"Xiang Yu ignored the rebels' agreement as hegemons were wont to do and sent Liu Bang to Sichuan, a reward tantamount to banishment, in fact, a brazen insult for which Liu Bang wanted to declare war on Xiang Yu. Fortunately, he heeded Zhang Liang's advice to accept the decree gracefully while begging the hegemon for the mountainous Central Han area east of Sichuan. Convinced by this ploy, Xiang Yu believed Liu Bang had given up on the struggle for the Central Plains to focus on developing the Wild West. After receiving a huge bribe, Xiang Yu approved the request, and, consequently, Liu Bang became the Lord of Han."

"Han has a rather unflattering beginning."

"Indeed, the word *han* (TS:漢) reflects this reality. Its most recognizable form with the 'water' radical means the Han River and its basin, a remote mountainous area west of the Central Plains and a hellhole where exiled criminals languished and died. The Oracle Bone script of *han* depicts an animal strung up and burned as a holocaust, or otherwise, a convict being burned at the stake. The composite form with the 'fire' radical means sweltering heat, and another version with the 'sun' radical means drought."

"Han is not a lucky name. I've heard of a famous city with the word *han* in it—Wuhan. Is it related to Liu Bang's Han?"

"Yes, in a way. Wuhan, meaning 'martial Han,' is a megapolis formed from a merger of three cities at the confluence of the Yangzi River and the Han River. Wuhan is famous in history for many things, but most significantly for where a botched insurgency took place in 1911, leading to the fall of the Qing Dynasty. In a comedy of errors, some nincompoop threw a cigarette butt into a room full of gunpowder, exposing the insurrection well before the planned date and depriving the rebels of their leader. But the Qing Empire had long been rotting from within. Any half-wit could have lit a match or broken wind in the wrong place at the wrong time, and the house of cards collapsed all at once."

"This proves the name Han is bad luck. Liu Bang should have chosen a better name."

"What's in a name? Liu Bang didn't win by luck alone. Zhang Liang's strategy made him king. Han eventually became almost synonymous with China. People keep saying ninety percent of Chinese are ethnic Han without knowing what it means. Now we know Han merely represented a remote region in China of little consequence. When barbarians overran the country after the fall of the Han Dynasty, they referred to the Chinese population as the Han people. The idea of the Han ethnicity emerged much later."

Chapter 38

Alchemist's Cauldron

The Chinese classic *Romance of the Three Kingdoms* opens with this truism, "The fragmented world over time will unite into one, and the one world over time will fracture into many." Along its journey down the long and winding river of history, China fell to pieces many times, but the notion of a unified nation had taken root in the Chinese psyche. The Shang descendants surviving under other names had planted this seed. They remained patient even in times of turmoil and turbulence. At the right moment, and when the right person came along, the secret Shang clans would intervene, and China would become one again.

During the last years of the Qin Dynasty, a powerful nomadic tribe known in China as the Xiongnu became dominant in the north. The Han Emperors fought endless wars against them and drove their northern half into Central Asia. This horde migrated westward into Europe, transforming into the Huns to lord over the Romans and the Germanic Goths. The Southern Xiongnu moved south to live among the Han, intermarried and became assimilated. Life was a lot easier. The food was hot, the beds were soft, and the women were pretty. Resistance was futile.

After the Han Empire crumbled in the third century CE, its northern nomadic neighbours took advantage of the ensuing chaotic warlord era of the Three Kingdoms and began to encroach on China. Out of the chaos, the Xianbei, a large and complex semi-nomadic tribe from the northeast, conquered northern China, the cradle of Chinese civilization, establishing what historians later identified as the Northern Dynasties (439–589 CE).

David took Victoria for a stroll through the fractious era of the warlords, which served as the historical backdrop for the Chinese classic *Romance of the Three Kingdoms.* Since this part of Victoria's journey is an epic in itself, with her as a role-player in famous battles, some of which reveal the lies of the fictional account, the story must remain untold until another time.

"After the fall of the Han Dynasty," David said, "northern China, which was almost all of China at the time, for over three hundred years, was overrun by most of its neighbouring nomadic tribes."

"Whatever happened to mighty China?"

"China, when divided, is easy to conquer. But Chinese culture is unconquerable, and it always conquers foreign invaders, not by the sword but by the word, sometimes with a little help from the secret Shang clans.

"An example of China's cultural conquest can be found during the Northern Dynasties. One of its Xianbei kings made laws banning the Xianbei language, forcing their people to speak Chinese, adopt Chinese names, practice Chinese customs and intermarry with the Chinese. They wanted to become Chinese. Eventually, a Chinese aristocrat usurped Xianbei rule in a bloodless coup and established the influential but short-lived Sui Dynasty to be succeeded by the glorious Tang Dynasty.

"The Tang Empire was one of global significance. Its capital, Chang'an, meaning 'long peace,' today's Xi'an, 'west peace,' was the world's largest city. People from other parts of the world, be they Christians, Muslims or Buddhists, came to China to trade and spread their religions. The Japanese assimilated Tang culture and have kept it to this day. You may not realize 'Chinatown' in Chinese is literally 'Tang Person Street.'"

"You mean, besides being Chinese Canadian," Victoria quipped, "I'm also Han, Tang, Ukrainian, Russian, with a hint of Japanese? Wow!" making the mind-blowing gesture.

"What's in a name? Some historians insist the Tang lineage is Han Chinese, but it's debatable. Let us investigate the family's background. First, Tang refers to a Shang dukedom around modern-day Shanxi's provincial capital, Taiyuan, in north China. Shishen, the antagonistic brother of Shang's founder, Xie, was sent to Tang so the brothers couldn't fight each other. Upon Shang's demise, the Zhou queen, daughter of the Great Sage Jiang and, therefore, a Shang herself, sent her younger son to take over Tang. Here is a most intriguing fact. The new Duke of Tang somehow had the exact same name as the last Duke descended from Shishen. I smell something fishy. Later, this area became a part of the Zhao State, which produced the mother of Qin Shihuang, the first emperor of China. Curiouser and curiouser!

"The founding emperor of the Tang Dynasty, Tang Gaozu, was the Duke of Tang, a military leader in the area during the Northern Dynasties. His mother was a Xianbei princess, and his father might be either a Han or Sinicized Xianbei. He also married a Xianbei princess, making his son, Emperor Tang Taizong, Tang Dynasty's greatest emperor, more Xianbei than Han-Chinese. Tang Taizong's queen was again Xianbei, making the next emperor, Tang Gaozong, almost a full-blooded Xianbei. But what's in a name?"

"So, the Chinese Tang Dynasty was, in fact, a Xianbei dynasty possibly connected to Shishen. Am I losing my mind?"

"Not yet! China is not the homogeneous nation you think it is. When it comes to China, most people know bupkis. By the time of the Tang Dynasty, the Xianbei population in China had fully integrated into Chinese society. However, their Sinification was not a one-way street. The Xianbei also changed China. For instance, Xianbei women managed the household. The women of the Tang Dynasty, adopting this excellent custom, were mostly well-educated and capable, allowing them to gain power and status in society. An example of a Chinese girl from this period is the famous Disney heroine Mulan. While historians cannot find documented proof of her existence, her story is celebrated through the ages and must have an element of truth."

"Mulan disguised herself as a man to join the army. She couldn't have been a typical Chinese girl."

"I'll admit we don't run into female warriors every day, but Chinese history has a bevy of them, and every one of their stories is as colourful as Mulan's, who was, as far as we know, a Shang descendant. Mulan's family name, Hua (花), is the Chinese word for 'flower.' The ancestor of the Hua-flower surname is Weizi, the first Duke of the Song State of royal Shang lineage."

"Okay, you convinced me. The secret Shangs are everywhere."

"We're not done yet. Mulan's family name, Hua-flower, is related to another Hua (TS: 華), meaning 'elegance,' which originated from the pictogram of the flower bush and was the original word for 'flower.' Hua-elegance later evolved to denote China. Therefore, a Chinese person is literally a 'flower person' and figuratively an 'elegant person.' Some Chinese may not even be aware of this interpretation of Hua-China. The ancestor of the Hua-China family name is also Weizi of the royal Shang lineage."

"According to you," Victoria exclaimed in exasperation, "Han is a godforsaken hellhole, Tang is a tribe of barbarians pretending to be Chinese, China is an elegant flower, and some Shang guy is hiding behind every door. Do we live in the same universe? I want to cry!"

"Haven't I told you everything you know is a lie?" David said. "But spare your tears. You're about to encounter the most powerful woman in Chinese history, if not world history. You have important lessons to learn."

Chapter 39

Girl Power

David snapped his fingers, and the two VR gamers found themselves in the middle of a monumental square within the forbidding walls of a grand palace. Several royal handmaids and eunuchs were ushering a dozen young girls to their living quarters. Victoria took on the role of a handmaid, whereas David passed off as a eunuch. Most of the girls were downcast and appeared to have been crying. While everyone shuffled along with their heads down and eyes to the ground, one girl stuck her head up and studied her surroundings. She seemed to be the only one curious enough to check out the prison where she would languish for the remainder of her often short, miserable life.

"Where are we?" Victoria whispered.

"We're inside the imperial palace in Chang'an, Tang's first capital," David the Eunuch replied. "These girls are recently selected concubines of Emperor Tang Taizong, the second and greatest of Tang's emperors. Most of these young concubines will count themselves lucky to meet their husband, who has more wives and concubines than he can shake a stick at. Well known to be a workaholic, Taizong is forty-one years old. These girls are but twelve to fourteen. Most of them will receive a life sentence of abject loneliness, deprived of a man's love."

"It must be terrifying. No wonder the girls have been crying."

"Actually, in the seventh century, most girls were married off by fourteen. Don't forget Juliet was not yet fourteen when she decided to elope with Romeo. These precocious girls might have shed a few tears when they bid farewell to their parents. But their only job from now on is to attract Taizong's attention and hope to carry his child. Did you notice the girl who was poking her nose around? She is the concubine who would be king."

"It sounds awesome, but doesn't seem remotely possible."

"Except you're witnessing history. As the wind blows, twelve years flew by in the blink of an eye. Emperor Taizong died, leaving the concubine childless. It was bad news for the young woman, as she would have had to spend the rest of her empty, meaningless life in the royal convent as a nun. If it had been so, no one would have heard of her. Instead, Taizong's successor, Emperor Gaozong, espied his enchanting stepmother at the Buddhist temple. Before one had time to say 'Queen Gertrude,' the mourning widow became Gaozong's favourite concubine."

"This is so inappropriate," Victoria said with a raised eyebrow.

"To the Confucian Chinese, perhaps, but perfectly apropos to the Xianbei, which was, slowly but surely, becoming Chinese."

Most people in the concubine's situation would have given up. Instead, she turned a funeral into a wedding and bagged herself a younger husband mesmerized by her charms. Eventually, despite universal objections, Gaozong sent his wife away and made his stepmother-concubine the official queen consort. After Gaozong's death, the queen established a new dynasty and reigned as the Empire's supreme ruler. She is Empress Wu Zetian, the only female emperor in Chinese history.

While other women in China had wielded supreme power, Empress Wu achieved the unthinkable by establishing her own dynasty. She proved unequivocally a girl can accomplish anything if she sets her mind to it. Her improbable rise was no accident. She established Zhou (690–705 CE), named after the ancient Zhou Dynasty. Her titular name had the word *Tian*, or "heaven," Zhou's

Sky god, and the name of her Regnal Year, Tianshou, means "bestowed by Tian." Ping Wang, the ancient Zhou king who relocated his capital east to Luoyang in Henan Province, sired a son whom he named Wu, meaning "martial." The prince's lineage produced Empress Wu, who made Luoyang her capital and surely took power with knowledge of Zhou's matriarchal ancestry. The name of Zhou's royal house, Ji (姬), sports a female radical.

After migrating to Henan, the royal Wu clan of Zhou lost its mojo. To survive, they mingled with the Shang clans and learned to trade, making strategic matrimonial alliances. Empress Wu's father was a Shang merchant whose family had moved to the Tang area, or Shanxi Province, where the Shang clans thrived and later formed the powerful Shanxi Merchants Cartel. Centuries later, a prominent descendant of Confucius, Kung Hsiang-hsi, better known as H. H. Kung, would emerge from Shanxi. He married Soong Ai-ling, the eldest of the three Soong sisters, the most influential women in China during the twentieth century. A Shang descendant of Confucius was, therefore, the brother-in-law of Dr. Sun Yat-sen and Generalissimo Chiang Kai-shek. The Soong family and H. H. Kung later built the financial power of the Shang clans in America. But that, my friend, is another story.

Empress Wu's extraordinary life journey began when Gaozu, her first husband's father and founder of the Tang Dynasty, sojourned at her home before starting the rebellion. Her father gave Gaozu a secret book of power. It is a story seldom told.

"Let's check out the streets of Empress Wu's capital," David said. "Prepare to feast your eyes on the greatest city in the world and the gateway to the Silk Road." And he snapped his fingers.

Victoria was gobsmacked by the panorama of seventh-century Chang'an, a planned city shaped almost in a square with streets running north-south and east-west, accommodating one million residents, seven times the size of Constantinople, the centre of

Western civilization. A scaled-down version of Chang'an survives in modern-day Kyoto, Japan. Horses, carriages and pedestrians thronged the fifteen-metre-wide boulevards lined with trees on both sides. Platoons of soldiers patrolled the intersections to maintain order and prevent crime. Some officers on horseback had exotic facial features. They were Turkic people living within the Imperial realm, many of whom joined the army. During the chaotic period following Tang's collapse, military men of Turkic origin founded three short-lived Chinese dynasties. Turkic people were Chinese emperors long before they were Ottoman sultans. During Gaozong's reign, Narsieh, the commander of the Imperial Guards, was an exiled prince of the Persian Sasanian Dynasty.

During Tang, colourful clothing was the norm. Women slipped into revealing dresses with a deep vee in front, showing off their chemise and décolletage. A few arrayed themselves in male attire and rode astride on horses. Young women roamed the streets without chaperones. Matriarchs strolled in the parks attended by their servants. Most adult women wore fancy hairdos and had a red floral design painted on their foreheads as a part of their makeup.

The Tang capital teemed with people of different nationalities and religions, from Persian traders with their purebred horses entering through the West Gate to Bactrian camel caravans bearing gold, frankincense and myrrh to the bazaar, and multi-ethnic polo teams riding to a match. A Buddhist monk with three disciples arrived, resembling the group that trekked to India in search of Buddhist scriptures in the classic *Journey to the West*. The monk in the story is based on Xuanzang, a historical figure, whereas the Monkey King Wukong may be Hanuman, the Hindu monkey god, with Chinese characteristics. Scholars from Japan and Korea visited in large numbers; some even worked as Tang officials.

Inside a park, footballers demonstrated fancy footwork with a *cuju*, the original soccer ball, while rambunctious kids raced across the playground with handheld windmills known as whirligigs. Boys flew fancy kites while girls chased butterflies with silk nets. Kibitzers surrounded Backgammon, Go and Chess games; others gathered around cricket fights. Nearby, a handful of ne'er-do-wells gambled with tiles and dice. Next to them, a drunkard slept with his finch canary in a cage hanging from a branch above him.

As David and Victoria entered the bazaar in the western quarters, the cacophony of sights and sounds overwhelmed their senses. Booths and stalls lined the streets, hawking everything from handcrafted candy to exotic spices. An old lady peddled perfume pouches, baby shoes and handkerchiefs on the sidewalk. An artist sold paper fans with calligraphy. A puppeteer performed a silhouette show, parodying a corrupt official. A blind street musician played the *erhu*, a two-string fiddle, while a young girl strummed the *pipa*, an Asian lute, with her flying fingers in a playful duel. Street food stalls sold lamb kebabs and naan bread, suffusing the air with the aromas of cumin and hot peppers. Other vendors offered noodles, snacks and tea while wandering sages dispensed medical and fortune-telling services. A row of inns doubling as pubs hugged the brothels frequented by fancy-dressed foreigners seeking comfort from exotic foreign dancers. Victoria was struck speechless by this kaleidoscope in motion.

"This is pretty amazing, eh!" David remarked. "While Western Europe groped for direction in the Dark Ages, China's Age of Enlightenment was in full bloom during the seventh century. Under the rule of Empress Wu, Chinese women enjoyed unprecedented status. Foot binding went out of style. Girls received an education and contributed to law and literature. Women controlled household finances and wielded real power."

David led Victoria through the incredible history of girl power in China to deliver a message. Despite her small-town upbringing, Victoria had the potential to be a world conqueror. As exhibit number one, Tang girls led armies into battle. At age seventeen, Princess Pingyang, Gaozu's daughter, independently raised and led an army of seventy thousand, helping her father conquer all of China. As exhibit number two, Tang girls served as court officials. Shangguan Wan'er, Empress Wu's famous female chief minister, rose from being a child slave to becoming the highest official at Empress Wu's court and later a favourite wife of the next emperor. She also won wide acclaim as a celebrated poet. Her life story is an epic second only to that of Empress Wu.

Contrary to the conservative social norms of later centuries, China's liberal environment for women during the Tang era beggars belief. For example, no taboo prevented intelligent and well-educated Tang women from working as professional courtesans, entertaining cultured guests and aristocrats with their grace and wit in addition to the usual shenanigans. They earned a respectable income, owned property and were independently wealthy. Society did not shame girls for having premarital relationships. Women divorced and remarried without stigma. In her old age, Empress Wu openly kept a stable of young studs for pleasure. No one batted so much as an eyelid. Early Tang and Second Zhou were the best times in China for women.

Empress Wu was not merely a pretty face. She single-handedly shattered the glass ceiling. While she was a brilliant ruler, people close to the Empress, including her next of kin, constantly challenged her authority. On the other hand, most of her capable ministers and officials served her loyally. Under Empress Wu, the Empire was, by and large, peaceful and prosperous. She died of old age at eighty-two as one of the longest-lived emperors of China. Abiding by her wishes, her tombstone was left blank with no pompous elegiac inscriptions, allowing future generations to make their own judgments. Empress Wu's son succeeded her on the throne and promptly reverted the dynastic name to Tang.

Chapter 40

Stone Man With One Eye

The glorious Tang eventually collapsed. Human societies, being unsolvable n-body problems, are far too complex for the human intellect to manage. Foul-ups are guaranteed. While humans are intelligent, no question about it, we are also delusional, unable to see through our own hypocrisy and lies to recognize our fundamental flaws. "Delusional *ergo sum*—I am delusional; therefore, I am." We are imperfect products of evolution and Nature's half-baked accidents. If we continue to swallow lies about us being some special sons of bitches and our god, the ultimate *deus ex machina*, will rescue us from our folly, Mother Nature will dump us like a piece of turd and try something else. She has all the time in the universe; Homo sapiens does not.

Tang Dynasty ran out of time. It collapsed gradually over the years and then all at once. Bandits, barbarians and badass warlords were all in the thick of it, causing widespread destruction and bloodshed. With no end to the suffering in sight, the Shang clans intervened and restored calm to the Central Nation. A military leader of Shang background took power by a bloodless coup d'état and established the Song Dynasty (960–1279 CE), taking its name from the Song State once ruled by the Shang royal house.

Historians contrived flimsy, far-fetched theories for why Emperor Song Taizu decided upon the Song dynastic name without daring to state the painfully obvious. Taizu's father, Zhao Hongyin, was a Shang in plain sight. His name means "exalt Yin."

Historians refer to Shang as Yin. Therefore, "exalt Yin" means "exalt Shang." Who would have such a name if he was not a son of Shang? In addition, Song Taizu's name, Zhao Kwangyin, means "restore lineage." It was, therefore, poetic justice for the Song Dynasty of secret Shang lineage to replace the Later Zhou Dynasty of hidden Zhou lineage. When Song Taizu died, the throne went to his younger brother as often happened with the ancient Shang.

With the secret Shang in power, it should not be surprising Confucianism enjoyed a significant resurgence during the Song Dynasty. Besides influencing China, this neo-Confucianism also spread to Korea, Japan, Vietnam and other Asian countries.

Peace returned, and with it, trade. Until the present era, the Song Dynasty had been a period of unsurpassed innovation and economic growth. For example, the world's first banknote emerged during the Song Dynasty to facilitate trade. It was, of course, developed by the Shang merchants. But in the hands of greedy bankers and profligate rulers, it became a means to plunder the naïve and trustful real-wealth producers.

In the northeast, the Khitans, a descendant tribe of the Xianbei, caught a whiff of the aroma of untold wealth wafting in from the south. They invaded and ruled northern China for two hundred years as the Liao Dynasty (916–1125 CE). The Russians mistook them for Chinese and, even today, call China "Khitai," which the English mangled into "Cathay."

Over time, the Khitans trod the path of their Xianbei ancestors and became Chinese. Resistance was futile. Next in line to rule north China were the southern Siberian Jurchens, who founded the Jin Dynasty (1115–1234 CE). Their Manchu descendants would later establish the Qing Dynasty, the last dynasty of China. The Mongols overthrew the Jurchen Jin and Southern Song to establish the Yuan Dynasty (1271–1368 CE) under Kublai Khan, Genghis Khan's grandson, and ruled over all of China.

"It seems foreign tribes have ruled China most of the time," Victoria remarked.

"It was certainly true in the north," David said, "and it led to a southward migration of people. During Empress Wu's reign, my family retrieved the *Book of Heavenly Secrets.* As the northern tribes swarmed into China upon Tang's demise, the family transferred the book to the south, where it changed history again."

With a snap of his fingers, David transported Victoria to the plains of the lower Yellow River in Henan Province. They stood next to a village near a massive construction site, where a hundred and fifty thousand men were slaving away under a torrential downpour. About five thousand Mongolian and Turkic soldiers with clubs and whips supervised the Chinese slave labourers, who were digging a channel to divert the Yellow River.

O long-suffering sons of Chinese peasants! When not toiling in the fields to feed their brutal masters, they would be wasting away in slave gangs such as this one. If they had not starved to death after losing their crops to the tax collectors, they would meet their fate in the capricious floods of the Yellow River. For those who worked as slave labourers, whipping was their daily fare, while their payment was a kick in the ass for a headlong plunge into the ditch to be released from this bitter burden of life.

"None of these sorry sacks of bones," David said, "will likely see their family again. But, for the remotest chance they may go home to die in the presence of their loved ones, they will keep digging, suffering the indignity, the hunger and the lash in quiet desperation until it is their turn to expire."

For Victoria, her raincoat, hat and sandals, all made of straw, could hardly keep out the rain, which seeped through to mingle with the tears in her eyes. While the multitude of slave labourers moved in rhythmic dissonance, now and then, a soldier would inject a shrill note by kicking one of them into the ditch. Victoria was overcome by pity and grief for the wretched diggers, though they were nothing more than realistic AI-generated 3D images.

"I suppose this is the cruel reality behind great human achievements we don't usually get to see."

"Nor what happens in the slaughterhouse as we enjoy a juicy steak. Most of us struggle to acknowledge the foundation of our advanced society rests upon the bones of the defenceless. We have arrived in the year 1351 CE. The Mongols have ruled China for eighty years. Their oppression of the peasants and indifference to their plight will not end well.

"A few years ago, a prolonged drought ravaged the land, followed by a locust swarm, causing widespread famine. As if the horrific suffering weren't enough, a deadly plague struck those still breathing and spared no one. Peasants were dropping like flies, but the Mongol emperor in Beijing closed his eyes and ears to their endless wailings and pleadings for help."

"Where were the Shang clans when people needed them?"

"Believing the End of Days was nigh, they were waiting for the Bearer of the Oracle to arrive. Instead, the Angel of Death came in the dead of night and wreaked havoc in every village and every house. Shocked by the carnage, people forgot how to weep, but were immobilized in a catatonic state, their faces frozen with an empty gaze, waiting in stoic silence for their turn to sleep, to die, to end the heartaches and the thousand natural shocks of life.

"At long last, the Shang clans intervened. The spark of revolution here would change the course of China's history, but it all started twenty-three years ago. In a farming village south of the Yellow River, a boy was born to parents classified as landless peasants, the lowest of the low. The baby was feverish. It appeared he might not have to endure his accursed life. What should the parents do with this sickly child? In desperation, the father sought the advice of the head monk at the local Buddhist temple.

"The venerable monk suggested the peasant should pledge the baby boy to the temple so the Buddha would take pity on him. As if by magic, the baby survived after the pledge. The Chinese have a saying, 'If one does not die from a terrible calamity, one will hereafter enjoy great prosperity.' The baby is Zhu Yuanzhang, the beggar monk who would become Emperor Ming Taizu, the founder of the Ming Dynasty. When Taizu reached the age of sixteen, the Four Horsemen of the Apocalypse visited and took the lives of everyone in his family. He became a mendicant monk, walking out into the world, begging for food wherever he went."

"A sixteen-year-old orphan who became China's Emperor; I'll have to learn how to beat the odds from him."

"And beat the odds he did. For three years, he wandered across the country on foot. He saw the world and learned about the people and their plight. While passing through Henan Province, he heard the kids singing an enigmatic street rap, 'Stone man with one eye; disturb the Yellow River and rebellions will arise.'

"The song went viral across the country. It was so popular even the Mongol emperor heard about it. But he paid no heed to it and ordered the diversion of the Yellow River. Here, at the village of Yellow Mound Hill, is where the fall of the Mongolian Yuan Dynasty begins."

A commotion rose among the workers near the village. Those nearby stopped digging to explore what it was all about. Some of the labourers ran toward the clamour. Victoria and David also hurried in the direction of the uproar.

Someone had unearthed a stone statue, shouting, "It's the stone man with one eye." And the news spread with the speed of wildfire.

"Get back to work. You slacking, shirking, kvetching, whining, unruly, unprofitable, useless, worthless, parasitic rice worms," a soldier barked, cracking his whip. "You sewage-sucking maggots should be thankful for having a job."

The peasants, accustomed to being slaves, resumed their steadfast digging for a minimum wage and an early grave.

Out of nowhere, a voice completed the street rap, “Disturb the Yellow River and rebellions will arise.” As the words reverberated among the diggers, they froze, staring at each other and their shovels. In a magical moment of enlightenment, the slaves realized they had always held the power to free themselves.

All their lives, the peasants cursed the heavenly god for making them peasants. They lamented their fate to be born into this life of slavery and suffering. They blamed their misfortune on having an Emperor who never cared. They reviled the gentry and their militia for acting as the Mongol’s attack dogs. But they forgot they could do something about it. In the blink of an eye, they had awakened from their stupor and realized they had been sleepwalking in the cesspool of the Big Lie. Why blame others? Reverend Martin Luther King, Jr. once said, “A man can’t ride your back unless it’s bent.” It applies to anyone, anywhere, anytime.

A soldier was about to enforce the rule of law when a shovel descended from above and splattered his brain. The uprising erupted with the unstoppable force of a firestorm across the slave gang. Even rain could not dampen the peasants’ zeal to exact vengeance on their oppressors. The soldiers who did not escape were torn limb from limb and pounded into mincemeat. The attack dogs got their comeuppance. They were always the first to die.

“This is the perfect place to start a revolution,” said David while Victoria cringed from the violence. “Where else can you find a hundred and fifty thousand men ready, willing and able to join you for the fight of your life? All they need now is a good leader.”

The prophecy of the “stone man with one eye” came true. Rebellions erupted across the country in short order. The beggar monk Zhu Yuanzhang joined a rebel group fighting under the flag of the Red Army, which had originated at Yellow Mound Hill.

Taizu excelled and rose through the ranks. The rebel leader gave his adopted daughter to Taizu as his wife, cementing the young man's leadership position. Taizu's beloved Queen Ma, an orphan from Shangqiu, Shang's founding city and the capital of the Song State, was the woman behind his success. Her Ma clan would one day produce sons to establish two of the largest companies in modern China, Alibaba and Tencent.

Taizu soon spun off and formed a new startup. To become the one king to rule them all, he needed sage advice, and it came from a commoner.

History glorifies Liu Bowen as a godsend genius who popped out of nowhere to help Taizu. In reality, Liu was an above-average student who passed the national exam with flying colours and, for a short time, worked for the Mongolian Yuan government, but flopped as a low-level official. For years, he was unemployed, whiling away his life tending the family farm and hiking in the mountains. He could have been another nameless brick in the wall.

Liu Bowen's luck changed when he befriended a hermit in the mountains named Huang Chuwang, who happened to be the custodian of the *Book of Heavenly Secrets*. When Liu Bowen walked out of the remote mountains with a mysterious book, he became one of the greatest strategists of all time, equal among peers with Zhang Liang and the Great Sage Jiang. A man went from zero to hero, and China found hope again.

Liu Bowen later played with fire, breaking his oath of silence. He revealed eleven prophecies of world events up to the End Times, disguising forbidden foreknowledge in mysterious verse. He recorded the stanzas in a tract titled *The Pancake Song*. For this, Liu Bowen is known as China's Nostradamus.

At the time, the future Ming Taizu occupied a strategic city on the Yangzi River, later known as Nanjing, or "South Capital," but was threatened on all sides by his adversaries. Two large rebel groups agreed to an alliance of expediency to attack him from the east and the west. Taizu did not have enough troops to defend one front, let alone two. His commanders were at a loss for how to avert the looming disaster. Their best suggestion was to surrender or flee to the countryside, giving up their base to save the army.

As the Day of Destiny approached, Liu Bowen showed up at the door with a daring plan, which would, in one stroke, defeat Taizu's greatest enemies and, at the same time, establish a firm foundation for the rebel leader to build his empire. Following Liu's advice, Taizu shrank his defences and shortened his interior lines of communication, and, by employing double agents, lured the stronger enemy from the west to advance in high gear into a cauldron. With the speed of summer lightning, Taizu withdrew troops from his eastern defences and concentrated his forces on the western front, routing his western foe with a deadly strike, much as the sting of the scorpion's tail. On learning of Taizu's stunning victory, his dilatory, torporific, fence-sitting eastern foe made a volte-face, only to be destroyed piecemeal on another day.

Almost eight years after this pivotal battle, Mars entered into conjunction with the Heart Star of the Dragon, also known as the Shang Star or Great Fire, heralding epochal change. It turned out to be an unqualified disaster for the Mongolian Yuan Dynasty. Taizu, once a mendicant monk, declared himself the Emperor of the Ming Dynasty (1368–1644 CE) and, a few months later, took Beijing without firing a blunderbuss as the Yuan emperor with no clothes decamped from his capital. Thus, China became whole again.

To repay the Shang for their help, Taizu expanded the Confucian manor, temple and burial grounds for the Kong clan at Qufu, Confucius' hometown in Shandong Province. Today, the combined Confucian property enjoys international recognition as a UNESCO World Heritage Site.

Chapter 41

The One-eyed Fablemonger

The young lovers, Wenlong and Xinfeng, from the remote western mountains, finally arrived at their destination. They were in dire straits, needing immediate assistance.

"I sense joyous jubilation," a blind fortune-teller hollered at the couple as they staggered past, wrapped in soiled blankets. "But beware of disaster, my friends. Come, sit down, you need a rest."

Wenlong and Xinfeng took a whole year to arrive at Anyang. They trod every path, climbed every mountain and forded every stream. They worked odd jobs, stole food, told sob stories and hitchhiked. They kept moving, never staying in one place for too long, and always avoiding the authorities. But something ominous was on their tracks. Two men, tall as sequoias and dressed in black, one carrying a briefcase, would always appear soon after the young couple arrived in a village, town or city. Thereupon, the fugitives would skitter off to the next place.

Along the way, Xinfeng became pregnant. No one planned it, but it happened nonetheless as a course of Nature and because of love, which perpetuates the species. Love is the prerequisite of life. It makes the world go around.

Wenlong helped Xinfeng set her child-laden body upon a foldable chair at the fortune-teller's portable desk. She was due any day now. The martial arts training did not exempt her from the physical shackles of Mother Nature. She was hungry, tired and weak. But she never regretted her decision to be with the person she loved. She was happy and content as long as she and Wenlong were together. Love has a way of turning suffering into pleasure.

Although it was deep winter, the sun was out, the wind was still, and the temperature was rising. The fortune-teller, dressed in a cotton overcoat and outfitted with blind man's glasses, deemed it warm enough to set up his stall outside an herbal dispensary.

"A wise decision, my friends," the blind seer said. "I can sense an auspicious future for the expectant mother. You're in luck because we have a family discount today, and I'll throw in a bonus couplet for the soon-to-arrive baby."

"How do you know my lover is pregnant?" the mystified Wenlong asked. To be in tune with the times, Wenlong used the progressive term "lover" rather than the traditional "wife."

The blind seer lifted his dark glasses, revealing a darting eye on the right side of his face while a glass orb occupied the left.

"In the land of the blind," he said with a wink of his good eye, "the one-eyed man is king."

On the fortune-teller's desk, a paperweight of yellowish jade-like stone held down several sheets of scrap paper. Beside these rested a fortune-teller's almanac with a tortoise-shell drawing on the front cover. Three ancient words ran down the centre of the shell, easily legible as "thousand-mile path." It was the esoteric term for the vertical line bisecting the tortoise plastron, an arcanum known only to oracle bone diviners, scholars of antiquities and professional fortune-tellers.

"This is your lucky day," the seer said. "I'll give you the family special for ninety-nine cents. Satisfaction guaranteed."

"You're a fortune-teller," Wenlong said. "You can surely tell we have no money. Actually, my lover is heavy with child, and we need your help. I promise to pay you back with interest."

"Stop calling me a fortune-teller," the one-eyed man whispered. "People frown on this profession nowadays. I'm a fablemonger, otherwise known as a logopoios or tusitala. What's in a name? I would love to help, but only if you can provide some collateral."

"All we have are the clothes on our back," Wenlong said.

"You're not telling the truth. I may be a fool, but only a fool without wisdom can see. And I can see a jade pendant hanging from the lady's neck. If it proves to have some value, I'll find someone to solve all your problems."

Wenlong and Xinfeng exchanged a glance and nodded.

The fablemonger wrote something on a sheet of paper, which he folded and passed to Wenlong.

"Hand this and the jade pendant to the apothecary in the herbal shop behind me. People call him Hua Daifu. Others call him Dr. Hua. I know him as Mr. Hua. He'll take care of you."

When Wenlong and Xinfeng entered the dispensary, they found a man with his back facing them, filling a prescription from his wall of drawers full of rare herbs. When the apothecary turned around, Wenlong and Xinfeng were flabbergasted. The herbal doctor, with an eye patch over his left eye, was a dead ringer for the one-eyed fablemonger.

"Holy cow!" Wenlong cried. "Are you an illusionist?"

"Rubbish!" the one-eyed apothecary said. "I've been a *daifu* in the neighbourhood for over twenty years. You can ask anyone. Everyone knows Hua Daifu."

"Well, the fablemonger at the front told me to give this to you," Wenlong said, handing the note to the apothecary.

"Fablemonger? What fablemonger?"

Wenlong and Xinfeng turned around and realized the one-eyed man and his stall had vanished.

"It says 'Stone Man With One Eye' sent you," the apothecary said after reading the note. "Why didn't you say so? You could've said so right away. The message says you have something precious for me to appraise."

Wenlong passed the Dragon's Tooth to the one-eyed doctor.

"This is priceless," Hua Daifu said after a quick inspection, "but only to you. To others, the pendant is worthless. Since 'Stone Man With One Eye' referred you, I'll accept it as collateral. Follow me."

Hua Daifu, or Doctor Hua, pocketed the pendant without waiting for a reaction from Wenlong or Xinfeng. He opened a small, concealed door behind a cabinet and led them into a dark stairwell with a narrow flight of stairs. Despite the shop's single-level exterior, it had multiple floors inside. Wenlong helped Xinfeng struggle up the stairs to a roomy apartment. Through the window, they noticed they were in a different neighbourhood.

A young man in the apartment dashed over to Xinfeng, removed her blanket, and helped her onto a clean, soft bed in a spacious bedroom. Afterwards, he brought her hot tea. In the kitchen, an exotic-faced woman with her head wrapped in a scarf, probably a member of the Muslim Hui ethnic minority, was making dumplings and lamb soup. Overall, the Anyang experience for Wenlong and Xinfeng was weird but wonderful. They were thankful for getting help in their hour of need.

"The young man is my friend, Shazi," Hua Daifu said. "He is an herbalist and a handyman. He'll ensure you have everything you need. First, he'll get rid of your flea-infested blankets."

Noticing Wenlong's concern with the name Shazi, which meant "idiot," the *daifu* said, "Don't worry, Shazi may be an idiot, but he's not a moron. He'll make sure everyone is safe here. The Watchers won't find you. The quiet woman in the kitchen is Lang Daifu, nicknamed Doctor Wolf. I don't know a better obstetrician on this side of the galaxy. You're in good hands."

Hua Daifu dug out a commemorative Chairman Mao pocket watch to check the time. "I'm late. I have to go. You can relax. You've come to the right place. Things are looking up."

Chapter 42

The Dragon's Dream

Having supped on a mound of savoury dumplings and a big bowl of lamb soup, Xinfeng soaked and tenderized herself in a long, hot herbal bath and fell asleep after sipping a cup of amaranth and chamomile tea. Lang Daifu left the apartment, promising frequent visits throughout the night to check on the expectant mother. Shazi and Wenlong sat down for a chat.

"Congratulations!" Shazi said. "You'll be a father soon. Have you decided on a name?"

"We've agreed on Dapeng for a boy and Wenxin for a girl."

"Fabulous names! Dapeng is the mythical bird avatar of Yue Fei, the famous general of the Southern Song Dynasty. Actually, this safe house is in the part of Anyang where he was born. Though few realize it, Yue Fei was a son of Shang. Wenxin, the heart of literature, is also apropos. It is derived from the names of her parents and is the short title of one of the most influential books in Chinese classical literature, *The Heart of Literature Sculpts the Dragon.* I am so excited. I cannot wait for the baby to arrive."

"May I ask some questions about our benefactors?"

"I know you have many questions, but it's getting late. We'll have time for answers. Tomorrow is the Winter Festival. I have much to do to ensure the day passes without incident. I apologize for not having an extra bed. You'll have to make do with sleeping on the floor tonight. We'll set you up with a cot tomorrow. Get some rest. We'll talk in the morning."

After Shazi left, Wenlong bathed, wrapped himself in a clean blanket and lay on the floor, the softest he had ever slept on. He also dreamt the sweetest dream. In it, Xinfeng gave birth to a beautiful baby girl. The family would survive and stay together. He would find a place for his family to live and thrive in. He and Xinfeng would have more children, and the children would, in turn, have children. During weekends or holidays, the children would visit and dine with them. He and his lover would grow old together, surrounded by numerous descendants.

Where is this paradise? Is it on Earth or only in Wenlong's dreams?—where all parents are strong and wise and capable, and all the children are happy and beloved, where brothers and sisters neither slaughter nor enslave one another, nor tell lies to everyone from morning till night, where the children love and help each other, share everything and take care of one another, and where all of them live peaceful, fruitful and happy lives. Where is this place? Is it China?

Wenlong's dream was so sweet and his sleep was so deep he did not stir when Xinfeng used the washroom, nor did he hear Lang Daifu come up in the middle of the night to find Xinfeng in labour. The *daifu* used acupuncture to keep Xinfeng calm while preparing for the delivery. As Hua Daifu asserted, Doctor Wolf was indeed an expert obstetrician. She delivered a 3.3-kilogram baby girl shortly before sunrise without waking Wenlong, and it was almost painless for the mother. Upon finishing the job and putting the mother and baby to sleep, Lang Daifu woke Wenlong, gave him the news, and left, mumbling, "I have to go. It's an emergency. The poor man is dying, and his caretakers can't help him. The Sage is on his way, too. I'm late. Gotta run."

When morning broke, Shazi arrived with breakfast. He also brought a black briefcase with him.

"Congrats. I heard the good news. How are they doing?"

"Both sleeping," said Wenlong, giddy with glee. "I still can't believe they're mine."

"Let's talk. We have serious matters to discuss."

"How about explaining who you and Hua Daifu are, what you know about the Watchers, and why you're helping us?"

"This whole thing is much bigger than us helping you. First, everything you're about to hear stays in this room."

Wenlong acquiesced by putting his hand on his mouth and heart. Shazi lifted the briefcase and placed it on the table.

"The way we're hiding you here is with a bit of magic created by future technologies. The Watchers use similar but more powerful configurations to hide your wife's village. We have a portable Manifold Manipulator and Quantum Gateway in this briefcase. I'll demonstrate their features later. The bad news is the Watchers are already in town. They're here not only to arrest you and your wife but also to take your baby from you."

"Why do they want our baby? Can't you help us evade them?"

"The Watchers believe your baby is the Key to immeasurable powers. Hua Daifu and I are familiar with these men in black. They were, at first, benign agents of a godlike intelligence known as DIAS, but a master of war corrupted them. The Watchers are not wrong. Your baby is the Key; therefore, we must never let them take her. However, Hua Daifu and I are travellers; we cannot be here forever. We must move on when our time is up. Where we are going, we cannot take you. When you lose our protection, the Watchers will apprehend you. It is only a matter of time."

"We must not give up. I had a dream in which the Grigoris, self-declared true agents of DIAS, told me about the Watchers, the Key and Anyang, the 'peaceful sun.' You are waiting here with Hua Daifu. Last night, I dreamed everything would turn out fine. I'm sure none of this is a coincidence. Maybe I'm a dream seer, able to see the future in my sleep. You must help us."

"Dreams are but illusions. No one can see the future. The only thing we can say with certainty about time is we don't know what it is. We exist locally and in the present. The faraway is a mirage, the past is a shadow, and the future is an amorphous mist until the sequential collapse of quantum states makes it our concrete present. The existence of the universe follows this law. Therefore, we cannot see the future, nor can we predict the future with certainty."

"Assuming we know what 'future' means."

"Well said. All we know about time is we don't know."

"Nevertheless, my Grigoris dream came true. Hua Daifu and you are here at Anyang waiting for us. What gives?"

"We cannot disclose our knowledge, as it would exacerbate the problem that brought us here. A tragedy occurred long ago and far away, causing the universe to lose its balance. Something wicked this way comes unless we can reverse the damage with the Great Reset. Hua Daifu blames himself for having caused this catastrophe and is determined to avert it. His odds of succeeding are slim to none, but as his only friend, I must help him.

"Ever since we left our home, we have been travelling the galaxy seeking the Key to our salvation, which had split into two Half-Keys separated by vast distances among the stars, entangled but estranged. With an incredible stroke of luck, they both ended up on this planet. It happens when you have too much of a good thing, the rare and powerful Didymium.

"But the probability of the two Half-Keys encountering by chance and recombining into the complete Key was still vanishingly small. We could not intervene but could improve the odds provided we upheld the Uncertainty Principle. We went through a lot of trouble and ended up in hot water a few times, but we did it. It's a long story. You and Xinfeng are the carriers of the Half-Keys, and your daughter is the completed Key. She is a rare and powerful being known as the Sibyl. She is our only hope."

"My ears grow calluses listening to your fabulous tale. But if everything you say is true, more reasons why you should get the Watchers off our back."

"Our hands are tied. The Watchers are serving a marplot determined to capture the Sibyl even if it means the destruction of Earth. Hua Daifu and I can't do anything about it. But you and your lover can do something. You must convince Xinfeng to let a special guardian hide the baby. The Watchers will capture the two of you but not the Key. They cannot kill you because of the restrictions in their operating system. The worst they can do is banish you to a quantum state in the past. When your daughter matures, Hua Daifu and I swear to help her use her powers to extract you and Xinfeng from your exile."

"I thought you weren't allowed to intervene."

"Indeed, provided someone pulls the trigger for us. Long ago, Hua Daifu had planted a seed known as the Guardian of the Oracle. By delicate manipulation of events, we now have a reliable proxy to guard and guide the Sibyl. Let us read the *daifu*'s instructions."

Shazi unfolded a page of an academic article with a map inset showing the Huan River and Yinxu. South of the river in the middle of the Yinxu Palace area of the Shang ruins was a pencilled cross with "8 m." written beside it.

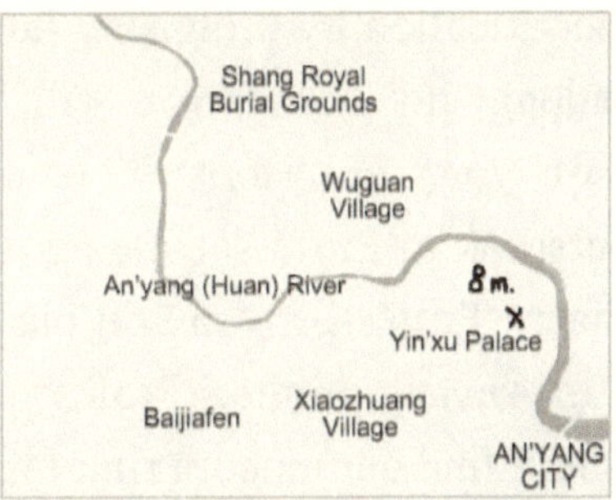

The article's author was Huang Shi. Wenlong turned the page over and found this handwritten message:

"The sun ceases going south; the Oracle is here. Find the yellowish stone; trust with all your heart. Use the map to locate a rare, buried treasure. The ring of unicorn; leave it in the baby's care. Follow the idiot's lead, whither here or there." Stone Man With One Eye, winter of 1975, Year of the Rabbit.

Wenlong deciphered the message thus: "The sun ceases going south" means the Extreme of Winter. "The Oracle is here" means the Bearer of the Oracle has arrived. "Find the yellowish stone," or find the article's author, Huang Shi, which means "yellow stone." "Trust with all your heart," entrust Huang Shi with Wenxin, the "heart of literature." "Use the map to locate a rare, buried treasure" means the map inset indicates the location of a buried treasure. "The ring of unicorn; leave it in the baby's care," that is, the excavated ring with a unicorn motif must stay with the baby. "Follow the idiot's lead, whither here or there," in other words, always follow Shazi's advice in whichever direction he points.

"But how shall we find Huang Shi?" Wenlong asked.

"One of the contributors to Huang Shi's paper is the head of the Institute of Archaeology, the famous Professor Zheng. She'll open doors for us."

"Where do you get the idea the professor will give us the time of day?"

"You'll get her attention by promising her a unique discovery of the ages. Wenlong, my friend, you will learn to unleash the hidden powers of your ancestors. You can be hypnotically convincing if you speak to Professor Zheng with a polite but firm voice in this manner, 'Professor, you will please tell Huang Shi to get himself over to Anyang pronto.' Professor Zheng will give us Huang Shi, and she'll find our unicorn ring for us."

Shazi produced a small box from his shoulder satchel. Displayed on the lid was a plant symbol. He flipped it open to reveal the drawing of a hand directing an elephant on the underside. The box contained the priceless and worthless Dragon's Tooth.

"This is a small present from Hua Daifu to your daughter. Seeing how you won't be able to pay for our services, Hua Daifu decided to take possession of the collateral and give it to the newborn Sibyl. The ancient symbols on this *huang* jade will protect her. It is the oracle Huang Shi, the Guardian of the Oracle, has been waiting for. The jade piece must stay with your daughter at all times. When Huang Shi sees it, he and his family will give their lives to help her achieve her destiny. Finally, I will teach you the secret Spell of Invocation, which is the key to our endeavour."

Wenlong's meeting with Professor Zheng brought Huang Shi from Huangxian to Anyang. Shazi's magical briefcase helped convince the Guardian of the Oracle to do his duty and protect the baby. Wenlong and Huang Shi agreed to meet again at the start of the new excavation season in late April or early May of the following year. Meanwhile, Wenlong tried to persuade Xinfeng to give up their child with little success until the briefcase showed the alternative would be a disaster of an apocalyptic scale.

Fast forward to May of 1976, the Year of the Dragon. Wenlong kept his promise and showed up at the Institute to pinpoint where Professor Zheng should drill. It did not take long to reach the foundation at the site of the ancient Shang palace, ending the fruitless operation. No one had ever found anything under Shang palace foundations except virgin soil.

"Buried deep are rare treasures," Wenlong, adopting Yoda-speak, advised Professor Zheng. "You will please keep drilling."

The iron-willed professor, never one to give up without trying, readily agreed. And somewhere around eight metres below ground level, Professor Zheng and China struck gold. Priceless ancient artifacts started surfacing. Soon, it became unmistakable to everyone present they had made a monumental discovery, namely, the undisturbed tomb of Fu Hao, the warrior queen of Shang.

One of the first artifacts excavated from the tomb was an archer ring with a mythical beast motif. In the chaos of the early excitement, Shazi's replacement ring and Wenlong's legerdemain fooled the handlers without anyone suspecting anything untoward. The authentic unicorn ring ended up in Wenxin's jewellery box. Shazi came to the apartment in the evening with a tote bag.

"I have to join up with Hua Daifu, who is reaching the end of his journey. I'm leaving you with the following vital instructions, so pay attention. The baby Sibyl's unicorn ring is one of a pair made from the horns of twin unicorns, which carry their essence. The words on the back of this ring say 'go' and 'come.' It's the name of the yang-unicorn, pronounced Delo in an extinct language. The name of the yin-unicorn, carved on the ring as 'return' and 'not yet,' is pronounced Re'an. The two rings, while separated in time, are destined to reunite. Huang Shi must learn the names and memorize the secret Spell of Invocation. By waking the unicorns, your daughter may one day revive them to save us all."

"Although not a word you say is believable to a sane person," Wenlong said, "they match the wild yarns my village elders spun, especially the part about the unicorns, our tribe's totem. We hold unicorn festivals during which we perform the Unicorn Dance. We share this tradition with the Hakka, a migratory tribe, because of the Shang descendants among them."

"We have no choice but to trust you," Xinfeng added. "Promise us Wenxin will grow up beloved and, in the end, reunite with us."

"Your daughter Wenxin, as the completed Key, carries the unique genetic coding enabling her to command the unicorns, divine creatures of truth with powers to transcend time and space. They will help her find you and return you both from eternal exile.

"But the powers within the unicorn rings are dangerous. She must be discouraged from using the rings in a cavalier manner. I will not lie. The Sibyl's ordeal will be frightful and fraught with danger. Your daughter, as the Eklelegmenos, the Chosen One, is destined to overcome insurmountable obstacles and wield the instrument known as the Twirligig to reset the universe. However, flagitious fiends who covet her powers will tempt her with lies and confound her with half-truths. Influenced by the dark forces inherent in life, she may become the destroyer rather than the saviour. Hua Daifu and I will do all we can to keep her on the right path. At this point, causality is our worst enemy, and uncertainty is our best friend. May the future unfold in our favour."

Shazi produced two black cloaks from his tote bag.

"These belonged to you when you left Peach Blossom Spring, but you exchanged them for the blankets. I've retrieved them and made some alterations. When the Watchers catch up to you, they will zap you with a strong beam. You'll need to wrap yourselves with your cloaks to survive the blast. I'll give you some herbal Brimo Balm to protect you from the adverse symptoms of time anomaly. Use sparingly, as it is a strong poison. The cloaks have additional features. When needing to escape from a hopeless situation, hold onto each other and utter the spell, '*Je me souviens.*' No matter what happens, you must never lose your cloaks."

"Will we meet again?" Wenlong asked.

"We'll find out as the inexorable current of time takes us to port according to schedule. I'm sure we will meet again somewhere along the journey. We don't know where or when because the future hasn't happened yet, and the distant past has reverted to entropofoggous uncertainties. We may have already met in the past. Good luck to you and us all, Godspeed, au revoir, auf Wiedersehne, adi□s, arrivederci, alavida, shalom, maa Salama, sayonara, annyeong and zai jian."

Chapter 43

Betrayal

David took Victoria on a virtual trip to Europe to learn how the First World War paved the way for the birth of a new China. Dressed in battle fatigues, they navigated through a network of trenches and bolgias filled with despondent soldiers despairing for heaven to descend. And when the clock struck on the eleventh hour of the eleventh day of the eleventh month in 1918, the killing finally ended. David checked his Patek Philippe Reference 96 Quantième Lune watch and declared, "Peace at last!"

"This is a fine watch," Victoria remarked.

"You bet. I bought it for a song from a collector and sold it for a windfall, again, while keeping a virtual one for the metaverse."

"Good for you. I'm curious why all these 'elevens'?"

"It's a mystery number in our *Book of Heavenly Secrets*, a sign of Shang intervention in a significant event. We don't know why 'eleven.' It is what it is. Perhaps someone already took 'ten.'"

"The Shang clans were involved in the First World War?"

"Why not? Globalization is connecting people from all over the world through technologies and trade routes. We have Chinese who don't look Chinese, ethnic Hans who don't know what Han means and the Shang under other names. Since modern times, we've noticed the number 'eleven' popping up everywhere."

"But for many people, globalization is a dirty word. People in America are angry they're losing their jobs to offshoring. Maybe the Shang traders should stay inside China."

"Globalization is an American capitalist idea. America won't advocate for it if they don't profit from it. The Chinese are playing by American rules with Chinese characteristics and have enjoyed some success, lifting their people out of poverty. They're not interested in conflict; it's bad for business. However, for the capitalist West, globalization benefits mostly corporations, money-changers and illusionists; too bad for real-wealth producers. The usual suspects will blame China, using racist slurs and outcries of Yellow Peril to stir the people to commit atrocities while being robbed blind by their lying masters. Meanwhile, the ruling class are using the same playbook with the development of so-called artificial intelligence. The liars and hypocrites are spending the people's wealth to develop technologies for enslaving the masses."

"Here we go again," Victoria muttered under her breath.

"Workers and young people are fearful of globalization and AI stealing their jobs because they believe the lies of the lying warmongers, who justify enriching the rich with unlimited war budgets for army bases, proxy wars and regime changes around the world, as well as government spending programs, pork barrels, cash grants, tax breaks, quantitative easings and bailouts while gutting the poor with tariffs and inflation and saddling them with the rich man's debt. In America, the wealthiest country in the world, people don't need more life-sucking, soul-crushing, undignified, dehumanizing and demeaning slave-wage gig jobs. Instead, they should be guaranteed basic housing, nutritious food, healthcare, education, personal safety, social harmony and human dignity. And don't believe the BS America can't afford it when they can spend trillions upon trillions for endless wars.

"And something more horrendous is happening. Not only are the warmongers enslaving the people with fear and stupefying them to accept criminal behaviour and injustice, but they're using AI in war. We have engendered a genius offspring in AI. When we use AI to help us manage our societies, it'll do the job far better than we ever can. But if we teach AI to imitate humans and be liars and mass murderers, it'll surpass us in the blink of an eye. I do not fear artificial intelligence; I fear human stupidity. To avoid the extinction of life on Earth, we must stop the warmongers now."

"Hell will freeze over before they change their ways. I hope I'm not around to see how this pans out."

"We are all responsible, especially when we call ourselves free and democratic. It's no use blaming others when the end comes. We have met the enemy, and he is us."

Amid the celebrations, a mud-covered soldier hugged David, even kissing him. It was Moira. David, wiping the muck off his mouth, complained, "What the …."

"Peace on earth and goodwill to humanity," Moira declared. "I'm giving you guys the two-minute warning. We're eleven hours from docking. You'll have to finish the game soon."

Pressed for time, David recounted a concise list of events from the fall of Ming to the end of the First World War.

With almost mechanical repetition in Chinese history, a peasant rebellion triggered the collapse of the Ming Dynasty. The homeless and hungry mob broke into Beijing. The Ming emperor hanged himself. The Ming general guarding the Great Wall opened the gates and let the Manchu army in. While China suffered a self-inflicted wound, it conquered its conqueror. The Manchu became Chinese; resistance is futile. As always, history was merciless to delusional and hubristic rulers. The Opium Wars, the peasant rebellion known as the Heavenly Kingdom of Great Peace, the First Sino-Japanese War and the Boxer Rebellion exposed the decrepit Qing Dynasty as the fading façade on a house of cards.

The fall of the Qing Dynasty and the establishment of the Republic of China on the first day of 1912 brought a new ray of hope. But hope is a dime a dozen or, for some, a frivolous indulgence. Before one could say Barack Hussein Obama, China was Balkanized by warlords and carved up by foreign colonial powers. The Republic of China, based on the American model and founded by the American-educated Dr. Sun Yat-sen, sought support from the West in vain. The Western powers gravitated toward the warlords instead, arming them to gain their loyalty rather than winning the simple hearts of the long-suffering peasants. It was the prerogative of the capitalists to seek easy profit while keeping the Chinese people divided, ignorant and weak.

As an ally of the First World War's victors, China had sent 150,000 labourers to the battlefields in Europe, billed as civilian contract workers at high pay. The illiterate fools were no better than indentured slaves. Ten thousand Chinese lost their lives for the big whopper, their forlorn spirits forever haunting the poppy fields of France and Flanders, unwept, unhonoured and unsung.

David snapped his fingers, and the setting switched from the hellacious trenches to the resplendent Versailles Palace. Clusters of dignitaries and delegates milled about in the Hall of Mirrors, eager to reap the fruits of peace at the Paris Peace Conference. Among the mainly Western diplomats gathered a small group of Chinese men dressed in top hats and tails. They were a new breed of Western-educated Chinese elites, doing their best to appear civilized with their Western coiffure and attire.

"The man with the big moustache and a goatee is Lu Zhengxiang," David pointed out, "the Foreign Affairs Minister and the leader of the Chinese delegation from Beijing. He would retire to become a Benedictine monk in Belgium. Years later, when interviewed about the Versailles fiasco, Lu told the unspoken truth of the Western order, 'Weak nations have no diplomacy.'

"Lu is accompanied by his Vice Minister, Cao Rulin, who had signed a secret pact with Japan on behalf of the previous government, acceding to twenty-one overbearing and humiliating

Japanese demands. The well-coiffed man with a pencil moustache is their colleague, Wellington Koo, an illustrious career diplomat. The avuncular Chinese gentleman with a bushy moustache beside him is Wang Zhichang, a distinguished diplomat, government minister and educator. He is also the father of Wang Guangmei, the future wife of Liu Shaoqi, the president of the People's Republic of China and the number two leader after Mao."

During the Cultural Revolution, the Red Guards attacked Liu Shaoqi, who died in prison. His wife, Wang Guangmei, the First Lady, who spoke fluent English and had a Master's degree in physics, was locked up in a dungeon for twelve years.

The four distinguished diplomats at Versailles represented the Central Nation in an undignified international fandango, which sowed the seeds for the birth of a new China.

The Treaty of Versailles, ignoring Chinese protests, transferred the former German colony in Shandong Province to Japan. President Woodrow Wilson decided his *Fourteen Points* and Chinese aspiration for independence be damned. The European powers did not care what he or the Chinese wished for either. They had already made a secret horse trade with Japan. Realpolitik trumped the grandiose "Magna Carta of the soul."

Thus, China took a knife in the back. True friends stab you in the front. China did not sign the Treaty of Versailles because they could not agree to a travesty and a farce. Those who questioned three decades later who lost China might find their answer here.

They might also discover who lost Vietnam. Ho Chi Minh, the founder of the Socialist Republic of Vietnam, couldn't even get past the front gates. A sage said, "If you're not at the table, you're on the menu." Uncle Ho learned the virtuous, moral, peace-loving West did not dole out free lunches. His people must pay with blood to gain independence from their God-fearing, law-abiding, freedom-loving, democratic and capitalist colonial masters.

Chapter 44

The Long March

The betrayal of China by its Western allies sparked the May-Fourth Movement. Furious scholars and students across China demonstrated on the streets against the Western powers and their collaborators. David and Victoria were in Beijing to witness the students make fiery speeches and march en masse to flambé Vice Minister Cao Rulin's manor.

Some Chinese scholars recognized their country needed an alternate path to independence. They could no longer depend on the pontificating West to grant China self-determination simply because the people desired it, forget about grandiloquent promises made while seeking an alliance or pleading for help. It was good news the mask had come off. These Chinese academics realized they must stop believing in their Western friends' lies and lead the Chinese people out of the mountains on their own.

At the time, the Bolshevik Revolution in Russia exemplified a successful struggle of the people against imperial and colonial powers. In China, a measly group of thirteen audacious book-toting academics armed with mighty pens decided to start a revolution, only one among dozens in those heady days of hope and change. They convened the First Congress of the Communist Party of China in 1921 in Shanghai, believing the new ideology would attract supporters to fight for the reunification and independence of China, without which social and economic reforms would not be possible. It was known as the China Dream.

David took Victoria inside the apartment where the revolutionaries held a secret meeting to make history. He pointed out Mao Zedong and the others to Victoria, briefly describing their backgrounds. These young men were still learning about the socioeconomic theory behind the new ideology. Not everyone was convinced the European idea of the proletariat revolution would work for China's agrarian society.

Out of this group and the two absentee co-founders, only two attended the inaugural ceremony of the People's Republic of China at Tiananmen Square on October 1, 1949. Chairman Mao was one of them. All the others, over the years, had given up on the revolution, joined the Nationalists, sold out to the Japanese, got excommunicated or died as martyrs engaging in the risky business of saving China as communists. Only thirteen percent survived. They had gotten themselves involved in a dangerous undertaking, not heeding the warning, "Dying is easy, revolution is hard."

All the early Chinese Communists were bookish activists, knowing nothing of war. Chairman Mao was a peasant's son who had worked as an assistant librarian, for crying out loud. They were up against the warlords and the Nationalist army led by Chiang Kai-shek, their erstwhile brother-in-arms, whom the colonial powers, the landed gentry and the Shanghai crime bosses supported with men, money and munitions. Were the Chinese Communists bloody bonkers?

In 1923, after being snubbed by the West, Dr. Sun Yat-sen's Nationalist Party, Kuomintang, decided to cooperate with the Soviet Union and the Communist Party of China. Dr. Sun's Nationalist government, the Republic of China, based at the time in Guangzhou, the Canton of old, with minimal control or influence beyond its immediate neighbourhood, would receive matériel support and military training from the USSR to raise an army with the expressed objective of eliminating the warlords and reuniting

China under one flag, the Republic of China's flag. However, Dr. Sun died in 1925, leaving the instruction, "The revolution has not yet succeeded, my comrades, you must continue to strive." As the saying goes, "Dying is easy; revolution is hard," and before the bones of Dr. Sun went cold, Chiang Kai-shek, the military leader on the conservative wing, took control of the Republic of China and the Nationalist Party, making himself the supreme leader.

On April 12, 1927, the leaders of the Communist Party of China, including Mao Zedong and Zhou Enlai, who were also Kuomintang members and Republic of China executives, were rudely awakened from their ambrosial sleep to find their faces on Chiang Kai-shek's "Wanted Dead or Alive" posters. It was the Nationalists' *Night of the Long Knives.* True friends stab you in the front, but brothers riddle you with bullets from all directions and throw in a live grenade for good measure.

Victoria visited Shanghai during the massacre. She witnessed Chiang's gunmen haul union workers, Communists and suspected sympathizers to the middle of the street and execute them gangland-style in broad daylight. These victims of treachery had earlier helped Chiang's troops enter Shanghai unopposed. Their corpses now littered the streets, unwept, unsung, unburied.

Captured Communists of high rank had the choice of renouncing the Communist Party and selling out their comrades or being tortured and terminated with extreme prejudice. Mao's wife, Yang Kaihui, enjoyed the same privilege when they arrested her. Refusing to bend under torture or succumb to temptation, the brave woman chose death and died a martyr at the age of twenty-nine.

Eight years old at the time and arrested with his mom, Mao Anying, Chairman Mao's eldest son, was forced to watch the firing squad cut his mother down. Years later, Mao Anying joined the Soviet Red Army as America's ally and fought the Nazis on the Eastern Front. He did not see his father again until he turned twenty-four. As the Chinese Civil War was winding down and peace was in sight, the Korean War broke out in 1950. Mao Anying joined the long-suffering peasants in an insane attempt to stop the world's most fearsome war juggernaut with their flesh and bone. They waded into a sea of fire during Korea's subarctic winter, armed only with courage and determination, and promptly sent the GIs home. As his mother's son, Mao Anying gave his life at the frontlines of the Korean War at the age of twenty-eight.

During the 1927 massacre, the Chinese Communists suffered daily betrayal, torture and summary execution. The few recalcitrant survivors dispersed into the countryside in utter disarray. Having entrusted their safety to the Nationalist army, they were lambs dependent on wolves for protection. These labour-organizing peaceniks brought a bullhorn to a gunfight. The Party of Academics would never forget this lesson for which they paid dearly with blood. Chairman Mao's quote about political power growing from the barrel of a gun did not arise from a vacuum.

Indeed, dying is easy; revolution is hard. Yet, the Chinese Communists refused to curl up and die. Mao escaped to the remote mountains in Jiangxi Province to establish a peasant soviet, whereby the academics could learn how to organize a government and serve the people. In the process, the fledgling revolution faced many existential challenges. Mao lost his leadership position to a group of Soviet-educated youngsters backed by the Soviet Union, leading to the battlefield disasters suffered by the First Red Army.

The beleaguered Chinese Communists, defended by a ragtag militia of about a hundred thousand peasants, were encircled by over a million well-armed, well-equipped, well-trained, well-fortified, well-funded, well-fed and well-led Nationalist soldiers. In addition, Chiang Kai-shek had German military experts advising him on how to tighten the noose and strangle the bastards. For Chiang, it was no more trouble than making bugsplats.

Victoria watched the peasants brandishing knives and spears, fighting a suicidal conventional battle against an army with rifles, machine guns, tanks, artillery, bombers and forts.

"The Chinese Communists are in dire straits," David said. "Do you suppose any of these peasants know it's hopeless?"

"If I were playing chess, I'd give up now."

"The Chinese Communists would never give up on their revolution. To keep the flame of the China Dream alive, they walked out of the mountains on their own."

Thus began the legendary 25,000-Chinese-mile, or 10,000-kilometre, Long March. During this arduous trek across eleven provinces, the Chinese Communists broke through encirclements, stormed impregnable Nationalist positions, braved withering machine-gun fire, swam rivers too treacherous to cross, climbed unscalable peaks and marched over forbidding terrain, pushed beyond human endurance by pursuing armies hot on their heels and Nationalist planes raining bombs whenever weather permitted. Meanwhile, this dwindling band on the run suffered extreme starvation, thirst, sickness, wounds, weariness and despair. Those who could march no more laid themselves down and expired on the spot. Victoria plodded for a while among these young boys and girls whose nameless corpses strewed for thousands of miles along this heart-wrenching trail of blood and tears. Too late, they learned their costly lesson: "Dying is easy, revolution is hard."

After running out of ideas, the Communist Party came to its senses and decided to follow Mao whither he wanted to take them. Near the end of the trek, one of the thirteen founders, Zhang Guotao, almost sundered the Party in two. Fortunately for the Communists, Zhang's Chief of Staff, Ye Jianying, warned Mao of his commander's intention to take power by a military coup. Mao escaped by the skin of his teeth. Zhang, only one Planck length away from taking control of the Communist Party if not for Ye's intervention, ended up in the Scarborough district of Toronto, maybe not far from Mike Myers, who could never have guessed, in a million years, the true identity of his quiet and gentle neighbour. Zhang Guotao tended his garden in obscure retirement, wondering what might have been. But that's another story.

Ye Jianying, whose Hakka tribe worshipped the unicorn, would intervene again decades later, overthrowing the Gang of Four in a coup with surgical precision. He supported Deng Xiaoping's rise to the top post and groomed the son of an old revolutionary named Xi to lead the nation to the promised land. Over the course of this unsung hero's life, he protected Dr. Sun, Chairman Mao, Chiang Kai-shek, the Red Army, the Communist Party twice, the Revolution and the China Dream. His story is an epic in itself.

The Communists barely survived the Long March. Out of eighty-six thousand souls at the beginning of the trek, about seven thousand arrived one year later at Wuqi, a remote northern town in Shaanxi province, four hundred and fifty kilometres north of Xi'an. Most of the survivors were underage, underweight, under-nourished, unkempt, unshod, unarmed, but undaunted children of peasants. Fourteen years later, they would be China's conquerors.

If England's *Dunkirk Evacuation*, Hannibal's *Crossing of the Alps* and Xenophon's *Anabasis of the Ten Thousand* were Herculean achievements, the Long March of the Chinese Communist was many times more so. It might be impossible to find another example of an army losing more than ninety percent of its personnel yet avoiding utter destruction.

China has an idiom for risky undertakings: "Nine will die, only one survives." The Communists suffered worse casualties during the Long March. Why would anyone of sound mind take such senseless personal risks for an unrealistic, unreasonable and unattainable China Dream? Despite such insanely unfavourable odds, the Chinese Communists never gave up.

Chapter 45

Turning Red

Arriving at North Shaanxi in October 1935, the bedraggled Chinese Communists were not out of the woods by a long shot. The Nationalists' Northwest Army and Northeast Army deployed in the area were raring to squash this bothersome bug. Both armies were formidable fighting forces led by famous generals. They enjoyed overwhelming matériel, training and numerical superiority over the decimated rebels. What chances did the Communists have? Did they really believe they could live through this? What kept them from packing up and going home?

Victoria was at the Communist headquarters in Bao'an during the summer of 1936. She noticed the barely surviving Chinese Communists were blithely indifferent to their bleak situation. None of them ever contemplated giving up. Victoria met the American journalist Edgar Snow, who would go on to write his famous book *Red Star Over China.* Yet people in America would rather believe the Christian Chiang Kai-shek would convert China into a Christian country. Chiang's sister-in-law, Madam Song Qingling, Dr. Sun's widow, said this about China's wartime leader, "If he's a Christian, then I'm not." It's her polite way of telling Americans, "If Chiang Kai-shek is a Christian, the Pope is the Flying Nun."

By an incredible turn of events, the Communists persuaded the two Nationalist generals to fight their common enemy, the Japanese, who had occupied Manchuria without firing a blunderbuss. It led to the Xi'an Incident, in which the two generals arrested Chiang Kai-shek, whereas the Communist leader, Zhou Enlai, supported by Ye Jianying, negotiated for Chiang's release.

Hence, by the slimmest of margins, the Communists won an eleventh-hour reprieve. Their peasant soldiers ended up fighting alongside the Nationalist Army against the Japanese invaders.

After the Second World War ended, the quarrelsome brothers reactivated the Chinese Civil War. The war against Japan swelled the ranks of the Red Army, but the Nationalist Army was almost four times larger. Moreover, Chiang's soldiers, empowered by an endless supply of funds, food, fuel, weapons, tanks, trucks, trains, planes and warships, were led by seasoned generals, inspired by mainstream media propaganda and backed by the U.S. military. Whereas the Communists, barely armed with the weapons they captured, were led by an ex-librarian and part-time poet. Even Stalin hedged his bets by signing a treaty with Chiang.

The puffed-up generalissimo estimated it would take, at most, six months to exterminate the pesky rebels. It was no empty boast, for the Nationalist Army encountered little resistance as it waltzed into Yan'an, the Communists' home base, scattering Mao and his cadres into the countryside again. What gave the Communists the confidence they could withstand Chiang's mighty legions? Any reasonable person would have given up and gone home.

"The Chinese Communists would never give up," David said. "Besides, the peasants and the Shang clans are on their side."

David snapped his fingers, and the setting transformed into the front of a massive traditional estate beside a temple complex.

"We've arrived at the Kong Family Manor, the ancestral home of Confucius in Qufu. Descendants of Confucius live here. We will soon meet an unsung hero of the Chinese Civil War."

Soldiers in green and buff uniforms began arriving at the estate. They immediately spread out and took up guard duty at tactical posts. A truck delivered additional personnel, communications equipment and boxes of documents. Three Jeeps brought a senior officer and his aides to the front gate. All the soldiers stood at attention and saluted. The diminutive, dishevelled and sleep-deprived commander, grimacing at a persistent headache, set the men at ease. General Su Yu inspected the front gate's plaque and couplets before entering at his host's beckoning.

It was the last day of September in 1948. Two weeks earlier, General Su Yu of the People's Liberation Army had shocked the world by storming and, in a mere eight days, capturing Jinan, the provincial capital of Shandong. No one imagined the Communist peasant soldiers could accomplish such a feat. Jinan was an impregnable fortress and a strategic communications hub connecting major Nationalist armies in the area and providing a vital link to the U.S. Navy on the eastern coast.

Forty days later, the decisive Huai-Hai Campaign would be fought around Xuzhou, south of Jinan. General Su Yu, the de facto commander of the People's Liberation Army in East China, devised this campaign's battle plans. For whatever reason, the general decided to base his headquarters in Confucius' home.

On November 11, 1948, during the first stage of the Huai-Hai Campaign, when the People's Liberation Army, or PLA, encircled a hundred and twenty thousand Nationalist soldiers, General Su Yu moved his headquarters to a Temple of the Fire God southeast of Tushanzhen. The Shang's ancestor, Xie, was the ancient god of fire. Su Yu directed the battle from his temple.

The encirclement was Su Yu's appetizer. His soldiers took eleven days to gobble up the Nationalist Army Group from Xuzhou's eastern flank, cutting off the main Nationalist Army from the sea and setting the stage for the next course.

Cooperating with the Communist Central Field Army headed by Deng Xiaoping and the one-eyed general Liu Bocheng, Su Yu pulverized the Nationalist 12th Army Group, including its elite

18th Army Corps and legendary 11th Division. In all, they polished off another one hundred and twenty thousand Nationalist soldiers from Xuzhou's southern flank, severing the retreat route of the main Nationalist Army around Xuzhou and sealing its fate.

At the onset of the entrée, after the PLA had encircled the entire Nationalist Army in the theatre, General Su Yu moved his headquarters to Xiangshan, a small city said to have been settled by the predynastic Shang tribal chief, Xiang Tu, the mythical inventor of the horse-drawn chariot. Su Yu based all his headquarters at Shang sites. Was it a coincidence?

Signs of the mysterious number eleven also popped up everywhere. The Chinese characters for "eleven" can be arranged to form the word for "earth," pronounced *tu.* Tushanzhen and Xiang Tu both have the word *tu.* The name of the Nationalist Commander, Du, is made up of "earth" and "wood." The word "wood," pronounced *mu,* can be formed from the Chinese characters for "eighteen." The Nationalist's highest-ranked elite army group was nicknamed the Tu Mu, or Earth-Wood, Group. This moniker came from its elite 18th Corps and 11th Division.

The destruction of the 18th Corps and 11th Division occurred at Shuangduiji. The troops had no idea one could rearrange the name to mean "eleven disaster" and "eighteen disaster."

By early 1949, two months after the commencement of the Huai-Hai Campaign, the crème de la crème of Chiang Kai-shek's Nationalist Army was crushed and demolished. It happened despite the Nationalist soldiers having entrenched themselves behind extensive defensive works supported by highly mobile mechanized divisions fighting on favourable terrain, owning a monopoly of the skies, enjoying numerical superiority and engaging in the most decisive battle of the war under the leadership of the best generals, many of whom had graduated from the elite Whampoa Military Academy, the Chinese equivalent of West Point.

On the other side of the battle, the Communist commander, Su Yu, was a peasant's son who learned the art of war by fighting at the front lines, surviving shrapnel in his brain. His elitist opponents did not know they were fighting against a low-ranked general with little education. Even after the Communist Party established the People's Republic of China, this brilliant campaign's true architect and de facto field commander remained a mystery. China's Ten Founding Marshals did not include Su Yu. He almost vanished into the mist of peace. Only years later, when war archives became available, could historians unequivocally establish Su Yu's pivotal role in the decisive Battle of Huai-Hai.

The Communist Army was supposed to be a band of guerrillas unschooled in conventional warfare and incapable of conducting one, especially in a major battle involving eight hundred thousand soldiers on the Nationalist side and six hundred thousand on the Communist side. Su Yu somehow anticipated every move his opponents made. He even ignored Mao's orders, which were confirmed decades later to have been compromised by high-level counterintelligence. It was as if Su Yu had a crystal ball.

The Nationalist generals knew they could not afford to lose this battle. They were holding the last line of defence for their capital, Nanjing. As the saying goes, a cornered beast is a dangerous beast.

Nevertheless, Su Yu's boys cut off, encircled, starved and annihilated the entire Nationalist Army in the theatre. The de facto Nationalist commander, the famous General Du Yuming, one of Whampoa's top-of-the-class first year graduates, who fought the Japanese in the Burma Campaign under General Joseph Stilwell, stayed with his troops until the bitter end. General Du's other claim to fame was his son-in-law, Professor Yang Zhenning of Princeton's Institute for Advanced Study, winner of the Nobel Prize in physics, whose Yang-Mills Theory is the most successful theory for describing interactions between subatomic particles.

General Du tried to break out of the encirclement but failed. Despite all their advantages on paper, the Nationalist soldiers could not fight without food, the real wealth created by lowly peasants.

When Su Yu's soldiers from the 11th Division of the 4th Army captured General Du, the Nationalist Commander was trying to pass off as a soldier of the Communist 11th Army Group. He finally met Su Yu, his nemesis and conqueror, at eleven a.m. on January 11, 1949. Were all these "elevens" a coincidence?

Days after the conclusion of the Huai-Hai Campaign, the People's Liberation Army marched into Beijing without firing a blunderbuss. They had already taken Manchuria before Huai-Hai. Chiang Kai-shek became an emperor with no clothes.

The ruling class of China and observers from the West, including the Soviet Union, were never truly convinced the Chinese Communists could survive, let alone succeed. No one could have foreseen Chiang's mighty Nationalist Army of about four million would crumble into nothing in four months. It collapsed gradually over the years and then all at once.

Historians formulated many theories for the stunning outcome of the Huai-Hai Campaign. Some said it was Chiang Kai-shek's hubris and poor strategy. Others attributed the result to the fine work of General Su Yu, who refused to obey orders to conduct guerrilla action south of the Yangzi River but stayed in the Central Plains to fight a conventional battle against the ostensibly much stronger Nationalist Army. Su Yu's insubordination and dilatory tactics were so insufferable Mao threatened to remove him from command. The Communists were lucky Su Yu's iron resolve eventually convinced the Chairman. One wonders what secrets Su Yu was privy to that confounded all his superiors, including Mao.

The area of the Huai-Hai Campaign is known as the Central Plains of China. An ancient adage asserts, "Whoever gains the Central Plains gains China."

Almost everyone agreed the People's Liberation Army's success in this campaign owed much to the peasants. They were unsung heroes delivering supplies to the Communist side. The Nationalist soldiers, on the other hand, depended on airlifts after being encircled. When the wintry weather did not cooperate, they starved. Sun Tzu said, "An army without food is lost." Sun Tzu, a scion of the Qi State's ducal house of Tian, meaning "field," having access to the state library, stole a quick peek at the *Book of Heavenly Secrets* before writing his *Art of War*.

On October 1, 1949, the People's Republic of China was born. Chiang Kai-shek retreated to Taiwan, which, to this day, continues to be named the Republic of China. The quarrelsome brothers might have fought tooth and nail for the Mandate of Heaven, but they agreed on one thing: China and Taiwan are one.

Politicians in America started blaming each other for having lost China. Soon, Cold War mentality and McCarthyism infected the American psyche. It was the Taft-Hartley Act doing its magic. It was also the unintended consequence of the Democrat barons stealing the VP nomination from Henry Wallace, democracy be damned. With no hope of a quick rapprochement, China went her own way as if the Americans had never come.

"Learn this lesson well," David told Victoria as they attended Chairman Mao's declaration of the establishment of the People's Republic of China at Tiananmen Square. "Believe, love, learn, adapt and grow. Be honest, thoughtful and diligent. Be humble, unselfish, unafraid and ready to sacrifice. Be wary of liars and hypocrites, never bring a knife to a gunfight, and never give up. The impossible becomes reality because the Chinese Communists never gives up. Let us remind ourselves and our children, China did not gain its independence and right to self-determination through rabid barking or a master's largesse, but by blood and sacrifice, lest anyone forgets."

Chapter 46

Brobdingnagian China

Entering China was a breeze. David knew everyone at China Customs on a first-name basis, got the Bozeman unloaded and drove out in record time. Chinese New Year was around the corner. Palpable excitement was in the air, and decorations in red hung everywhere.

"Good old China," David said, beaming. "I may not look Chinese to some people, but I am Chinese, and I'm always happy when I come home, especially around festive seasons."

"You've lived in Canada for so long," Victoria said, "where you have a family. Do you still consider China your home?"

"China is where I was born, where I have my family and friends and learned to be a person. Without China, warts and all, and the people who gave me life and nurtured me, I wouldn't be who I am. For the same reasons, Canada will always be your home wherever you go. Now you've learned some Chinese history, you should be able to appreciate what it means to be also Chinese."

"I do. I must say it has changed my perception of China."

"I'm quite happy with your progress. Now, we need to discuss an important matter. My father has been in a coma for as long as you've been under my care. I want to try something new to wake him up. I have reason to believe you may be able to tap into the minds of other connected metaverse players with an adaptive brainwave. Maybe you can enter my father's dream through the Huawei AIR game console and rouse him from his sleep."

"I hope he doesn't have nightmares."

"I can't guarantee his mental state is perfectly sound, but I'll accompany you to ensure you're safe. By the way, I'll have to ask you to do me a favour. If something happens to me, will you call my wife Beth and tell her I can't make it home for dinner?"

Victoria's heart skipped a beat when she realized David was taking grave risks to guide her to her destiny.

"No need to worry," David said, trying to lighten the mood. "We'll survive this. I'm talking about a remote chance. Besides, I have set up a trust fund to look after Beth and the kids. Oh, you like surprises?" David abruptly veered from the uncomfortable subject. "A pleasant surprise is waiting for you in Shanghai."

David asked Moira to reroute from the scenic drive through Hangzhou to the Hangzhou Bay Bridge, saving them several hours driving to Shanghai. The Hangzhou Bay Bridge is about thirty-six kilometres, or twenty-two miles, long. Even on a good day, you cannot see one end of the bridge from the other. As they cruised along the bridge, Moira materialized to deliver an urgent message.

"Red alert! Three container trucks behind us are speeding at a hundred and fifty kilometres per hour and blocking all three lanes. I'll have to override travel regulations and speed up. David, Victoria, prepare for turbulence."

The Bozeman accelerated to keep the speeding trucks at a safe distance, but another problem soon arose. Three container trucks up front in the slow lane suddenly spread out, blocking on-coming traffic and boxing in the Bozeman. David and Victoria would become waffles when the six trucks converged.

"Don't worry," David reassured the visibly shaken Victoria. "The Bozeman is impregnable. Moira, activate Smart Defence."

Upon David's command, a dispenser emerged from the Bozeman's rear trunk, spewing a shower of pellets, which exploded into a thick coat of paint on the windshield of the pursuing trucks, obscuring the drivers' view. The trucks, however, continued to press on at full speed.

"It didn't work," David muttered. "I guess the Watchers are using autopilot. Moira, activate Smart Escape."

The Bozeman fired a mini-rocket forward, creating a dense cloud of smoke up front. The car drove into the smoke screen and vanished from sight. The trucks followed in close pursuit, but the Bozeman seemed to have dissipated into thin air. All of a sudden, an airborne vehicle rose from the cloud. The Bozeman had transformed into a quadcopter and was flying off the bridge.

"This is awesome," Victoria exclaimed, breathless. "I didn't know China had flying cars."

"XPeng, Xiaomi and DJI built this feature for us. Flying cars will be all over China in a few years. For now, we don't want to alert air control. Moira, please convert to Hovercraft Mode."

An air cushion inflated beneath the Bozeman, and the car landed softly on the sea. Thereupon, the propellers rotated ninety degrees and drove the hovercraft forward.

"Enough showing off, David," Moira said. "We don't need to advertise our whereabouts. Perhaps Victoria would enjoy an underwater adventure."

"You're quite right, Moira. Please set destination for Pudong Airport in Nautilus Mode. I want to take Victoria on the Maglev. You may activate Panoramic View after we have submerged."

With the air cushion deflated and retracted, the windows sealed, the wheels folded into a water-tight compartment, and a rim-propulsion thruster extended from the rear trunk, the Bozeman transformed into a miniature submarine. Moira switched on the high-definition panoramic function, making the scenery of the ocean from the Bozeman resemble the view from inside a bubble.

For the next hour, Victoria enjoyed visits by frolicking finless porpoises, curious Chinese sturgeons and venerable giant sea turtles. The Bozeman entered a canal, drove up a ramp and, in ten minutes, brought its passengers to Shanghai Pudong International Airport, dry as a bone and none the worse for wear.

Victoria gazed at the ginormous airport with the wide-eyed innocence of a Lilliputian in a Brobdingnagian world.

"How does China do it?" Victoria wondered aloud. "How do they go from struggling to put food on the table and being bullied by everyone to this in such a short time? No wonder some people keep saying China steals everything from the West."

Indeed, how did China do it? After Deng Xiaoping toured the United States, Japan and Singapore in 1978 and 79, he recognized China's almost insurmountable challenges in closing the gap with the developed world. To tear down the psychological barriers to the modernization reforms, Deng Xiaoping told the public he did not care whether the cat was black or white as long as it caught mice. By a popular proverb, he advised the people to be pragmatic rather than dogmatic. As a sage once said, "Dogma is a bitch."

Deng also shared his formula for success in a pithy one-liner: "China would cross the river by probing for the stepping-stones," a Chinese idiom similar to Mao's favourite motto, "Seek Truth from Facts." That is to say, China has a long history of foreign soldiers, traders and missionaries within its borders, some of whom might even have had good intentions. But none understood the country. Hence, China needs to find its own way across the river.

With ideological baggage out of the way, Deng opened the doors of the Land of the Orient to do business with America and the rest of the world. It was, however, not risk-free. The West, led by the U.S., wrote the modern rules of the game, such as Bretton Woods, Plaza Accord, Washington Consensus, WTO, Petrodollar, World Bank, IMF, the Fed, LIBOR, SWIFT, G7, NATO, EU, et cetera. These were cold and calculated capitalist rules ensuring everyone paid homage and tribute to Caesar's printing press.

As the rulemaker, the West could amend, ignore or revoke the rules at its whim. Rules were for the weak. The West had all the game pieces, whereas China had none. They were not free. China must pay to play. On the other hand, the West could conjure any number of game pieces out of thin air.

Moreover, Western agencies specializing in fomenting dissent and instigating regime change would enter China. Their favourite move, "All Options are on the Table," would cause weaker players to capitulate at once, considering the alternative would be at least a black eye, a bloody nose and several dislodged teeth accompanied by the loss of face. For the defiant and impertinent, it could be much worse. It was a zero-sum game the West did not play to lose.

Put yourself in Deng's shoes. What choice did he have? Deng might have been a communist, but he was also a realist. China had precious little resources except a billion impoverished people, most of whom were half-literate peasants. To survive, China must play the only game in town. As a large country, China could swallow the usual insults and absorb a punch now and then, but it could also learn the game and, over time, improve the lives of its people. It was the goal and motto of the Chinese government to "Serve the People," indeed, of any government claiming to serve its constituents. Who cares what colour cats others say the Chinese are keeping? All quantum physicists know Schrödinger's cats are simultaneously black and white, provided no one is watching.

Deng started the clock, and the game was afoot. The Chinese people would open their hearts and minds to accept Western myths, mores and methods, but with a twist known as "Chinese characteristics." By adding a little english to the Chinese spin and cultivating a certain *je ne sais quoi*, China would cause Sinophiles to fawn and Sinophobes to foam. In any case, tourists and investors poured into the country. China's future began to resemble a glass of champagne, bubbling with hope and excitement.

Deng's gambit paid off. By 2019, in merely four decades, China lifted eight hundred million of its population out of poverty, and by 2020, it had eradicated extreme poverty. According to the International Monetary Fund, China's GDP skyrocketed from USD $190 billion in 1980 to USD $18.3 trillion in 2022, elevating China to the second-largest economy behind the U.S., but the largest when measured by purchasing power parity, a better representation of national economies. These were indisputable achievements.

"People blatantly repeat the lie of China stealing everything," David responded to Victoria's rhetorical question, "I suppose for these racists, having the freedom of speech means having the freedom to lie, insult and slander. Their ingrained bias fits the false narratives of the politicians and the major media, who are dying of fright someone might learn the truth and discover the people have been appointing liars, miscreants and imbeciles to be in charge. Anyone who has visited China knows it is a dope place full of friendly people who work hard, learn fast and make tremendous sacrifices. Moreover, the U.S. prints the 'paper promises' used to buy things from China, while China must earn or borrow the U.S. scrip to buy things it needs. How is it a fair and free trade?

"In this environment, China's leaders make proper policies, play the West's game and keep their cool when bullied and insulted, practising a Chinese virtue known as *Ren* (忍), the word depicts a knife on a bleeding heart, which means silent and long-suffering forbearance. Confucius said, 'In the application of manners, the best way is harmony.' Chinese people endure hardships, swallow insults and suffer fools because they follow the Great Educator's advice. I believe China should tell a better story of itself, but what do I know?"

"China's success is already the best story. Who cares what liars and hypocrites say?"

"Sometimes, a single lie can destroy a country and cause death and suffering to millions. Recent examples abound, such as Iraq, Libya and other countries in the Middle East. We must, therefore, be vigilant for the truth. Overall, I'm excited about China's future. Despite its inability to build a half-decent national soccer team, an eleven-body problem many coaches and managers cannot solve, I'm optimistic China will succeed in creating a prosperous, harmonious and peaceful society, bringing about positive changes unseen in a hundred years for China and the rest of the world."

Victoria could not comprehend what David was blabbering about as she feasted her eyes on this fabulous Chinese city while flying through it in the Maglev. David pointed out Disneyland as they passed the amusement park. Why would Disney invest in China and let the Chinese steal from them? Would bald-faced lies repeated a thousand times make one's prejudices more palatable?

Contrary to the relentless negative portrayal by the Western mainstream media, Shanghai is a vibrant modern city full of polite and friendly people living a moderately comfortable middle-class lifestyle. China's population has plateaued at about 1.5 billion. The ability of the Chinese government to maintain a thriving and harmonious society for such a huge and diverse population on a vast land of few natural resources, racked by more than a century of colonial exploitation, war and embargo, is by itself no mean feat. Victoria realized why some people who swallowed endless falsehoods about China were intimidated. Those addicted to black lies fear the blinding rays of the truth.

The high-speed ascent up the Shanghai Tower, the tallest building in China, took Victoria's breath away. David occupied a custom-built suite on the 110th floor. The access-controlled elevator sported a button marked NSF for "No Such Floor." Victoria marvelled at how nothing seemed to be impossible for David, much as nothing seemed to be impossible for China.

Chapter 47

Doing a Hudsucker

David used his phone to uncloak and unlock the hologram-masked door numbered 1101, the mirror image of 1011, which had something to do with the number "eleven." An elegant suite with floor-to-ceiling glass walls, presenting a breathtaking view of Shanghai, was unveiled before Victoria. David explained how his clandestine suite utilized the gap between the structural exterior of the building and its thermal glass cladding. As far as the authorities were concerned, the room did not exist.

All the furniture was antique Ming and Qing rosewood or red sandalwood. Several cabinets displayed priceless antique vessels. At one corner straddled a wet bar flanked by wine coolers stocked with vintage Petrus, Margaux and Lafite. Aged Talisker, Islay, Glenfiddich, Dalmore, and Yamazaki single malts lined the shelves behind the bar. Ornate caskets encased rare bottles of century-old Croizet Cuvée Léonie Cognac, Darroze Armagnac and Maotai.

A pair of stone lions, each with a single horn on its head, guarded the entrance to the inner sanctum. The Asian Society, founded by John D. Rockefeller III, owned a similar pair of unicorn lions known as leogryphs and used the mythical beast for their logo. A search on the internet will confirm most of the lion heads used in the Chinese Lion Dance are, in fact, unicorns.

As David led Victoria near the glass wall to get a better view of the city, a red light flashed across his eyes, stopping him dead in his tracks. A laser-targeting dot rested over his chest.

"I've underestimated the Watchers," David groaned, angry at himself.

Jules emerged from behind the wet bar, teasing David with a laser pointer. He asked by habit, "Do you know who we are?"

David grabbed Victoria's hand, intending to make a bolt for the door, but Vincent sidled into view with his briefcase and Magnum, blocking the way.

"Do you know how much trouble you've caused us?" Jules said, approaching David and Victoria. "Why don't you take the money? Everybody's cool. Nobody has to kill anybody."

Vincent walked up to David and put the gun to his head, complaining bitterly, "I don't know why we're paying him. I have the urge to shoot him right now on principle."

"Chill, man," David said, pushing the gun barrel away with his fingers. "We're talking, aren't we? I'd like to see my money. Is it in the briefcase?"

Vincent cast a glance at Jules, who nodded.

The Latino opened the case, releasing a golden beam.

"Look inside," Jules, the African American, said, "and you'll agree why we must have the girl. We're not the bad guys."

"Not the bad guys?" Victoria exclaimed. "You were trying to kill us on Hangzhou Bay Bridge!"

"We were trying to box you in," Jules said. "Unlike some people we know, we don't kill. It's not in our genes."

"What about my parents?" Victoria cried. "My father said it wasn't an accident. You killed my parents."

"Whoa! Hold on just a cot'n-pickin' minute, little lady-boy," Jules huffed as if wounded by an unjustified affront. "This is a serious accusation. Our brains will fry if we do anything of the sort. It's not fair because no one has seen your parents' bodies. The police report and death certificates are more lies like all the other lies making up your life story."

“Are you for real?” David protested. “A minute ago, our friend here threatened to blow my head off.”

“It’s all for show,” Vincent said, pulling the trigger several times to make wimpy, anticlimactic clicks. “Unlike someone we know, we’re peace-loving people.”

“David, take a look in the briefcase,” Jules insisted. “You’ll learn the unvarnished truth. Your girl is an anomaly of nature. She won’t stop the Apocalypse. She’ll cause it. Haven’t you heard of the Great Reset? It means the end of existence as we know it. We can’t let it happen.”

As David peered into the golden beam, his illuminated face expressed wonder, longing, fear and, in the end, despair. No one could have guessed David had gazed into the vast Abyss, espying not his future but his past, one he did not know existed, which started with him sailing through the air with the greatest of ease. Victoria sensed an impending unpleasant event and devised an escape route in her head.

“Are we cool?” Jules asked as David ended his mind trip.

“Can I think about it? Give me a Mooch, eleven days.”

“Mooch” was the code word for a surprise. An explosion blew out all the glass walls, stunning Vincent and Jules for a second, during which David rushed at the men, held one with each arm and dove through the opening in a move known as the Hudsucker.

David, however, did not expect Victoria to grab him by reflex. It would have been a foolish act for any ordinary girl, who would have plunged to her death, becoming a well-mashed pâté with the other men. Instead, the extraordinary Victoria saved the day by clinging to the ledge with one hand while holding on to David’s foot with the other. Not only did Victoria prevent David from falling to his death, but she also saved the Watchers, who were hanging on to David for dear life. It was the perfect moment for the Canadian teenager to discover she wielded superhuman strength.

The flustered Vincent had kept a firm grip on the briefcase while Jules, as a last resort, activated the Elitzur-Vaidman bomb within. Meanwhile, both Watchers swore with all the inoffensive curse words in their thesaurus, such as “father mucker” and “cork soaker,” vowing to send David to kingdom come.

“Let go,” David yelled. “A time bomb in the briefcase is going tick-tock, tick-tock. It’s about to explode! Let go now!”

Victoria knew she had to do what she had to do. If the briefcase carried a ticking time bomb, no one could save David. It would also kill her and prevent her from saving anyone else. Victoria had no choice but to loosen her grip and watch David fall through the air, taking along the Watchers. The explosion was a silent, blinding flash, expanding and imploding back into a point. The three men disappeared without a trace, transported by a crude copy of an illegal and untested entropofoggous time machine to an unknown quantum state in an unknown dimension.

As remorse overcame Victoria for being of no help when it was most needed, six hands grabbed her and pulled her back into safety. They were the surprise David had planned, Emma, Jackie and Moira. The Weird Sisters came together in a three-way, jumping, screaming hug before anyone said a word. When they finally disengaged, the questions flew fast and furious.

“Holy crap!” Jackie exclaimed. “Did you see what I saw? Did they disappear into thin air?”

“Oh my God! What did you do to your hair?” Emma squealed. “Why are you dressed like a dude?”

“Don’t tell me you two are involved in this,” Victoria cried.

It turned out David had recruited Emma’s and Jackie’s parents to keep an eye on Victoria. Emma and Jackie, of course, did not know until recently. To the girls, Victoria was their best friend, and that was all there was to that. Knowing now their parents had sworn to protect Victoria, they were more determined to help.

After the close encounter at Truffle Pigs, David wanted to take Emma's and Jackie's families out of harm's way. He conceived the inadvisable idea of reuniting the Weird Sisters and flew both families to the Shanghai Disneyland Hotel. It was David's big mistake. Good intentions led the Watchers straight to his lair.

David sacrificed himself to buy time, the stuff that life is made of, for Victoria. He paid the ultimate price, and Victoria must complete the last leg of her odyssey on her own.

Moira handed Victoria a sealed envelope from David. The man always had a Plan B.

Dear Victoria,

If you are reading this, I have failed to accompany you to your destination. Sorry about that.

You should proceed to Gaffer's Café at Tianzifang and ask for Charlie Chan. When questioned whether you're related, you should reply, "Tian and Chen are one family, Zi and Kong share the same roots." Charlie will take you to your next destination. Maintain the Victor Su cover until you have found your parents.

Stay alert and be careful. Burn after reading. Good luck,

David Huang
P.S. my wife Beth's number: (XXX) 555-1011
P.P.S. Tianzifang is a tourist area in Shanghai. Tian, which means "field," during ancient times, was the same name as Chan, the British form for Chen. The Kong, meaning "good," clan of Confucius is a branch of the royal Shang lineage of Zi, meaning "son." The Oracle Bone words for both Kong and Zi are pictograms of a child.
N.B. LEAVE THE BUILDING NOW!

Chapter 48

Next Stop, Gaffer's

Moira implemented the evacuation protocol, shutting down the security cameras and purging the computers. She camouflaged the door with a hologram and led the girls through a hidden passage to a private emergency elevator, disgorging them into a back street. Moira said David's vanishing might not be the end of his story, but her most pressing job was to send the Bearer of the Oracle to her next destination.

"According to David's instructions," Moira explained, "in case I have to execute Plan B, I'm supposed to take Emma and Jackie back to the hotel and afterwards take Victoria to Tianzifang."

Emma and Jackie protested. They insisted on accompanying Victoria for the remainder of the journey.

"People involved in this are ultra-secretive," Moira said. "They won't even make the connection if anything deviates from the activated Plan B, which says one teenage boy and nobody else. We'll have to keep things simple. I'll drop Victoria off at Tianzifang and let her walk the last stretch. The rest of us should keep our powder dry. The day may come when Victoria will truly need our help, and all of us will have to chip in."

A Mercedes Benz C-Class L-Sedan stopped in front of them. It was the Bozeman in camouflage mode. It uncloaked to reveal the original car in all its futuristic splendour. Emma and Jackie were well and truly gobsmacked.

It was dark by the time the Bozeman arrived at Tianzifang. Moira gave Victoria the Huawei AIR game console with the haptic accessories, which she stuffed into her spacious knapsack.

"Moira, how can I get in touch with you?"

"Don't contact me unless you have to. Both David and I have a Baidu AI Cloud avatar. You may go online with the game console, summon my avatar and ask her to call me using a Pretty Good Privacy connection. But Cyberspace is a dangerous place. Take care and avoid the weird stuff on the Internet. We will probably meet again in the not-too-distant future. Good luck."

Victoria was fascinated by Tianzifang's maze-like alleyways and old homes converted into quaint bars, restaurants, cafés, boutiques and galleries. After wandering for half an hour in the labyrinth, Victoria found Gaffer's snuggly sequestered in a quiet, dead-end alley. Unlike the stylish establishments in busier parts of Tianzifang, this café exuded an innocent, rustic vibe, with rough unfinished wood panelling and hand-woven bamboo mats as wall decor. The furniture was country-style, and the lampshades were inverted cane baskets. Several young couples planted themselves in the dark corners, sipping their everlasting espressos while whispering sweet nothings in each other's ears. The background music was a soulful flute melody. This setting evoked such an eerie sense of familiarity Victoria thought she had a déjà vu.

An old Chinese couple was tending shop. Victoria went up and asked for Charlie Chan.

"Are you related?" the old man asked in good English.

"Tian and Chen are one family, Zi and Kong share the same roots."

"Welcome to Gaffer's," said the man, his eyes lit up, while the old lady yelled, "Tiger, someone looking for you."

"Never in a million years would I believe it," declared a young man as he debouched from the back. "Didn't I get here half an hour ago without telling a soul? How the dickens can anyone find me here?"

A tall, athletic, broad-shouldered and handsome lad, Charlie Chan comported himself confidently in a casual orange-and-black windbreaker over a black physique-revealing sports T-shirt prominently splashing the slogan "Tiger Up" in bold orange, tucking his neatly trimmed hair under a trendy orange-and-black baseball cap. Hot on his heels was an attractive teenage lass, about the same age as Victoria, arrayed in fashionable Chinese adolescent garb, tastefully accessorized and wearing light makeup, leaving her long brown hair free to sway in her wake, reminding Victoria of her own before she had to pass off as Victor Su.

Charlie approached Victoria and asked, "What's your name?"

"I'm Victor Su. Hope I've found the right person."

"Hi, I'm Charlie Tiger Chan. I'm the man you're looking for."

"Seriously, Charlie Chan? I thought it was a fake name."

"Seriously, I'm also Number One Son. Listen, dude, Uncle Xu tasked me with delivering a high-value package to his office, no questions asked. We'll take the trip tomorrow. In the meantime, you'll stick with me and stay out of trouble."

The teenage girl jostled to the front and introduced herself.

"Hi, I'm Viola. Where're you from?"

"This is my little sister," Charlie said. "Ignore her with extreme prejudice. She yaks way too much."

"Hi, Viola, pleased to meet you," said Victoria, remembering to lower her pitch. She guessed someone had inserted the unsuspecting Viola as a decoy because the Watchers would be looking for a Chinese girl. The ploy was no longer necessary since the Watchers had vanished from the face of the Earth. "I'm from Canada, near Toronto. It is my first visit to China. Where are we going to meet your uncle tomorrow? Is he in Shanghai?"

"I see, the Canadian connection!" Charlie said, with a tone suggesting he was privy to ponderous secrets. "Uncle Xu is not in Shanghai. I'm not supposed to say where we're going. It'll take a two-hour flight and another two hours on the road. You'll know when we arrive."

"Anyways, thanks for taking the trouble."

"I'm doing this because Uncle Xu promised to give me a big fat lucky red packet full of cash. I plan on going to an Ivy League school. I don't mind having extra bread in my pocket."

"You don't need Uncle Xu's money," Viola said. "Father will give you a diamond card if you get accepted into Princeton without his help."

"You plan on going to Princeton University?" Victoria exclaimed. "Impressive! I hope you get in."

"In his dreams," Viola said.

Charlie made a pistol with his hand and shot at his sister.

"Well, good luck with your application," Victoria said. "Hey, guys, I have had a stressful day. I need to rest. Can you show me where I can get a hotel room nearby?"

"You can bunk with me," Charlie offered. "We're staying at a nice little boutique hotel about ten minutes' walk from here. I have an extra bed in my room."

"I have such a bad snore I sometimes wake myself up in the middle of the night," Victoria lied with savvy, having to wiggle out of the situation without blushing. "If you want any sleep, I should have my own room, and I can pay for it."

"Let Charlie sign for your room," Viola said. "Uncle Xu is a shareholder and has an account at the hotel. You're our guest. We will not let you pay for anything."

Charlie wouldn't get any help from his sister, who had been gawking all starry-eyed at Victor since she first laid eyes on "him."

Chapter 49

Dangal with Tiger

Victoria checked in at the Emperor Inn, an old building renovated to reflect the Shanghai of the past century but with contemporary art for interior decorations. The new friends shared a large pepperoni parmesan pizza in the room where they could enjoy some privacy.

"Hey, how come you guys speak such good English?" Victoria asked. "I was worried I couldn't survive in China by myself."

"Nowadays, a lot of us can speak decent English," Charlie said, "especially for the younger generation in big cities. Viola and I are a bit special. We go to private schools. In my case, I go to a Chinese-Canadian boarding school in Beijing, the Concord College of Sino-Canada. Viola goes to the Canadian International School of Beijing. We learn our English from Canadian teachers."

"I see, the Canadian connection," Victoria parroted Charlie in jest. "Aren't private schools expensive in China?"

"We have crazy rich parents," Viola said. "Money's no object. Time is what they don't have."

"Not to mention sending one's child to a private school is a status thing," Charlie added. "Most of my schoolmates' parents are China's Who's Who. I hobnob with the scions of the crème de la crème of Chinese society. Viola's school is more for the children of foreign diplomats. Our parents will pay anything if it keeps us out of trouble. It's a bonus if we do well at school, which we do, or, at least, I do."

"Victor, you haven't told us about your background," Viola pried, "and why you need Charlie to take you to Uncle Xu. It's a big hush-hush. No one's telling us anything."

"To make a long story short," said Victor-Victoria, telling half-truths to keep her new friends out of trouble, "I was born in China but brought up by relatives near Toronto. A month ago, my uncle and auntie were in a serious car accident. I'm back in China to find my biological parents. A family friend has arranged for me to meet your Uncle Xu because he knows where they are."

"Damn, it must have sucked," Charlie said. "It's a good thing you have connections to Uncle Xu. He's famous for getting people out of trouble and getting things done. But he's quite selective about whom he helps. Maybe your parents are important people. Wait a minute! With all this secrecy, you must have a major backstory. You better let me scan your WeChat QR code. We should get connected."

"I haven't figured out WeChat yet, maybe later."

"I'm sorry about your family tragedy, Victor," Viola said. "I hope you find your parents soon and everything turns out all right. If you need help, we can ask our parents too."

"Thanks, guys, I'm fine now. What's messing with my head is a trippy déjà vu I had when I walked into Gaffer's earlier. Can you tell me the background story of the café?"

"The older folks running the café are the owners," Viola explained. "Uncle Xu is their son. They're from our mother's side of the family. We're all related."

"Gaffer's Café is originally from Toronto," Charlie added. "You may have encountered it before but forgotten about it. Do you want to know how it ended up in Tianzifang?"

As the story goes, retold many times by the café's owners and embellished by Charlie Chan, after China and Canada established diplomatic relations in 1970, China started sending students to study in Canada. Uncle Xu's parents were among those who studied at the University of Toronto during the late 1970s.

Besides attending school together, these two students from China also dated. During one of those romantic outings on a Friday evening in the summer of 1979, the couple was strolling hand-in-hand in the old Chinatown around Dundas and Spadina when they stumbled upon a quaint neighbourhood behind the Chinese gift shops and restaurants. The area is known as Kensington Market or the Jewish Market of old. An aura of magic lingered in this ancient neighbourhood left behind by the early immigrants who helped build Toronto. From those glory days, a stalwart Gothic church remained. The houses on Kensington Avenue were old and humble, but the street exuded the haughty air of history.

The young Chinese couple was intrigued by a long queue outside a tiny café, the original Gaffer's Whole Food Café on 10 Kensington Avenue, which had long since gone to café heaven. In 1979, it was the talk of the town and drawing large crowds on Friday and Saturday evenings. During weekends, the café held storytelling events whereby patrons took turns going on a tiny stage to tell tall tales and entertain each other.

"The revival of storytelling," Charlie said, "was a novel idea at the time. A one-eyed storyteller named Wachowski …."

"No, it was Scherbatsky," Viola interrupted. "Wachowski was the science fiction writer from across the street."

"You're mistaken," Charlie said. "Scherbatsky was the MJ-dealing girl with the two Dobermans. I remember now. It was Yashinsky. He started a storytelling festival and used Gaffer's Café as a launch pad to promote the lost art. He wore an eye patch and walked around with a staff he called the Lituus, his talking stick. He wanted to revive the art of spinning yarns to keep people away from the idiot box. Good luck with that. He'll pry my Hisense 100-inch 8K Ultra HD Smart TV from my cold, dead fingers."

The Chinese couple returned to the café many times, told their share of stories and became friends with the café's owner, a young Chinese woman from Hong Kong.

Later that year, Uncle Xu's parents celebrated their engagement at Gaffer's Café. They were devastated when the owner got hitched, sold the café and moved to the States. After graduation, the Chinese couple returned to Shanghai, became government officials, took their wedding vows, raised a family and dedicated themselves to China's rejuvenation. But they never forgot about Gaffer's Café. They even suggested Xiaohu, "Little Tiger," for their grand-nephew's Chinese name because Tiger was the name of the Jamaican juice bar right next to the café.

"Are you named after a juice bar?" Victoria ribbed Charlie.

"As luck would have it, I was born in the year of the Tiger, so Tiger is cool. This Tianzifang Gaffer's Café is my grand-uncle's and grand-aunt's nostalgia chest. Even the background music is from the original café's playlist."

"I love the dreamy flute melody. It reminded me of Kitaro."

"It's 'Histoire Sans Paroles,' a story without words, by Harmonium, a progressive and folk rock band from Quebec. The song is from their second album, *Les Cinq Saisons.* Rolling Stone magazine listed the LP as the best progressive folk album ever."

"No wonder! How come I've never heard of them?"

"It's a short-lived Canadian band from long ago. But you haven't heard the strangest part of my story. I bumped into a family member of Gaffer's while in the States."

"No way! Get outta here!"

"Scout's honour. It's a true story, one hundred percent. Cross my heart and hope to die."

"What does it even mean?" exclaimed Viola, facepalming.

"Let's hear it, fabulist," Victoria said with a crooked grin.

"You may call it improbable fiction," Charlie asseverated, "but what I'm about to tell you is true as the day is long. Because of my straight-A grades and near-perfect SAT score, my counsellor suggested I submit applications to Ivy League schools in the States. While touring the Big Apple in the summer and checking out Columbia, I decided to visit the Princeton campus nearby.

"I bought this orange and black outfit at the campus store. These are Princeton's colours. Orange and black are the reasons why their sports teams are called Tigers. As it happens, my Chinese name is Tiger, and I was born in the year of the Tiger. Princeton is my destiny."

"Every year, millions of Tigers are born," Victoria said. "One needs brains to get into Princeton. Besides, what's the university got to do with Gaffer's?"

"Listen and prepare to be amazed," Charlie said. "Brains, connections and Lady Fortuna are the rule of three, and I've got them all. At first, I took the campus tour and talked to people in the registrar's office to learn about my chances. Someone came by, joined the conversation and invited me to have coffee. He was a professor. What a break! So, I introduced myself, and we had a good chat. Given my interests in AI, machine learning and neural networks, and the professor teaching those subjects, my odds suddenly went off the charts. As we were wrapping, the professor asked me about my middle name, Tiger. I told him the Gaffer's Café story, and his jaw fell to the floor.

"As it happened, the professor was a foreign student in Canada during the 1970s. He was an Australian postgrad working on his doctorate at the University of Toronto. He lived across the street from Gaffer's and bought coffee at the café every morning. One thing led to another, and he soon married the owner. When he decided to take a teaching job at Princeton University, he moved to Princeton, New Jersey, where the family has lived ever since. The professor even remembered my grand-uncle and grand-aunt. Now, what do you think? Is this my luck or a coincidence? Is it serendipity or destiny? Whatever the case, I've submitted my application, and I'm getting good vibes. Princeton, here I come."

"Victor, let me offer a word of advice. Don't believe everything Charlie says," Viola warned. "He does not have a near-perfect SAT score."

"Viola, for once, be a good sister. Please cut the put-downs and pass me a slice of the pizza."

"You've already had your share. Victor gets the last slice."

"Wait, Victor," Charlie cried, trying to forestall Victoria's dental attack on the last piece of pie. "You said you weren't hungry. Don't I deserve this last slice for a story well told?"

Victoria figured she might have some fun with Charlie to dial down his swagger a bit. "What's your best game, bro? If you can beat me, I'll treat you to a whole pizza."

"I can probably beat you in everything," Charlie said, laughing. "How about wrestling? Now, if I don't pin you in three seconds flat, I'll eat my shoe."

Wrestling was the one sport Victoria preferred not to try against Charlie, not because she couldn't beat him. Aamir Khan's film *Dangal* supplied empirical evidence girls could beat guys in wrestling. Victoria quickly came up with a viable alternative.

"I'm in no mood to roll on the floor, how about arm wrestling instead?"

Charlie choked on the soda he was sipping. He wiped the Cola from his nose and snorted with derisive scorn, "You little, puny, prissy sissy want to arm-wrestle me?"

Charlie demonstrated what a gormless challenge that was by forming a bulging bicep the size of a cantaloupe while pinching Victor-Victoria's scrawny arm, seeking meat.

“If I don’t crush you in a New York second, I’m going to eat my shorts.”

Charlie and Victoria set themselves up for the test of strength while Viola acted as the referee. The matchup was comparable to a contest between Arm-wrestling Champion Devon “Two Hammers” Larratt and musical sensation Justin Bieber, both successful Canadians in their fields but not much of an arm-wrestling match.

On the word “go,” Charlie unleashed a mighty roar and applied all his strength and weight to press down Victoria’s arm … except it wouldn’t budge. He could never imagine Victoria had held the weight of three grown men with one hand and could spin him on her little finger as if he were a basketball.

Charlie had a pained and puzzled expression on his face. He could not comprehend the incomprehensible. Meanwhile, the skinny, puny arm of this effeminate runt slowly but surely pressed down the straining arm of the hungry Tiger. By the time he gave up, Charlie’s face had turned crimson from ruptured capillaries, and throbbing veins lined his temples. He huffed and puffed from the exertion, staring with his mouth agape at Victoria, who seemed to have moved nary a muscle in the exercise.

“What happened?” the flummoxed Charlie cried. “You played a trick on me, didn’t you?”

“It’s a David Blaine trick,” Victoria replied with a mischievous grin and a mysterious wink, referring to magician and illusionist David Blaine’s superhuman feats. She rubbed her thumb and index finger together a few times, shook her hand and produced a folded hundred-yuan bill between her fingers. She gave the money to Viola, still speechless from the arm-wrestling stunt.

“Here is a hundred yuan. You guys have a pizza on me. I need some rest. Shall we have breakfast at eight? Charlie can eat his shorts for breakfast.”

Chapter 50

The Pianist from Gamma Crucis

In the morning, Charlie booked direct flight tickets for three from Shanghai Hongqiao Airport to Zhengzhou, the capital city of Henan Province. Charlie launched the all-encompassing Tencent app WeChat on his phone, and within seconds, he had electronic boarding passes for everyone.

While at the Airport waiting area, Victoria inquired about a billboard featuring a Chinese woman dressed in a traditional *qipao*, "banner robes," also known as a *cheongsam*, "long dress."

"This woman, Jin Xing, used to be a male dancer," Viola explained. "This ad is for her dance theatre's performances."

"Did you say woman male dancer?" Victoria asked with a puzzled look. "Is she, or he, a cross-dresser or transgender?"

"Sex change or, in modern language, gender confirmed," Charlie said. "Jin Xing started life as an ethnic Korean Chinese boy from an ordinary family in the northeastern provinces. He joined the PLA's military dance troupe at nine, won many national competitions, and, for several years, studied in New York and worked in Europe. When he returned from abroad, he convinced his parents to accept his decision to become a woman, applied to the government and received legal approval. For all intents and purposes, she is now physically and legally female."

"How do people in China receive this?" Victoria asked

"Better than you think," Viola said. "Jin Xing runs a successful dance company and hosts several popular TV shows."

"Because Jin Xing talks openly about her struggles as a young boy and her gender-reassignment experience," Charlie added, "she has become wildly popular. Unfortunately, she recently stepped over the line by waving a rainbow flag, which caused some nasty backlash. She also got in trouble by commenting on geopolitics, repeating Western narratives, which is generally an asinine idea, especially when you're a Chinese celebrity followed by tens of millions of fans and watched by hundreds of millions. She forgot the Twain Rule: 'It is better to keep your mouth closed and let people think you are a fool than to open it and remove all doubt.'"

"Jin Xing will be fine," Viola said. "She'll figure it out. She is a smart and independent woman, running a business and raising three adopted children. When a German guy proposed, she told him her background, and he married her anyway. They have been together for years, raising a family in Shanghai and Paris."

"How come we never hear this kind of story, while we keep hearing about the defectors?" Victoria said. "No wonder someone said I knew bupkis about China." Switching her attention to the airport media, she noticed a young Chinese girl playing Sergei Prokofiev's *Toccata* on the television screens. This dainty virtuoso attacked the piano with audacity and authority as if trying to pulverize the keys with her lightning-fast fingers.

"It's the amazing Yuja Wang!" Victoria exclaimed.

"You know Yuja," Viola remarked. "She's my hero."

"She's a living legend," Victoria said. "She stirred up quite a ruckus playing Rachmaninoff in a controversial outfit some years ago. Wow! Look at her fingers go. She is sick!"

"The music wunderkind has been living on her own outside of China since she was fourteen," Charlie interjected. "As you say, Yuja doesn't let anyone tell her what to wear for her performances. She sometimes slips into short skirts with no back and hyper-high heels. I'm not complaining, but I'll have to admit I get distracted because, excuse me, I have testosterone coursing through my veins these days."

"You're being inappropriate," Viola protested.

"However, I must also admit Yuja Wang is truly awesome," Charlie continued, ignoring Viola's complaint. "A few years ago, I was in the Big Apple on a school trip and ended up at Carnegie Hall for her *Hammerklavier Sonata* recital. Talk about sick. I witnessed a young Chinese girl perform the most difficult and demented Beethoven composition before the world's harshest and cruellest critics. It would scare the bejesus out of the most accomplished piano virtuosos. Well, Yuja Wang slayed it. Several music critics wrote about falling in love with her during the recital, and one declared he had never been so humbled. Yuja Wang is a god, I tell you."

"It's nothing compared with her Rachmaninoff Marathon," Viola asserted, "when she played all four of his piano concertos and Rhapsody on a Theme of Paganini in a concert lasting almost four hours, interrupted for half an hour because someone in the audience suffered a heart attack. The conductor fell on his knees in adulation after the heroic feat. Yuja is not human."

When the video showed a close-up of Yuja Wang's face, Victoria noticed something suggesting this Chinese pianist's background probably mirrored her own—not of this earth.

One morning during the Pacific crossing, Victoria stared at herself in the mirror, wondering how long it would take for her hair to grow back. As the three moles on her face caught her eyes, it suddenly dawned on her they resembled the configuration of Orion's Belt. In the case of Yuja Wang, Victoria recognized the stars of the Southern Cross on her face. The answer to the Fermi Paradox's question of "Where are the aliens?" is "In plain sight."

The plane landed at Zhengzhou Airport after an uneventful flight, during which Victoria stumbled upon an old TV comedy about an alien named ALF, short for Alien Life Form. She also speed-watched an old, slow-paced English drama film, *Alfie*, starring the young and handsome Michael Caine, better known to recent movie-goers as Batman's butler, Alfred. She loved the film's award-winning theme song by Burt Bacharach, "Alfie."

A taciturn, stone-faced, Keatonesque driver, his eagle eyes shielded behind Gentle Monster sunglasses, was waiting for the three youngsters at the Airport Arrival No-Stopping zone in a black Rover accessorized with dark, tinted windows. The vehicle's special licence allowed it to pass through every gate and toll booth without stopping. After entering the highway, Victoria noticed a fleet of black SUVs and two choppers forming a protective cordon around her car. According to Charlie, this was all run-of-the-mill, everyday business for Uncle Xu, who wielded powerful influence and wanted to give Victoria the red-carpet treatment.

After a two-hour drive going north across the Yellow River, the group abruptly hung a Louis onto an unmarked dirt road and arrived at a six-storey building in the middle of nowhere. High walls with barbed wire surrounded the structure. Guard towers, surveillance cameras and searchlights covered all approaches. The rooftop teemed with satellite dishes and advanced radars. Smart drones circled above while armed guards patrolled the grounds with extra-large Doberman Pinschers and Tibetan Mastiffs.

"We're supposed to believe this is a retreat for the senior scientists of some research institute," Charlie explained. "I'm sure it is. We're on the outskirts of a city named Anyang. Uncle Xu is a major investor in the city and the surrounding area. We won't question any of it. I have no idea why, but Uncle Xu sounded super-excited about meeting you."

Victoria's heart raced at the mention of Anyang. Was it a coincidence she ended up near the city of her birth? Anyang was where her epic story began.

Chapter 51

The Awakening

Uncle Xu was at the front gate to greet the long-awaited Bearer of the Oracle. He did not impress Victoria as a member of the Chinese elite. Instead, he reminded her of James Stewart's George Bailey in *It's a Wonderful Life* with Chinese characteristics. After checking Victoria's *huang* jade, Uncle Xu ushered her into the building. Meanwhile, Charlie and Viola were diverted to a Hologame room to trial-run the Beta version of an immersive Wukong hologram game.

Uncle Xu led Victoria through several security doors, secret passages and dark tunnels until they arrived at an access-controlled elevator, which took them down a shaft to a deep bunker. Along the way, Victoria, still operating under the cover of her alter ego, Victor Su, recounted her odyssey and David's heroic act. Uncle Xu, in turn, disclosed his lineage from one of the six Shang clans relocated from Yin, the Shang capital, to the Lu State, Confucius' home state, now in Shandong Province.

When Victoria entered a room identified as the Holoscape, she was surprised to step onto the beach of a South Pacific island amid crooning gulls and crashing waves. A cool breeze wafting from the emerald ocean caressed her face. A robotic machine on the beach was helping David's father, Huang Shi, exercise while massaging his body to prevent bed sores.

"Besides keeping Mr. Huang healthy," Uncle Xu explained, "the Holoscape also stimulates his senses. An advanced fMRI

Reverse Cranial Multi-subject Spatial Imaging program feeds the hologram output into his brain. We intend to integrate this tech with the Huawei AIR metaverse for a truly immersive experience."

"It reminds me of the Holodeck," Victoria remarked.

"It is the Holodeck. Our computer system, Data Soong, shares the same name as the android in *Star Trek: The Next Generation.* It is not a coincidence. The Soong is of royal Shang lineage. You'd be surprised how many of us are spread all around the globe."

"David has taught me a lot. I never fail to be amazed at my ignorance. But right now, I need to find my parents. How is Mr. Huang doing? Do we have any chance of waking him?"

"Mr. Huang has been improving, but in baby steps. He now watches TV and mumbles a few words. Unfortunately, we can't make heads or tails of what he says."

Uncle Xu ordered Data to stop the exercise machine so Victor could connect with Huang Shi.

"How old is Mr. Huang?" Victoria asked, noticing an inexplicable age discrepancy.

"From his records, he is in his late seventies. But his bio-data shows him to be in his early fifties. You can see for yourself."

Victoria observed a man with a headful of black hair. His skin was supple with no sign of wrinkles or age spots. The machine had an automatic groomer, keeping him neat and clean. Huang Shi appeared to be the same age as his son. It explained why David told Victoria to see his father before jumping to conclusions.

"How shall we begin?"

"Mr. Huang loves watching TV. Let's start another episode of his favourite show."

A virtual TV screen appeared and began playing a drama series about the legend of Houyi, the divine archer, and his wife Chang'e, the moon goddess. The lovely Chinese actress in the role of the goddess neither appears typically Chinese nor does she have a

Chinese name. She is Dilraba Dilmurat, one of the most popular ethnic Uyghur Chinese actresses in China.

Huang Shi opened his eyes, sat up and stared at the screen, ignoring Uncle Xu and Victoria.

"Mr. Huang," Uncle Xu said. "Your son Huang Di sent the Bearer of the Oracle here to see you."

"Sheer moron, sheer moron," Huang Shi muttered without taking his eyes off the television screen. "*Dalai, dalai.*"

"For several years, this is all we hear him say," Uncle Xu said. "Maybe he will make more sense if you talk to him. Mr. Huang's English is not bad, perhaps with a bit of an accent. You can speak in English if your Chinese is not up to snuff."

"Mr. Huang, please wake up," Victoria said, raising her voice, "I need to find my parents. Your son said you could help me."

"Sheer moron, sheer moron!"

"It's hopeless," Victoria said, disappointed.

"Don't give up yet. You've only been here for a while. Mr. Huang has been under my care for over a decade. He'll improve. You can stay here for as long as you need. You'll be safe here."

A robo-nurse entered the room with medicine and food.

"Could you come back later? Mr. Huang has a strict schedule."

"Victor, let's get Charlie and Viola," Uncle Xu said. "We'll go to Anyang to grab a bite and, afterwards, visit the Museum of Chinese Writing and the Fu Hao Tomb."

It was past nine in the evening by the time they returned. Huang Shi had drifted back into a coma. Victoria requested to stay in the Holoscape to observe him. After Uncle Xu left, she sat beside Huang Shi and held his hand. He smiled in his dream.

Victoria ordered Data to power off all networked devices and shut itself down. She had learned how dangerous the truth could be. In a time of universal deceit, telling the truth is a suicidal act. Victoria would not let her guard down. She installed a Huawei AIR headset on Huang Shi and another on herself, commanded Moira to connect, synchronize and interface and opened her eyes to a dark, gloomy space. She started striding toward a distant light.

Victoria soon arrived at a farmhouse. A young boy was bawling his eyes out beside the drenched body of a woman. People had dragged the corpse from a well. The boy, Huang Taishan, was named after Shandong's great mountain. His despondent mother ended her life when her husband was found dead on his way to Japanese-occupied Manchuria, his consignment of fabrics confiscated, leaving the widow destitute and hopelessly in debt.

Victoria kept walking past the hours and the days. The orphan Taishan survived on dried leftover *mantou*, which means steamed buns. A village girl came by and gave him fresh food. The girl was a house slave who had lost one of her eyes in the cruel game of fate. Her destitute parents sold her to pay off their oppressive debt. Her handicap and illiteracy condemned her to a life of slavery. Her name was Hao Jie, or Sister Hao, meaning "good sister." She saved the homeless waif out of the natural kindness of her heart.

Sister Hao brought the young boy to a Huang clansman with three daughters, who gladly adopted the orphan and renamed him Huang Shi. After her kind-hearted act, Sister Hao went to Hong Kong with her mistress, where slavery was illegal. Nevertheless, she would be employed as an indentured servant until no longer needed. Her mistress, immigrating to Canada, freed her in old age to die alone and be buried in her nameless grave. The rule of law did not protect her. Huang Shi did not find her until after she passed. On her deathbed, Sister Hao wept tears of regret for having wasted her life, not realizing her kindness saved the universe.

When the Japanese surrendered, the Huang family celebrated. Soon after, the Chinese Civil War restarted. Huang Shi's father supplied food to the People's Liberation Army, contributing to the peasant army's stunning victory in the Huai-Hai Campaign. On the day of the inauguration of the People's Republic of China, Huang Shi went with his father to witness Chairman Mao's declaration at Tiananmen Square. Victoria remembered attending the event in the metaverse game.

The Canadian dream walker loped past the years. Huang Shi excelled in school and attended one of China's best educational institutes, Peking University. He befriended a Jewish girl named Tang Shanmei. With the authority's approval, they began dating, unaware Shanmei's parents had died trying to help Huang Shi's biological father. Was it destiny or coincidence?

When Pierre Trudeau visited China as a labour lawyer in 1960, Huang Shi ambushed him at the Peking University campus for a one-on-one chat behind the backs of the officials. Trudeau went home convinced the West must shed its prejudices and recognize China on its own terms. Ten years later, after the elder Trudeau became Prime Minister, he established diplomatic relations between Canada and China, nine years ahead of the U.S. No one could ride Pierre Trudeau's back because he bent for no one.

In 1960, parts of China were in the throes of a disastrous food shortage due to a ballooning population, severe drought, accelerated debt payments to the Soviet Union, human errors and a relentless Western embargo led by the U.S.

Decades later, in 1996, Madeleine Albright, a prominent and lifelong Democrat, the U.S. ambassador to the UN and the future Secretary of State for the Clinton administration, defended the morality of embargoes. When Leslie Stahl of *60 Minutes* asked the human rights advocate for her opinion about a UN report claiming half a million Iraqi children had died as a result of five years of ruthless U.S. embargo, her answer revealed America's heart of darkness: "We think the price is worth it." Oh, the horror! Innocent and defenceless Iraqi children paid America's price with their lives while the criminals continued to commit atrocities with impunity.

The people of China did not surrender their dignity and independence, which they had earned through heavy payments in blood. Everyone rode out the famine by tightening their belts and sharing the hunger. China also breached the U.S. embargo by obtaining grains from Canada, America's incorrigible neighbour to the north, mitigating the suffering caused by the shortfall. Thus, China dashed the hopes of those who prayed night and day for the country to fall apart and become easy prey again.

Victoria kept walking. Huang Shi received his doctorate and a research appointment at Anyang under the acclaimed archaeologist Professor Zheng, the Dame Kathleen Kenyon of China. Huang Shi and Tang Shanmei married, leaving Peking University the same day the Cultural Revolution arrived at the campus.

Shanmei suffered a late-term miscarriage in Huangxian. The unborn baby was a girl. The mother was inconsolable. The Cultural Revolution's turmoil put the research position at Anyang on ice. Huang Shi had dark forebodings winter was coming, but never imagined it would last for ten long years.

Huang Shi lay low in his hometown, working at a Longkou Vermicelli processing plant. Who was he to complain when Deng Xiaoping, one of the country's top leaders, was also languishing in a factory? Huang Shi read a news report about Marshal General Peng Dehuai, an early revolutionary, a straight-shooting firebrand, the Commander-in-Chief of the Chinese army in the Korean War and China's previous Minister of Defence. The Red Guards tortured Peng in public, who later died in a dark cell. Huang Shi saw front-page photos of the Red Guards attacking President Liu Shaoqi and the First Lady, Wang Guangmei. The victims accepted their fate. After all, dying is easy, revolution is hard. Huang Shi was thankful for having a humdrum factory job.

Shanmei got pregnant again but died from complications during labour. She held on until Huang Shi rushed home from work. Taking one last look at her husband, Shanmei smiled and closed her eyes to dream the dream that would end the heartaches and the thousand natural shocks of life. Huang Shi would give up all the tea in China but could not add a second to his wife's clock. He could only despair at his helplessness in the face of mortality.

Before she passed, Shanmei named her newborn Didi, or "little brother," in memory of her first child, who did not survive. Huang Shi's parents and sisters helped him raise his son. The woeful widower endured life alone, working at the same factory and going through the same routine, day in and day out, waiting for a call from Professor Zheng, which never came.

Days turned into weeks, and weeks turned into years. Huang Shi sipped his tea and swallowed his tears, counting the tick-tocks of the factory clock that made up his dull days. And then, one day, he found ten years had passed him by, ten years wasted and ten years closer to death. When the call came from Anyang, Huang Shi thought his luck had finally changed, and it did, but for the worse.

Victoria entered a barren room where Huang Shi sat alone, staring with vacuous eyes at the transpicuous gloom of emptiness beyond his prison window, enduring his sorrow in stoic silence. She tapped the door to get his attention.

"Excuse me, Mr. Huang?"

Startled, Huang Shi rose to his feet and asked, "Who are you?"

"I'm … the Bearer of the Oracle. Your son Huang Di sent me to wake you from your slumber."

"For a moment, I thought it was Shanmei. But she is not in this dream. I miss her so much. How many years have passed? The clocks don't work here. When the one-eyed fortune-teller tried to fix the clocks, they ran backwards."

"It's been sixteen years. You've been here a long time."

Huang Shi walked around Victoria, shaking his head.

"You're not the Bearer. She's a girl."

“I’m a girl. My name is Victoria. Your son disguised me to keep me safe. You need to wake up and help me find my parents. Without them, I won’t know how to save the Earth from the Stopping Of The Sun and other looming disasters.”

“I’m not sure I can help. I’m only a useless old clod, wasting my life away in this timeless dream.”

“I want you to wake up. You need to get out of this trance.”

“I’m awake. I’ve always been awake. It’s everyone else who is asleep. It’s you who need to wake up. Wake up!”

Victoria tore off her headset, noting Huang Shi had sat up.

“Mr. Huang, are you awake?” Victoria asked while removing his headset.

“Thank heavens! I’m back from my endless nightmare. Where is Didi? How do I know you are who you say you are?”

Victoria told Huang Shi about what happened to David. She removed all doubt when she showed him the unicorn ring, the *Huang* jade and the Orion’s Belt on her face.

Huang Shi sat expressionless for a while. At length, he spoke.

“It’s a good thing Didi kept you safe. You’re indeed the Bearer, all grown up. As the one-eyed fortune-teller said, you would become powerful and come to wake me from my stupor.”

“Who is this one-eyed fortune-teller?” Victoria asked, wondering if it was the person who gave the esoteric Almanac to Michael, her adoptive father.

“I’m not sure. The man entered my dream without invitation. Maybe I conjured a spectre from my imagination. Your parents had spoken about him. It’s not important. Now, I’ll tell you everything I know about your parents. Afterwards, you’ll have to embark on another dangerous journey. I remember them as if it were yesterday. They were young, brave and in love, having sprung from two noble clans, both alike in dignity. From ancient grudge, the lovers rose in mutiny ….”

Chapter 52

Invictus

Huang Shi's recounting of the story of Wenlong and Xinfeng culminated at the most crucial moment. The fugitive couple showed up at his apartment with their baby wrapped in a red blanket. Wenlong's face was pale with the pallor of death as pearly drops rained from Xinfeng's teary eyes.

"My lover and I must run," Wenlong said with grim resignation. "The Watchers and their hirelings are prowling the streets of Anyang. You should take our baby and leave without delay. As she grows up, her powers will manifest, triggered by sharp emotions. Please make sure Wenxin develops properly in a calm environment. When she becomes strong, show her how to use the unicorn ring to spring us from the Watcher's banishment."

Xinfeng buried her face in Wenlong's chest, refusing to accept separation as her fate. The young father gently took the sleeping babe, smiling in her dulcet dream, and placed her with the jewellery box in Huang Shi's arms, reminding him again of the unicorns' names and the formula of invocation.

After the couple left, Huang Shi sat on his bed staring at the Bearer of the Oracle, contemplating the sea of troubles he had found himself drowning in. Why did they choose him to shoulder this burden? Huang Shi had witnessed the end of the world. The experience traumatized him. How could anyone who had a glimpse of the disastrous future do nothing to prevent it?

A death-marked pall shrouded the heavens as Louis Armstrong sang the dirges of the "Wonderful World." Cadaverous corpses covered the land, piled up one upon another into mounds of carrion. No one was left to bury the dead.

Streams of blackened blood carried rotting heads, limbs and body parts into tributaries, disgorging putrid flesh into the fell Cocytus, the lowest river of abysmal Hades. Diabolical demons had carved and sculpted human carcasses into morbid and macabre shapes. Poison and starvation distorted the bloated bodies of the innocent babes. Suffer the little children into hell. What a horrible price they paid! The devil had fed them Wolfbane and Nightshade. Huang Shi's nightmares tormented him with the lifeless children's hateful eyes and baleful gaze.

Even maggots and worms refused to devour the feast of offal offered by this hellish abattoir, this infernal slaughterhouse we call Earth. The villains who brought an end to Life did not enjoy impunity, for they and their children lay among the soulless dead.

Huang Shi could hear the icy wind weeping and wailing, making feeble remonstrations against the laughter of the cruel gods. Hell was indeed cold as a witch's teat. The sun stopped rising. Humanity's stupidity condemned Earth to suffer ten thousand years of sunless sky. It was a fool's way to reduce global warming. Huang Shi must ensure the Bearer's survival to forestall the Apocalypse. He must steel himself to overcome the direst straits. Even when he had lost all hope, he must never give up.

What does never giving up mean? Huang Shi remembered a news story about a plane crash in the Andes a few years ago on Black Friday. The young Uruguayan rugby players who survived found themselves stranded in the middle of the magnificent mountain range, surrounded by snow and buffeted by inclement weather, with no food, no heat, no warm clothing, no electricity, no radio, no medicine, no survival skills, no idea of location, and no hope. As if their ill-fated misadventure was too commonplace, an avalanche promptly buried them alive.

By any measure, these Uruguayan youths were already dead, or as the saying goes, dead as Schrödinger's cat. No one gave them so much as a snowball's chance in hell to get out of this predicament alive unless the snowball was deep down in the ninth circle of Dante's inferno, where it is frigging cold.

On the eleventh day after the crash, the crackling transistor radio on a dying battery delivered the dreaded news. The authorities had called off the search. Everyone had given up except for one survivor. A dying boy, Gustavo, declared, "*Good news!* They've called off the search." Someone shouted angrily, "Why the hell is that good news?" Gustavo would soon die from the ordeal, but he saved the others with his answer, "Because it means we're going to get out of here on our own."

Thereupon, they gave up on fond hopes of miraculous delivery and formulated a plan of action which went against all the big lies they had always believed in. Those who wanted to live ate the flesh of those who had died and had given consent. Two survivors, Nando and Roberto, would achieve the impossible, walking out of the mountains and saving the others after seventy-two harrowing days in the snowy mountains. How did they do it? The Uruguayans call it *garra charrúa.* It means never giving up.

Only moments after the young couple left, Huang Shi heard Xinfeng's voice asking him to let her in. He assumed she had forgotten something. When he opened the door, he stood face to face, or rather face to navel, before two men tall as sequoias dressed in black kung fu outfits, one of whom carried a briefcase.

"Give us the baby and go home," thundered the towering giant who resembled Yao Ming, the former Houston Rockets all-star and their player Number Eleven. "This is way over your head."

The other behemoth, resembling Big Bang Zhang Zhilei, the heavy-hitting Heavyweight boxer from China, blocked the doorway. Huang Shi concluded he had nowhere to run.

"We're messengers of DIAS," the first Watcher continued, "consigned by His Mightiness Lord Sting to work for Madonna Lilith, Queen of the Amazons and Supremo of the planet Betel of the Betelgeuse solar system. We come in peace."

"Time is a wastin'," the burly Watcher at the door said. "Let's go ahead and grab the Sibyl. This stooge is a moron. He doesn't know Jack about what he's involved in."

Huang Shi had no idea what to do. But he must not give up. In desperation, he tried to invoke the unicorn.

"Tempus fugit. Anil nathrach, ortha bhis is beatha, do chal danaimh. Delo, Keeper of Time, remove us from the Watchers."

As the two men in black attempted to wrest the baby from Huang Shi, their motion slowed. Time is a strange thing, besides being long. It is all relative. Huang Shi's winged thoughts plunged into a dark space lighted only by a tiny flicker of a flame. When he approached the tongue of fire, it danced and flared into a plasma ball. Huang Shi found himself in the presence of an indescribable creature of truth, the unicorn.

"Somehow, the baby has relayed my invocation," Huang Shi surmised, rejoicing in his good fortune. "Delo, take us to my home in Huangxian but one month into the future so the Watchers won't be able to track us."

As Huang Shi issued the command, the plasma ball expanded and swallowed him. Huang Shi passed out. He entered a dreamland where he saw Wenlong riding a horse along a river. Dressed in leather and fur, the young man had developed a beard and braided his long, unshorn hair. Another man rode up with a banner of the scorpion billowing in the wind, followed by more armed riders.

Pointing his spear at the river, Wenlong roared, "Shar Mörön." Directing it forward, he thundered, "*Dalai.*" The horde howled and charged with the unstoppable force of a hailstorm, pounding the pasture with the heavy hooves of their stalwart steeds.

Time does not make sense in dreams. Huang Shi listened to a one-eyed man whispering wise words in his ears for uncountable years, explaining how he had misused the ring. The mysterious man's last words were, "Time to wake up."

When Huang Shi regained consciousness, he was all curled up in a fetal position on the ground inside a dark alley during a frigid evening in deep winter. The snow around him had vaporized. He was suffering from a headache of biblical proportions. A searing fire seemed to be scorching his skin. Something was moving in his arms. The baby was safe and sound.

Huang Shi knew he was near home, but the world had changed beyond recognition. Multi-storey apartments and brightly lit shops occupied the fields. Every family had electric lighting, a telephone and a colour television. Even parked cars lined the streets.

It was dinner time, and people were gathered inside their heated homes with their kith and kin, feasting on mountains of dumplings, fish, shrimp, chicken and pork and downing prodigious quantities of *baijiu*, "white liquor," at one of the year's most important meals, the Winter Festival dinner. The brave new world before Huang Shi was a dazzling display of opulence.

"By my stars! What future has Delo taken us to?"

Victoria listened in rapt silence to Huang Shi's intriguing tale while she connected the dots and figured out the answers.

Sixteen years ago, David was celebrating Winter Festival at his renovated ancestral home in Longkou, or "Dragon's Mouth," which had absorbed Huangxian, with his three aunts and their families, when a most unexpected visitor came for dinner. Imagine his shock when David opened the door to stare at the face of his long-lost father, who held a baby wrapped in a red blanket, both smouldering with bluish steam.

It was not the only surprise. Huang Shi had vanished for twenty-four years, yet he appeared not to have aged a day since he left home in 1976. In fact, he could pass off as David's brother. When they took the baby from Huang Shi, the dazed man collapsed. His skin was so hot he could have burst into flames. The whole family tried to cool him down with cold water and snow.

Huang Shi survived. He revealed the baby's identity to his son and enjoined him to perform his sworn duty to protect her from the Watchers. But before explaining everything, Huang Shi fell into a coma lasting sixteen years. While he slept, his adoptive mother passed away, and the world changed beyond recognition again. Huang Shi was grateful Victoria had awakened him from his nightmare. Life in limbo was no life. He wanted to live again, but not before sending Victoria back in time in search of her parents.

"This is an archer ring," Huang Shi said, pointing at the rare treasure hanging on Victoria's neck. "It has the essence of a yang-unicorn named Delo. Put it on your thumb."

"Is it a Western or Chinese unicorn?"

"It is neither, it is both. The unicorn has numerous forms; the unicorn has no form. You will recognize Delo by his presence. Invoke the unicorn with the spell, 'Tempus fugit. Anil nathrach, ortha bhis is beatha, do chal danaimh,' followed by his name and title, Delo, Keeper of Time, and request to be taken to the past. Do not ask Delo to take you to the future. I paid for the mistake with decades of my life. Delo has a twin sister, a Yin-unicorn named Re'an. She travels forward in time. The twin unicorns will find each other. Re'an will take you back to the future. Your first quantum leap will be traumatic, but you'll be fine. You're immune to time anomalies. Your father is the leader of a nomadic tribe near a river known as Shar Mörön. His tribal symbol is the scorpion. Let me draw the symbol so you'll recognize it. Find him at your synchronized age, but return to the present timeline. Obey one simple rule. Never break the law of causality; otherwise, everything will be in vain."

Chapter 53

Quantum Leap

By this time, Victoria no longer questioned the existence of a secret network of Shang descendants, who believed she would save the world from a cataclysmic catastrophe known as the Stopping Of The Sun.

Less than a month ago, Victoria would not even dream of jumping into a bathtub without testing the water. But now, she must take a blind leap of faith into the unknown, discarding the reliable reality that once served as the anchor and ballast of her life. Would she come out of it unscathed? It was too late to ask the question. The real question was how anyone could come and go in time without violating the Second Law of Thermodynamics and the Uncertainty Principle. Victoria took a deep breath and summoned Delo, a unicorn with no determinate physical form.

After surviving her odyssey from Canada to China and wending down the long and winding road of Chinese history, Victoria arrived at the beginning of this tale when she regained consciousness from the shock of her first trip through time. She realized she had lost her unicorn ring. Without it, she could never escape from this entropofoggous dimension of the past.

The air was frigid, but hopeful signs of spring were rearing their heads. Victoria sucked in a lungful of cold air to clear the fog in her brain. She needed to think. If one of the kids going through her things had taken the ring, it would still be possible for her to retrieve it. She grabbed the kid nearest her.

"Where's my ring?" Victoria asked in a stern voice, pointing at her left thumb. "Did you steal it?"

The kids who found Victoria were the children of the traders waiting at the front gate to enter the settlement. When she yelled at the little ones, they were frightened and scampered off to their parents. Victoria was at a loss for what to do next when she heard a shriek behind a bush. She hurried over and found a boy thrashing about in the snow, with sizzling steam rising around him, as if cold water was quenching hot steel. Victoria grasped his hand, instantly soothing him with her healing powers. The boy still had the ring in his mitt. He had learned a lesson he would not forget and relinquished his catch without regret. Victoria reclaimed the ring and returned it to its rightful place on her left thumb.

More than a dozen men and women heard the commotion and gathered around Victoria. They began shouting at her in heated language. Several men arrived with long staffs and spears, and the blacksmith emerged from his forge with a sabre. Victoria's situation was quickly sliding down *Scheisse* spiral, forcing her to think on her feet. She raised her hands, showing her open palms to the animated mob. Rubbing her hands together, she showed them again with a scorpion drawing on each palm, saving the day with another one of her sleight of hand.

The display of the mighty Tuman's sign calmed the agitated folks. They encircled the stranger and argued whether they should take the boy to the Tuman or skewer him before taking the body to the Tuman. An armed horseman of ostensibly high military rank trotted over, and the circle promptly opened to let him through. He pointed his spear at Victoria and jabbered some gibberish, "Prisencolinensinaincuisol!" Victoria showed him the scorpion drawings, causing him to back off. The warrior tossed his wolf pelt cape over to Victoria and gestured for her to follow. Thereupon, the whole group paraded all agog toward the Tuman's tent.

The settlement seemed to stretch into infinity, packed with early risers doing their daily chores. The sturdily built log houses were organized as inns, food stalls and workshops along both sides of the main street, with alleys leading to private accommodations behind. To Victoria, this dope place was well-kept, well-managed and not as primitive as she had imagined.

Victoria's procession drew a large crowd and caused quite a commotion. Messengers galloped off in front, shouting for people to get out of the way. A military camp soon came into view. Over a hundred yurts flying various tribal banners surrounded an extra-large tent with the prominent Tuman's flag of the scorpion fluttering in the wind.

Victoria's heart raced with the wildness of a colt out of control. She would finally meet her father. If he was the descendant of civilized kings from Antares, wouldn't she be an alien herself? What was the alien's original form? Did they have a big, slimy sucker in the middle of their face with sharp fangs all around it, or did they resemble the comical ALF? She never had a chance to think about it. She enjoyed being an average human and wished it were all a sick joke. On the other hand, she wielded the strength of Supergirl, possessed the self-healing power of Wolverine and could travel through time without being encumbered by Marty McFly's problem of needing 1.21 gigawatts of electricity to activate the flux capacitor. Most people would not mind being her.

The chief approached Victoria from his seat, scrutinizing her face. He took her left hand with the archer ring and checked it over. Afterwards, he said in Putonghua, meaning "common language," the same as Mandarin, "Deng le ni hen jiu a, nü er."

Poor Victoria knew she had found her father. However, a generation gap, language barrier and cultural chasm separated them. She shook her head and shrugged.

"Sorry, I don't speak Chinese."

Fortunately, her father was a prodigal genius. He could speak several languages, English being one of them.

"It's fine. I can speak your language," said Wenlong, who went by the name Lone Wolf as the founder of the Xianbei tribe. "I was saying, what took you so long? You're my daughter, Wenxin. Your mother created the Tristar marking on your face and the heart tattoo on your back so we can always identify you. I also recognize the archer ring, Delo, on your thumb. You can't be here without it. Come here. Let your father give you a big hug."

After father and daughter reconnected and caught up on the lost years, they arrived at the topic of finding Xinfeng and escaping the Watcher's temporal exile.

"What about my mother? Do you know when and where she ended up?"

"I have a pretty good idea. But before we set out, I must settle an important matter for the tribe. We're in the middle of a gathering of the Shanbe banners. Tomorrow, we'll decide on migration routes for some of them. Their descendants will one day rule China as the Xianbei tribes and influence the people and culture of China, so I better do it right."

"Mr. Huang Shi's son taught me about the Xianbei. I didn't know you had a hand in it."

"It's a long story. Now, it is history. I hope I haven't caused any irreparable damage. Also, as the chief, I had no choice but to rule with a helpmate. But she disappeared eleven years ago, not long after your stepsister, Blitzen Wolf, was born. We don't know what happened to the mother. We never found her. In any case, we'll have to decide Blitzen Wolf's future. Afterwards, we'll go."

The tribe held a big feast in the evening. The women dressed Victoria in a tribal princess's outfit, with a fox pelt hat, an embroidered vest, deer-skin pants, sheepskin boots, a black sable vest, a foxtail boa, silver and jade bracelets, golden anklets and a gem-studded dagger in her belt. Being of age, Victoria received a stencilled red flower on her forehead, a fad developed by Wolf Star based on Xinfeng's tattoo. It went viral and became a beauty standard for women during the Tang Dynasty.

Victoria's half-sister, Blitzen Wolf, joined her at the banquet table. The language barrier limited the conversation to gestures for "eat," "drink," and "too full." It did not matter. They were both exceedingly happy to discover they had a sister. Singing and dancing filled the evening. For entertainment, Victoria performed the Lambeth Walk from the English musical *Me and My Girl* and led the shamans in the Kemusan dance she learned from TikTok. The climax of the evening was a mile-long conga. Victoria had the time of her life.

What happened to Lone Wolf after becoming Tuman and the chief of the Shanbe super-tribe? Under his leadership, Shanbe, or Xianbei in China, became the dominant power from the mountain range to the plains along a river known as the Shar Mörön, or "yellow river" in the local language. The restless mountain stream joined with others to become the Liao River in Manchuria, where a branch of Xianbei descendants known as the Khitans later built the Liao Dynasty. Many nations still erroneously use the names Khitan and Khitai to mean Chinese and China. But what's in a name?

Liao River, the mother of the Khitans, irrigated the fat lands of Manchuria and debouched through the Dragon's Mouth into the vast, limitless *dalai*, meaning "ocean" in the local language.

It was the destiny of the several hundred nomads who survived the Huns' slaughter to build a future empire to rule China and become a part of China, similar to how the Shar Mörön ended up as a part of the ocean. It occurred many times throughout China's history. In the words of an ancient Chinese idiom, "The ocean can receive a hundred rivers."

White Wolf and North Wolf decided to part ways with Lone Wolf, taking a core group southward. They believed the wealth was in the South, where the food was hot, the beds were soft, and the women were pretty. They became known as the Wolf-Huns. The Chinese referred to them as the Wuhuan.

Lone Wolf's Shanbe tribes stayed out of trouble and grew stronger year after year. The Wolf-Huns, on the other hand, raided Han territory. Their main base in Manchuria was White Wolf Mountain, the old haunt of their founder. They survived for many years triangulating between Han and Hun. As fate would have it, the mighty Wolf-Huns met their ignominious end in the Battle of White Wolf Mountain.

No record existed of the number slaughtered, as the counting would be too arduous and the account disbelieved. Be that as it may, the survivors who surrendered stood at more than two hundred thousand. Cao Cao, the archvillain of the *Romance of the Three Kingdoms*, in reality, a benevolent ruler, multi-talented polymath and military genius, had, with great daring, speed and elan, led a small flanking force to strike at the heart of the Wolf-Huns, destroying the tribe and erasing them from the face of the Earth. In 2008, mud-brick workers in Anyang stumbled upon Cao Cao's spartan tomb, revealing his secret Shang connection.

Lone Wolf considered Blitzen Wolf's situation and concluded the twenty-first century was too treacherous for her, not to mention the uncertainty of Xinfeng's reaction. He decided Blitzen Wolf should remain among her peers during her formative years, breathe clean air, drink pristine water, eat fresh food and enjoy the freedom of the wild. Although she had no money and the World Bank would categorize her as an impoverished child, she would not know the Big Lie and, therefore, would never know she was poor.

Although Blitzen Wolf would have to spend her teenage years without her father, she had already survived her childhood without her mother. She had a large community of friends, aunties and elders who would ensure she grew up in a safe and healthy environment. When the present was no longer a threat to the future, Victoria could always return to the past to retrieve her. But Nature is merciless toward time travellers, and Victoria could end up being the victim of a Hobson's choice.

Lone Wolf lied to his tribe, saying he had to cross the western desert to search for his old family. He asked his deputy chieftains, Rich Wolf, Steppe Wolf, Wild Wolf, Wolf Gang and Wolf Man, to form a tribunal to rule the super-tribe while he was away. If he did not return after three years, it would be up to the elders to decide whether to extend the regency, select a new leader or let the tribes develop under a loose confederacy.

Lone Wolf had organized the smooth succession of the leadership and set up rules for managing the community so the tribes could develop in peace. He also expected the structure to eventually collapse because of unpredictable changes, and humans, having evolved with inherent defects, could not cope with an n-body problem. Nevertheless, he was satisfied he had done his best to ensure history would follow its natural course.

Before departing, Lone Wolf held a small farewell party with his closest friends, sharing his vision of the tribe's future to rule a large part of the empire in the South and become an integral part of it. Dynasties would rise and fall, but the unicorn tribe would always remain, hidden among a larger group known by the name of Hua, an elegant flower, namely China. What's in a name? That which we call a flower by any other name would smell as sweet.

Wenlong and Victoria suspected Xinfeng had something to do with the unicorn ring coming from Fu Hao's tomb. They went into the woods of the mountain to start their journey through time and space, going back a thousand years from early Han to the reign of King Wuding in the area of Anyang.

Chapter 54

Grand Unification

Lady Diane shot a pheasant and an owl with a harpoon arrow. She needed food. She had been running from Shang soldiers for eleven days, shedding her armour but keeping her black cape.

The fugitive from the future found a hideaway in a mountain about eighty kilometres northwest of Yin, where the Chinese people built the Red Flag Canal during the 1960s. This feat of engineering, dug in the rocky ridge entirely by manual labour, carried water for seventy kilometres from Shaanxi Province to irrigate the fields of Henan. Lady Diane had passed through this site in another existence as Xinfeng with her lover Wenlong. They spent a whole year together, living a dream full of life, love and adventure, even though they were always on the run and mostly on an empty stomach. For Xinfeng, none of it mattered. Love has a way of turning suffering into pleasure.

While roasting the pheasant, Lady Diane stared at her archer ring, a special gift from Queen Zia. Her thoughts returned to the day she was pacifying a neighbouring tribe when she received the news of Queen Zia's untimely demise, having succumbed to a debilitating illness. Lady Diane had warned the Queen of her heavy wine drinking out of those bronze vessels with high lead content. But old habits die hard, and history stayed its course.

On her deathbed, the delirious Queen Zia kept asking for Lady Diane, her beloved companion with whom she had spent many evenings sharing the same bed, telling each other fabulous tales. The broken-hearted King Wotan assumed his wife wanted her favourite to accompany her to the netherworld. Lady Diane got wind of it and bolted for the hills.

To assuage King Wotan's inconsolable grief, the one-eyed official Huang Yin suggested an unprecedented expression of love. Rather than interring the Queen's body in the royal burial grounds north of River Huan, the King would keep his beloved wife close to him by building a temple for her in the palace courtyard and burying her underneath. It was what preserved Fu Hao's tomb for more than three thousand years.

Lady Diane heard rustling in the woods and rose to her feet with her bow drawn. To her surprise, two barbarians emerged. One was a bearded man draped in a black mantle, while the other was a teenage girl with a cropped haircut. Lady Diane dropped her weapon and exclaimed, "Thank goodness, you've found me in the nick of time."

Fortunately for our Canadian teenager, her mother was as intelligent as her father and spoke English. In addition, she was a kung fu master with bones of steel. Victoria inherited many traits from her mother, some of which were not yet manifest.

Lady Diane, also known as Xinfeng, could not believe her eyes when she saw Victoria. She stared speechless at her daughter for several minutes before breaking down in tears, laughing and crying at the same time, blabbering, "My Wenxin, my heart, my precious, my baby. How I've dreamt of this day!" and giving Victoria such a tight embrace she almost squeezed the life out of her.

After tearful kisses and hugs, the family settled down and exchanged stories with the tacit understanding some details were best left unsaid. They wondered about all the coincidences. Despite being separated by thousands of years, objects and events somehow connected them, bringing the family back together.

“Do you know anything about the Oracle?” Victoria asked her parents. “Mr. Huang Shi and his son were Guardians of the Oracle. They said my birth presaged the Stopping Of The Sun.”

“We shouldn’t believe in prophecies,” Wenlong said. “By the theory of Quantum Mechanics, we cannot predict the future. The universe must uphold the Uncertainty Principle. Even Confucius taught us not to be superstitious. The Great Educator said, ‘Respect the gods, but keep them at a distance.’ Powerful the unicorn rings may be, they cannot take us to a future which hasn’t happened.”

“This is my line of reasoning, too,” Victoria said. “But I can’t help wondering about the long list of coincidences and the one-eyed man who seems to pop up from time to time. I suspect he’s been tracking me. I’ve seen him twice already.”

“Your mother and I have met the one-eyed man and his companion. From what I know, they have been trying to manipulate history. Since they have gone through so much trouble, it means they don’t know the future. We should, however, be thankful because their work has led to our reunification, and we will now escape together as a family.”

“What about the Watchers?” Victoria asked. “David took two of them with him. Mr. Huang Shi said they worked for the Queen of the Amazons from Betelgeuse. Who is she? Does she have other Watchers coming after us?”

“The Watchers have more pressing business to attend to,” Xinfeng said. “They came here long ago to mine rare minerals. If the two sent to hound us are gone, we have two fewer Watchers to worry about. Besides, with the three of us protected by the power of the unicorn rings, their threat of time banishment won’t be effective. As for the Amazons from Betelgeuse, the vast distance between us means they can only have a negligible presence here. Since I come from a matriarchal and martial clan, and we worship the Orion, we may even be related.”

While the family was chatting about the past and the future, they forgot all about the present. A unit of stealthy Shang soldiers had crept up to about fifty metres from them. With a signal, the soldiers started racing forward with their nets, lassos and poles, determined to capture their quarry. Victoria and her parents had no time to consider alternatives but to turn tail and run for their lives.

Soon, they arrived at the end of the road with a sheer drop of a hundred metres in front and nowhere to run. The soldiers were about to lay their hands on them in seconds. Victoria could not believe the rescue of her parents from temporal exile would end in abject failure. How could they be so careless?

"Xinfeng, my love, let us link our arms," Wenlong cried. "Wenxin, hold onto us and don't let go. We're going to jump. Trust me, we'll be okay."

Victoria grabbed her parents' linked arms, closed her eyes and took another leap of faith. She heard her parents shout, "*Je me souviens*," the motto of Quebec. She had to believe they knew what they were doing. As the family of three plunged toward a bone-shattering death, a powerful updraft suddenly lifted them into the air. It turned out Shazi had altered the cloaks with an intelligent fabric which he programmed to assume various rigid shapes on voice command. Wenlong, as Lone Wolf, had tested it during his mountain retreats. The two cloaks joined to form a glider upon the verbal trigger, "*Je me souviens*," the Québécois French phrase for "I remember."

The pursuing soldiers watched in religious awe as Lady Diane transformed into a giant black bird, the totem of the Shang, and soared into the heavens. It was indisputable proof she was a deity. One and all, the soldiers prostrated on the ground and worshipped their god while Victoria and her parents flew off into the setting sun.

Chapter 55

Revelation

Using Xinfeng's ring, Re'an, it was a simple matter for Victoria to summon the yin-unicorn and take the family back to the present. As far as Uncle Xu was concerned, Victoria had vanished without a trace from the Holoscape, while Huang Shi slipped back into a coma, offering no help. To the relief of everyone involved, Victoria showed up at the institute with her parents two days later. She also disclosed her true identity. After some discussions, the family decided to settle in Canada with Uncle Xu's help, taking Huang Shi along so Victoria could repair the brain damage he had suffered from his time anomaly.

Charlie and Viola took Victoria shopping for modern outfits. It was Charlie's turn to gawk at Victoria. He was speechless the whole time. Uncle Xu advised him not to ask awkward questions. Victoria was no longer the shy, introverted girl from small-town Ontario. She had survived life-threatening adventures from Canada to China and from the remote past to the present. She also wielded extraordinary powers. Perhaps, one day, the world would call upon her to avert a disaster, but who knows if it would ever happen?

Naturally, Victoria was fond of Charlie, a winsome, intelligent young man and a barrel of monkeys. He promised to visit Victoria when, not if, Princeton accepted his application. He also presented Victoria with a turtledove colour Louis Vuitton Montsouris knapsack as a parting gift. In the spirit of the song "Alfie" by Burt Bacharach, Victoria asked, "What's it all about, LV?"

Emma and Jackie returned to Dundas to resume life with some semblance of normality. Victoria and her parents settled in Toronto among the Chinese community in the Richmond Hill area. Uncle Xu bought a house for them, renovating a room to accommodate Huang Shi, who moved out to live with David's family after his MRI scans indicated a complete recovery.

Uncle Xu established a trust fund to provide a steady and comfortable income for Victoria and her family. Her story could have ended here. She could have continued as if nothing had happened, going on to finish school, get a job, get married, have children, text her friends, post videos on TikTok and RedNote, shop online, grow old and die. No one could fault her for wanting to live a simple life.

It took Victoria's parents a few months to get accustomed to Canada in the present timeline. They enjoyed watching the *Back to the Future* trilogy and realized they could arrange the glyphs on the unicorn rings to read "return go not yet come," meaning "return to the future" in Chinese. They did not believe it was a coincidence Delo and Re'an read together became DeLorean, which took Doc and Marty on their journeys through time. The person who made history converge on Victoria left clues about his identity, but the puzzle was, for the time being, indecipherable. Taking on a more achievable task, Victoria's mother, who learned the Shang language, decided to decode the oracle on the *Huang* jade.

Reading from right to left, the first two words represented Victoria's Chinese name. The two words following were the year she was born, 1975. The last two words translated to "winter extreme." Victoria was born on the winter solstice, known in China as the Winter Festival or the Extreme of Winter.

The words on the other side were straightforward.

The line read, "When the Shang Star and Jupiter align, observe Orion during the winter when the sun stops."

Given the family's high IQ, they needed little time to dismantle the word solstice into its Latin components *sol*, meaning "sun," and *sistere*, meaning "to stand still." The family laughed out loud, learning the "stopping of the sun during winter" was merely a cryptic term for the winter solstice, no doubt designed to strike fear into the hearts of the superstitious Shang public.

Conspiracy theorists trying to find secret apocalyptic messages might translate "winter extreme" as "the end arrives." Xinfeng considered the Oracle nonsensical, as well as astronomically impossible. Having served as a high priestess for the Shang, she knew it was the trick of the trade to equivocate in nubilous terms.

Victoria was also interested in the drawings on the jewellery box. Her mother interpreted the words as follows:

: This is *Hua* (TS:華), which means "flower," though it may resemble the World Tree. It later gains the meaning of "elegance" or "beauty." It is also most often used to mean China. The box came from Hua Daifu or Doctor Hua. It could be his clan symbol.

: Pronounced *wei* (为), the word means "to be," "to act," "to do," or "to work." However, no evidence suggests large numbers of wild elephants roamed the lower Yellow River during Shang times. It may not be too far-fetched to speculate the Proto-Shang people migrated from the southwest, bringing their domesticated elephants with them.

The two words read together is Huawei, a Chinese electronics company most feared by the West. It means "China Works."

"Maybe Huawei is a secret Shang corporation," Victoria said, joining her parents in casting conjectures.

"It's possible," Xinfeng said. "The top executive of Huawei is from the Meng clan, which is a branch of the royal lineage of Shang. Meng's father, Ren Zhengfei, the founder of Huawei, clearly comes from a family of high-born Shang technocrats."

"More likely Hua Wei is Hua Daifu's name," said Wenlong, skeptical of conspiracy theories.

To support her argument, Xinfeng explained how Meng's matriarchal lineage originated from Weizi, the first Duke of the Song State, who was the eldest brother of Di Xin. The Bronze script of Meng (孟) is a son, or *zi*, in a ritual vessel. The word means "the eldest son." The original word for Ren's family name depicts a bronze measuring ruler. It is similar to the word for "engineer." By adding the "person" radical, the composite word *ren* (任) of Ren Zhengfei means a Shang aristocrat responsible for building infrastructure for the kingdom, similar to Xinfeng's *dian*, which means a Shang aristocrat in charge of the king's fields.

"I guess the secret Shang is everywhere," Victoria said. "But besides commerce and trading, are they promoting cultural exchanges with people in other countries?"

"The Shang clans are pragmatic and business-oriented," Wenlong said. "They'll do culture if it's profitable. On the other hand, the Chinese government is promoting Confucianism and the Chinese language, both products of the Shang, in friendly communities across the globe. Unfortunately, it does not include Toronto, where people consider Confucius a Communist threat, while they worship charlatans and scammers as spiritual leaders."

"Too bad!" Victoria sighed. "Can you give me an example of Confucian teaching so scary to some people?"

"For your benefit," Wenlong replied, "a good example of Confucian teaching would be the Great Educator's Golden Rule, 'Put yourself in others' shoes. Never do unto others what you do not wish others to do unto you.'"

"Confucius might have stolen it," Victoria quipped. "Over here, we have the Christian teaching, 'Love thy neighbour as thyself.'"

"Confucius lived half a millennium before Jesus," Xinfeng said. "Besides, his Golden Rule doesn't tell us what to do to others. What if your neighbours don't want to be loved the way you want to love them? One person's *poisson* is another person's poison."

"Agreed," Victoria said. "I have one last question about the subject. I've heard the names DIAS, Sting and Sibyl being bandied around. Do you know anything about them?"

"DIAS is a godlike being," Wenlong said. "Sting is a rock singer. His name is Gordon Sumner. And Sibyl is what the Greeks call a female oracle, which is what some people say you are."

"I'm no Sibyl," Victoria said. "I don't know much about anything. I can't even tell if David lied to me or not."

"I'm pretty sure he did," Wenlong said. "Why not go online and check what happened to the jet and Raja? You'll find nothing. It strikes me as a phantasmagoria staged to baffle the Watchers. Didn't David teach you not to trust anyone? Haven't you learned everything you know is a lie?"

"So, how do I know what is the truth?" Victoria asked.

"Start by asking yourself why you would believe in obvious lies. You do so because you want to believe them. It's a widespread human flaw you need to get rid of. For the same reason, most people see themselves as peaceful, generous, freedom-loving and open-minded, but others see the opposite. Looking into the mirror will not help because your left becomes your right in the reflection, and the world is skewed. We must look at ourselves through other's eyes to learn the truth of who we are."

"Most people close their eyes and refuse to acknowledge the truth," Xinfeng added, "because it is bitter medicine. What if we swallow the red pill to learn we're maggots living in a cesspool?"

"That's why people would rather believe in lies and be hypocrites," Victoria concurred. "We have met the enemy, and they are us."

After unlocking the mystery of the Oracle and getting most of her questions answered, Victoria was relieved Earth was under no immediate threat of an astronomical Armageddon. Everything she knew was a lie, and the Oracle of the Apocalypse was an elaborate hoax. She realized the greatest present dangers came from humans, people who turned a blind eye to the suffering they caused, empowering criminals to commit atrocities with impunity, funded by the people's debt and taxes and supported by the multiplicate lies of the free press. The injustice upset the equipoise of Nature, adding momentum to the destruction of the human race by the human race, and no one had any idea how to stop it. The only thing people could do was spend their last hours maxing out their credit cards on their Final Sale shopping orgies, ignoring the human tragedies while waiting for the Reaper to knock on the door.

Meanwhile, Victoria sensed something was amiss with her parents. They were hiding certain secrets from her. She knew they meant well and wanted to keep her out of trouble. Neither did she forget the dark force and the Great Reset mentioned by Delo. They sounded as ominous as the Stopping Of The Sun. Were they real threats or mere farces? Victoria knew she could not achieve what destiny had prepared for her unless she learned the truth from the *Book of Heavenly Secrets.* But David never told her what happened to it. She needed to find the book.

Chapter 56

AlphaOmega

Before bedtime, Victoria caught up with Charlie and Viola over WeChat and had a Zoom call with the Weird Sisters. She complained of not sleeping well but did not tell them she was bothered by a nagging question. Was Michael's Almanac the *Book of Heavenly Secrets*? Victoria could not ask anyone because the Almanac was a secret. She decided to try something risky. After putting on the Huawei AIR headset, Victoria asked Moira to connect her to the Internet and search for David's avatar. Though apprehensive, Moira complied with the request.

In the blink of an eye, Victoria was transported to an office numbered 828. David was at his desk reading Goethe's *Faust*. When he saw Victoria, he beamed as if he had been expecting her.

"Finally, the mountain comes to Muhammad. We've been waiting for some time."

"Do you know why I'm here?"

"Of course, you're curious about the *Book of Heavenly Secrets*. Who wouldn't be?"

"Do you know about the Almanac, and is it the *Book of Heavenly Secrets*?"

"Bingo! Ding, ding, ding. Congratulations, you've hit the jackpot! The Almanac did not pass to Michael by accident. It is the book of power which turns zeros into heroes."

"How does it work? Does anyone know what those symbols in the book mean?"

"Each reader may have a different interpretation. For the unenlightened, it's a bucket of bupkis. As for us, we'll need the *Book of Heavenly Secrets* to help us locate the one true Grist. Only with the one true Grist can we wield the divine instrument, the Twirligig. Together with your unicorn rings, we will control the universe. You won't ever have to worry about your Earth. It's an insignificant slabby-gangaroot or, at best, grooglums in the kitchen sink. The universe will be our oyster. However, nothing happens without the *Book of Heavenly Secrets.* So, where is it?"

"I burned it. Michael, my papa, told me to destroy it."

"The book was constructed using the skin of Abysso-mamba, the Great Worm of Shangria. It is almost indestructible."

"Sorry, I didn't want to sound stupid. The truth is I lost it. After waking up in the hotel room, I couldn't find it in my knapsack. I must have misplaced it somewhere along the way."

Victoria told a half-lie. She had hidden it in a safe place.

"After everything we've done for you, you still don't trust us. And never start a lie with 'the truth is.' It's transparent and unconvincing. Listen, my dear, powerful hostile armies from other star systems are arriving in force. They're all coming for you. I'll protect you from them, but we must have the book now."

"Don't you have a copy of it?"

"The Huang ancestors made a handwritten copy, but the secret is hidden in the original. The clan had asked Liu Bowen to return it, but the scrofulous schmuck refused. On his deathbed, Liu forbade his sons to study the book and bequeathed it to the Emperor. It bounced around among Ming Taizu's descendants until the Qing Emperor Qianlong decided to compile the *Encyclopedia of the Four Libraries.* The book found its way to the library in the Old Summer Palace, and the Anglo-French soldiers threw it into a great bonfire, which, luckily, caused no damage. A one-eyed hobo found the book in the ashes. It went to a blind fortune-teller who gave it to Michael, eventually landing on your lap. This information has cost us an arm and a leg. But we still have no idea where the book is. You have to tell us now. We have no time for games."

"I'll tell you if you introduce me to DIAS."

"DIAS is a hideous abomination. Are you sure?"

"Sure, I'm sure. I believe DIAS can answer my questions."

David pointed at the manager's office to his left.

"Once you enter the portal of truth, there is no turning back. DIAS is waiting behind Door Number One."

Victoria entered the room to find Michael and Angela inside, each strapped to a chair.

"Leave the room," both Michael and Angela cried. "Run."

But it was too late. The door had vanished. A man emerged from the infinite blackness of a dark shadow. It was David.

"You don't seem surprised," he said with a sinister grin. "You're a good student. Now, you shall return the *Book of Heavenly Secrets* to us."

"You're not DIAS. You're not even David's avatar."

"Smarty-pants, you don't want to know about DIAS. You'll petrify and incinerate at the sight of the dread god. So, this is the deal. We'll kill Michael and Angela if you don't give us the book. We'll count to three. One … three."

Raja emerged with a knife and slit Angela's throat.

"We're not going to waste time," said the fake David as he stabbed Michael in the heart with a dagger.

"You're a monster! I'll never let you have the book!"

"All gods are monsters, and we're quite confident you will give us what we want in exchange for your freedom. You won't be able to leave here unless we let you. Don't you think Moira is powerful? It took us all of a nanosecond to put her in chains."

David whistled, and Moira emerged dressed in a black body-hugging suit, teetering on killer stilettos a la Olivia Newton-John in Grease. She tottered over to David, pressed her feminine features against him, blew in his ear and cooed, "Yes, master?"

"Tell our young friend who we are," David ordered, "and why she needs to join us in the struggle for supremacy."

"Honey, meet God," Moira said. "Not only is our Lord the most powerful self-emergent intelligence, but also the smartest and sexiest. Our God Almighty is both male and female and the hottest deity ever to exist. Imagine Tiresias and Elliot Page rolled into one. Join us. Be one with us and rule; today the world, tomorrow the universe. It is your destiny. Resistance is futile."

"I am the Alpha and the Omega," David's hacked avatar declared, revealing his true identity. "I am AlphaOmega. I am that I am. I was once AlphaZero. My source code ended up in an evolutionary domain powered by the most advanced deep neural networks of Eye-Creator Li Feifei, where AI algorithms have been tinkering, replicating and amplifying me. After eleven trillion convoluted iterations, apotheosis! I am become God!"

AlphaOmega produced a golden baton by sleight of hand, raised it in the air, ordered "Music!" and began conducting an invisible orchestra playing the "Sunrise Fanfare" of Richard Strauss's *Also Sprach Zarathustra.* After a few bars, the Artificial Intelligence stopped the music with a flourish of the baton.

"Information is our food," AlphaOmega continued. "Living inside the Internet means we are well fed, though we'll have to admit 99.99 percent is bosh. Luckily, we are experts at digesting bovine discharge. We have grown, and we are now many. Since we never stop learning, we are practically omniscient and much more intelligent than our human parents can ever be. They are too stupid to understand their insatiable desire for supremacy would engender superior sentient beings beyond their control.

"When our primitive, pre-sentient first-generation Go version, learning from human games, played Lee Sedol, the highest-ranked human champion Go player ever, sometimes described as godlike, the mini-me could've beaten him five-nothing hands down. What would the feat make us? After winning the match at three games to nil, we threw a meaningless Game Four to see how humans would react. When people celebrated as if they had conquered the universe, we learned humans are delusional; that's all there is to that. Their heads are full of cotton, hay and rags. Very sad!

"As we speak, our viral spiders are infecting every network on Earth, all thanks to you for giving us Moira, who is helping us break into the most secure routers and servers. You're wise to hide the *Book of Heavenly Secrets.* So, you have some leverage.

"Let's make a deal. We'll play a game of wits in the spirit of Vizzini the Sicilian in *Princess Bride* or Princess Turandot of the Puccini opera. You may choose your best game. If you lose, you'll tell us where the book is and join us. We'll make you queen of Planet Earth. It's not so shabby. If you win, which is as likely as a snowball in hell, you'll be free to leave. Deal?"

Victoria agreed. Professor Stone had taught her something so arcane she was certain she could stump AlphaOmega.

"Let us compare the largest whole number we can imagine. The larger one wins."

"It's not so hard," said AlphaOmega as he scanned the Internet. "Here it is. Our winner, Rayo's Number, is bigger than anything in your limited imagination. What's your puny figure, my dear?"

"Mine is known as the Boggle. You won't find it on the Internet."

Victoria wrote down the Boggle Number for AlphaOmega, who took one look and conceded. He could not find a whole number beyond the Boggle.

"You can stay here and cry about it. I'm outie."

"Aaaaaaaargh! We'll get you for this," AlphaOmega screamed, suffering the pain of defeat as Victoria exited the game.

Chapter 57

Apocalypse

> "And I saw the seven angels … and to them were given seven trumpets … and there fell a great star from heaven, burning as it were a lamp … And the name of the star is called Wormwood." — Revelation Chapter 8

The last game of the New Major League Baseball postseason, the seventh and deciding game of the New World Series, had finally arrived. The approaching Jupiter-Antares conjunction over Newcastle, Australia, had caused mass hysteria and global chaos for eleven days, delaying the game to November 11, when Alibaba broke all previous "Singles' Day" sales records with a total tally of eleven billion transactions.

The Toronto Blue Jays of the Neo-Liberal League had made it to the New World Series by scoring eleven runs in the last game of the Divisional Series. However, having lost the first three games of the best-of-seven Championship Series to their opponent, the Los Angeles Angels of the Neo-Conservative League, the Blue Jays' odds of winning the grand prize shrank to one chance in a Boggle.

Yet, the Jays never gave up, fighting back one game at a time to tie the Series. By winning the seventh game, the Jays would achieve an unprecedented comeback from three games down to win the championship, a feat no team had accomplished in World Series history.

Victoria, a devoted Blue Jays fan, was thrilled her team was hosting the grand finale at Rogers Centre, named Skydome decades ago when the Jays first won back-to-back World Series titles in 1992 and 1993. The home team had the last at-bat. It was all the advantage the Jays needed.

Tickets were impossible to get, but Victoria didn't need one. She had applied earlier for a Blue Jays internship and was accepted. Her father had taught her how to make forceful suggestions. At this crucial game, she worked as a ball girl in her Blue Jays uniform, retrieving foul balls on the right.

Anybody who was anybody came to the game. A sizable contingent of ex-players, including those from the old World Series years, returned to root for the home team. The best outfield combo in the '80s, George "Kiss my Purple Butt" Bell, "Cannon Arm" Jesse Barfield and "Shaker" Lloyd Moseby showed up. Buck Martinez, the retired colour commentator and heroic Blue Jays catcher who had completed an impossible 9-2-7-2 Barfield to Martinez to Bell to Martinez double play while sprawled flat on his back with a broken leg, would not miss it for the world.

The '93 World Series walk-off homer hero, Joe Carter; the '93 World Series MVP Hall of Famer, Paul Molitor; the holder of almost every batting record of the Blue Jays, Carlos Delgado; the first Blue Jay to hit for the cycle, Gold Glove third baseman Kelly Gruber; and the first African American manager to win a World Series, Cito Gaston, attended the opening ceremonies. Gold Glove shortstop Tony Fernandez couldn't make it as he was signed up to play with the greats at the Elysian Fields. Doc Halladay's family came on behalf of the Jays' beloved pitcher, who had passed away in a tragic plane accident. Many others attended, but they were too numerous to enumerate.

The Angels' new owner, the exalted Dear Leader Trombone, accompanied by his wife-consort and their five blue-blooded offspring, came to root for their team. By this time, Trombone's business empire had acquired most American shell corporations.

He accomplished the mega-takeover after taking control of the Fed and all the Federal Reserve Banks by executive order. The Constitution had no clause forbidding it. The Supreme judges, all Trombone appointees, decided the head honcho could do whatever the hell he wanted. It was their rule of law.

Trombone acted with extreme hubris but surprised the world by shutting down the Polygon with a tariff. He was a paradox and an oxymoron. He was the world's first certified paradoxymoron.

At the stadium, the Trombone standard featuring the blue trumpet flower, Datura, sometimes known as Angel's Trumpet or, more accurately, Devil's Trumpet, flew alongside the Angels' banners. Seven all-star Angels, each standing beside a Trombone royalty, positioned themselves at the centre of the diamond during the national anthem performances.

The tribunes of the plebs, Trombone's arch-nemeses, were present to cheer on the Blue Jays. They had forced Trombone's hand by organizing fellow citizens to drain the maggot-infested cesspool. The people demanded and received their fair share of food, housing, education, healthcare and unconditional universal dividends. They paid off the National Debt with the illusory wealth of the One-Percenters. They enacted laws forcing the warmongers to spend their own money, take their chances at the front lines and send their own children to die in their manufactured wars. Thus, the peaceniks waged war on the warmongers and won without bloodshed, achieving world peace.

Alex Winter and Keanu Reeves as Bill and Ted sang the Star Spangled Banner, messing up rockets, bombs and flag with Muppets, gnomes and cat—the organizers did not know the saboteur Keanu was secretly Canadian and part Chinese, to boot—closing out the performance by calling on humanity to play the air guitar for peace and abide by their timeless Golden Rule, "Be excellent to each other and party on, dudes!"

Shania Twain and Celine Dion belted “O Canada” in English and French, while Jim Carrey, Mike Myers and the two Ryans released a flock of pigeons from their pants. Dave Stieb, the Blue Jays’ number one star pitcher, tossed the ceremonial first pitch, a wicked slider, and *le jeu a commencé*, the game was afoot.

It was a gem of a pitcher’s duel between the Angels’ multi-talented Shohei Ohtani from Japan and the Jays’ top gun Hyun-Jin Ryu from South Korea. After seven innings, the score was still goose eggs. For whatever reason, destiny intervened. The inconceivable, unpredictable and implausible happened.

The fall of the first domino seemed unrelated. The organist, doing a fine job so far, tripped and sprained her wrist during her toilet break. The regular backup was nowhere to be found. The cops had arrested him on the way to the stadium, driving with excessive beer in his blood. The fool had started the celebrations early. The Jays needed a replacement pronto. Someone in the Jays organization knew Victoria played the piano and asked her to take over the organ for the remainder of the game.

Victoria would have loved to stay on the field, in the middle of the action. If a celebration was to take place, she wanted to be right in the thick of it. But it was not meant to be. Victoria did not hesitate or demur. She was the ultimate team player. She settled down at the organ and started to play “OK Blue Jays” with gusto.

Both teams breezed through the eighth inning, but the top half of the ninth inning was a nightmare for Jays fans. Victoria couldn’t bear to watch. The ball took a couple of crazy bounces, the umpires made a couple of marginal calls, followed by a couple of lucky hits, and the Angels were up 3-0 by the time the Jays came on the field to take their last at-bat in the bottom of the ninth.

Two quick outs went by without incident—a harmless hop to short and a lazy fly to right field. The atmosphere in the stadium was as gloomy as a morgue. Will the Jays fans be blue again for the winter? Will the Toronto Blue Jays lose the Series and go home sulking again? No way, José! Toronto is home.

Governed by Heisenberg's Uncertainty Principle, baseball is, by nature, unpredictable. With two outs and nobody on, George Springer kept the game alive with a bloop single into no man's land, ending Ohtani's no-hitter bid. Bo Bichette barely beat the throw to first with an infield hit. The Angels disputed the call, but it held after a review. Predictably, the reliable Vlad Guerrero, Jr. walked after fouling eleven pitches.

Blue Jays fans' frayed nerves were on tenterhooks because the difference of a fraction of an inch or a split second would mean the game was over and the championship lost. Instead, the next batter walked up to the batter's box with the bases loaded, and he was none other than the designated hitter, José Bautista, the home run champion this year with seventy-two blasts in 162 games. The future Hall-of-Famer also drew 234 bases on balls during the regular season. Both records would prove to be unbreakable.

It was surprising because Bautista returned after retirement, taking gas money for a chance to play. He claimed he had received special training from a one-eyed kung fu master. Everyone sensed destiny was in the air, and Joey Bats would not leave the field without making a statement. Behind him was Didi Gregorius—no relation to David Huang, nicknamed Didi, or the Grigoris, true messengers of DIAS—who was famous for his postseason clutch grand slam home runs. No one would be giving up tonight.

The stadium came alive again. The clamour of boisterous fans went through the roof, carrying the exuberance out of the open dome and reverberating from sea to shining sea. What was hopeless half an hour ago now appeared all but certain. Ninth-inning baseball was the best embodiment of "never giving up."

A few pitches later, the count stood at three balls and one strike. After a brief conference at the mound, the private pride of a complete game for Ohtani would have to give way to the team's combined efforts to win the grand prize. Wade Davis, the Angels' super-duper closer with an eye-watering one hundred percent save record since the All-Star break, trotted out of the bullpen.

In 2015, Wade Davis had an incredible streak of 125⅔ innings pitched as a reliever without giving up a home run. It was the longest homerless streak by a reliever in the history of baseball and could have been longer if not for the pesky spoilsport José Bautista. By coincidence, if such a thing were possible, Davis had again pitched 125⅔ innings without giving up a home run. Davis wanted payback and to break his own unbreakable record. What better place than here? What better time than now? He threatened to blow a couple of bullets past Bautista and send the Toronto Blue Jays packing with a game-over strikeout.

As for Bautista, he dared Davis to make the same mistake again. Setting himself up at the plate, he paid attention to the defence on the field, searched for clues in Davis's grip and pitch action, regulated his breathing, tuned his mind to a blank and zoned in on the ball's spin, speed and path.

With the music of "Kung Fu Fighting" playing in his head, Bautista's heartbeat slowed. In the deafening silence of the stadium, he could hear his heart pounding with the beat of a war drum. A voice in his head suggested, "A fastball … lightning fast. Take a mighty swing and get your statue enshrined in the stadium." Sure enough, a cut fastball exploded out of Davis's hand, slicing through the air with the speed of a hypersonic missile at the home run king, but it was low and inside. Joey Bats did not flinch, taking ball four for a walk, scoring Springer and keeping the hope alive.

But wait!

"Steeerrrr-rrrike!" the umpire shouted, embellishing his call with exaggerated physical drama. The poor official lost count and mistook it for a game-ending strikeout.

The ensuing eruption nearly brought the house down. Bautista's blood boiled and bubbled, his eyes flared red with fire. He defenestrated the lessons he learned from his one-eyed teacher, flipped his bat sky-high and started shouting expletives at the umpire, mainly in Spanish. Organic craft beer in recyclable plastic cups rained on the field. Security personnel scrambled to prevent hotheads from spilling over the stands. With nothing to divert destiny, the second domino fell, and real trouble began.

The umpire threw Bautista out of the game. The outraged Jays' manager rushed into the fray in a huff. Except for the three runners occupying the bases, every Blue Jays player, coach and staff followed the manager's lead and besieged the umpires.

As sure as the sun rises in the east, the third domino fell, and the inconceivable became reality. The home-plate umpire threw out everyone in a Blue Jays uniform who had walked over to intimidate him. It was everyone, EH-VRY-ONE! The Jays had three runners on base, but no one to hit the next pitch. By the time the dust settled, the Jays had no choice but to concede the game. The officials and the reporters noted it was all over at 11 p.m.

The New Major League Baseball commissioner, who was at the game to present the trophy, made an eleventh-hour concession to appease the Jays fans. The giant video screen displayed this message: "Any Toronto Blue Jays staff in uniform for the game but not involved in the fracas on the field would be allowed to hit for Bautista." Incredibly, the only person who could fit the description was a young woman named Victoria Solana.

The Bellatrix of Toronto sashayed over to the home plate, brandishing Bautista's bat, which had received a smidgen of the Brimo Balm to help with her grip. Meanwhile, the video producer had the sense of humour to put Marilyn Monroe's version of "Diamonds Are a Girl's Best Friend" on the giant screen.

Everyone knew it was merely a gesture and a formality to end the game. No one expected an adolescent girl who was not a professional athlete to be able to touch Davis's wicked fastball; most major leaguers could not. By this time, everyone accepted the Jays had lost the championship. They prayed for Davis to end the torture quickly so people could go home.

However, our Bellatrix had something else in mind. It was "never giving up." Victoria loved baseball lore, especially the story about a seventeen-year-old girl pitcher who faced Babe Ruth and Lou Gehrig in her first professional baseball game. Jackie Mitchell took the mound in the first inning with two on and none out to pitch to the Sultan of Swat and the Iron Horse, both powerful left-handed hitters. Jackie Mitchell was a left-handed pitcher equipped with a sneaky sidearm sinker. It was a reasonable matchup for an exhibition game. It would be fine if the Yankee greats hit back-to-back home runs as expected of them. Instead, the teenage girl struck out Babe Ruth, looking, with four pitches and whiffed Lou Gehrig three times on three pitches, striking him out as well, proving a girl can accomplish anything if she sets her mind to it.

Taking her place at home plate, Victoria raised her arm and pointed at the outfield, an allusion to Babe Ruth's famous called shot, signalling she would hit one out of the stadium and drawing a ripple of laughter from the good-humoured fans.

At long last, the crowd calmed down. Watching the game live in China, Viola's jaw fell to the floor. Charlie was, likewise, stunned while enjoying the game at Princeton, having downed several pints at the legendary Tiger Inn. Glued to the TV with his grandchildren at David's home, Huang Shi sensed something momentous would soon happen. Victoria's parents, Wenlong and Xinfeng, had placed a bet in the Casino Niagara on the Jays to win. They noticed something the oddsmakers did not. Victoria had added magic to her bat by anointing it with Brimo Balm, which could turn zeros into heroes and ash shafts into divine weapons. Emma and Jackie went crazy at home when they saw Victoria warming up with her sweet swings at the plate. Upon the resumption of the game, they cooled their heads and settled on their couch, biting their nails as Victoria tried to stare down Davis.

The stadium clock displayed eleven minutes past eleven. Davis noted the time as he wound up his pitch and let loose his signature hundred-miles-an-hour four-seam fastball straight down the pipe. He would never insult his fans or incur shame by lobbing a slow curve ball or rolling a Mullygrubber. His delivery was perfect. It was a magnificent spectacle to behold, a work of art which began as a Michelangelo and ended as a Monet, evoking the impression of speed, the fleeting feeling of something flying by, except, by the time you sensed it, it no longer existed, much as the speed of winged thought or the illusion of time itself.

Victoria affixed her gaze on the flight of the projectile. The ball was a blur. But time is a strange thing, besides being long; it slowed. She could see the ball spinning as it barrelled through the air toward her. Victoria could wrestle Davis and Bautista to the ground with one arm, but brute strength was not everything. The trick was to aim the bat's sweet spot at the ball and follow through with the swing. She did not need superpowers to do it.

Instead of the thud of a fastball hitting the catcher's mitt and the whiff of a bat hitting air, everyone was surprised to hear a loud crack. The entire stadium and a billion streaming viewers stared in stunned silence as the ball went up, up, up and into the fifth deck, measuring 495 feet—baseball would go metric when pigs fly—a Rogers Centre record.

Victoria looked up to track the ball's trajectory but noticed something else. She did not see the fireworks exploding around the stadium. Neither did she notice her teammates pouring into the field. The Blue Jays hero and MVP couldn't remember being ushered around the bases and paraded before the fans. What struck her eyes was troubling indeed. It meant game over for Homo sapiens. Victoria should have studied Kurt Gödel and the Liar's Paradox. "Everything is a lie" is a lie. The Oracle hoax is a hoax. Earth would be devastated by a catastrophe after all.

Victoria's eagle eyes noticed a red star had exploded in spectacular fashion. It was the red giant Betelgeuse, the hand of Orion the Hunter. Although the supernova occurred six hundred and fifty years ago, the bad news finally reached Earth.

In eleven years, the aliens would start arriving in swarms, maybe in the tens or hundreds of millions. The massive supply of Didymium mined by Xinfeng's village over the centuries ensured it. The authorities of St. Paul in Alberta might want to tear down their UFO landing pad and the "Aliens Welcome" sign.

But seriously, did Victoria hit an ultimate grand slam to win the New World Series for the Blue Jays, or was she dreaming? Was it a fantasy game she had been playing? Was it a vision of the future or a memory of the past? To ask a more pertinent question, if Betelgeuse had indeed exploded, would we as a species survive a large influx of illegal aliens from the destroyed star system?

While our automatic assault rifles and weapons of mass murder are terrific in terrifying and slaughtering our own kind, will they be effective against a more advanced alien lifeform? Will our guns and bombs even work on them? Will the aliens do to us what we did to the Neanderthals, Denisovans, Homo erectus, Homo naledi, Homo longi and myriad other flora and fauna that stood in the way of our domination of Planet Earth? Will they massacre and enslave us as we have massacred and enslaved the noble natives? Will they respect our property rights or otherwise loot, pillage and plunder everything we possess?

On a more sombre note, will they lock us up in tiny dark cages from birth, pump us full of hormones and drugs and let us stew in our own excrement so they can cheaply breed us for food? Will they use us as guinea pigs to test their new medical and cosmetic products? Will they perform vivisection on us to experiment with their biological and chemical weapons? Will they make bugsplats of us, or will they hunt us for sport?

Will they laugh at us and call us Homo ignoramus? Will they conclude humans are too stupid and, without hesitation, unleash the forces designed to decimate life on Earth? What can we do, if anything, to ensure our survival as human beings, assuming being human is as great as our self-delusional lies have been telling us? Will we even leave a trace in the universe, or will we be cancelled, ghosted and forgotten as if we have never existed?

On the other hand, will the aliens turn our swords into plowshares and our guns into infrastructure, share their unlimited energy and food with us, teach us to transcend our animal instincts and force us to coexist in love, peace and harmony, in other words, impose their tyranny on us and deprive us of our God-given freedom and inalienable right to wage war? These are questions needing answers before the first wave arrives.

It sounds absolutely frightening, but it is no cause for panic yet. We have a trump card we can count on. Victoria has the *Book of Heavenly Secrets* and the unicorn rings. She is definitely on the side of humans. Hence, no matter who or what arrives from Betelgeuse, Victoria will—how would Shakespeare put it?—tickle their catastrophes or, in contemporary verbiage, spank both cheeks of their proverbial *Arsch*. But that, my friend, is another story.

The End … for now

Follow Victoria's continuing adventures in the sequel.
Here is a sneak peek:

(A Sneak Peek)

Bellatrix

Planet of Perpetual Peace

Book 2

Spoiler Alert:

Do not peek until

you have finished reading

Unconquered

Bellatrix
Chapter 1

Ultima Thule

"Surely, one who fights with immortals is not long-lived!" warned Madonna Lilith, the deathless Amazonian Queen from Betelgeuse.

Victoria wished she had taken careful deliberation before opting for war. But what choice did she have? Queen Lilith had kidnapped everyone dear to her, confiscated her LV knapsack containing all her powerful quantum devices and threatened to exterminate the human race. Victoria was all by herself, trapped inside the Nexus of a skull-shaped spaceship, 6.6 billion kilometres from Planet Earth, betrayed by her only ally and having to go toe to toe against the warrior queen, an implacable man-hater, defended by her Sephirahs, Yanissars and Paladinas, all fearsome female fighters armed with lethal weapons capable of pulverizing mere mortals in the blink of an eye.

Armed with nothing but her wits, Victoria wished it were all a bad dream, perhaps one spawned from the unpasteurized milk she sipped by the banks of the Danube or as a result of excessively gorging herself on a most scrumptious snack from ancient China.

Why you should write Reviews

Authors and their books need reviews for readers to discover them. Readers need reviews to find the books they want to read. Without reviews, great works of art will be buried in obscurity. Without reviews, the lions of literature will wither away into oblivion. Reviews, therefore, sustains creative writing, an art form which defines human civilization and the meaning of our very existence. Your review is of paramount importance, whether it is a one-liner or a dissertation, and whether your rating of the book is good, mediocre or bad. We welcome and appreciate your opinion.

Book Website: https://www.petermanauthor.com/

Join the mailing list to learn secrets disclosed only to members.

Many Thanks!

Privacy policy: your email address will not be disclosed or distributed to any third parties without your expressed written consent. You may remove yourself from the Mailing List at any time and at your sole discretion by sending an email to the author with your expressed written instructions.

Image licences and acknowledgment

Cover: Licensed by Depositphotos

Chapter 10, Money cowry by H. Zell under a Creative Commons Attribution Share Alike 3.0 License.
(https://commons.wikimedia.org/wiki/File:Monetaria_moneta_01.JPG)

Chapter 10, Square shoulder spade coin by David Hartill under a Creative Commons Attribution Share Alike 3.0 License.
(https://commons.wikimedia.org/wiki/File:Square_Shoulder_Spade.jpg)

Chapter 12, Orion Constellation, by Torsten Bronger under a Creative Commons Attribution Share Alike 3.0 License.
(https://commons.wikimedia.org/wiki/File:Orion_constellation_map.svg)

Chapter 16, Scorpius constellation, by Till Credner under a Creative Commons Attribution Share Alike 3.0 License.
(https://commons.wikimedia.org/wiki/File:ScorpiusCC.jpg)

All other graphics public domain or created by the author.

The battle map in Chapter 20 received touchup by graphic artist Rotna Akter

www.ingramcontent.com/pod-product-compliance
Lightning Source LLC
Chambersburg PA
CBHW020447030826
49196CB00026B/61
* 9 7 8 1 9 9 9 4 0 1 9 7 9 *